DAKOTA

*Four Inspirational Love Stories
on the Northern Plains*

Lauraine Snelling

BARBOUR
PUBLISHING, INC.
Uhrichsville, Ohio

Dakota Dawn © MCMXCIII by Lauraine Snelling.
Dakota Dream © MCMXCIII by Lauraine Snelling.
Dakota Dusk © MCMXCIV by Lauraine Snelling.
Dakota Destiny © MCMXCVI by Barbour Publishing, Inc.

ISBN 1-57748-355-3

Published by Barbour Publishing, Inc., P.O. Box 719, Uhrichsville, Ohio 44683 http://www.barbourbooks.com

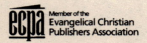

Member of the
Evangelical Christian
Publishers Association

Printed in the United States of America.

DAKOTA DAWN

Chapter 1

Nora Johanson leaned her forehead against the sooty train window. It seemed as if they had not climbed a hill nor traveled through any woods in the last forty years. "Don't be silly," she chided herself. "You haven't been on this train for forty years, it just feels that way." She glanced over at the corpulent man sprawled in the seat across the aisle. She certainly didn't need to worry about her mutterings waking him—snores fit to wake hibernating bears puffed at his walrus mustache.

Besides, he would not have understood a word she said since he obviously did not speak Norwegian and her few, carefully learned English phrases were not understood by most people she met.

She dug a cloth out of her carpetbag and scrubbed at the window, the dirt reminding her of how desperately she wanted a bath. If only she could have bathed in Minneapolis. But she was down to her last few coins and could afford only a small hunk of bread.

What will you do? What will you do? The question beat in time with the clacking train wheels, ever bearing her west. Farther from her beloved mountains and fjords of Norway but closer to the arms of the man she had promised to marry. At fifteen she had been so sure of their love. Now, she could barely remember him. She scrunched her eyes shut to conjure up a picture of Hans Larson, but it was easier to see his handwriting on the letters they had exchanged over the last three years.

She carefully drew off her natural wool, knitted mittens and opened her purse to count the coins that were left. One, two, three, four. *Uff da.* No blessed angel had multiplied them while she dozed. Four pennies—all that was left of the money Hans had sent to her.

Her stomach rumbled.

In the last letter, Hans had said it was plenty. But then he had not counted on the overly long, storm-tossed sea passage. Or the tedious wait with the thousands of other immigrants on Ellis Island in this year of 1910. Or the blizzard that stopped the train for twelve hours.

Her stomach rumbled again. Would they never come to another town?

Nora fought back the tears that seemed to hover like persistent bees at the back of her eyelids. She sent a silent plea upward. *Please, make the town hurry.* Or maybe it was the train that should hurry. Whatever.

She leaned her head against the back of the seat. Visions of home danced through her mind. Home—with her family crowded around the white-clothed kitchen table, laughing, teasing, telling funny stories.

A sob caught in her throat. Her sister Clara had promised to come to the new land too, as soon as Nora could send her passage money. And her brother John. When she closed her eyes she could see them so clearly. She shut off the memories with a snap. *Think only of the better times,* she told herself. Remembering her loved ones, all bundled up and waving good-bye at the train station in Oslo, cut too deeply.

She blew her nose and wiped the errant tear away. As Mama had always said, "The good Lord will be with you and guide you when we can't." But right now Nora needed a human hug, one that she could touch and feel, and even hear. She sneaked a peak at the man in the other seat. She certainly could hear him. The train trip had not kept him awake.

She focused her attention again to what was out the window. The snow did not surprise her—it would be weeks yet before spring came to the hills and valleys at home. It was just the unending flatness of the land. The only rises were the drifts that piled against the buildings and sometimes stopped the train. Several times, the railroad men had been forced to dig through the drifts so the train could continue. It would have helped if the men had allowed her to assist them in digging instead of just looking at her as though the wind had frozen her brain. Her brothers would have tossed her a shovel and dared her to outdig them.

She caught a sigh as it was escaping her throat. *Think about Hans,* she ordered herself. *Think of what a fine man he is, how wonderful it will be to have a home of your own and milk cows again. Think of his promise to buy some chickens in the spring.*

Will there be flowers by the house? she wondered, closing her eyes to see them better. *Roses. I'll have pink ones and red, maybe even a scarlet climber.*

Just before she nodded off, she jerked upright. This time through the window she saw the sinking sun fling banners of orange and red, vermillion and gold across the sky. The heaped high, gray clouds were now burnished to shine and glow like the very gates of heaven. As the fiery red sun slipped below the horizon, the clouds faded to lavender and purple—and back to gray.

One thing this flat land does exceedingly well, Nora thought, *is sunsets.* She had never seen such a display—not even over her beloved mountains in Norway. As she watched, she dared not blink in fear that she might miss a single hue.

"I'm sorry, Miss," the woolen-coated conductor said as he paused at her seat. At least he spoke Norwegian. "But we'll be an hour later than I thought." He dragged out his gold watch and peered at its face. "Somewhere around ten, I expect."

"Mange takk, thank you," Nora nodded with her words.

"Surely your young man will check at the station, so he'll know our arrival time."

Nora nodded; she seemed to be doing a lot of that. Why didn't she feel the consolation the man was trying to offer? Was something wrong with her hearing? "I. . .I'm sure he'll—Hans'll be there."

Not true, a little voice inside her whispered. *You're sure he won't be there to meet you.*

Nora forced her lips into a smile and thanked the man again. She kept herself from turning around and watching him as he made his way down the length of the car, swaying with the movement of the train. He had boarded the train in Chicago and was beginning to seem like an old friend. The music of her own language cemented that feeling. She had never dreamed she would be at such a loss for words because she spoke only Norwegian.

She started to take out her dictionary but put it back because the light was so dim. She had not been able to concentrate on learning new words for the last two days anyway. Since the Norwegian woman she had traveled with left the train in Wisconsin, Nora had practiced English with no one.

Seeing her reflection in the darkened window, she smoothed a few stray hairs up and tucked them under the thick, golden braids she wore coronet-style. She shook her head. "You really need to brush and rebraid your hair," she whispered to the woman in the glass. "And take a bath." She used her handkerchief to dab at her tongue and rub off a spot on her cheek.

In the reflection she could also see a portion of the car behind her. Polished wood on the walls and ceiling gleamed in the lamplight; the brown fabric of the padded seats was worn in spots; some of the passengers had drawn their window curtains closed against the cold and dark. Not Nora, though—she hated to close herself in any more than was necessary. The car had looked comfortable in the beginning, but these five days of being cooped up had worn on both her body and spirit.

It seemed like another week had passed before the conductor returned, announcing, "Soldall. Next stop, Soldall." He stopped beside her. "You take care of yourself, now." He reached up and swung her bag down for her from the overhead racks. "I've already made sure your trunk will get off when you do. I just hate to see a pretty thing like you. . ."

Nora could feel her cheeks flame at his compliment. *"Mange takk.* I thank you for all you've done. I. . .I'm. . ." She lifted her chin. "I'll be just fine."

While the train slowed, Nora searched for lights. Surely everyone in the town had not gone to bed already. But, as the train huffed and screeched to a halt, she saw only two lights off in the distance—only two. There must be more than two houses in town; Hans had said this was a big town.

She pictured his letter and tried to remember how his voice sounded. "It's a large town for the area. We have stores, a hotel, a Norwegian Lutheran church and. . ."

She shook her head to keep herself awake. After all, it was ten o'clock at night.

A lone gaslight hung above the door to the train station. Nora paused a moment at the head of the steps leading down to the platform. It had started to snow again; tiny hard pellets rattled on the roof of the metal car. The square window of the station glowed like a beacon against the blackness of the outside peppered with whirling snow.

The conductor held out his hand. "Be careful going down these steps, Miss," he said with a ready smile. Even with his muffler, he shivered in a draft of bitter wind. "Don't appear anyone's here to meet you." He looked over his shoulder as if hoping that someone—anyone—would make a liar out of him.

Nora bit her bottom lip and forced her mouth into a smile. "I. . .I'm sure Hans will be here. I'll wait for him in the station." She trembled at the thought of another falsehood. She wasn't sure he would be there at all. In fact, she was terrified to admit the nagging feeling she had that something was not right.

"You better ask Oscar, the stationmaster, to come pick up your trunk. It'll get buried if this keeps up." He motioned to a black square farther up the station platform.

The train whistled, as if impatient for the delay.

"You take care of yourself now." The conductor helped her down the last step. "Get right inside before you freeze." He waved his lantern, picked up the metal stool, then stepped aboard as the wheels of the train squealed back to life. "God bless."

Before she could get her scarf wrapped up over her nose, the pelleted snow stung her cheeks. *If this is what March is like in North Dakota, what will January be like?*

"Please, God, let Hans come soon," Nora whispered as she

peered off to the sides of the station building that seemed to hunker down against the swirling snow. Darkness, so black it reached out for her, sent her skidding across ice-coated planks towards the square of light. *"Uff da,"* she muttered as she slipped and slid, barely keeping her feet.

The wind helped her push the station door open, but it swirled her black woolen skirt and tugged at her scarf before it retreated in defeat. She slammed the door shut and leaned against it. Why did she feel like she had just battled and barely won? Her wish had been that Hans would be waiting inside to surprise her. He had liked to do that—surprise her and make her laugh. But, when she stared into the darkened corners of the room, she felt the dream fade and disappear.

The stationmaster certainly did not resemble Hans in any way. Short and thin seemed the best words to describe him, from closely clipped hair, to feet that barely touched the floor when the man sat at his desk. He had not risen to greet her, but Nora realized right away it was not because of bad manners. The man listened to the telegraph with both his hands and ears.

Nora nodded back at him, left her satchel by the door, then wandered over to the potbellied stove near the station desk. She loosened her scarf and let it drape around her neck. While the room temperature was warmer than outside, the heat from the stove failed to reach the door, or the corners, or the benches lining the center of the room.

His tapping finished, the man gave a little hop to get down from his chair and then he limped forward. "May I help you, Miss?" He reached into a back pocket to retrieve a handkerchief. After blowing and wiping his reddened nose, he peered over his metal-rimmed glasses and, starting at her feet, measured her height with his stare.

Nora felt like the giant troll in one of her sister's stories. "I. . . I'm Nora Johanson, from Norway." His intense gaze caused her to falter. "I. . .I wired ahead. Hans Larson, my betrothed, was to meet me tonight. I'm. . .ah sorry, the. . .ah train was late." Why didn't the man say something? Anything? She unclenched her hands in her mittens and extended them to the warmth of the stove. Right now her cheeks felt like they had been sunburned.

Maybe he had not understood a word she had said. She pointed to her chest and repeated her name, louder.

"You don't have to shout." The little man backed away.

Nora breathed a sigh of relief—he had answered in Norwegian. "Did you receive my wire?" she asked.

He nodded.

"Did you give it to Hans Larson?"

The stationmaster shook his head.

"Did Hans contact you?"

A nod. "Close to a week ago. Said he'd return in a day or so. Too far out in the country for me to deliver it." The man limped back to his desk and shuffled the papers in a wire basket. He pulled one out. "Here it is."

Nora felt something clench around her stomach and twist. Hans didn't even know she was arriving today. How could he have met her? She licked her dry, chapped lips. What would she do now?

"The hotel's right up the street. I can take you there on my way home." The man returned to the stove and closed the damper. He set the teakettle to the back and peered through the isinglass windows to check the coals. A grunt seemed to express his approval.

"I. . .ah—" Nora could not force the words past the lump in her throat.

"Ja?" He paused on his uneven journey to the coatrack.

"Sir, I have no money for a hotel." Nora felt like crawling under one of the benches. "The trip took much longer than we planned, than Hans planned. Perhaps I can sleep here, until Hans comes, that is. Maybe he'll come first thing in the morning. I won't bother anyone and. . ." Her voice trailed off.

"Oscar."

"What?"

"My name's not Sir, it's Oscar."

"Ja, *mange takk*. Mister Oscar, I. . ."

He was shaking his head again. "Not Mister Oscar. Oscar

Weirholtz. But everyone just calls me Oscar. You can, too."

"*Mange takk.* I—" Nora could feel the tears clogging her throat and stinging her eyes. She clamped her lips shut and looked upwards to ward off the waterworks. She would not cry!

Oscar stopped buttoning his coat. "No money at all?"

Nora shook her head. "Four pennies."

"Well that old goat at the hotel won't give a room to anyone who can't pay in advance." He shook his head. "And, no, you can't stay here. Against the rules of the railway. No one can be here without the stationmaster or another employee of the Great Northern Railroad."

Nora now knew how an animal in a trap felt. *Dear God, what will I do?* The prayer slipped past her strangled thoughts in spite of herself.

"I know." Oscar reached for his hat. "I'll take you over to Reverend Moen's house. Mrs. Moen will take you in and she'll know how to contact your young man. You'll like her." He turned down the kerosene lamp, leaned over the glass chimney, and blew out the flame.

"Oh, my trunk." Nora stopped in midstride. "It's still out by the track. I forgot all about it."

Oscar groaned. "Can't it wait. . .no, I suppose not." He struck a match and lit another lantern hanging by the door. When it flared satisfactorily, he set it on the floor and pulled mittens from his pocket. "Come on, then. You'll have to help me. We can probably skid it on the ice, but best be careful." He grabbed the wire handle and, swinging the lantern, stepped outside into the black and cold.

Nora pulled her scarf up over her nose and followed him. When they reached the trunk, he handed her the lantern and grabbed one of the rope handles. "You push."

After they broke it loose from the ice, the trunk slid easily. Nora followed behind until they came to the step and then she set the lantern down and hoisted along with Oscar. The trunk screeched its way over the threshold.

"We can leave it here," Oscar said, nodding toward the wall.

"One of the men will bring it down on a wagon in the morning."

"Ja, that will be fine," Nora brushed the snow off the top of the trunk so no moisture would seep inside it. Her quilts, hand-embroidered linens, and household treasures painted with rosemaling designs had not left much room for her clothing. She dusted off the last of the white powder from the trunk and then shook her mittens clean. *"Mange takk.* Thank you very much. I am sorry to be so much trouble."

Oscar nodded, checked the stove and, picking up the lantern, led the way out the door, carefully locking it behind him. "No, here, I'll take that." He held out the lantern in exchange for her heavy bag.

Nora looked down at the small man and hid a smile; she stood nearly a foot taller than he. As he swung off through the stinging snow, the bag bumped against his gimpy leg. She hurried to keep up with him so the lantern could light both their paths.

When they stepped from behind the station, the wind snatched at her scarf and huffed to extinguish the flickering light. Dark buildings lined the street now carpeted with white snow.

Oscar strode down the center of the road. "Less ice this way," he shouted to be heard above the whistling wind. While the falling snow stung all the skin it could find, each gust of wind made the visibility worse.

Nora knew that this storm was a playful kitten compared to the fierce lions of Norwegian blizzards. Hans had written her of the howling winds and whiteouts of the North Dakota winters of the past, of the cold that cracked trees and killed anyone careless enough to be caught out in it. Her homeland and North Dakota had one thing in common—winter could be deadly.

She shivered at the thought. Was that why Hans had not been back in town? Had there been a terrible blizzard? She shook her head. This new snow was only ankle deep and while snowbanks lined the street, there did not appear to be deep drifts of snow.

Oscar puffed beside her. Nora wished she could repossess her bag, but she hated to hurt the man's feelings. He had been so kind to her.

"Here we are," he said. He opened a gate on their left and walked up a path to a porch that spanned the entire front of the house. Oscar stepped forward and, after setting her bag down, thumped on the door.

Nora felt like crawling over the porch railing and hiding down under the straw banking the sides of the house. How terrible to wake people in the middle of the night like this. And bringing a stranger, at that.

"Don't worry, Miss." Oscar turned to her with a smile. It was as if he had read her mind. "The Moens, they'd skin me alive if I didn't bring you here. You needn't worry about your welcome. And they'll probably know about your young man, too." He pounded on the door again.

Nora flinched at each thump of his fist. A light flickered and gleamed beyond the curtain-covered window.

"I'm coming." A deep voice sent shivers up her spine.

Dear Lord, please make this man willing to take me in. I don't know where else I could go this night. She banished thoughts of "no room at the inn" and swallowed hard. This certainly was not going the way Hans's letters had promised, or like her daydreams on the long trip.

The door swung open and a tall man wearing a dark, belted robe shielded the flame of the candle from the wind. "Come in, come in. You must be freezing out there." He stepped back and held the candle high. "Oscar, whom have you brought us this time?"

"Who is it, dear?" A woman's voice floated down from the hall.

"Hello. I'm John Moen, pastor of the Lutheran church here in Soldall." He shut the door behind them and extended a hand to Nora. "That voice you heard, that's my wife, Ingeborge. She'll join us in a minute. And you are. . . ?"

Nora could not decide whether to shake hands with her mittens on or take them off first. She drew off the right one and extended her hand. "I'm Nora Johanson, from Bergen, Norway. I've come—"

"And who is this?" A tiny, rounded woman with her blond hair in a long braid down her back, beamed up at Nora. Her smile removed any doubt of trespassing on their hospitality. "Whom did you bring us, Oscar?"

"I'm sure they'd tell us if you'd give them a chance," Reverend Moen said, with a twinkle in his eye and love in his voice.

Ingeborge laughed, a merry sound that not only invited smiles from those around but made resistance impossible.

Nora felt a sigh start down in her toes and bubble upward to bring a quiver to her bottom lip. "I. . .I'm Nora Johanson, from Bergen, Norway. My betrothed, Hans Larson, was supposed to meet me at the train, but I suffered all kinds of delays during my trip here. I wired him a message, but—"

"But he didn't pick it up," Oscar finished for her. "I hoped she could stay here until we notify her young man."

"Ja, sure, you know that she can."

Nora intercepted a look between husband and wife. "Only for tonight," she said, feeling a sharp stab of unease. "I'm sure I can find transportation out to Hans's farm tomorrow. I don't want to cause you any trouble."

"No, it's no trouble." Ingeborge shot another look at her husband and reached up to unwind Nora's long knitted scarf. "You give me your coat and come on over by the fire. Oscar, would you like a cup of coffee before you start home?"

"No, no, that's fine. I need to get along. It's late." He turned to leave and paused. "Is something wrong?"

"I'm afraid so." John studied the floor for a moment, then looked at his wife. At her nod, he continued. "You said you were engaged to Hans Larson?"

Nora nodded. A tiny arrow of fear sneaked between her ribs, stabbing her heart.

Ingeborge reached out to take both of Nora's hands in hers.

"I'm so sorry to be the one to tell you this," John paused again as if fighting to get the words out. "But we buried Hans two days ago. He died of the fever."

Chapter 2

It won't be much longer now." Doctor Harmon looked up at Carl Detschman, the pacing father-to-be. "If'n ya can't stand still, get on out to the other room. You men are all alike. You say you want to help and then you make matters worse."

"I'm sorry." The tall man with eyes the faded blue of sun-bleached skies tore his fingers through his thatch of wheaten hair. "I just never—"

"That's the problem, you men never—and I never shoulda asked you to help, but Anna here insisted. I shoulda stayed by my rule—no men ever in the birthing room. Go on out and tend your cows or something."

"But this," Carl waved his hand at the woman he loved, the woman who had now been in labor for a day and a night. "How much more can she stand?" Torn between leaving like the doctor said or staying to help if he could, Carl resumed his pacing.

At a groan from his patient, the doctor stopped lecturing the man and turned back to the woman lying limp on the bed, slowly recovering from the small dose of laudanum he had administered to her.

"All right, my dear. You've had a bit of a rest now, so let's get this baby born." The doc handed a dry towel to Carl as the younger man dropped back to the bedside to take his wife's hand.

"Anna, my heart, you must be strong," Carl murmured as he wiped her brow and smoothed back the tousled hair from her white forehead. Fear nearly strangled him at the sight of her slowly opening eyes, now sunken back in her head.

"Carl!" With the attack of another contraction, her hot hands

18

gripped his. Her body arched off the mattress. She bit back the scream that twisted her face in agony. Even in her near-delirium, she kept quiet so she wouldn't waken their three-year-old daughter who slept peacefully in her own room.

"Oh, my God!" Carl said in a prayer. He knew that in spite of his great physical strength, there was nothing else he could do but pray.

"Push! Push!" The doctor shook his head when he realized his words failed to penetrate the fog she swam in. "Prop her up on the pillows. When the next contraction begins, you yell 'Push' at her and give her every bit of strength you have. I can see the head—if you can just give her the strength to make it through this. You understand?"

Carl nodded and placed his hand on his wife's bulging belly. "Come now, Anna, my love. This is the time." He kept up the soothing murmur even as he felt the contraction begin.

"Now," the doctor ordered when Anna's body tightened again.

"Anna! Push, now! Like you've never done before. Push, Anna!" Carl felt her fingernails dig into the palms of his hands. Her teeth ground into the rag the doctor had placed between her jaws. Sweat poured into her eyes and down to her ears. *God, please! Help us!* He was not sure if he had shouted the plea aloud or screamed it in the hollows of his mind but, at that very second, the doctor grunted his approval.

"You can rest now, my dear." The doctor held the slippery infant in his hands. "You have a son."

Carl leaned his cheek down on Anna's forehead. "You did it, my beautiful love, you did it. You wanted a baby boy and now he is yours." He kissed her forehead, then her cheek.

"Come on, little one, breathe." Doctor Harmon slapped the baby on the buttocks. "Breathe!"

"Wha. . .what's happening?" Anna's voice was so weak, Carl nearly missed it.

"Nothing, everything's fine. You just rest now." Carl murmured reassurances, all the while never taking his eyes from the battle waging at the end of the bed.

The doctor turned the baby over and rubbed its back. Finally, he pinched the minute nose and blew into the baby's mouth.

A cough, faint but gurgling. A moment of silence and then a weak, indignant cry.

"Stubborn, just like his father." Doctor Harmon's shoulders slumped. He placed the infant on Anna's chest and proceeded to cut the umbilical cord, all the while murmuring in a singsong voice.

Carl was not sure if the man was comforting the baby, the mother, or him, but he did not care. He finally allowed his shoulders to relax and the tears to flow. They had made it; they had a son. He knelt by the bed and gently touched the baby's head. He wrapped his other arm around Anna's head.

"Is he all right?" Her voice barely stirred the heavy air.

"Ja. He's fine."

Her eyes fluttered open. One hand crept up to lie across the tiny back. "He's so still."

"Resting like you must." Carl stroked her hair back from her forehead.

"Not yet," the doctor said. He picked up the slippery baby and wrapped him in a soft blanket. "Here, Carl. You put him in the cradle by the fire. We, Anna and I, have more work to do here."

Carl pushed himself to his feet and took his tiny son from the doctor's hands. How could anything so small cause such problems for his mother and yet be so perfect?

"All right, now. Let's get this over with." The doctor had no sooner finished saying the words when along with the afterbirth came a bright red flood that drenched the sheets.

No matter what he did, the bleeding refused to slow. No matter how desperately Carl pleaded with her to hang on and railed at the doctor to do something, nothing helped. Within a few minutes, Anna Detschman quietly slipped away. She never woke again to cuddle the son she had wanted so much.

Carl sat numbly by as she breathed her last. A pain—the likes of which he had never known before, clogged his throat, his chest, his very life. This could not be happening. Just yesterday, his Anna had been laughing, promising Kaaren a new baby brother. And now. . .

"I'm so sorry, son." The doctor leaned his head against the wall. "I don't know what else I could have done." He turned and, bending over, gently pulled the sheet up over Anna's now peaceful face.

Carl folded the sheet back down. "Just leave us alone." His manners caught up with him. "Please."

"Of course." The doctor turned toward the door, then went to the fireplace and picked up the cradle. "I'll wait outside." He left the room, closing the door behind him.

Carl sat on the bed staring at his wife, his love. Only moments ago, she had been there, fighting for the life of their son, and now. . .now she was gone. Anna, the laughing center of his life. . .of their home and family. Gone, leaving him and their children behind. With a gentle finger, he stroked her hand and her pale cheek.

"Oh, Anna. How could you leave me? What kind of a God would let you suffer so and then take you away when we need you so desperately?" He raised his eyes to the ceiling. "Why?" Sobs racked his body as he put his arms around her shoulders and clutched her to his chest. Together they rocked as if he could bring back her life force by sheer willpower.

An hour—an eon later—Carl staggered from the room and collapsed into the rocking chair by the stove. A striped gray cat left the warmth of her box behind the iron stove and rubbed against his leg.

"What will you do?" Doctor Harmon asked from the shadows of the other rocker.

Carl dropped his hand from his eyes and peered into the shadows. "Oh, Doctor Harmon. I. . .I'm sorry. I guess I forgot you were here." His own voice sounded like it came from a far distance.

"I understand." Before he spoke again, the doctor allowed the silence to lengthen. "Oh, Carl, if only I knew of ways to keep tragedies like this from happening. I want you to know how terribly sorry I am."

Carl nodded. "Ja. I know."

"I know you can hardly think now, but that baby there needs some nourishment and soon. Do you know if Anna had some bottles ready. You know, just in case. . .ah. . .of an emergency."

Carl lifted his head. The weight of it took all his strength. "I. . . umm. . ." His breath sighed out like the bellows of a forge. He waited as if expecting someone else to answer. "I don't know."

Just then, a weak wail grabbed their attention.

"See what I mean?" Doctor Harmon touched the cradle with his foot. "Where would the bottles be?" He spoke slowly and precisely, enunciating each syllable as if Carl were hard of hearing.

"In the pantry, there. . .the door to your left."

"And the milk?"

"Out in the well house." Carl rose from his chair and stumbled to the outside door. He slid his feet into the boots waiting on the rug by the door and lifted his coat from the hook. After pulling a knitted stocking cap over his ears, he turned the knob on the door.

"Don't you need a lantern?" the doctor asked.

"Oh, yes." Carl placed the palm of his hand on the doorjamb and leaned his forehead against it. He felt like he was lost in the dark and someone had just blown out the only light.

"Would you like me to get the milk?" Doctor Harmon left his chair and came to stand by the door.

"No. No, I'll be. . .I'll get it."

The baby wailed again, louder this time.

"You see to him, all right?" Carl dug a match out of the box and lit the lantern sitting on the shelf. Without another word, he pulled the door open and staggered out into the dark.

Icy pellets of snow drilled his face and swirled about in the lantern's glow. He kicked the drifted snow away from the well house door and yanked it open. Compared to the freezing wind outside, the cool house felt warm. He pulled a bucket of milk from the nearly frozen water and, after latching the door, headed back to the house.

The doctor, with the swaddled baby in the crook of his arm, had stirred the embers of the fire and added more coal to it. "Water from the reservoir's still warm," he said as he looked up to greet Carl. "I think a cup of coffee would do us both good."

Carl blew out the lantern and hung up his jacket. Bathed in the golden glow from the kerosene lamp on the table, the doctor looked right at home. Carl filled the bottle on the table and set it in the pan of water the doctor had placed off to the side of the range.

When the baby began to fuss, the doctor patted his back and crooned a song in rhythm with the gentle swaying of his own body. "Here," he said, when the bottle seemed warm enough. He handed both baby and bottle to Carl and nodded toward the rocker. "Set yourself down. You both need the rest."

Carl settled down and pushed the nipple into the tiny, rosebud mouth. The baby pushed it out and turned his head, searching for a breast. After several more failed attempts, Carl handed the baby back to the doctor. "You try." He flung himself out of the chair and went to stand at the frosted window.

The baby began to cry, a soft sound that quickly grew into a wail. A voice from the back bedroom joined in the chorus. "Pa-a-a. Ma-a-a."

Carl shrugged his shoulders and dropped his hands in defeat. "Coming, Kaaren." He strode down the hall. "It's all right, *liebchen*." He sat on the bed and hugged his three-year-old daughter close. "There's nothing to be afraid of."

"Where's Ma?" the towheaded child sniffed and rubbed her hand across her eyes. "I want my ma."

Carl hugged her close. "Your ma's busy," he whispered. "You have a new baby brother."

"Ummm." Kaaren nestled into his chest. She popped a thumb into her mouth and, after one pull, relaxed into the sleep of the innocent.

Carl laid her back down. He could still hear the baby crying.

"He refuses to suck on this thing." The doctor waved the bottle in the lamplight. "He won't last long if he doesn't eat."

"Do you know anyone who could wet-nurse him?" asked Carl.

The doctor shook his head and tried again to get the infant to take the bottle.

Carl raked his fingers through his hair until the white-blond strands stood straight up. "What am I going to do?"

The doctor pushed himself to his feet. "How about harnessing up my horse while I rewarm this and try again. I'll get to town right about sunrise and I'll see if I can find one of the women to come out and help you. They're always better at this than I am. Maybe Widow Nelson can help. Naah. She's gone to Fargo to take care of her sister."

Carl ignored the doctor's mutterings and dressed again for the cold outside. Lantern in hand, he opened the door and left, shutting it quickly to keep out the cold.

The barn warmth welcomed him as he slipped in through the small door. The doctor's old bay horse nickered a greeting. Even that simple touch brought tears to Carl's eyes. To keep from throwing himself down on the mound of hay and letting the tears ravage him, he concentrated on each step of the job at hand.

Pick up the harness, settle the leathers in place, buckle the straps, and lead the animal out of the stall. Back the gelding between the shafts. "Sooo now, easy, boy." *Don't think. Don't feel.*

Why was he so clumsy? Because of his gloves? He dashed the back of the knitted fabric across his eyes.

Secure the shafts to the breast piece. Open the main double doors. He continued giving himself orders, as if all this was new to him. Then, he backed the horse and buggy out into the freezing wind. After retrieving his lantern and closing the door, he led the horse up to the house.

He trudged along, knowing he would rather have stayed in the barn. In there, life was as it should be. Life, not death. But duty called him back to the house.

Carl blocked the thought of his wife lying in their bed.

Think of something else. Think of nothing.

The house was silent.

"Shhh." The doctor laid a finger across his lips. He was dressed for the outdoors, his hat pulled down over his ears. "He's asleep." He pointed to the cradle by the stove. "I got him to take a bit. I'll try to find someone for you. In the meantime, try giving him some each time he wakes up. If he gets hungry enough, maybe he'll eat."

"Thank you, Doctor." Carl extended his hand. The older man clasped it and covered their joined hands with his other.

"You're welcome, son. I just wish I coulda done more." The man hefted his worn black bag and slipped out the door.

Carl listened to the jingle of the harness as the horse trotted down the lane. Only the whistle of the wind, seeking entrance through tiny cracks, disturbed the silence of the house. The awful silence.

Chapter 3

Nora felt like a glacier pressed upon her shoulders.

"Oh, my dear, I am so sorry." Ingeborge guided the younger woman into a chair. "Such terrible news and right off when you first arrive like this." She pulled up a stool and perched immediately in front of her guest so as to hold Nora's shaking hands.

Nora heard the men talking by the door as from a great distance. She forced herself to concentrate on the caring woman before her. What had she said? Anything that needed an answer? Hans had died. He was dead. Shouldn't she be weeping? But the sorrow was more like that of losing a dear friend, not the love of one's life. She was sad. Of course. But it did not seem to touch her—not inside where heart and love dwelled.

Instead, the thoughts that set her body shaking raced one on top of the other. *Whatever will I do now? Wherever will I go? Who will take care of Hans's farm? Could I live there?* She pulled herself back from looking over the precipice of her future and focused on the tender smile of the woman in front of her.

"I. . .I'm sorry, I seemed to have wandered off somewhere." Nora leaned back in the chair and drew in a deep breath. She felt the shudder start at her toes and work its way up until even her teeth rattled.

"Are you cold? Can I get you a blanket? The coffee will be ready shortly." Ingeborge rubbed Nora's icy hands.

Nora heard the door close and Reverend Moen approach. She studied her hands, warmly clasped in Ingeborge's as if to keep the outer world at bay. Her own hands, so large with long fingers and so smooth due to the long weeks of idleness. Ingeborge's hands, small and reddened from the work of her house. Maybe she could help the Moens for a time.

But Hans's cows and the horses. Who was taking care of them since he had passed away? He had said he had no near neighbors.

She reached to unbutton her coat. Here she was, dripping all over the spotless kitchen. What kind of visitor did things like that?

"I'm sorry for dripping snow on your floor. What you must think of me."

"No, no. You mustn't worry. You've had a great shock. Here, let me take that." Ingeborge pulled herself to her feet and reached for Nora's dark, wool coat. "Let me hang this over a chair by the stove so it can dry. Your scarf and mittens, too."

Nora felt like a small child obeying her mother. How comforting. She went through the motions but her mind insisted on darting around like a cornered animal. Hans—her friend of so many years—was gone. When she thought of their growing up together, she felt the tears beginning in the back of her throat. What about his parents? At the thought of their dear faces, the tears overflowed.

She covered her face with her hands, trying to stifle the sobs that shook her shoulders. Oh, the dreams that died along with a loved one. The happinesses that now would never be.

She felt a hand smoothing her hair, heard a gentle voice murmuring condolences. Words that ran together with no meaning, save that of love. She rested in their comfort.

When Nora leaned her weary head against the back of the chair, Ingeborge took a steaming cup of coffee from her husband and handed it to the young woman. "Drink this, it will help. I don't know if you use sugar, but I sweetened it to lick the shock."

Nora nodded her thanks and wrapped her hands around the mug. She sipped carefully. The aroma seeped into her pores, as the warmth cupped between both her hands and now sliding down her throat overcame the shivers.

"Did you know Hans well?" She looked from one Moen to the other.

Reverend Moen nodded. "We knew him, but we were not what you might call friends. He attended our church a few times when he had first arrived. This is a small community, so everyone knows everyone else."

"Did he talk much about his farm. . .our farm? You see, I'm concerned about the cows and horses, that someone is caring for them." Nora caught one of those looks passing from husband to wife again. An uncomfortable silence thrummed between the three of them. Nora took her courage in hand. "Is something else wrong?"

Reverend Moen inhaled deeply. "You asked about *his* farm?"

Nora nodded. "Hans wrote in his letters about the two-storied house and big barn, three milk cows, and a team of gray horses he'd already purchased. He said that last year he built a windmill so I wouldn't even have to pump water. He said. . ." Her voice trailed off. She had been babbling like a brook in the spring. She rubbed the smooth edge of the cup in her hand.

"Ach, you poor child." Ingeborge patted Nora's knee.

"Please, tell me." Nora whispered her plea.

Reverend Moen drew up a straight-backed kitchen chair and folded his lean frame down onto it. He shook his head. "I am so sorry to be the bearer of bad news tonight but. . .well. . ." He drew in another deep breath. "Hans Larson worked as a farmhand for the Elmer Peterson family, south of town. He lived in their bunkhouse with the other hired hands." He shook his head. "Hans didn't even own the horse he rode."

This is too much. I cannot bear all this. Nora's thoughts weighed her down. She wished she could sink through the leather seat of the rocker and down into the floor. "Are you. . .you sure? My Hans Larson was tall, yellow hair, and a smile that broke your heart. He—" She forced her mind to think of something different about him. "He had a scar from a burn on the back of his right hand, from when we were children."

Reverend Moen nodded. "Yes, that's whom I am talking about. The same Hans Larson, from Bergen, Norway. He arrived about three years ago."

The crushing iceberg settled on her again. Nora bit the inside of her lip to keep it from quivering. No Hans. No farm. "Well, then, at least there are no animals suffering from neglect." She attempted a smile in the minister's direction but failed miserably.

Instead, she studied the muted colors in the braided rug at her feet. Anything was better than looking at the faces of the two sympathetic Moens. How could she have been such a fool?

"You mustn't blame yourself. . .I mean. . .how could you have known anything else clear back in Norway? You trusted his letter, like you should have." Ingeborge leaned forward from her perch on the stool. "Besides, he was such a charming young man."

That he was, thought Nora. His charm was one reason she had fallen in love with him. Or had she fallen in love with love, with the adventure of coming to the New World? She drank some more of the sweet coffee; its warmth seemed to melt that glacier she felt resting on her. After draining the coffee mug, she glanced around for a place to set it down.

Ingeborge took the empty cup. "Would you like some more?" Nora shook her head.

"Then, if you'd like, I will show you to your bed. I'm afraid you must share it with our seven-year-old Mary. She'll be surprised when she wakes up in the morning, but Mary loves company."

Nora felt the words flowing over her like a healing draft. She did not have to make any decisions tonight. Maybe tomorrow she would be able to think better. Maybe tomorrow God would work a miracle and take this all away. Maybe tomorrow she would awaken from this terrible dream and be back with her beloved family.

"Good night, then." She nodded to the man adjusting the damper in the great black iron stove. "And, thank you."

"I've already taken your bag upstairs." He clattered the round lid of the stove back into place. "Sleep well. Things always have a way of looking brighter in the morning, even when times seem the darkest."

"Mange takk." Nora followed Ingeborge up the steep stairs. Halfway up she paused to rest. She had not realized how exhausted she was. Each step seemed like a mountain, with her feet so weighted she could barely lift them. She stepped with her right

foot, then her left, each dragging the other until she reached the upper hall. Soft light from Ingeborge's candle beckoned from the room on the left.

"If you sit in that rocking chair, I can help you with your boots." Ingeborge turned from arranging the sleeping child in the bed. "Have you a nightgown in your bag?"

Nora nodded as she sank down into the chair. Waves of weary sadness washed over her. She felt like she had been pounded by waves down in the fjord on a stormy day and was being pulled out to sea. Ingeborge's voice came from far away. She felt herself sinking.

"Now, let's just get you in bed before you fall asleep in the chair." A gentle hand tugged her upright. Nora did as the voice commanded. She stood, stepped, turned, and sank into the feather bed that rose up to greet her. She heard her mother's voice, *"Now mind your manners,"* but Nora could not force the required *"Mange takk"* past the sleep that clogged her throat and eyes.

"God bless you, my dear. I'll leave the candle here in case you need it." Ingeborge smoothed the hair back from Nora's forehead just like she had done to her daughter. The feather-light touch was the last sensation Nora felt; she was at home, in her mother's care.

Light, bright as though from a thousand flashing diamonds, filled her eyes. She blinked against the brightness, then slowly opened her eyelids. To the left, sun streaming through the frosted window-pane made her blink again. She turned her head to the right.

A solemn stare from bright blue eyes met her own. In a blur of spinning braids and a voice to wake the deaf, the child fled out the door.

"Ma, she's awake!" echoed in the hall.

Nora stretched her hands over her head and pointed her toes to the end of the mattress. Oh, how good it felt as she rotated her shoulders.

The night before came crashing back. Hans was dead. Hans had lied. What was she to do now? She felt like pulling the covers over her head to blot out the sun and the new day. Instead, she lifted her head and looked around the room. Covered by colorful patchwork quilts, she had not noticed the cold through the night. A small rocker held a rag doll, which kept company with the grownup one. By the bed, a pitcher and matching bowl painted with pink roses sat on top of a dark oak commode. More pink roses climbed trellises up the wallpapered walls. . .the same pink roses she had dreamed of for her new home.

"Enough of that," she ordered herself when she could feel a lump beginning in her throat. "As Ma always says, 'The good Lord has His eye on the sparrow and us as well.' " She threw back the covers and planted her feet firmly on the braided rug of many colors. "This is the day that the Lord hath made. I will rejoice and be glad in it."

She bit back the quiver in her chin. She had said that verse every morning since her confirmation, but today it was difficult to say. So she said it again—more firmly. "This is the day that the Lord hath made." She heard footsteps coming up the stairs. "I will rejoice and be glad in it."

Ingeborge tapped on the door before entering. "What a marvelous way to start the day." Cheeks red from the heat of the cooking stove made her blue eyes sparkle even more. "You must have been sleeping hard since Mary came down without waking you."

"Oh, I did. . .sleep well, that is."

Ingeborge poured hot water into the pitcher on the stand. "Now you can wash and, when you're ready, there's breakfast waiting."

"Ma. . ." A young voice floated up the stairwell.

"That's Knute. He's five. You've met Mary. . ."

Nora nodded.

"Ma-a-a."

"Goodness. With these four of mine there's always something." She turned in a swirl of skirts but paused at the door. "You come down when you're ready now."

Nora pressed a hand to her chest and shook her head. She felt like a whirlwind had just blown through the room. She crossed the room and closed the door. Now, she would finally have a real washing.

In spite of the heating grate in the floor, she shivered in the cold room as she hurried through her bathing. Wishing for clean clothes, she thought of her trunk still at the station. But that would come later. She pulled on her clothes and the long black wool stockings. While warmer, she no longer felt so clean. She shook out her shirtwaist and black wool skirt before buttoning them in place.

With her hair brushed and rebraided, she felt more like a young woman who had boarded the train for a new country. Actually, she was feeling better than she had felt for days. In spite of her difficulties, she hummed under her breath while she made the bed and wiped the water from the oak stand.

As she made her way down the stairs, she could hear young voices. Her stomach rumbled, reminding her of how long it had been since her last meal.

She turned to the right and stopped at the entry to the kitchen. Two children sat at the oval oak table in front of the window, reading their lessons. They looked up when they heard her tread. Nora smiled at them both and then at the picture Ingeborge made. The baby was nestled in her arms while a chubby little girl played with the cat at her mother's feet.

An ache began somewhere in the middle of Nora's heart. This was what she had dreamed of. . .and now that dream was shattered. She resecured the smile on her face and buried the ache under the ashes of her yesterday. As Ma and the Good Book said, "Weeping may endure for a night, but joy cometh in the morning."

And this was definitely morning—she glanced at the grand-father clock by the door—but not morning for much longer.

"I'm sorry to be such a lazybones, I. . ."

"Not at all." Ingeborge shook her head. "You needed the rest. Now, I know you must be starved." When she started to get up, Nora laid a hand on the woman's shoulder.

"No, you stay there with the baby. Just tell me where things are and I will fix my own. The coffee smells wonderful." She reached into the glass-faced cupboard for a cup. A loaf of bread sat on the counter, next to a crock of jam.

"Thank you, my dear. Everything is right in front of you. We'll be having soup for dinner in about an hour or when Reverend Moen returns. He had some calls to make."

While Nora sliced the homemade bread, Ingeborge introduced her children. "Mary is the oldest at seven, Knute is five, Grace is three, and James here is five months." She dropped a kiss on the rosy cheek of the baby asleep in her arms. The gentle rocking of the chair creaked its own song, in counterpoint with the kettle singing on the stove.

Nora sighed blissfully as she took her first sip of coffee and bite of the jellied bread. She placed two thick slices on a plate and carried her breakfast over to the table. "Do you mind if I join you?" she asked the children.

The two with hair so blond as to be white, hers in braids and his bowl-cut, stared at her solemnly. Mary broke the ice with a grin. "I didn't think you were ever going to wake up."

Not to be outdone, Knute piped up. "Did you like the train ride?"

"He always wants to go on the train." Mary closed her book. "But we never have." She leaned her chin on her stacked fists. "Ma said you went on a ship, too."

Nora set her plate and cup on the table, then pulled out a high-backed oak chair. "Yes, I did. Both a ship and a train." She sat down. "Now, why do you like the train so?" She leaned forward to look Knute right in the eyes.

"It is so big and goes so fast."

"Big and fast. Big and fast." Mary shook her head like big sisters everywhere.

Nora smothered a grin behind her coffee cup. "Someday, I'm sure you'll have a train ride."

"Now, you children go play in the other room," their mother ordered. She rose to her feet and laid the baby in his cradle. "Miss Johanson and I would like to visit."

"Yes, Ma." The two obediently slid to the floor and, gathering their books, ran laughing down the hall.

"No running in the house."

"Yes, Ma." A giggle floated back to the peaceful room.

Ingeborge poured herself a cup of coffee and brought it over to the table. The orange-striped cat followed her and wound herself around Nora's ankles. The toddler followed the cat and tugged at her mother's skirt to be picked up.

Nora felt a tug at her heart. "What beautiful children you have." She leaned over and scratched along the cat's arched back. "It is so wonderful here."

"Thank you." Ingeborge settled little Grace on her lap and leaned back in her chair. "Mary and Knute should be at school, but there have been so many children sick that they closed the school for a time. I thank the Lord each day for keeping us safe and healthy. The fever seems to come like a fiend from the north and before you realize it, people are coughing to death. That's where John is now. Someone else died during the night. And the doctor was at a difficult birthing. But there seems to be nothing he can do for these poor ones. Some get well but many don't."

"We've had those in Norway, too. But not so much this last year." Nora got up and refilled her coffee cup.

"Ach, what a terrible hostess I am," Ingeborge moved as if to get up.

"No, you stay there. This is the least I can do when you take in a stranger like this." Nora sat back down. The cat leaped up into her lap and settled itself for a nap.

"The cat likes you; the children like you; I like you. That means we all agree. You are welcome to stay as long as you need to." Ingeborge stroked little Grace's silky white hair; the little one's eyes drooped closed and a thumb found its way into her mouth.

"You have no idea how much your offer means to me, but I must earn my own way. With all the illness, isn't there someone who needs a strong back and willing hands?"

"I don't know." The older woman wrinkled her brow in thought. "Can you teach school? There is a town not far from here that is looking for a schoolteacher."

Nora shook her head. "I think not. I have no certificate and, besides, I don't speak English. Does everyone around here speak Norwegian?"

"No, there are Germans and Swedes and several Norse dialects. You would have to learn English." She thought awhile. "You're not thinking of returning to Norway then?"

"I have no money."

"None at all?"

"Four pennies. That is why Oscar brought me here last night. I couldn't afford the hotel." Nora sipped her coffee. "Do you suppose they need anyone at the hotel? I can cook and clean."

Ingeborge shuddered. "I know the Lord says not to speak ill of anyone, but we can't let you work there. We'll ask John when he comes home. Surely he'll have an idea of what to do."

Nora stroked the soft fur of the cat purring in her lap. It was true, animals and children always took to her, especially the wounded. Back home she loved teaching Sunday school for the little ones. If only she did not need English to teach school in North Dakota.

The clock bonged the first notes of twelve.

"Oh, my land. John may be home any minute." Ingeborge roused the sleepy Grace and, after a quick kiss, set the child on the floor. "Mary, time to set the table. Knute, the coal bin is nearly empty."

"Let me help." Nora set the cat down in Grace's arms and patted the little girl on the head. She glanced out the window. "Here comes Reverend Moen. He's just opening the gate."

Nora helped Mary set the table and, with everyone flying to do their jobs, the dinner was on the table by the time the father had hung his coat on the coatrack by the door and had washed his hands. The children scrambled into their places, Grace into her high chair, and, when the adults sat down, everyone joined hands for grace.

The familiar words of the table prayer transported Nora back to the warm kitchen of her family's farm. She swallowed a tear and sneaked a peak at the child in the high chair beside her.

Grace murmured her own unintelligible words along with them all. But her "Ah-men" rang loud and clear and her proud grin prompted giggles from the others.

Their father eyed them sternly, but they caught the twitch in his cheek.

Nora tried to suffocate her chortle, but a glance at Ingeborge struggling the same way did her in.

When they all laughed, Grace announced "Ahh-men" again and banged her spoon on the table.

Reverend Moen reached over and removed the spoon from the child's hand. "Ja, that was good." He smoothed her hair back with the back of his knuckles. "Now you must eat your dinner like Mama's good little girl." He looked around the table. "As you all must."

Conversation lagged while everyone devoured the soup, both first and second helpings. When they finished, Ingeborge brought cookies and coffee to the table.

"Now. Did Mary and Knute do all their lessons?" Reverend Moen gazed at each child, then his wife.

"Mostly," Mary answered.

"That's not enough. You go get your books and bring them to the table while we talk. Knute's, too." When the children were settled and the coffee poured, he turned to Nora. "And now, how are you?"

"I'll be all right. This all takes some getting used to."

"Yes, it does. I want you to know you can remain with us as long as you want."

"*Mange takk.* But we, Ingeborge and I, were talking about—do you know anyone who needs a. . .someone like me to help them? Ingeborge said you might have heard of someone who is sick or a family that needs. . .well, I can cook and clean, manage a house, a barn." Her voice began to fade away. She took a breath. "I'm not afraid of work."

Reverend Moen leaned back against the chair. He looked up at the ceiling, his brow creased in thought. The clock ticked loudly in the silence. "There are so many that need help but they can't afford to pay anyone. Times are harsh here on the prairie." He rubbed the bridge of his nose with a long finger. "I'll ask Doctor Harmon if I see him this afternoon. We'll be having another funeral in the morning. Old Peder Stroenven died during the night."

"Ach, this is so hard." Ingeborge shook her head. "The young and the old are always hit the hardest."

Nora glanced out the window in time to see a horse and sleigh stop in front of the gate. "You have company."

Reverend Moen pushed back his chair and rose to his feet. "You'd best make some more coffee. Whoever it is will be cold clear through if he's driven far. The cold is fierce even with the sun shining."

He strode to the door and pulled it open before the knock sounded. "Why, Carl Detschman. How good to see you. Come right in."

Nora felt lost immediately. The greeting was in English. She looked up to find frozen blue eyes staring at her. Then the man's gaze flickered back to the pastor. Their conversation continued.

The man handed a well-wrapped bundle to Ingeborge and pushed a very young girl forward also. Then he touched his hand to his forehead and left. The door closed behind him.

"Oh, the poor man." Ingeborge sank down in a chair and began to unwrap the bundle. A tiny red-faced infant emitted a wavering cry. Tears formed in the little girl's blue eyes and ran down her cheeks.

"Pa!" she cried and ran to the door. "Pa!"

"What is it? Can I help?" Nora sprang to her feet.

Ingeborge settled herself in the rocker. "Carl's wife died last night in childbirth and he can't get this mite to take a bottle. John said we'd help. Why don't you bring the little girl here? Her name is Kaaren."

"Now, we'll have two funerals tomorrow." Reverend Moen stood in front of the window. "Dear Lord, when will this cease?"

I wonder if this is the family I am to help, Nora thought as she went to the stove for the coffeepot. *Mr. Detschman is certainly a man with more than his share of troubles.*

Chapter 4

"Oh, that poor man." Nora felt her heart break for him.

"Pa-a-a." Kaaren tried turning the doorknob to follow her father. Tears streamed down her face as she
twisted on the slippery knob.

Nora rose and knelt by the child. "Your pa will come back.
Come here and let me dry your tears."

Kaaren pulled away and wailed more loudly.

Nora sat back on her heels. If only she could speak the language.

Reverend Moen stooped beside her. "Come, Kaaren, you
must give this up now. You'll make yourself sick with such tears."
He lifted the little girl in his arms and patted her back.

"Pa, I. . .I want my. . .my pa."

Nora rose to her feet, thankful that the Moens spoke both
Norwegian and English. However would she be able to work for a
family that did not speak Norwegian?

"Mary, you take Kaaren and show her your dolls," John said.
He set the crying child down again and linked the two girls' hands.
"Kaaren, you go with Mary. Knute, why don't you help entertain
our visitor, also?" When the children wandered off to the other
room chattering, he turned back to Nora.

"Carl said he needed to get back to take care of his livestock.
That's why he left so hastily. He also said he'd bring Anna, that's
his wife, in for the funeral tomorrow."

"Oh, that poor, poor man." Nora shook her head. Visions of
stern, blue eyes in a strongly handsome face returned to her. So
young for such a tragedy. She totally forgot her own situation while
praying for his.

"God be thanked that Carl didn't lose his son, too," Ingeborge added.

"That is true. But for right now—" Reverend Moen studied the toe of his boot. He inhaled deeply and sighed in weariness. "I need to go over to the blacksmith and ask him to prepare another box. Then locate someone to ride out and help Carl. He looked about at the end of his tether." Reverend Moen reached for his coat and hat. He paused. "You know anyone besides yourself who could wet-nurse this baby, Inge?"

Ingeborge looked up. "What? Oh dear, I don't know, not right now."

After the man left the house, Nora began clearing the table. Had the good Lord answered her prayer already? Here was someone, literally on their doorstep, who needed help. And he needed help now! Granted, she could not nurse the baby, but maybe she could persuade him to take a bottle. Maybe after Ingeborge nursed him a few times to get his strength up—the thoughts leaped and tumbled over one another.

"There, now," Ingeborge said with a sigh of relief. "The mite finally found out what he's supposed to do." She pushed her rocker into its creaking song. "Who else might still be nursing a baby? We've had no newborns around here for a time."

Nora reached under the sink for a metal pan. After slicing several curls off the hard lye soap bar and into the pan, she poured in steaming water from the teakettle. Then, she added the dishes. All the while her thoughts tumbled on. She could work for Carl Detschman, of course she could. That way she would earn money for her passage back to Norway. She could go home. What kind of wages would he pay? Maybe he was unable to pay like the others that Ingeborge mentioned. What then?

Memory of her mother's voice blew cool reason through the confusion in her mind. *If you are doing God's will, He will make your path straight.* I don't only need it straight, Nora thought, I need the bumps taken out and a good road map. What am I supposed to do?

"There." Ingeborge nestled the infant up on her shoulder and rubbed his back for a burp. "He should feel much better now."

"What did they name the baby?" Nora finished drying the dishes and putting them away.

"Peder. Peder Detschman. Such a strong name. He will have much to live up to." The baby burped in her ear. "There now, little one." She cuddled him in the crook of her arm; the rocking chair continued its song.

Nora heard the beginning stirrings of Ingeborge's baby waking in the cradle by the rocker. She hung the dish towel over the bar behind the stove and, picking up the iron handle, lifted the round stove lid and set it to the side. Red coals glowed in the firebox. She picked up the small, metal scoop on top of the coal bucket and dug out several dusty, brown pieces of lignite, the soft coal of North Dakota, and scattered them over the red embers. After replacing the lid, she dropped the scoop back into place.

The baby in the cradle announced that he was ready to be picked up now—and eat.

"Will you have enough for him?" Nora nodded toward the cradle.

"We'll make do." Ingeborge put both arms around the baby in her arms and made as if to stand. She looked from the bundle in her arms to Nora and then back down. "Here, you take little Peder and lay him in the cradle after I take James in for dry diapers."

Nora leaned over to take the infant from the older woman's arms. As she straightened, she studied the baby wrapped so tightly in his blankets. When his eyelids fluttered and the rosebud mouth yawned, she felt her heart fly right out of her chest and open wide to the tiny baby.

"Oh, you are a darling, baby mine," she crooned to him as she rocked him carefully in her arms. Without a thought, she hummed him a lullaby, learned at her mother's knee. She hesitated to put him down, this mite who was starting life with no mother. He needed her.

If only she had milk for him. But she did not. Her practical side won out, and she laid him on his stomach in the cradle.

Peder squirmed and mewed like a newborn kitten. When

Nora gently rocked the cradle and resumed her sweet song, his body relaxed and he drifted back to sleep. Nora knelt by the cradle, reluctant to take leave of her charge.

She smiled as Ingeborge returned with her contented baby perched in her arms. James waved an arm and, turning his face, began rooting at his mother's breast.

"Ja, you are hungry again." Ingeborge settled herself back in the rocker. "With two of these young men, I know what a ewe with twins feels like." His sucks and gurgles proclaimed his relief that he was finally being fed.

Ingeborge chuckled as she stroked the baby's round, still-bald head. "This one, he's not shy about letting his mama know when she is neglecting her duty. He seems so big, especially when I hold him right after little Peder." She trailed a finger down the baby's rosy cheek.

His blue eyes concentrating on his mother's face, James waved a chubby fist and reached for his mother's mouth. She nibbled on his fingers and then kissed them.

Nora felt an ache in her heart. If only she and Hans. . . She rose to her knees and then to her feet. As she dusted off the back of her skirt, she dusted away the regrets. Hans was now a memory, and any dreams of him and their life together should be put to rest in the cold ground, like he had been. That sounded so easy.

"Ingeborge, would you like a cup of coffee?" She swept away the thoughts, firmly planting a smile on her mouth, a mouth that would rather quiver.

"Yes, please. Here I am so remiss. What kind of a hostess do you think I am?"

"A very busy one," Nora replied with a smile. "Since I'm not able to perform your special task, let me take over some of your other ones."

"There are cookies in the round blue tin on the second shelf," Ingeborge motioned to the cupboards with her chin. "Why don't you set out enough for everyone and call the children? They have been playing so good. There's milk for them in the pantry."

Nora did as asked, taking a peek at the sleeping infant every time she passed the cradle. He was so tiny. As soon as the table was set, she walked through the sitting room, scarcely taking time to admire the stiff, horsehair sofa and matching chairs. She could hear the children laughing through a door at the opposite end of the room.

"There are cookies and milk on the table," she said, pausing in the doorway.

Smiles greeted her from the two girls sitting cross-legged on a counterpane, surrounded by dolls. Mary cuddled a porcelain-faced doll with curly, blond hair and dressed in blue dimity. Kaaren clutched a rag doll as if it would be taken from her; she turned to look up at Nora.

On the floor, Knute stopped his train rumblings and screechy noises and sprung to his feet. "Cookies, yumm." He brushed past Nora in the doorway.

"Knute, put your train away," Mary called after him.

As he trudged back into the room muttering under his breath, Mary took Kaaren's hand. "Come on. There are cookies and milk." When spoken in English so she could understand, Kaaren smiled and, still hugging the doll to her chest, slipped by Nora in the doorway, careful not to touch her—or look at her.

What does she think I am, the big bad troll? Nora thought while waiting for the hurrying boy to put his toys away. *Just because I talk Norwegian instead of English. Poor little mite, how will she bear it with no mother? I wonder if they've told her yet. How do you tell a little one like her that her ma won't be coming back anymore? How can she even understand. . .when I don't?*

Nora followed after the children, wishing she could gather little Kaaren close and take away the tears that would be coming.

And come they did, as soon as Kaaren saw Ingeborge nursing her baby, James, in the rocking chair. "I want my ma-a-a." Huge tears spilled from her eyes and rolled down her cheeks. When Mary offered her a cookie, Kaaren pushed it away and continued to cry. She scrubbed her fists into her eyes and leaned her forehead onto the edge of the table.

Nora scooped the little girl up in her arms and sat back down on the vacated chair. She rocked back and forth, cuddling Kaaren against her chest and murmuring words of comfort. She stroked the fine, blond hair and wiped away the tears as they continued to course down the pale cheeks.

"Hush, now," she crooned. "You'll make yourself sick with all these tears. You've cried so many we'll all float away on a puddle."

Mary left her chair and brought one of the crisp sugar cookies to Kaaren. She took the younger girl's hand and placed the cookie in it. "My ma makes the best cookies anywhere. You'll like this." Mary took a big bite of the cookie in her other hand and grinned between chews. "See?"

Kaaren sniffed back her tears and took a bite. As she solemnly nibbled at the rich cookie, she kept her gaze on Mary. Sniffs punctuated the bites.

Nora looked over the little girl's head to see Ingeborge smiling and nodding. The baby had finished eating and was now playing poke-a-finger-in-my-mother's-mouth, a favorite mother-baby game since time began. She could hear him cooing, imitating his mother's sounds and, once in a while, adding a contagious belly laugh.

She continued the soothing rocking motion and laid her cheek against the child's head leaning on her chest. Who would care for this dear little one? Could it be herself? How would she propose this idea of hers? Just step forward and say, "I know you need help with your children and I need work"? She mentally shook her head. Should she talk this over with Ingeborge? But what if she disapproved? Why would she do that? Nora felt like she had two people arguing in her head.

"Mary, why don't you and Kaaren play with James while I start fixing supper? Bring the quilt in from the foot of the bed and all of you can play on the floor." Ingeborge held her baby under his arms and bounced him on her knee. "I could sit and play with you all afternoon and then what would your pa say? He'd like to have supper ready when he comes home." The baby gurgled in agreement.

While the children played on the floor, the women shared the cooking chores. Nora peeled carrots and potatoes to add to the already cooked pot of chicken that Ingeborge had brought in from the pie safe on the screened-in back porch.

"Then, we'll make some dumplings and supper'll be all ready." The older woman glanced at the clock bonging by the door. "We have time to make applesauce cookies. Would you like to help me?"

"Of course." Nora rinsed off her hands and bent over to check the cradle where Peder was making the squeaking noises of a baby awakening. She set the cradle rocking gently with the toe of her shoe. "Hush now, little one. You must sleep longer."

"Ja, so I have more milk for him." Ingeborge set a tan earthenware bowl on the table and began adding ingredients. As she measured and stirred, she kept up a running introduction of the residents of Soldall for Nora's delight and amusement.

Nora felt like she would be able to recognize her prospective neighbors just from Ingeborge's mimicry. "What can you tell me about Carl Detschman?" Nora asked, after giggling at another of Ingeborge's tales of life in Soldall.

After sliding a sheet of cookies into the blackened oven, Ingeborge paused. The creak and slam of the oven door snapped her back in motion. "Ja, that poor man. He has his hands full now. And it is so hard for him to ask for help." She shook her head, like so many other women who wish they could do something but did not know what.

Nora waited, continuing to drop the cookie dough onto another flat baking pan.

"We've known Carl since he arrived in Soldall six years ago. He was just starting out after buying old Mr. Einer Peterson's farm. Einer had died that summer from the consumption. He'd been sick a very long time."

Nora had a hard time to keep from interrupting. She did not want to hear about Einer Peterson.

"Carl came from Minnesota, somewhere down by St. Paul, so he has no family around here. He was already betrothed; that was such a disappointment to the young ladies in our church. You could just see their eyes light up the day he walked into services. Such a handsome young man."

Nora could agree with that even though she had seen him when he seemed frozen in the middle of an ice chunk.

"And the voice of an angel. When he sings those hymns—why he just lifts the rest of the congregation and leads us into heaven." Ingeborge winked at Nora then picked up the full sheet of cookies and slid it onto the bottom rack in the oven. With one finger, she touched one of the cookies on the top rack to see if it was done. When the cookie indented rather than springing back, she turned the cookie sheet around 180 degrees and closed the oven. "Now, where was I?"

"About what a voice Carl has," Nora reminded her.

"Oh yes, and such nice manners. You know his ma taught him well. He brought Anna to meet us when they returned after the wedding. They were married at the end of harvest. It was a very good year, I remember. He'd ordered a new wagon to drive her home in, painted all red and green with shiny yellow wheels. That wagon was really a sight."

Nora did not want to hear about the wagon, either.

"He's a hard worker, that Carl. Einer, because he was so sick, had let the farm run down. But by the next year, Carl had painted the barns and even the house. I said Carl is a hard worker. Well, his Anna was, too. It was a shame they didn't get more acquainted with the community. But they worked from dawn to dark."

Ingeborge opened the creaky oven door and removed the top sheet, placing it off to the cool side of the range while she moved the bottom sheet to the upper rack.

"Oh, Ma, those look so good." Mary and her three shadows lined up by the table, ogling the cookies as her mother lifted the fragrant goodies from the pan to the table.

"Wait until they cool a bit." Ingeborge pushed away an inquisitive finger. "My, they do smell good, don't they?" She sniffed appreciatively.

Nora agreed. The apple-cinnamon aroma filled the room. She dug a finger into the dough and, after putting the dab in her mouth, sucked her finger clean. She looked up, guilt evidenced in the heat coating her cheeks when she saw Ingeborge watching her.

"I know, I'm setting a bad example for the children as my ma always said, but. . ."

"No buts, child. I usually can't resist myself. But here, why don't you try this instead?" She picked up a hot cookie and brought it over, along with the empty pan. "You eat this and I'll finish." She turned back to the table. "Go ahead, children. Just be careful you don't burn yourselves." The three did not need a second invitation.

"Thank you," they chorused and joined James back on the quilt.

"No! No! He's too little." Nora flew across the room to scoop the baby up, safe from the cookie Kaaren was going to shove into his mouth.

The little girl burst into tears that turned into wails. "Ma-a-a. I want my ma."

Realizing he did not know who the strange person was who had snatched him up, little James joined Kaaren, puckering up and letting loose with a wall-shaking howl.

Mary and Knute stared from one to the other, forgotten cookies clutched in their hands.

Ingeborge dropped the spoon of cookie dough and, in the process of spinning around to help Nora, bumped the cradle with her toe.

With both the noise and motion, Peder yowled almost before he awakened.

"There, there." Nora tried to quiet the screaming baby in her arms with one hand and comfort the little girl with the other.

"Whatever is going on in here?" Reverend Moen stepped through the door. "I could hear the noise clear out to the street."

Ingeborge gathered James from Nora and hid her laughing face in the baby's chubby neck. James quieted immediately.

Mary patted Kaaren on the back, trying to comfort her but to no avail.

Nora looked from the little girl to the baby yelling in the cradle. Whom should she go to first? When Reverend Moen squatted down in front of the two little girls, Nora picked up the screaming infant. She put him up to her shoulder, joggling him and crooning comfort at the same time.

"What's for supper?" John asked after calming Kaaren and picking her up. Together, they leaned over the fresh cookies on the table.

Nora and Ingeborge stared at each other—supper was not ready.

Ingeborge threw her hands into the air and laughed. "Chicken and dumplings but, even with two cooks, it'll be a while."

"I can fix the dumplings since I can't take care of this one's needs." Nora continued swaying with the still-snuffling baby.

"Good." Ingeborge turned to her husband. "And, if you'll take care of your young son here, we can proceed. Mary, why don't you and Kaaren set the table?"

"Oh, the cookies." Nora reached for a pot holder as she handed Ingeborge the baby. The smell of burning chased the cookie fragrance from the room. All the cookies on the back corner of the pan had changed from light brown to smokey black.

"I'm so sorry to burn—" Nora felt her cheeks flame again.

"Oh, well. The birds needed something to eat, too," Mary said over her shoulder as she led Kaaren and Knute from the room.

Ingeborge chuckled. Nora bit her lip. John grinned from one woman to the other, his eyebrow arched above his right eye. Laughter filled the room and bounced off the darkened windows.

Just like home, Nora thought. *Oh, how I've missed the laughter.*

Ingeborge settled herself in the rocker and started to nurse the baby. She flipped the baby's quilt over her shoulder and set the chair rocking.

John pulled out a chair and, after sitting down and bouncing James on his knee, reached across the table for another cookie. "How good to come home to such a happy place." He took a bite of cookie and closed his eyes in bliss. "Now, if only I had a cup of coffee to wash this down." He looked his young son in the eye, as if asking his opinion. "Wouldn't that be about right?"

Nora leaped to grab a cup and fill it to the brim. If she wanted to hire out as a housekeeper or helper, she had better begin to anticipate what a man arriving home would want.

"I hope that is hot enough." She placed it in front of him. She watched him with anxious eyes as he sipped then nodded.

"Good. Now I start the dumplings."

On her way back across the kitchen she stopped to check the fire and added more coal. After moving the cooking pot to the hotter part of the stove, she raised the cover and gave the contents a stir with the wooden spoon that rested in a saucer on the warming oven.

While she mixed and stirred the dumplings, Nora listened to the conversation between the pastor and his wife. Thanks to Ingeborge's delightful descriptions, she recognized many of the people John talked about. The conclusion of both doctor and pastor: No one was available to nurse this new baby. Also, they had not talked to people about hiring Nora.

"Maybe tomorrow, after the funerals, I'll have a better idea for you," Reverend Moen told Nora. "In the meantime, we are grateful to have you here."

"Especially since all I seem to be doing is feeding babies." Ingeborge lifted baby Peder to her shoulder and patted his back.

Nora took her bowl to the stove and, after raising the lid of the steaming kettle, plopped the spoonfuls of dough onto the bubbling chicken. "There now." She resisted the habit to taste her cooking and set the kettle farther back on the range so it would simmer.

That evening, after a dinner lightened with laughter, the family remained gathered around the table for the father to read from the Bible and lead family prayers. Nora relaxed against the back of her chair, caught up in the rhythm and beauty of the Beatitudes.

"Blessed are they. . ." The words rolled off Reverend Moen's tongue and brought a lump to Nora's throat. It was so easy to picture herself back home and pretend this was her father reading. "Blessed" was one of her mother's favorite words.

Nora opened her eyes to lock herself into the present. These people—this family—were indeed the merciful. To take her in as they had and make her feel so much a part of them. "Thank you" hardly seemed sufficient for all the gratitude she felt.

When he prayed for Carl Detschman, she joined her thoughts and prayers with his. And for little Peder, sleeping so soundly and blissfully in the cradle at their feet. Kaaren nodded on Nora's lap, as did Grace on Ingeborge's. But, when the "Amen" came, all the little ones joined right in.

"I'm going to take Peder to bed with me so we can keep him warm enough. Nora, I'm sorry to ask this, but will there be room for Kaaren with you and Mary? Grace is still using the crib and I dislike making a pallet on the floor in case she throws off her covers."

Nora hugged the little one on her lap even closer. "No, that will be just fine."

"Come on, Kaaren, you get to sleep with me." Mary bounced to the floor and, grabbing the little girl's hand, dragged her up the stairs.

"Me, too," Grace wailed, trying to scramble down from her father's lap.

"All right, all right." Ingeborge threw her hands over her head. "You go on up with the others." After Grace trudged partway up the stairs, Ingeborge whispered, "We'll bring her down to her crib after they all fall asleep." She gave Knute an extra hug and sent him up after the others to his room across the hall. "I'll be up in a bit for prayers."

Nora rose to her feet and began clearing the table. "Maybe I should have Mary teach me English," she said as she stacked the plates. "She switches between English and Norwegian like she's speaking one language. I know the Bible says not to envy, but I wish I knew two languages like that." She carried the dishes to the sink.

"Ja, and Kaaren speaks some German since her mother and father speak both languages. These little ones learn quickly." Ingeborge dipped water from the reservoir to fill her dishpan. "Tomorrow, we'll all begin teaching Nora English. You'll help, too, won't you, John?"

Reverend Moen looked up from his Bible and the papers beside it. "I'll be happy to, after the two funerals." He rubbed his forehead with the fingers of one hand. "So many we are losing. And this isn't even what you'd call a bad year."

"Did you talk with Carl again today?" Ingeborge crossed the

room to rub her husband's neck and shoulders.

"No. I asked Einer, who works down at the feedstore, if he could go out and let Carl's neighbors know he needed help." He leaned his head forward. "That feels so good."

Nora took Ingeborge's place at the sink and continued with the dishes. She bit her tongue against asking if she should go out and help Carl. When he came for the children, that would be the right time.

After they had shuffled all the sleeping children into the right beds, Nora studied the faces of the two girls sleeping together. Kaaren's hair was darker, more like honey than towhead white like Mary's. Freckles dotted Kaaren's turned-up nose, and the trace of a tear still lingered on one pale cheek.

Poor little lamb, Nora thought as she lifted the covers and slipped into the bed. So young to be left without a mother. No wonder she cried herself to sleep. Nora snuggled down into the feather bed and tucked the quilt around her shoulders so no cold air could sneak in.

How long would it take her to earn passage home to Norway? Could she be there by Midsummer's Eve? At home she shared the bed with her sister Clara, not two little girls who looked enough alike to be sisters.

"Dear Lord," she whispered, "please let Carl Detschman hire me so I can go home soon." But her last thoughts were not of home. Instead, a tall, blond farmer walked through her dreams and the land he strode was flat.

Chapter 5

By noon the next day, Nora had a headache.

"You're trying too hard." Ingeborge patted the younger woman's shoulder as she walked by. "You can't learn to speak an entire new language in one day. Even with all of us helping you."

"But I feel like. . .like as soon as I have a word locked in my head, it takes off like a lamb running from the barn up the hill after its mother." Nora rubbed her aching head.

"Well, the table is set and dinner is all ready, so why don't you sit down with a cup of coffee and close your eyes a few minutes? Both babies are sleeping and I'll read a story to the others in the parlor." Ingeborge suited actions to her words and left Nora sitting in the rocker in front of the stove.

Nora tipped her head forward, stretching the muscles as far as she could, then leaned it back against the rocker. With one foot she set the chair in motion. The hum of the fire and the creaking-rocker song were as soothing as a cold compress on her forehead.

The fragrance of bread, fresh from the oven, and the stew simmering on the stove, mingled with the bite of the lye soap with which they had washed diapers. Strung on a line behind the stove to dry, the diapers added their own peculiar odor.

The cat meowed at her feet then leaped up in her lap and arched its back against the palm of her hand before circling three times to find its comfort spot. As Nora stroked its back, the cat's rumbling purr added harmony in bass to the kitchen quartet.

The drumbeat of her headache left her temples and escaped up the chimney pipe.

After several minutes of comfort, she heard boots scraping

snow off on the step, then a fist knocking on the door. Nora swept the cat to the floor and rose to answer the summons.

Up close like this, Nora realized how tall Carl Detschman really stood. Even with the difference of the porch and house floors, he towered over her by nearly a head. Tongue-tied because she could not speak his language, Nora just stepped back and motioned him to enter.

At his *"Guten tag,"* Nora bobbed her head. She was amazed. It sounded so much like Norwegian. Would they really be able to communicate?

"Come in, come in." Ingeborge and the children joined them at the door.

"Pa!" Kaaren threw herself into her father's waiting arms. She locked both arms around his neck as if defying anyone to try to remove her.

Carl Detschman stood and took off his hat but refused to venture farther into the room. He pointed to his snowy boots and shook his head. "Is Reverend Moen here?"

"Any minute now," Ingeborge shooshed the other children back. "He had another funeral this morning and then a call to make. How may I help you?"

"I. . .that is, Anna. . ."

"Ma? I want my ma!" Kaaren placed her hands on both sides of her father's face and turned him to look at her. "Please, Pa."

Nora did not need to speak English to understand what the little girl was saying—the look on Carl Detschman's face said it all.

"Can you keep her. . .them. . .until after the funeral?" Carl asked after shushing his daughter.

"Of course. We'll talk more then. But why don't you come in and sit down to wait for Reverend Moen? What will you—"

"I can't." He drew himself straight, hugged his daughter, whispered in her ear, and handed her to Ingeborge. "I just can't." He turned and yanked open the door, the cold draft sending the women's skirts back against their legs.

The look on his face imprinted itself on Nora's mind. *Lost and angry. What a heavy burden,* she thought.

"Why didn't they have both funerals this morning?" Nora asked after they had settled the children again. Kaaren sniffed back tears once in awhile—and hiccuped.

"Because Carl and Anna are German," Ingeborge snapped, "and some people in this town are hateful." She hid her mouth with the back of her fist. "Forgive me, I didn't—I shouldn't even think such things. But, much as Reverend Moen preaches to love thy neighbor, some people think that doesn't include anyone who isn't Norwegian." She shook her head. "Sometimes, being the pastor's wife isn't easy, let alone being the pastor."

"So, will anyone come to mourn with him?"

"Ja, a few."

"Why don't you go and I'll stay here with the children? Just being with you is a comfort, and I know he needs that."

"Ja, that is a good idea. Thank you." Ingeborge used the edge of her apron to wipe something from the corner of her eye. "I should have fed Peder by then, and I won't be gone long if James wakes up. Now I know how difficult it would be to feed twins."

Everyone ate dinner with serious faces and little talking.

"Mary, you help Miss Johanson with the dishes," Ingeborge reminded her daughter as they all rose from the table. "We won't be gone very long and I'm depending on you to show what a helper you can be."

"Yes, Ma."

"We'll bring Carl back for coffee and maybe others who attend the funeral. So would you please set out the coffee and cookies?" Ingeborge pressed a forefinger against her lips. "I have some *søtsuppe* in the pie safe also. You could bring that in and thaw it out over the stove. That, warmed, will taste good."

"Oh, I haven't had that for so long." Nora continued to clear the table. "My mother uses all kinds of fruit in hers."

"And we have cream to pour on top." Ingeborge lifted her black wool coat from the wooden coat tree and pinned on her black veiled hat while standing in front of the mirror. "Now, you children be good for Miss Johanson." She bent and kissed each one, including Kaaren. Then, waving her fingers, she went out the door.

When Kaaren started to fill up with tears again, Nora lifted the little girl in her arms and spun her around. Laughing together, they all trooped into the kitchen. She handed each of the children a dish towel and as she washed each dish and cup, she handed them one at a time, to each child. Mary led the game of naming every item in English with Nora repeating the word each time. After the dishes were done, they continued the game by naming things around the room. When Nora forgot the word for table, they chorused it together; when she remembered stove and oven, they cheered.

After setting the table again and finishing the preparations for company, Nora sank down into the chair and, lifting Grace to one knee and Kaaren to the other, gathered Mary and Knute as close as she could. *Oye* was eye and *toyebryn,* eyebrow. The game continued just like teaching a baby he had a nose and mouth.

They were all laughing over nothing when the door opened with a blast of cold air.

"But you must have some help," Reverend Moen was saying as they stamped snow off their feet and entered the house. "You can't take care of all your livestock and the children, too. How will you manage?"

"I don't know. I. . ."

"Here, now. See how nicely Nora has prepared things for us. Let's just sit down to eat and talk things over." Ingeborge helped the younger man off with his coat and hung it up with her own. "You can't go off without something warm in your belly."

Nora flew to set the coffeepot on the table and dish up the *søtsuppe.* Mary carried the cream pitcher and set it in front of her father.

"Pa!" Kaaren attached herself like a limpet to her father's leg.

"Is no one else coming?" Nora asked Ingeborge in a voice only they could hear.

Ingeborge shook her head. "It was getting late and they needed to get home before dark."

Nora finished the comment in her mind. *Or so they said,* whoever "they" were.

"Why don't you leave the children here for a few more days," Reverend Moen suggested after everyone was served. "Peder is getting stronger, but we haven't found a wet nurse for him, yet. And Kaaren is doing fine here. What do you say, son?"

Carl glanced over at Ingeborge as if asking her permission.

"Ja," she said with a nod. "I feel that is best, too."

"I appreciate what you are doing, but I—"

"No buts, then. It is settled." John clapped a hand on Carl's shoulder.

Nora refilled the coffee cups and wished she knew for sure what they were saying. In a moment of silence, she took all of her courage in hand and announced, "I could go out to help Mr. Detschman with the house and the children. If we get Peder to take a bottle, there wouldn't be any problem." She stopped to look at the Moens' faces, took a deep breath and continued. "You said there wasn't anyone else and. . .and this way I could earn my passage money back home. . .to Norway. . .that is. . .if Mr. Detschman can afford. . .ah. . ." This time she could not pick up the words again.

"Certainly not!" Reverend Moen shook his head. "Why he couldn't—you couldn't—"

"What he means to say is that you're not married," Ingeborge interposed softly, "and if you, as an unmarried woman, went out to work for Carl, your reputation would be ruined. No one would ever marry you."

"But. . .but. . ."

"Thank you, Miss Johanson." Carl answered after Reverend Moen translated the conversation for him. "But they are correct."

Nora tried to remember the good reasons she had thought of earlier but, in the face of their unified disapproval, she fell silent. She had thought things might be different here in the new country, but the old customs still held sway.

"I just thought this might be a way out of a difficult situation for both of us." She raised her chin and sat up even straighter. "I need work and you need a worker." She thought she saw a ghost of a smile soften his mouth and eyes, but she must have been mistaken—when she looked again, the glacier had taken over his eyes and voice.

"I thank you for all your kindnesses. I'll return on Sunday for church and to pick up the children, if that will be all right." Carl whispered in his daughter's ear and set Kaaren down on her feet. When she clung to him, he gently disengaged her fingers. "I'll see you on Sunday and then we'll go home," he promised.

"Thank you again, Miss Johanson." He nodded in her direction and, after shaking hands and thanking the others, he shrugged into his wool coat and bent over to plant a kiss on his daughter's wet cheek. "You be a big girl now."

"Pa!" The forlorn child leaned her head against the door after it closed after him. "Ma-a-a. I want Ma."

Ingeborge scooped the whimpering child up into her arms. "Your ma has gone to live with Jesus in heaven, little one." She kissed away the tears and crooned soft words until Kaaren quit crying.

He never even looked at the baby, Nora thought, as she and Mary cleared the table. *And I still think mine was a good idea.*

Up in her room that night, before falling to sleep, Nora carefully penned a letter to her family. When she told them about Hans's passing away, she did not mention the lies. She described the trip and the Moens. And said she would be looking for work.

She fell asleep thinking of eyes the blue of a glacier ice cave, shimmering in the sun. But the eyes were so sad as to bring tears to her own.

Saturday, the entire house had to be cleaned and the food prepared for Sunday. Nora and Ingeborge worked with a rhythm that showed how close they had become. The naming game continued with new words thrown in to make sentences.

"This is a table," Nora said as she waxed the shiny surface. Kaaren and Mary clapped their hands. "This is a chair." Big smiles. "This is a. . ." Nora raised her hands in the air and shrugged.

"Rug," the girls chimed. "This is a rug."

"And it needs to be shaken. Take it out on the back porch," Ingeborge told her daughter. The two little girls picked up the corners and carried the woven rag rug out the back. "And shake it good."

Late in the afternoon, Ingeborge sat nursing baby Peder and Nora had the children gathered around her, telling them a story of trolls. Even Kaaren laughed at the funny faces and voices Nora used for each character. When the story was finished, Nora hugged each of them and set the two littlest girls off her lap.

"You will make a wonderful mother," Ingeborge said after the children trooped off to play. "You are so good with the little ones. And what a help you've been to me. I'm spoiled already."

"Thank you. You make me feel like one of the family."

They rocked in companionable silence. Little Peder burped once into the stillness and continued his soft nursing noises.

"What will happen to Carl?" Nora finally asked, softly. "How will he manage?" She knew she should refer to the man as Mr. Detschman, but he could only be Carl in her mind.

"I don't know." Ingeborge leaned her head against the back of the rocker and stared up at the ceiling. "He has family in Minnesota, but he doesn't think any of them can help. His sister is still too young to come out here and the others all have families of their own."

"What about a bottle for Peder?"

"We'll start him on that tonight. I wanted to give him as much breast milk as possible." She lifted the baby to her shoulder and rubbed his back. "Since he's so much stronger now, I think he'll be all right."

"Then I can feed him." Nora looked across the dimming light to her friend in the other chair.

"That you can. He'll have two bottle-feedings before we go to bed and then I'll nurse him in the middle of the night." She chuckled softly. "God certainly knew what He was doing when He created mothers and babies. This one is such a love." She trailed a finger across the baby's closed fist. Her sigh seemed to come from deep within her heart. "I love babies so." She kissed the baby's cheek and looked up. "Here, you hold him for a while and I'll get the supper going."

Nora accepted the bundled infant and settled him into her arms, like Ingeborge had done in her arms. She watched the baby's eyelids flutter and the perfect little mouth pucker and relax. "He is so beautiful." How could one do anything but whisper in the face of such a miracle?

Several hours later, she felt the same awe but only more so when she got the baby to take a bottle. While he fussed at first, he finally sucked on the nipple and settled down to feed. Nora felt like she had climbed the highest mountain near the farm at home.

Sometime later, in the middle of the darkest night, Nora awoke to the sniffling and tears of Kaaren, crying for her mother. Nora gathered the sobbing child into her arms. With hands of love, she brushed the straggles of hair from Kaaren's face and wiped away the tears.

"I. . .uh. . .want. . .my. . .ma. Why doesn't she come?"

Nora murmured responses in her own language, wishing she could say the things in her heart to this grieving child. Ingeborge had told her that her mother had gone to be with Jesus. That she was not coming back. But how could such a little one understand that?

Softly, so she would not wake Mary, Nora began to sing. "Jesus loves me. . ." As the words and love in the song crept into that silent night, she felt the child relax against her shoulder. Jerky, leftover sobs that racked the small body tore at Nora's heart. "Yes, Jesus loves me. . ." She finished the song on a whisper and removed her arm from under Kaaren's neck.

"Heavenly Father, comfort this family," she prayed. "Bring back the love they've lost and, if You want me to care for them, please find a way. Amen."

Forgotten were the tears of the night as the two girls bounced up to greet the sun sparkling around the feathery frost patterns on the windowpane. They ran, giggling, down the stairs, leaving Nora to stretch and twist her body from one side to the other in the softness of the deep feather ticking. When she heard a baby crying, she leaped from the bed, put on her wrapper, and made her way downstairs.

Ingeborge was jostling James on her hip while warming a bottle for Peder, who was crying in Mary's arms in the rocker.

"And a good morning to you, too," Nora said with a laugh while relieving Mary of her squalling bundle.

"Good. Now I can take care of this one," Ingeborge sank gratefully into the other rocker. "He thinks his mother should drop everything the minute he cries. What a spoiled little boy."

Nora tested the warmth of the bottled milk on one of her wrists and then sat down to begin the feeding. Peder fussed a bit, not quite willing to take the bottle. "Come now. We did this beautifully last night. Ingeborge isn't going to be here to feed you anymore."

Peder looked up at her as if he understood every word she had said. When she prodded his closed lips with the nipple again, he took it and began to suck like she might take it away before he could fill himself.

Nora chuckled. What a precious baby. And smart, too, she could already tell.

"Mary, you set the table. We'll have mush as soon as I finish here, so put the cinnamon and cream on the table."

"Where's Pa?" Mary asked as she handed the bowls, one at a time, to Grace and Kaaren.

"Starting the furnace at the church. Then he's planning to work more on his sermon. I told him it was too cold over there and that he should come home to finish."

"And?" Nora set the chair rocking.

"And he's over there in the cold because he says he can't work with all the noise around here." Inge's glance around the kitchen included the chattering children as all four went about their chores, Mary firmly telling each one what to do. The teakettle sang merrily on the stove and, up until a few minutes ago, there had been two babies crying. "I just don't understand why he thinks this is noisy." Her eyebrows nearly met her hairline.

Nora laughed along with her friend. "This is the way homes are supposed to be. Someday, I want one just like this." She put the baby up to her shoulder and patted his back. "Just like this."

"With two babies at a time?"

"Well. . .maybe one by one."

The clock bonged eight times.

"We must hurry if we don't want to be late to Sunday school. Here, Mary, you take James while I finish making the breakfast. The table looks lovely."

While Ingeborge was giving out assignments, Reverend Moen let in a blast of cold air as he came through the door. "What a beautiful day we have," he said as he hung up his coat and hat. "Why it's ten degrees above zero and getting warmer. Pretty soon, the chinook will come sighing across the plains and, before you know it, spring will be here."

He rubbed his hands together, warming them above the stove. "Wait until you see spring here on the prairie, Nora. It is like no other season."

Nora, like a good guest, kept her doubts to herself. What could possibly be beautiful about this flat country? Now, spring in Norway—that was sight and sound to behold. The cracking thunder as the rivers broke loose from their winter dungeon and the logs cascaded down with the ice floes. The birds returning in flocks to darken the sky and the masses of green bursting forth from the soil as the sun shone longer each day.

The ache of homesickness caught her by surprise. To stem any tears that threatened to overflow, she swallowed the lump in her throat and rolled her eyes upward. Better remember that Old Man Winter still held her beloved homeland in his icy grip.

"I. . .I'll take Peder with me while I go get ready. Unless you need me for something else first?"

"No, no. You go on." Ingeborge shooshed her away with fluttering hands. She went back to stirring the mush that was thickening under her watchful eye.

"I'll hurry." With the baby in one arm and the pitcher of warm water from the reservoir in the other, Nora went up the stairs. She propped the infant against the pillows and continued talking with him as she washed her face and hands. Before she was half done, he had fallen asleep.

With Reverend Moen encouraging haste, they finished eating

and cleaning up in time to be bundled up and out the door, arriving at the church as the first of the other families were hitching their horses to the rails.

It felt like home to Nora and yet she felt strange and out of place. This was the first time in her life she had worshipped in a church other than the one at home. While people were speaking Norwegian around her, none of them were her relatives. At home her aunts and uncles and cousins, besides brothers and sisters, made up half of the congregation.

Nora smiled as each person was introduced. But she kept waiting for one man, Carl Detschman, to appear. He had said he would join them for church but he still had not arrived as the organist played the opening songs.

They had settled in the front pew. Nora rocked the baby in her arms, Kaaren was beside her, and Mary next. Ingeborge was shushing Grace and Knute. What a pewful they made.

Nora did not realize until the closing hymn how much she had been waiting for a tall, broad-shouldered farmer to join their group. She kept hoping he had sat in the back and, when they turned to leave, she thought she saw that familiar blond head leaving before anyone else. He had said he would join them for church. If it was him, why did he leave so quickly?

Peder had slept through the service, much to Nora's relief, but, when they stood for the benediction, he began whimpering. By the time she could get out the door, he had progressed into the demanding stage.

"I'll take him home and feed him," Nora whispered to Ingeborge as she passed the Moens in the greeting line at the front door. At the top of the three wooden stairs, Nora stopped for a moment to look again for Carl Detschman. Was that Carl driving his sleigh down the street?

"Don't be silly," she scolded herself on the short walk back to the parsonage. "It doesn't matter one whit to you if the man came to church or not. Once he picks up his children, you probably won't even see him again. Ingeborge said he was unpopular—an outcast —because of his German heritage. So just put a smile on your face and enjoy the day. You won't have to worry about whether this darling bundle of baby eats or not. It's his father's problem."

So, then, why did her bottom lip feel like it wanted to quiver? And what was that stupid lump in her throat? How could she let these babies go without someone there to take care of them?

She hurried through the door of the parsonage and slammed it shut behind her. In the time it took her to warm the bottle and settle down to feed the crying infant, the remainder of the family arrived home. They were chattering and laughing about their chores when a knock sounded at the door.

"Welcome, Carl." Reverend Moen ushered the visitor in. "I was happy to see you come to the service. Let me take your coat and hat."

"Thank you."

Kaaren made her usual beeline for her father's legs.

"Dinner is almost ready," Ingeborge said while bending down to remove the roast from the oven. "You're just in time."

Nora clutched little Peder tighter. *How have I gotten so attached to these two children in such a short time?*

"Miss Johanson, Reverend, Missus, can we talk for a few minutes? Right away?" Carl ducked his chin, then squared his shoulders. "Please?"

Ingeborge wiped her hands on the dish towel she had slung over her shoulder. "Of course. Mary, you take the children into the other room to play. Nora, Peder can go back in the cradle now."

Nora shook her head. She could not lay the baby down, not when he was to be taken away from her so soon. "I. . .I'll just rock him. He was fussing a moment ago."

"No—I mean, please, could you join us?" Carl motioned to a chair at the table.

Nora stood and, after laying Peder in the cradle as asked, walked to the table and sank down on one of the oak chairs. With the tip of her finger, she smoothed a spot on the table. Something strange was happening here.

"Miss Johanson, Nora, would you marry me?"

Chapter 6

Nora felt her chin drop—clear to her chest.

"I know this is sudden, but let me tell you what I am thinking. As the Moens said, you cannot come live at my farm without marriage. It would not be proper. But, if we were married, your living there and caring for my children would be all right. I will advertise for a housekeeper in the Fargo and Grand Forks papers and, when we find one, then we will have the marriage annulled and I will pay for your passage to return to Norway."

He waited while Ingeborge finished translating.

I can go home to Norway was Nora's first thought. *I would have a place to work* was her second, and *I won't have to give up these babies* was the third. *At least not for a time,* she amended. She closed her eyes, the better to think. *But marriage! An annulment?*

Her gaze flew to Reverend Moen's face. "Will this work?"

John rubbed his nose with the index finger of his right hand. "A marriage can be annulled only if it is not consummated."

Nora felt her cheeks flame at the thought. Surely Mr. Detschman understood that. . .that they would not share a bed.

"You and the children will share the big bedroom downstairs, where it is warm. I will fix a bed for me upstairs." Carl ducked his chin and stammered over the last words. "I mean, this marriage would be because. . .to. . .ah. . .save your reputation." His voice deepened to a growl. "That is all I have to offer."

Nora nodded that she understood. And what he was offering was enough for her. Since Hans had lied and died, she wanted nothing to do with North Dakota farmers. She would dream of returning home. This seemed to be a sensible solution.

"What do you think, Ingeborge?" Nora risked looking at her friend.

"I don't know." She looked from her husband to the man still standing, his hand now resting on the back of a chair. "You and the children can stay here for as long as you need."

When Carl understood her response, he shook his head. "I cannot lay such a burden upon you. You have already been good to me beyond duty."

"Let us eat our dinner and think about this plan of yours," Reverend Moen said. "You have not proposed an easy thing."

Nora let the conversation at dinner flow around her like a river around a big rock. It wasn't that she did not understand half of it, she just needed the time to think.

What would her mother say? *Surely I would be home almost before they could send a reply. All I need tell them is that I am caring for two small children for a farmer here who lost his wife. An annulment is like the marriage had never been.*

And I can go home soon. Back to the mountains, with green forests and white rushing rivers. Back to my family. . .Clara and Einer, Gunhilde and Thorliff. And little Sophie—she won't be all grown-up before I see her again. She pictured each of them in her mind.

Halfway through the meal, Peder began his waking whimpers. By the time Nora had a bottle warmed, he had progressed to red-faced demand.

Nora picked him up and whisked him off for a diaper change. Then, she took her place in the rocker and silenced him with the nipple. As the baby sucked, she let her mind roam back across the ocean again. But it refused to stay in Norway.

Instead, she thought of the baby in her arms. If she did not stay, who would care for him? And little Kaaren. She was still waking at night, calling for her mother. Would her father be able to care for her. . .and do all his farming, too? Spring planting would come and then how would he manage?

Her mind flitted to the man himself. He was so stern. Was this his usual way or was it due to his great sorrow? His children needed some love and light in their lives.

Of course, he could leave them with the Moens, like Ingeborge had suggested, but what if Nora went to work somewhere else? How could Ingeborge handle her home and all the children by herself?

After letting her thoughts race like a fox after rabbits, she tipped her head back. *Father God, what would You have me to do?* Her thoughts quit their scampering. She had prayed earlier for Him to work something out, hadn't she? Was this it?

When Peder finished eating, she rose and walked back to the table. "Ja, I will do this." She nodded as she spoke. "Carl Detschman, I will marry you."

"Today?"

She stared at him. Had she understood? She looked to Ingeborge for confirmation.

"I don't see what the rush is," Reverend Moen said, shaking his head. "Next week—"

"No. If we are going to do this, we will do this now." Carl kept his gaze on Nora's face.

Nora took a deep breath and let it out, along with all her hesitations. "Now."

"Let me warm up the church first." Reverend Moen rose to his feet and reached for his coat.

"No!" Nora cried, then repeated more softly, "no, we'll be married in the parlor, not the church. Since this wedding doesn't count anyway, I do not want the ceremony to be performed in the church."

"If you are certain." John hung his coat back up.

Nora nodded. She kept her gaze on the part in Kaaren's hair. She could not look up at Carl, not right now.

Although the ceremony was spoken in Norwegian, Nora heard the words with only the top part of her mind. The rest of her floated in a fog. She gave the proper answers when the Reverend Moen asked her to, but she never looked above the Bible clasped in his hands.

"I have no ring," Carl said, as he held Nora's hand. "But if you like, I will buy one the next time I come into town."

"No. That is not necessary." Why was there a lump in her throat? After all, this ceremony meant nothing. They really were not married—were they?

Carl and Reverend Moen loaded Nora's trunk into the wagon while the women gathered up all the children's things. Nora repacked her carpetbag and carried it downstairs to the front door.

"I can't believe this is happening." Ingeborge took Nora's cold hands in hers and held them together. "If you need anything, remember your big sister is always here to help you."

Nora tried to smile around the quiver in her chin—Ingeborge was anything but big. Leaving here was almost as hard as leaving home.

The women wrapped Peder in his blankets and then an extra quilt before following the men out the door. Carl had spread hay in the back of the wagon and, with extra quilts, made a nest for his family. Nora placed her hand in his and, using the runners for a step, joined Kaaren in the box. Ingeborge handed Peder in to her.

Carl swung up on the high board seat and unwound the reins from the whipstock. "Thank you, for everything." He tipped his hat to the Moens, who stood by the side, arms around each other.

"Come and visit when you can." He clucked to the team. With a flick of the reins, the horses started forward, the iron sled runners creaking in the snow.

The good-byes rang on the clear air. Nora waved from her shelter. Kaaren waved one last time, then snuggled down into the warm nest of quilts. She leaned her head against Nora's arm and, tipping up her face, smiled broader than Nora had yet seen.

The smile sent angels of joy dancing in Nora's heart. Surely she had made the right choice. She smiled back, then tucked the quilts more closely about them with her free hand. With the sun on its downward slide, the temperature was already dropping. She edged the long scarf draped around her neck up and over the hat she had pinned so securely in place. Hats like hers may be fashionable, but they were not worth anything in a snowstorm.

Carl hunkered down in his seat, offering little of himself to the wind. He flicked the reins again, bringing the team up to a smart trot. The way the sun was sinking, they would barely be home just before dark. He had not planned on spending so much time at the Moens'.

Oh Anna, he cried in the confines of his heart, *have I done the right thing? Little Kaaren needs you so desperately and so do I. The house is empty without you. I'd rather sleep in the barn where at least there is some noise with the animals.*

He covered his nose with the red scarf wrapped around his neck. "Come on, boys. Let's get home." The harness jingled soprano while the hooves thudded bass. The runner creaked in counterpoint, but the symphony was lost on the man hunkered on the driver's seat. He wandered in a frozen, desolate land where music and laughter were outlawed.

How would he talk with this woman he was bringing home? Granted, he had learned some Norwegian since coming to Soldall, and Norwegian and German had some similarities, but she had to learn English—he would insist. His daughter would grow up speaking English—no people would laugh behind her back. He remembered the cruelty of children, especially at school.

He shivered against the cold. But the cold within him was deeper than any weather could bring.

Nora, snuggled down in the bed of the wagon now turned sleigh, was nearly asleep when a halt jerked her upright. A dog leaped and barked beside them. They were stopped in front of a square, two-storied house, the kind that dotted the prairie like toys tossed out by a giant hand. A snowdrift reached like a dragging scarf clear up to one second-story window. She craned her neck around the rumps of the steaming horses to see the red hip-roofed barn, silo, and other outbuildings. A tingle ran up her spine. Mr. Detschman owned a fine farm.

Kaaren stirred from her sound sleep. "Are we home, Pa?"

"Yes, little one, we are." He leaned over the edge of the box and lifted his daughter out. "Here." He handed her a parcel. "Bring this into the house."

When Nora held out the quilt-wrapped baby to him, he took her arm instead and steadied her as she clambered down to the shoveled walk to the house, the infant clutched to her chest. She would have liked to have taken a few moments to look around, but dusk was on them, tinting the snow the bluish gray of eventide. She hurried up the path to open the door for Kaaren.

When she glanced back, Carl was throwing robes over the horses. *He must plan on unloading my trunk right now,* she thought. *I should go back and help.*

Peder squirmed in her arms. No, the baby came first. And it would not be long before the entire world would know that it was feeding time. Maybe the water in the stove's reservoir would still be warm enough to heat the bottle.

"Ma! Ma?" Kaaren yelled into the stillness of the empty house as soon as the door opened. "Ma, where are you?" She ran from room to room, calling, until she collapsed against the bed in the room off the kitchen. "Ma-a-a-a. I want my ma."

Nora felt like joining in the little girl's tears. How could she help this precious little one? And the baby who needed her, too—right now, if his utterings were to be quieted.

Where in heaven's name was their father?

She followed Kaaren into the bedroom and laid Peder in his quilts in the middle of the bed, unwrapping him only enough to allow him to breathe easily. Then, she scooped Kaaren up in her arms, holding her tightly while she cried. While she could not speak the language, words loaded with love and comfort could be felt by anyone. Could she be the mother they needed?

When Kaaren's sobs turned to sniffles, Nora set the child on the bed and, taking her hand, patted Peder's chest. "You do that," she said, depending on sign language. "Be good to your brother. Good, good." She nodded and smiled her approval as Kaaren gently continued the patting. "Keep on, more." Nora backed from the room, all the while smiling and nodding, and headed for the stove.

The reservoir water was still plenty warm, so Nora searched through the lower cupboards to find a small pan. She filled it half full with water, then went back into the bedroom for one of the baby's bottles of milk she had brought from Ingeborge's.

Nora could tell Peder was tired of being patted. His whimper had turned to a howl, so she picked him up. While rocking him in her one arm, she set the bottle into the warm water with the other hand.

"I do not know how all those women managed with just one arm for so many years," she muttered as she continued to lift the stove lid, add coal, replace the lid, open the damper, and comfort the hungry baby. "Your supper will be ready soon. Shhhhh." She swayed with the soothing rhythm that had been passed down through the centuries from woman to woman.

Kaaren wandered into the kitchen and hid her face in Nora's skirt, clinging to the fabric as if that, too, might be taken from her. Nora patted the little girl's hair with her free hand.

Where was their father?

With the baby finally nursing contentedly in her arm, Nora relaxed in the rocking chair. Kaaren stuck to her side like a barnacle on a rock. *I suppose I should make supper,* Nora thought as she rocked, *but what? You would think Carl would be here to show me where things are. That would be the decent thing to do.*

She looked around the room. *We could eat eggs if he has chickens. Is there any bread? Even toast and hot milk would be enough, at least for Kaaren and me.* She studied the white painted cupboards, the sink with a bucket below to catch the water. A red, long-handled pump was bolted to the outer edge. How wonderful, to have water piped into the house.

Lace curtains with red tiebacks brightened every window, both the smaller one above the sink and the double-sashed one on the other side of the round oak table. As in all homes, the large, black, cast-iron stove took up much of the space.

If the remainder of the house is as comfortable as the kitchen, Nora thought, *I'll love working here. And soon, I'll be able to take the ship back to Norway.*

With the baby fed, burped, changed, and put to bed in the cradle by the bed in the other room, Nora picked up the kerosene lamp she had lit, took Kaaren by the hand, and went exploring. The parlor, with both doors closed, was freezing, as was Kaaren's small bedroom in the back of the house. The little girl picked up a rag doll, hugging it to her.

"Come along, let's go back to the kitchen where it is warm."

To keep from wasting the heat, Nora closed all the doors behind them. Back in the kitchen, she found a door in the stair wall with a well-stocked pantry on one side and stairs down to the cellar on the other.

Kaaren stood in the doorway, one finger in her mouth and dragging the doll with her other hand. But she never took her gaze off the woman opening drawers and doors.

"Bread, good." Nora nodded as she talked to herself. "Jam." She gathered the items in her arms. "Butter." She opened a door on the end wall that was screened to the outside. "Ah, milk. But it's frozen." She handed the bread to Kaaren. "You carry this." Then she picked up the jug of milk. "Supper will be coming soon."

She set the milk to thawing in a pan of water on the stove while she sliced bread and set it in the toaster racks she had found hanging on the back of the warming oven. Then, opening the lid on the stove, she laid the rack over the burning coals. By the time the bread was browned, Nora felt toasted as well.

With the milk that had thawed and some toast with jam, Nora and Kaaren set themselves in the rocking chair and started to eat. Nora began the game. "This is. . . ?" She pointed at the bread.

"Bread. This is bread." Kaaren nodded and took a bite.

Nora pointed to the rich, red jam. "This is. . . ?"

"Jam." They grinned at each other as they chewed and swallowed.

First, they named the milk, the cup, the plate; and each time, Nora repeated the sentence. When they were finished eating, they remained in the chair, rocking slowly. Nora began humming a song her mother used to sing. When she was humming, she did not have to think about Carl Detschman or to where he had so rudely disappeared. If he was out doing chores, as was most likely, he could have come in the house first and showed her where things were kept. Kaaren settled back against Nora's chest and soon

70

closed her eyes. Before long, the small body slumped in sleep.

Nora had almost drowsed off when the thud of boots, kicking off the snow against the steps on the porch, startled her awake. She started to get up then thought better of it. If Carl Detschman wanted any supper beyond bread and milk this night, he would just have to sing for it.

Chapter 7

Peder demanded to be fed every two hours—all night and all the next day. By the third morning, Nora felt like she had been trampled by six teams of horses. If Carl had heard the baby crying, either night or day, he ignored it. That might be possible at night, since he was sleeping upstairs, but during the day? Granted, he was never in the house except for meals but. . .

The day before, Nora had passed the disgusted stage and now she was bordering on anger—if only she had the strength to even spark. She leaned her head against the door of the cupboard. Kneading bread took more power than she had thought—anything took more energy than she could summon.

Right now, the baby was sleeping. If she could only get Kaaren down for a nap, then she could sleep, too.

The thought of sleep nearly overwhelmed her. "But first you must finish the bread." Lately, she had found herself talking to herself more often than not.

She and Kaaren still played the naming game, but it was not the same as having a real, live, grown-up to talk with. Mr. Carl Detschman, though, spoke only in grunts; and language between them was not a barrier—there just wasn't any. How would she ever learn enough English this way?

She slammed the dough over on the floured surface and pressed it hard with the heel of her hand. Roll the dough in, press and turn, roll the dough in, press and turn. The rhythm continued.

At night, the temperature would fall to well below zero, so she kept both Kaaren and Peder in bed with her to keep them warm enough. During her nocturnal feeding forays, she would dream of warmer weather and how nice it would be if she could sleep straight through to spring.

She thumped the bread one last time, molded it into a round, and poked the dough with her finger. When the dough sprang back, she placed it into an earthenware bowl, covered it with a dish towel, and set the bowl on the warming oven to rise. After stirring the beans that were baking in the oven, she removed her apron and slung it over a chair.

"Come, Kaaren." She reached over to take the little girl's hand. "We're going to take a nap, you and I." She put her finger to her lips. "And we must be very quiet so Peder can sleep longer, too."

Kaaren put her finger to her lips and silently climbed up onto the bed. She scooted over to the other side, then sat on her knees. "Sing?"

Nora shook her head. "Sleep." She lifted the quilt and motioned to Kaaren to get under it. Kaaren flung herself back onto the pillow and lifted her feet, shoes still buttoned on, into the air.

"This is a shoe." Her eyes sparkled with anticipation.

"No. Sleep, not play."

Kaaren spoke more insistently. "This is a shoe."

Nora put her finger to her lips. "Shhhh. Ja, this is a shoe but now we sleep." She snuggled down and tucked the quilt around their shoulders.

Kaaren lay flat on the pillow, her eyes wide open.

Please, little one, Nora pleaded silently, *go to sleep. I am so tired my eyes won't stay open.* Under her breath she began to hum a song her mother used to sing.

Nora felt the warmth of the quilt steal over her. The little body next to her relaxed, along with hers. Her hum grew jerky until it faded away to nothing.

Somewhere in another world she heard a door close.

"Pa!" Kaaren flew out from under the covers and slid to the floor. "Pa!" Screaming voice, thundering feet.

Peder set up his own welcome, also at the top of his lungs.

Nora lay there with her eyes closed. Maybe Peder would go

back to sleep. Maybe Carl would take his lively daughter outside with him for a while. Maybe. She was too tired for any more maybes.

She pushed back the quilt and swung her feet over the side of the bed. Head in her hands, she waited for Peder to settle down again, but his demands grew louder.

"I'm coming." She slid her feet into her carpet slippers, pulled herself to her feet, and walked over to the cradle to pick up the hungry baby. With the baby in one arm, and pushing a strand of hair back into her braids with the other hand, she entered the kitchen to find Carl pouring himself a cup of coffee.

"I'm going into Soldall," he said in German, slowly so she could understand. "Don't worry about the cows if I return after dark. I'll be as quick as I can."

"I go, Pa? Please?" Kaaren wrapped both her arms around his leg, her face raised in supplication.

"No." He shook his head. "It's too cold outside for a little girl like you."

Nora stopped her bottle preparations and turned to look at him. He had spoken more words in the last two minutes than he had done in the last three days.

As he made his way to the door, Kaaren still clung to him. "Now, be a good girl. You can watch out the window." He stood her on the chair so she could see out.

Her lower lip quivered. A tear stood like a bead at the edge of one brilliant, blue eye. "Pa-a-a." The one word held all the woe of a little girl left behind.

Nora dug a cookie out of the jar. "Here. Your pa will be home soon." She placed the cookie in the limp hand and caught the child in a hug. Together, they watched the driver and team trot down the lane. Peder's cries increased in volume.

After feeding the baby, Nora punched down the risen bread dough and placed it on the cupboard where it would not rise so quickly. Then, she set the boiler onto the stove to start heating some water to wash the diapers. She could barely keep up with the baby's clothes. Once the diapers were boiling merrily, she set the boiler to the cooler side of the stove and, taking Kaaren by the hand, headed back for the bed. This time, there would be no interruptions.

Kaaren scrubbed a fist across her eyes to rub out the last of her tears and then turned onto her side and was asleep before Nora had finished settling the quilt.

"Thank you, Heavenly Father." Nora breathed the prayer as sleep claimed her.

By the time Carl returned from town, dusk had blued the snow. Nora was slicing bread when she heard the jingling of the harness. Was that joy she felt leaping in her midsection, just because the lord of the manor was home again? Well, maybe not leaping but more like stretching.

She shook her head at her silly thoughts. Her mother's words echoed for her. "Of kindness there is no equal." Calling Carl Detschman lord of the manor might not be kind, but it was true—wasn't it? The way he gave orders and without a smile—not even for his little daughter who needed love and laughter so desperately. But perhaps he had never been a smiling person. Many Norwegians were like that, too. Handsome, yes, but smiling, no.

She pinched off a small piece of crust and put it into her mouth. *I wonder what it would take to make Lord Carl smile?* The thought lasted until Carl entered the house, bringing in cold air, a sack of supplies from the store, and—

"There's a letter for you." Without even looking at her, he handed her the envelope.

"Mange takk." Nora's eyes devoured the handwriting—a letter from her mother. An ache in her chest made Nora press her lips together. She ignored the burning behind her eyes and tucked the beloved envelope into her apron pocket. She would save it for later, when she could read it alone. For now she must get supper on the table quickly so Carl could do his chores.

That night, after Carl had gone up to bed and the children slept, Nora poured herself a cup of coffee and sat down at the table where the light from the kerosene lamp was the strongest. With trembling fingers, she slit the envelope open and withdrew two sheets of paper.

She was almost afraid to begin reading. What if it was bad news? She shook her head and took a sip of coffee.

Dearest Nora,
*   I take pen in hand to tell you how much we love you and miss you.*

Nora put her head down on the table and allowed the tears to flow. The ache had grown to a roaring pain that tore at her heart and soul. How she missed those beloved faces. She could see her mother at the kitchen table, writing so carefully on the precious paper.

When she was able, Nora dried her eyes with her apron and read on. All were well. Her older brother, Einer, was courting one of the Kielguard daughters. They had all been out skiing. Father and the boys had been up in the forest cutting wood. Ice fishing had been good. How were she and Hans? Did she like North Dakota?

Nora wiped another tear from her eye. How surprised they would be when her letter arrived—shocked would be more like it. She read the letter again and sighed. Life took strange turns and twists—and when you least expected it.

Nora tried to catch a yawn but, instead, it nearly dislocated her jaw. If only she could stay awake long enough to write back. But, there was as much chance of that as a fox turning down a juicy chicken. She adjusted the stove damper, blew out the lamp, and made her way into the bedroom.

Please, Peder. Sleep longer. This had become her consistent prayer and plea, and tonight was no exception. She knelt at the edge of her bed and tried to pray, but even in so cramped a position, she nearly nodded off. Nora was asleep as soon as she pulled up the quilt around herself.

For the next week, Peder continued his demand for being fed every two hours and sometimes he screamed instead of sleeping between feedings. Nothing Nora did made him content. While he was not sick, he was not content, either.

"Hush, hush, my little one," Nora crooned one night in the wee hours when she would have much preferred sleep. She had tried singing to and walking the colicky baby, rubbing his back and then trying the rocker for a time. But she had been so tired that night she had even fallen asleep in the rocker with him and woke up in the morning, cold and stiff, when Carl came down the stairs to head for milking.

"I. . .I'm sorry," she whispered as she rubbed the sleep from her eyes.

He glanced her way but without looking into her face. With a barely perceptible nod, he turned back to the stove, added coal from the bucket, and opened the damper to bring up more heat.

She watched as he made his way out the door, looking like he carried a ten-ton load of coal on his shoulders. *"Uff da."* She shook her head. "What will become of him?" Even she, who did not know him, could see that the light in his eyes had gone out.

Nora stiffly stood with Peder in her arms and carried him to the bedroom. Together, they went to bed and—Peder started to whimper.

By the end of the next week, Nora could concentrate only on putting one foot in front of the other. Feed the baby, prepare a meal, wash the diapers, feed the baby—when would she be able to add sleep to the routine? At the same time, Kaaren grew fussy, her temper popping out in unexpected places.

Carl had just come in the house for dinner when his daughter tripped over the edge of the rug and banged her knee. *"Uff da,"* she said with a scowl.

"Speak in English," Carl ordered over his shoulder. He turned from the sink with dripping hands. "We speak English here."

"Nora doesn't." The little girl stomped her foot.

Nora hid a grin in baby Peder's blanket. She had understood what was said that time.

"Nora?" asked Carl.

"Ja." She turned to Carl with a look that dared him to say more.

Carl changed his mind. "We'll talk later," he spoke in German, slowly.

That will be a change, Nora thought as she filled the soup bowls at the stove. When she leaned over to help Kaaren with her bread, she heard the little girl muttering very, very softly.

"*Uff da, uff da, uff da.*" Her bottom lip stuck out and her eyebrows met each other in a line that Nora knew meant trouble.

"Nora, can I speak with you in the parlor?" Carl spoke slowly and nodded to the closed room.

With his back poker-straight and his hands clenched, Carl led the way into the freezing room. "Now." He stepped around her and closed the door. "Kaaren must speak English. No Norwegian."

Nora crossed her arms across her chest. She could feel her jaw tightening. She straightened her tired back and suddenly she did not feel quite so weary. "Ja!"

"You must learn to speak English."

"Ja!" Nora shook a finger in his face as all her mother's preaching against the evils of her daughter's temper flew right up the chimney with the smoke.

"Ja! You tell me to speak English! How I would love to; if only I could! Who is there to teach me? A three-year-old who is just learning to talk?" Nora tried to slow her words down so he could understand her, but it was like stopping a freight train. "I thought you would teach me—ja, you do not even talk. You don't talk to me. You don't talk to Kaaren. Maybe you talk to your cows!" With that, she spun around, yanked open the door to the kitchen, stomped through, and slammed it shut in his face.

The resounding crash woke Peder, who began to wail. Kaaren stared at her, eyes wide and chin quivering.

"*Uff da!*" Nora picked up the baby and carried him off for a change of britches. She heard Carl leave, gently closing the door behind him.

She sank down onto the bed, the fury draining away as quickly as it came. What had she done?

Silence hung in the air that night at supper and Nora could feel Carl watching her. Now she knew what a mouse stalked by a cat felt like.

Every morning Nora promised herself she would write to her family. At the end of each weary day, though, the letter still lived only in her mind.

One night, it seemed like she and her unhappy burden paced all night. Finally, she collapsed into the rocking chair. When she awoke, a quilt swaddled her from neck to toe. *Carl. He did this*, she thought. Warmth beyond that of the quilt seeped clear to her fingertips.

But her head ached, her nose dripped, and her eyes felt like they were glued shut. When she put Peder down in the cradle so she could begin the mush for breakfast, she started coughing.

The next morning, both Peder and Kaaren had runny noses and whiny voices. Nora coughed, Kaaren coughed, Peder coughed—and wailed.

By the next morning the baby's throat was so scratchy he could hardly cry. Nora had the kettle steaming on the stove. But, when she leaned her head over it and tried to inhale deeply, her coughing cut her off. If only she had some of her mother's special cold mixture.

The dog, barking outside, drew her to the window in time to see a horse and sleigh pulling to a stop in front of the door. Who could be calling?

Nora looked around the room. Dishes were still on the table; diapers were simmering on the stove; there was nothing in the house to serve with the coffee; her hair was not combed; the children were sick. She looked down at her dirty apron. What would they think of her?

While she took off her apron with one hand, Nora tried, with the other hand, to tuck some loose strands of hair up into her braids. She had finished neither when the knock sounded on the door. Reaching out with a trembling hand, Nora turned the glass knob.

"Oh, Ingeborge, I—a-a-achooo." The sneeze blew so hard it plugged her ears. She reached to get her handkerchief from her apron pocket, but the apron was dangling over the back of a chair. "Cub ind." She tried to smile but instead, at the sight of a smiling, friendly face, Nora collapsed into tears. She shut the door, groped in the pocket of the apron, then, in desperation, held the entire apron to her face.

"Oh, my dear, my dear. You look done in. How long have you been sick? How are the children?" All the while she murmured soothing sounds, Ingeborge patted Nora's heaving shoulders.

Kaaren stood, wide-eyed, in the center of the tumbled room.

"Here, now. You sit down in this chair and I'll get you a cup of coffee." Ingeborge pushed Nora down onto the chair. On her way to the cupboard, she removed her hat. With two cups of coffee in hand, she sat down in the chair next to Nora. "Now, tell me all that's happened." As Nora talked, Ingeborge removed her heavy wool coat and beckoned for Kaaren to come sit on her lap.

Nora poured out her miseries—the baby's eating every two hours, the colds, and, because of the coughing, her fear of the fever.

"And what about Carl?" Ingeborge smoothed the strands of hair off Nora's flushed, hot face.

"Him? I never see him. Only at mealtime. He never says anything. Only scolds me when Kaaren does not speak English."

"Me say 'Uff da.'" Kaaren nodded solemnly.

"Oh, you sweetie." Ingeborge hugged the child and kissed her cheek. "I could eat you up."

Kaaren smiled until a cough choked her.

"Well, I know what you need." Ingeborge stroked Nora's arm. "Bed. You wash your face and go crawl into bed. I can stay until late afternoon. I think some rest without worrying is what Dr. Harmon would order."

"Are you sure?" Nora croaked around the lump in her throat.

"I'm sure." Ingeborge slid Kaaren to the floor and then stood up. She took Nora's hand and pulled her upright. "Go, now."

"Peder. . . ?"

"I can see where you have things. We'll do fine. Now, go."

Nora did not need to be told a third time. She poured water from the reservoir into a basin, washed her face and hands, and stumbled into the bedroom. She took time to put on her nightgown and then crawled under the covers.

"Thank you, Lord," she mumbled before sleep claimed her.

The next thing Nora heard was a woman's voice singing. She blinked her eyes, wondering where she was. And who was that singing? She lifted her head and looked around the now-familiar room. What was she doing in bed at this time of day? She lay back down, her eyelids too heavy to hold open.

Next, she heard a baby crying. "Peder, I'm coming." She sat up and pushed back the covers. This time she felt awake. This time she remembered that Ingeborge had come to visit—and she was sleeping away their precious minutes together.

"Just in time for a cup of fresh coffee." Ingeborge greeted Nora's entrance into the kitchen with a wide smile. "You sit right here," she pointed to the rocker, "and we can talk some before I have to leave."

"Kaaren and Peder?"

"Both sleeping. You're right about that little one. He does not eat much at a time but he wants his bottle every two hours." She handed Nora the steaming cup. "Maybe it's the cow's milk that does not agree with him. Carl says he cries a lot."

"How would he know?" Nora felt ashamed as soon as she had said the words.

"Tell me, dear, how are things between you and Carl?"

At the kind words, Nora swallowed back the tears that threatened to flow. She rubbed a finger around the rim of her cup. "He won't even look at little Peder. He hardly talks to Kaaren but

81

then, when could he? He's never in the house. I do not know where he keeps himself all the time. Has a lot to do down at the barn, I suppose."

She leaned back in her rocking chair and, with a push, started the soothing rhythm. "Ingeborge, what am I to do?"

"Well, one thing I know. The only thing worse than a stubborn Norwegian is a hardheaded German. Right now, I'd say the man is grieving for his young wife and angry at God for taking her." Ingeborge sighed. "I think death is harder for our men than for us. They feel helpless, like they failed. And what can anyone do?"

"Ummm."

"Give him time and love."

Nora stopped the rocking with a thump. "Love? Remember the agreement? I'm going back to Norway as soon as I can."

"Now, now. I'm talking about the kind of love God asks us to give any suffering being. You have an abundance of that kind of love. I've seen it in all you do."

"Oh." Nora again pushed with her toe.

"Can you do that?" The question came softly.

Nora aimed a halfhearted smile at her friend. "It would be easier if he were around more."

"True. But perhaps that will change." Ingeborge pulled herself to her feet. "Well, supper is in the oven and the bread will have to go in pretty soon. I hung some of the diapers outside so they can freeze overnight."

"How can I ever thank you enough?"

Ingeborge took both their cups to the sink. "Just get better. Everything else will work out in God's good time."

The dog barking and a jingle from a harness announced a visitor.

"That must be my John now. He wanted to visit some of the members that live out in the country and that's why I could come today."

"How ashamed I am. I never even asked how you came to be here."

Ingeborge smiled and patted Nora's cheek. "Let's just give

God the thanks that He brought me here for you."

After Reverend Moen and Ingeborge left, the special glow that Nora felt around her heart remained. What a good friend she had. The special feeling stayed through the suppertime and after feeding Peder. Carl even played with Kaaren before Nora put the little one to bed. When she came out of the bedroom, he was sitting at the table, reading in the lamplight.

He cleared his throat. "Nora." His voice broke. He cleared his throat again. "Would it be possible that I teach you English? Here . . .in the evening? When you get to feeling better?"

Chapter 8

The break came a week later. Nora felt like she had been given a priceless gift. Peder slept for four straight hours in the afternoon and again that night. And he smiled at her when she bathed him. This little round face with the button nose that was usually screwed up in either anger or pain, now opened its mouth and let the sides flutter upwards.

Nora lost her heart. She felt it wing from her chest and join with the baby's. She dried him, between each precious little finger and toe, all the while murmuring love words and praising him when the smile came again, broader this time.

Nora wanted to tell someone. Kaaren? No, she was asleep in a much-needed nap. Carl? He should be the person to rejoice in his son's first smile. But he was out working on the farm someplace—who knew where—and, to this day he had never even peeked into the baby's cradle. He never asked about the mite or even said the baby's name.

She would have to settle for writing to her mother as soon as Peder fell back asleep. Her mother would understand the joy Nora felt. It was as if this little life were her very own. Her son. Her Peder.

Nora put a hand to her heart. A pain stabbed at the thought. No, she was only the housekeeper and, in only a few months, she would be returning to Norway. Another would see Peder crawl and take his first step. Carl would marry again and his new wife would take over the care of this home and this family.

The words she said to herself made so much sense. After all, they were the truth and the plan Carl had proposed. Why then did they hurt so much?

That night, when Nora and Carl sat down at the table for the English lesson, Nora found it difficult to concentrate.

First, Carl laid their earlier lessons on the table and they reviewed them. Then, she wrote something in Norwegian and, after making sure he understood what she wanted, Carl wrote the English word beside it. Then, he read it to her. She read the words and they repeated them until she said them correctly.

After the lesson, Nora gathered her courage. "Peder smiled at me today," she said slowly as she wrote the words in Norwegian.

Carl took the paper, read the words, and wrote them in English. After he said them in English, he waited for Nora's response. There was no smile, no change in inflection. Nothing.

Uff da, Nora thought. What an impossible man. She repeated the words aloud, but now they were just words—the magic she had felt with Peder's first baby smile was missing.

Why? Nora wanted to scream at him. *What is the matter with you?* But, instead she watched his hand. The hairs on the back of his hand glinted white in the golden glow of the lamp. They were strong hands with long fingers and hard callouses. How would they feel. . . ?

"Nora." The tone snapped impatience.

"Ah, ja?"

"The lesson? If you do not want to continue, just tell me. I have other things I could be doing."

She lifted her gaze to his.

Eyes stern, he repeated his words. "Peder smiled at me today."

"Ja, and his father might try the same," Nora said in Norwegian as she shoved back her chair and rose to her feet. She finished in English. "Good night, Mr. Detschman."

As she swept into the bedroom, she thought she heard a chuckle behind her, but she refused to turn and see. No, she shook her head, it must have been the wind.

The next morning, after waking only once during the night to feed the baby, Nora felt more like herself than she had for weeks. She had diapers washed and hung out before breakfast. There was a johnnycake baking in the oven, and Kaaren was giggling at Nora's funny faces.

When Carl walked in the door with a basket of eggs in one hand and a jug of milk in the other, Nora greeted him with a sunny smile. "Good morning, Carl. Would you care for your coffee now?" She spoke in English.

He brushed past her to set the eggs and milk in the sink and grunted.

No "Thank you." No "Congratulations." Not even a smile. Nora knew just how Kaaren felt whenever she stamped her foot. Only now she would prefer having a certain large, booted foot underneath her stamping. His grunt must have meant yes.

When she wrote to her mother that morning, Nora had a hard time thinking of anything good to say about her employer. She corrected her thoughts—"her husband." What a joke!

So, instead, she told them of March in North Dakota, of the Moens, about Peder's smiles, and Kaaren's antics. She did not write about the weeks of walking the floor and wiping runny noses; of no one to talk to; of the ache in her heart for Norway and home; of a little girl who cried at night for the mother that would never return. Of Carl. . .she said nothing.

A few days later, Nora woke to the sound of dripping water. She slipped out of bed, picked up her wrapper, and, while shoving her arms into the sleeves, went to stand at the window. Dawn had just cracked the dark gray of the eastern sky, tinting the clouds with a promise of gold. The icicles, hanging in dagger points from the roof, now dripped onto the snowbanks below.

Nora cupped her hands around her elbows. She could see the cottonwood trees bending before a wind, a warm wind—if her ears really heard dripping water. The chinook had arrived. Carl had told her about the warm wind that came unannounced from nowhere and melted the snow away. Spring was coming to North Dakota.

That morning, she hurried about her chores. Maybe for a change she could wrap up Peder and take the children for a walk down to the barn. She was so tired of staying cooped up in the house. "Today, I'll be free," she sang to Peder as she fed him. After all, they were all healthy again. And the fresh air would do them good.

"I'll be going to Soldall today," Carl announced at the breakfast table. "If you have your letter ready, I will mail it for you."

Nora nodded. She held her breath. Maybe he would ask her and the children to go with him. She watched as he ate his mush with rapid bites. The toast disappeared the same way. Nothing was said about their going.

"Carl, I—" Her words stumbled to a halt. She should not have to ask.

"Ja?"

"Ahh, nothing." She handed him her letter. "Thank you."

She and Kaaren waved in the window, but he never even turned his head. With a fluid motion, he stepped up into the wagon-turned-sleigh and flicked the reins. The harness jingled into the distance.

"Silly goose," Nora told herself. "What difference does it make if he is here or gone to town? You do not see him anyway." But the heavy feeling hung over her shoulders like the wooden yoke she used to carry two buckets of water to the garden.

While washing the dishes, she stared out the window. The sun still shone, the warm wind tickled the trees—nothing had changed. When she put the last cup away, the thought hit her. *You wanted Carl to show you around his farm.* She nearly dropped the cup.

"Who needs him!" She hung the dish towel over the line behind the stove. "Come along, Kaaren. We're going down to the barn."

"See cows?" Kaaren scrambled to her feet. "Horse?" She ran to pull her coat off the rack. "Pa's barn?"

"Ja, little one. Pa's barn. You must wait for me. We have to get Peder ready, too."

By the time they were all dressed and out the door, Nora could hardly keep from running down the carefully shoveled path. She wanted to fling herself into the snow and teach Kaaren how to make snow angels. Brownie, the cocoa-and-white fluffy dog, picked up on her exuberance and bounded over the snow, his tongue lolling. His sharp barks made Kaaren laugh, then made Nora laugh, then set a big black crow cawing from the top of the windmill.

"Bird." Kaaren pointed toward the sky.

"Ja, this is a bird." Nora agreed. "A—what is it called in English?" *Oh well,* she shifted Peder into her other arm and guided Kaaren before her. *On to the barn.*

Nora inhaled deeply when they stepped through the door into the barn's dim interior. She stood for a moment, letting the aromas wash over her. Cow and hay, grain and horses, manure, leather, all the odors so familiar, be they American or Norwegian.

One of the red-and-white shorthorn cows turned her head in her stanchion and lowed at the newcomers. Nora counted four milking cows. Walking farther, she saw the horse stalls. Overhead, a cat meowed and peered down through the open hayloft door.

The animals and barn showed Carl's good care. The manure had been forked out, hay was in the mangers, and the aisles were swept clean. Even with their dense winter coats, the cows showed evidence of having been brushed and curried. Harnesses hung in perfect order on pegs in the wall. Nothing was out of place.

Nora put the bundled baby down onto a pile of hay and, taking Kaaren by the hand, walked up to the first cow. "So-o, boss," she murmured to reassure the cow who turned friendly eyes their way. She reached through the boards of the stanchion and scratched the cow under the chin.

"See, Kaaren, this is how cows like to be petted." She took the little girl's hand and together they rubbed the cow's silky throat. The cow stretched her nose way out, the better to enjoy the caress. Squatting in the straw, cheek to cheek with her charge, Kaaren and Nora giggled together as the cow closed her friendly brown eyes in appreciation.

A bay gelding nickered when they came to his stall. He turned his head, pulling against the rope tied to his halter.

Nora looked around and saw the wooden grain bins against one wall. Together, she and Kaaren lifted a slanted lid to see the golden oats half filling the bin. Nora pulled her mittens off and scooped out a handful of the grain. "For the horse." Grain clenched in her fist, she motioned Kaaren to stand still while she eased her way past the horse's huge body to reach his head.

The horse lipped the grain from her hand and whiskered her palm, begging for more. Nora smoothed his forelock and rubbed under the halter behind his black-fringed ears. "Oh, you beautiful thing, you. You must be lonely with your friends gone. I wonder what your name is." All the while she talked, she rubbed and stroked. When she inhaled, the smell of horse reminded her again of home. Some things stayed the same, everywhere.

Sure now that the animal was gentle, she went back out and, taking Kaaren in her arms, brought her up to pat the horse, too. Her big hand guided the little one.

"Pa's horse." Kaaren giggled when the animal blew in her face. She wrapped her arm around the back of Nora's neck and leaned against her, cheek to cheek.

Peder began to whimper on his hay nest, so Nora gave the horse one last pat and left the stall. Down the aisle she found another stall, this one with two white hogs. She lifted Kaaren up to see over the wall.

"Pa's pigs," Kaaren announced.

By the time Nora picked Peder up again, he had switched from whimper to demand. "Hush, now. We'll go feed you, but you must be patient." They left the barn and dropped the bar into place behind them.

The windmill squeaked and turned in the wind above the low building that must be the well house. Off to the side of the barn other buildings waited to be explored, but Nora walked quickly between the snowbanks. Peder had been so good he deserved to eat right away.

Under the onslaught of the chinook, the snow quickly melted. Nora watched the calendar as Easter approached. One day, after serving fried pork chops for dinner, she made a decision.

"Carl."

He stopped drinking his coffee and looked at her over the rim of his coffee cup.

"Is Easter soon?"

He nodded.

"We go to church?" Nora hated to stumble over her words, but she knew he wanted her to speak English whenever she could.

He pushed his chair back and set the cup carefully down on the table. Jaw tight, he grabbed his coat and strode out the door.

"That must mean 'No.' " She stared after him. At least he could have answered. She had said the words right—hadn't she?

In spite of the thundercloud that seemed to have taken up permanent residence on Carl's forehead, Nora went ahead with her spring housecleaning. Her home must be shiny clean for the risen Christ. Laundry danced on the clothesline, rugs took their beating without a murmur, windows sparkled and welcomed their clean curtains.

On Saturday, while Carl was in town, she poured water into the washtub in front of the stove and, after giving Kaaren a bath, took one herself. She left the tub of water for Carl to use and disappeared into the bedroom with the children.

The next morning, the tub was gone. Nora wished Carl had rinsed away that stern look when he had washed his hair.

"Christ is risen, He is risen indeed." Nora whispered the words to the sun on Easter morning. "Thank You, Father, for loving us and sending Your Son to die. And rise again. He is risen."

When she thought of missing church, the organ, and the hymns, the joy of Easter dimmed. So, Nora refused to let the thoughts of what she was missing bother her.

Instead, in her mind, she repeated the words over and over, *Jesus Christ is risen today*. Even Carl's scowl when Kaaren spilled her milk failed to drown out Nora's inner chorus.

That evening after supper, Nora and Kaaren sat at the table reading a schoolbook Carl had brought back from town. Nora read the English slowly, but Kaaren did not mind. She pointed a chubby finger at the pictures, naming each object. When she got bored, she slid to the floor and ambled off to the bedroom.

A few minutes later, she came back, dragging her doll. She pulled on Nora's skirt. "Ma."

Nora felt her stomach fall clear to her knees. She focused hard on her book, hoping and praying that Carl had not heard. She scooped Kaaren up onto her lap. But the deed was done. She did not have to turn to see his face—his thudding footsteps on the stairs told her what he was thinking.

Kaaren put her tiny palm on top of the book, now closed, on the table. "Ma's book."

"Auntie Nora's book." She covered the small hand with her own.

Kaaren shook her head. She peered up at Nora with eyes the blue of a summer lake. "Ma's book."

With a shaking hand, Nora pressed the dear little head to her chest. What would she do about this latest folly? Did Carl think she taught Kaaren to say that? Didn't he know that she would never do such a thing? She leaned her cheek on the top of Kaaren's head. But then, what did Carl really know of her at all?

Nora crawled into bed that night with a heavy heart. How could a day that began with heavenly singing end on such a sour note?

Chapter 9

Two days had passed and he had not spoken to her. Nora felt her temper simmering like a kettle about to boil over. She stifled the urge to slam the lid of the stove back in place—or the oven door. In fact, she knew if she stepped outside after the sun went down, her cheeks would freeze in the smile she forced past her clenched teeth.

She heard her mother's soft voice. *"Ah, Nora, do not let the sun go down on your anger."* But Nora knew that that had referred to keeping a happy marriage. And this. . .this contract she was caught in certainly could not be called a marriage in any terms she knew of.

But this is what you agreed to, the cool voice of reason reminded her. *So you could go back to Norway, remember?*

"Talking to myself, hearing voices. You think my mind is going?" The gray-striped cat in her lap looked up and yawned, showing white dagger teeth and a raspy pink tongue. She stretched her front paws way out, claws digging into Nora's knee, then curled back up and resumed the rumbling purr that could probably be heard across the room.

Nora set the chair to rocking, letting her thoughts fly back over the last few weeks. Whenever she thought of Carl, his anger came to mind. Had she done anything to make him mad? Well, she tried not to, that was for certain, but he either snapped at her or ignored her. *No, that's not all true,* she corrected herself. *The English lessons have mostly been peaceful times.*

Was it his sorrow that made him so. . .so. . .she searched for the best word. Angry, yes. But lost? She stroked the cat's back. Lost, yes, but more like an animal that has been wounded and strikes out at anyone who tries to help. She nodded.

So, what do I do? She let her mind float again, like a thistle seed caught on a summer's breeze. The answer came strong and clear. *Pray for him. Pray for him daily. Pray for him when he spitefully uses you.* A verse from her confirmation time, part of the "blesseds" that she so loved.

Silence reigned in the kitchen, a peace that gilded each chair and shelf, that glistened on the stove, and sparkled in the window. Even the cat's purring ceased. Nora felt that peace slip into her heart and fill it to bursting. "Bless this poor hurting man, oh my heavenly Father. Bring healing to his broken heart and bring him back to You." She whispered the words, as if loud sounds might disturb the moment.

A meadowlark sang from the fence, its song fluting on the morning air.

Nora lifted the hem of her apron and wiped the corner of her eye. "Thank You." The words had to squeeze past the lump in her throat. "I promise to pray for Carl every day. Amen."

After supper that evening, Nora brought out her books and paper and put them on the table. When Carl came back into the house after having checked on the animals, Nora met him with a cup of coffee.

"Please." She nodded to the chair she had already pulled out and extended the cup with both hands. "English lessons I want."

"Nora, I'm really tired, I. . ."

Nora held the cup and threw all her heart into the smile. "Please."

"Oh, all right." Carl took the cup and sat down at the table. He took a sip and set the cup down on the table. "Let's see where we were."

Nora sent another "Thank You" heavenward and slipped into her own chair. She took up the pencil and wrote, "When do the roses bloom?"

Carl looked at her with a question in his eyes. "Roses?"

Nora nodded. "I love roses." She repeated carefully the word he had used.

Carl shook his head. "No roses here. Wild roses in June."

Nora shrugged her confusion. What did he mean?

"Let's review what we've done before." He pulled out pages they had written on in the past and pointed to the sentences. Nora had been practicing. She said them all correctly.

"Good." He nodded. One lock of golden hair fell over his forehead.

Nora had the urge to reach out and brush it back. Instead she pulled herself to her feet and went for the coffeepot to refill their cups.

Nora sat down and wrote another sentence. "I want to plant a garden."

Carl wrote the English and together they repeated the words. He nodded. "Soon. I'll plow up the garden, soon."

That night, as she knelt by her bed, Nora remembered her promise. She smiled to herself as she slipped between the covers—praying for the man wasn't so difficult when she didn't feel like pouring coffee on his head.

One morning, Nora had another surprise. Brownie's barking announced company and, when Nora threw open the door, the entire Moen family waved from their light buggy. Reverend Moen reined his horse to a halt and, after climbing down, helped Ingeborge and the children to get out.

Nora flew down the steps and met them on the walk. "Come in, come in. Oh, you do not know how happy I am to see you." Her words tumbled over each other like puppies playing in the sun. She hugged Ingeborge and reached out to shake hands with Reverend Moen. "Come in."

"You look wonderful," Ingeborge said as she tucked her arm into Nora's. "And how is that man of yours now?"

"Carl's out riding the fence line to make sure none of the cows can get out." She turned to Reverend Moen. "I'm sure he will be so happy to see you."

"Good. I'll return to gather my family later this afternoon.

Maybe he'll be back then." Reverend Moen set a basket on the porch and turned to leave. "You all have a good visit now."

They waved him away and walked into the house. "I brought you some things." Ingeborge handed baby James to Nora and went back outside for the basket. "If the coffee is hot, we can share the cookies right now." She plunked the basket on the table and began removing her gifts. "Jam, bread, *spekemat,* and cheese. One of the church members brought me this the other day. I thought you might appreciate it, too."

"Oh, like home." Nora sniffed the wrapped piece of strong-smelling cheese. "Thank you."

"And sour cream cookies. Mary cut them out for me."

"I put the sugar on," said Knute. "Come on, Mary. Let's play ball on the porch."

Kaaren took her finger out of her mouth long enough to shove her hands into her coat sleeves and followed the others out the door.

"Stay out of the mud," Nora reminded them. "Kaaren, you hear me?"

While a "Yes, Ma," trailed back, Nora looked at Ingeborge and shrugged.

"And here's the best gift of all." Ingeborge drew an envelope from the bottom of the basket.

Nora reached for the letter. "From home. Oh, thank you." She slipped it into her apron pocket to be read and savored later.

With baby James unwrapped from his quilts and lying on another one on the floor and Peder still sleeping, Nora and Ingeborge sat down with their coffee to catch up on the news.

They talked until it was time to fix dinner and continued to talk while preparing the meal. They were both feeding their babies when Nora heard Carl out on the porch, talking with the children.

"All right if these funny people I found on the porch go down to play in the hayloft after dinner?" he asked as he came in the door.

"That would be wonderful," Ingeborge replied.

Nora could not say a word—shock locked her tongue.

Dinner was a lively affair. And quick. Carl even gave up his second cup of coffee to take the children down to play in the barn.

"I have a favor to ask," Nora said when she and Ingeborge sat down again.

"What?"

"Will you write the English words to 'Jesus Loves Me'? I want to teach Kaaren to sing it, but Carl insists we speak English. So many things I can't give her because I speak Norwegian."

"Of course I will. But you are learning some?"

"Ja, Carl and Kaaren, they teach me." She went on to describe her evening lessons.

"And Kaaren calls you 'Ma'?"

Nora nodded. "Carl was not pleased, but I've tried to tell her where her ma is. And he will not talk with her about it. He hardly talks to her at all."

"What a shame." Ingeborge laid her hand on Nora's arm. "He used to have a wonderful smile—Anna would tease him into smiling and laughing. They were happy, those two."

"And now he says nothing. He works himself into a stupor. You should see the barn. I think he has scrubbed the walls and even the floor. I'm sure the machinery is the same. Every buckle on the horses' harnesses shines."

"Men are like that. Sometimes I think God gave us heavy work so we can live through life's sorrow. And men more so than women—they can't cry."

Nora nodded. She picked up her cup and sipped the cooling drink. "But crying and laughing again makes the sorrow easier to bear."

"Ja. That and praying."

The silence, sweet and comfortable, lengthened. The clock on the wall ticked away the moments. A robin sang from the cottonwood tree beyond the fence. Coal whooshed as it sank in the firebox.

Ingeborge roused herself first. "Now, to 'Jesus Loves Me.' Do you have paper handy?"

By the time Reverend Moen came to retrieve his brood, Nora had most of the English words to the song locked away in her heart. And, to refresh her memory, the carefully written words. After they left, she studied the letters. Maybe this new language was not so ugly after all.

That night, as she brushed the hayseeds from Kaaren's hair, she hummed the song. Kaaren chattered away about the hayloft with Nora listening carefully to pick out words she knew. "Pa's barn" and "hayloft" she understood, and giggles were a universal language.

Later, after the English language session was finished, Carl brought a box from the pantry and set it on the table. "Go ahead," he said with a motion. "Open it. These are seeds for the garden. I will plow tomorrow."

"Plow?" Nora tasted the strange word.

Carl wrote it down so Nora could look the word up in the dictionary. More and more she was able to find the words she needed by referring to the dictionary. She read the meaning. "To turn the soil with a tool."

"Then we plant?" She gestured to the seeds.

"After the ground dries. Then the harrow. Plant next week."

"Thank you." She turned her attention to the packets of seeds. While she could not read the labels, she did not need to. Peas, beans, corn, pumpkins—all were easily recognized. She held up one packet of very small seeds.

"Carrots." Carl identified it as well as the others. "Turnips, rutabaga, lettuce. Potatoes are down in the cellar. I'll buy onions when I go to town."

Nora nodded. Her fingers picked through the packets as if they had a delicate life of their own. Her own garden. She would plant and weed and water and they would have fresh vegetables. And some to preserve.

After her prayers for Carl that night, she slipped into bed with a smile still on her face. Her last thought wiped it away—by the time the garden was ready to eat, she would be on her way back to Norway.

She could not bear to remain in the house the morning Carl brought up the team hitched to a plow and started turning the soil.

Rich black curls of dirt folded over in perfectly straight lines running north and south. She reached down and picked up a handful of loam, clenching her fist and then letting the dirt crumble back to the earth. She breathed in the aroma of the rich soil, the promise of spring and of rebirth.

"Easy, now," Carl sang out to the team as they turned another corner. The harness jingled and the horses snorted as they leaned into their collars.

Nora watched when they started back toward her. Sun glinted off Carl's bright golden hair, the one lock falling over his broad forehead.

Like her, he raised his face to the sun, then brushed the strand back with his forearm. His shirt sleeves were rolled back, exposing skin already turning pink from the sun.

"Ma?" Kaaren tugged on Nora's skirt.

"Ja?" Nora left off gazing at the man on the plow and bent to see what Kaaren wanted.

"See?" Between two careful fingers, Kaaren held up an angleworm she had rescued from the turned earth. Nora held out her hand and Kaaren placed it on the flattened palm.

What is the English word here? thought Nora as she joined Kaaren in oohing over the creature.

"Show Pa?" Kaaren looked up, her eyes dancing with delight.

"Ja." Nora nodded. "And maybe he'll tell me what to call it," she smiled. Who could keep from smiling on a day like this one?

"I'm going into town," Carl announced the next morning after breakfast. "You need anything?"

Nora thought quickly. Kaaren needed new dresses and they were nearly out of sugar. How she would love to go along and visit with Ingeborge. Maybe he would ask her.

But Carl only wrote down the things she listed for him, including cloth for new dresses. When he drove out of the yard, he was by himself. She and Kaaren were left on the porch, waving good-bye.

"Come, little one. We'll bake some cookies and go down to the barn to see the new calf."

Kaaren stared wistfully at the barn. "Go in the hayloft?" She raised hopeful eyes to Nora. "Jump in the hay?"

"We'll see." Nora turned back to the kitchen. "Cookies, first."

Later, Nora wrapped bread and jelly sandwiches in one napkin, fresh cinnamon cookies in another, and poured milk into a pint jar. Then she wrapped Peder in a blanket and the three of them started for the barn.

The new red-and-white calf bawled from his pen as soon as they swung open the door to the otherwise empty barn. The cows were out to pasture, Carl was driving the horses, and the pigs could be heard rooting around in their lean-to at the side of the barn.

"Up." Nora pointed to the ladder, slanted from the floor to the door in the ceiling to the hayloft. She gave Kaaren a boost and stood beside the ladder until the little girl scrambled out of sight. Nora climbed up halfway and laid their lunch on the smooth boards of the hayloft floor. When she, with Peder in one arm, reached the upper floor, she stopped a moment just to look.

Rafters met in the peaked roof, high and dim in the dust-laden light. Much of the grass hay had already been fed to the livestock, but the densely packed fodder still covered about half the floor to a height of several feet. A pitchfork stabbed into the hay stood erect just like an empty flagpole.

Kaaren ran across the floor to the hay and slipped and slid until she perched on top of the mound. Then, she sat on the edge, legs straight in front, and, like sledding down a hill, slipped down the incline. She landed with a thump, giggling and calling, "See, Ma. Come, slide." She turned and scrambled back up. This time, she lay back flat and slid down again.

"Well, this hardly makes up for the hills in Norway, but we'll make our fun where we can," Nora muttered to herself as she laughed and encouraged Kaaren. When Nora left Peder on the hay and slid down the hay pile, Kaaren laughed and raced back up.

Nora lay back on the hay and looked up at the dust motes dancing in the light streaming through the high window. On the other end of the barn was a square door. It took up most of the wall and was meant to be opened to bring in the new hay. What a wonderful place to have a dance. When she thought about it, she missed the dances at home. People laughing, whirling, and tapping to the music. One thing Norwegians knew how to do—dance and have a good time.

Kaaren plunked down beside her. When Nora did not get up, the little girl snuggled down and laid her head on Nora's shoulder. "Hungry, Ma. Eat now?" She patted Nora's cheek with her grubby hand.

"Ja, we'll eat." With Peder propped in her arms and Kaaren sitting cross-legged in perfect imitation of her, they devoured their dinner. Between bites, Nora sang the first line of the new song she had learned. "Jesus loves me, this I know" rose to the rafters and echoed back to form a heavenly chorus.

When Carl returned home that evening, he brought in the supplies. One little sack he handed to Kaaren.

She carefully opened the top of it and squealed. "Candy. Yummm." She plopped down on the rug and stuck one piece in her mouth. Sucking on it took all her concentration.

Nora opened her package carefully, too. "So much?" She held up the light blue cotton material with small, dark blue flowers.

"You need a summer dress, too."

"Thank you." Nora held the fabric up to her cheek. "It's beautiful."

"You're welcome." He continued to move packages around until he pulled something out from behind the flour sack. He set the burlap packet on the table in front of Nora. "For you." He spoke like he had a rough patch in his throat.

She stared at him, wondering what else there could be. Carefully, she folded back the edges of the burlap. Inside, the roots still planted in a clump of moist soil, was the start of a rosebush. Tiny red nubbins, ready to sprout into new growth, glowed on three dark green, thorny stems.

Tears filled her eyes and blurred the gift. "Thank you." With the back of her hand, she dashed away the falling drops. When she raised her gaze to Carl's, he dropped his.

The silence vibrated between them like a fine piano wire tapped by the hammer. Unheard, unseen—the music crept into their hearts.

Carl cleared his throat and the silence tinkled to the floor to lie in quivering fragments. "Uhhmm." He started to say something but had to clear his throat again. "I'll be putting the horses away. . .and milking. . . . If you could have supper ready later?"

"Ja, I will." Nora whispered, never taking her eyes off his face. While there was no smile, she realized the lines between his eyebrows had smoothed away.

The next day, while Nora dug a hole by the front porch and planted her rosebush, Carl readied the garden spot. Now the soil was loose and flat, clods breaking down as the team and harrow cut pass after pass across the land.

"You can plant now." Carl reined the horses in and stepped off the harrow to stand in front of Nora. "The hoe is in the cellar." He made hoeing motions with his hands and pointed to the cellar door slanted against the side of the house. "After dinner, I'll begin plowing the fields." He pointed off to the east. Stubble from the previous fall lay gray on the land. "Wheat first, then oats, and finally corn. Maybe potatoes, too." He took off his broad-brimmed, black hat and the teasing breeze lifted his hair.

Nora stood transfixed. He glowed—burnished by the sun and the wind—his love for the land, part and parcel of his soul, shining from his eyes.

She looked out across the fallow land, flat as her eyes could see. A meadowlark soared and sang above them, its notes trilling down like bits of sunlight to be caught in her heart.

Later, serving the dinner, Nora laid one hand on his shoulder while she set a plate on the table in front of him. The need to touch him, to feel the strength of this man, welled up from that same place within her that hoarded the sunbeams. How right it felt.

"Thank you, Nora, for the good food." Carl pushed back his chair. "See you tonight."

Nora stared after him. Was God working His miracle?

Nora stacked the dishes in the sink and fed Peder. Then, taking a shawl, she settled him in it crosswise and, knotting two opposite corners together, formed a sling that she lifted over her head. She tied another shawl the opposite way and now the baby was clasped snugly against her chest.

With her hands free, she picked up the box of seeds. On the porch waited the hoe that Carl had brought up from the cellar. "Come Kaaren, we are going planting."

The sun had passed the midafternoon mark when Nora looked up from her labors at the sound of the dog barking. She shaded her eyes, looking off to the west where the sound came from. Two men strode across the field.

"We have company," she announced to Kaaren, who was busily digging a trench with a stick she had found. Nora watched them come closer. Dark hair, long, held back with a band. Dark faces, tattered shirts, leather leggings. One carried a rifle.

"Indians." Nora clutched the baby to her. All she had ever read and heard of the thieving, murdering, American savages flooded her mind.

Chapter 10

God, help!" Nora leaned over and grasped Kaaren by the hand, jerking her to her feet.

The Indians stopped at the edge of the garden. They stared at her.

She stared at them. Her heart pounded in her chest, loud enough she was sure that they could hear. "You must welcome strangers." Her mother's words could barely be heard over the bellows of her lungs.

Nora tried to swallow. Not even enough juice to spit, let alone swallow—or talk. What good would talk do anyway? What language did they speak? Certainly not Norwegian. She stepped forward like she had a board stuck to her spine. "Hello."

Black eyes did not blink. The taller one surveyed her from the crown of her braids to her boot tips that peeked out from under her black skirt and back up again, slowly. When he muttered something, the shorter one shrugged.

Welcome strangers, welcome strangers. What do you do when strangers come, especially if they are the type that might take your hair and scalp with them when they leave? She clamped her teeth against the bile that rose from her stomach, threatening to make her disgrace herself. *What do you do with company like this?*

Offer them food, of course. "You, eat? Drink?" If that slight motion of the tall one's head was agreement, Nora needed no second response.

"Come." She clutched Kaaren's hand and strode across the planted rows, girl in tow, head high. "Never show fear," was her father's advice for dealing with both strangers and animals. Nora

103

fought to hang onto those words of wisdom.

"Sit." She motioned to the porch steps and, without looking back to see if they obeyed, strode with Kaaren across the porch and through the door, letting the screen door slam behind her. She untied the sling contraption from around her shoulders and laid Peder in his cradle. Back in the kitchen, her hands shook so much she could scarcely pick up the knife. She sneaked glances at the door, sure that it would slam open at any moment and they would come to. . . She sliced bread and poured milk into cups. With bread, milk, leftover chicken that she had planned to have for supper, and cookies on the plates, she paused at the door.

The dark-skinned men sat on the stairs like she had ordered, leaning against the posts with their arms draped across their bent knees. One carved on a piece of wood with a knife that glinted in the sun. The gun rested against the outside of the porch, right near the owner's leg.

Please, God. . . Nora never finished the prayer as she pushed the door open and crossed the porch. "Here." She handed each of them a plate, then dug into her apron pocket for forks. When she held the silver out, they ignored her and ate with their hands.

Nora eased her way backward and, fumbling with her hands behind her, opened the screen door and slipped inside. She stood watching them through the screen.

The taller man scraped his plate clean with the bread and raised his cup in her direction.

"M–more?" If she could just quit stuttering.

He nodded.

She brought the jug out and refilled both their cups.

When they drained the cups, they set them and the plates on the floor. Slowly, they stood. The tall man picked up his gun. The shorter one slid his knife back into its sheath.

Nora now knew what the rabbit felt like when facing a fox.

"Thank you, Carl's new woman." The tall man spoke in better English than she did. He nodded—once. Their long strides eating up the ground, the two Indians headed east.

Nora felt a gurgle of laughter churning in her middle and

pleading to be let out. She stepped out onto the porch and bent to pick up the plates. As she stood again, she looked out across the land. The taller Indian raised a hand high in the air—and waved.

When she told Carl the story that night after dinner, she watched his face carefully. His lip twitched, his eyes crinkled. He had a dimple in his right cheek. When she repeated the Indian's "Thank you, Carl's new woman," Carl bent over double. The laughter exploded from him like a shot from a cannon; the kitchen echoed with his chortles.

Kaaren giggled along and banged her spoon on the table.

Nora sat back and let the music of his mirth flow over, around, and through her. She was not sure which she was laughing at more—her story or his enjoyment of her story.

When he wiped his eyes with the heel of his hands, she said with a lift of her chin, "He say better English than me."

Carl dug into his back pocket for a handkerchief, then he blew his nose and shook his head, laughter still quivering in his shoulders. "The tall one is called One Horse and his shorter brother is Night of the Fox. They've been walking through here ever since I bought the farm. Sometimes, I find a deer carcass as a gift. Sometimes, they sleep in my barn. You could say we've become friends the last few years." The grin split his face again. "All Indian stories you've heard, that was long ago."

"Next time I'll know."

The corners of his mouth remained tipped up all through the English lesson and while Nora tucked both Peder and Kaaren into bed. When Nora returned to the kitchen, she took her place in the rocker and picked up the pieces of blue-flowered material she had cut out for Kaaren's dress. In between stitches, she sneaked peeks at the man caught in the circle of lamplight. His smile had faded but so had the lines from his nose to his mouth and those in his forehead.

"Thank You, Father," she prayed that night on her knees. "He is so beautiful when he laughs." She rested her chin on her clasped hands. "But, next time, maybe he could laugh with me instead of at me." Her lips curved up at the thought. "But thanks, no matter what. I'm not choosy."

Before she drifted off, the rest of a Bible verse her mother used to recite floated through her mind. *"Be not forgetful to entertain strangers: for thereby some have entertained angels unawares."*

Funny looking angels, she thought. *And I was so scared.* She pictured the scene in the garden again. *But, it was worth it.*

Within a week, Nora had her garden planted. New growth on her rosebush jutted out several inches with more new leaves unfolding every day. When she looked toward the horizon, newborn grass sprouted, cloaking the unplowed land in green velvet.

"When you look across the prairie," she wrote her sister Clara, "you can see clear into next month. While I miss the mountains and fjords, I can see the beauty in this part of God's creation, also. It is not a forgotten land as I had first thought."

When Carl drove into town one day, he took her letter and returned with another. This one was in answer to his advertisement for a housekeeper.

"Bah. She can't speak English, either," he growled after dropping the letter onto the table. He flicked the paper with his fingers. "Why did she even bother to write? I said specifically that the woman must speak English."

When Nora brought out her papers for their lesson, he waved her away. "I'm too tired to concentrate on that tonight." He heaved himself out of his chair. "Good night."

Nora could hear his weariness in the measured tread with which he climbed the stairs.

Sitting under the lamplight, stitching away on Kaaren's dress, Nora searched her heart. Was it joy she felt when he said the woman would not work out? Surely not. Her dream was to return to Norway, and she would not be able to do that until Carl found someone to take her place.

Each day Peder seemed to do something new. He not only smiled now, but laughed when Nora blew on his round tummy. He waved pudgy arms and, when he reached for an object, sometimes he got it. When Nora laid him on a quilt either on the floor or outside on the grass, Kaaren would dangle a rubber jar ring or the bright red stuffed dog Nora had sewn for him. Hearing them laughing together always made Nora smile.

Carl ignored them.

"How can he?" Nora fumed one night after seeing him take a wide track around the two little ones on the floor. Kaaren was on her tummy, legs waving in the air while she and Peder laughed and chattered, her mimicking Peder's cooing.

One evening, Nora sat rocking and feeding Peder his bottle when she heard a thump, bump. . .silence. . .and then a scream to strike fear in any mother's heart.

Carl leaped to his feet, picked the screaming Kaaren up off the floor at the foot of the stairs, and tried to comfort her.

"No!" She arched her back and screamed louder. "Ma-a-a! I want my ma!"

Nora could see blood streaming from a wound above Kaaren's right eye. She stood, handed Peder along with his bottle to Carl, and took the little girl over to the sink. With a cold cloth pressed to the site to stop the bleeding, Nora murmured words of comfort. She turned to see Carl, wooden-faced, holding the baby stiffly in his arms.

Peder began to whimper, wanting the remainder of his supper. Without looking at his son, Carl walked into the bedroom, laid the bundle on the bed as if it were no more than a package from the store, and stalked out the door.

Nora struggled between vexation and pity. She wrapped a bandage over the tiny cut above Kaaren's eye. Then she retrieved Peder and resumed feeding him, still petting and comforting Kaaren.

Vexation swelled into fury. *That man! That insufferable, hard-headed, coldhearted*—she ran out of words harsh enough to describe him. *Who does he think he is anyway? Other people in this world lose their loved ones and they still love those left. How could he not love such a darling baby as Peder?*

"I will not pray for him tonight." She knelt by the bed, hoping to hear Carl's footsteps returning but was almost glad when they did not. "God, You don't *really* want me to pray for him, do You?" She listened to the silence. Outside somewhere, an owl hooted in its nightly hunting forays. The breeze fluffed the lace curtains at the open window.

She started to climb into bed. "Oh, fiddle." She knelt back down and scrunched her eyes closed, her teeth snapping together between words. "Please bless Carl and help him get through this time of sorrow. Make him love his sweet little son and. . ." She stopped to think. Nothing more came. "Amen."

She climbed back into bed and pulled up the covers. "So there." The silence crept back into the room. Was that God chuckling on the breeze? Nora turned over to sleep, a smile curving her lips.

With May, the beans leaped from the ground. Carrot feathers waved in their rows and the potatoes pushed up corrugated leaves to find the sun.

Nora leaned on her hoe, pride in her handiwork evident in the smile on her face. She pushed back the straw hat she had found in the cellar and wiped the sweat from her forehead. What her garden needed now was a slow-falling, soaking rain. She eyed the gray clouds mounding in the west. A lightning fork stabbed the sky.

"At least a storm can't catch you by surprise here," she said with a shrug. "And here I am talking to myself again. Better start giving myself orders, too. So get over there and take the wash off the line. It's been wet once today. It doesn't need to be wet again." She suited actions to her words and paused only long enough to watch rain fall in gray veils across the land. She dashed to the house with a full basket just as the first drops pelted the dust.

Carl galloped the team up to the barn, the harrow left in the fields. Nora stood on the porch. "What happened to him?" Brownie whined at her feet.

"Are you all right?" she yelled above the rising wind.

At his wave, she turned back into the house. Expecting him to come up for coffee, she stoked the embers and added coal to the fire. Maybe she should start an early supper. Even though the clock said four, the sky said dusk.

She crossed to the open door and through the screen door

watched huge, fat raindrops pound the earth. She shook her head. "Doesn't this country ever do anything gently?"

"Ma?" Kaaren meandered out of the bedroom, rubbing sleep from her eyes. She leaned against Nora's skirt until Nora picked her up and set the little girl on her hip.

Lightning forked beyond the barn and in a few moments thunder crashed. Nora stood in awe at the heavenly display. She heard the rain gurgle in the downspouts and into the cistern under the house. Lightning lit the sky again.

"Pretty." Kaaren leaned her head against Nora's shoulder. When the thunder boomed, she flinched, then giggled. Nora could already hear that the storm was moving to the east of them. Now, the rain fell in billowing skirts, gentle and kind. The cool breeze felt good.

She left the doorway and finished grinding the dark beans for coffee. By the time Carl stepped onto the porch, the aroma of coffee brewing floated out to meet him.

"Smells wonderful." He sniffed appreciatively and hung his hat on the rack.

"Pretty lights." Kaaren pointed out the window. "Big boom."

Carl tousled her hair with one hand before picking her up. "Did you like it?"

She nodded, her blue eyes grave. "Hungry, Pa?" At his nod, she smiled. "Me, too."

"Sit down. I have cookies. Supper will be soon."

This time, when Nora rested her hand on Carl's shoulder, she felt a tremor go up her arm—he had leaned into her gentle pressure. She finished pouring the coffee and took her own chair. When Carl smiled at her it was as if the skies had parted and the sun beamed down to melt the frost that had stilled the heart.

"Thank you," was all he said but, with the smile, it was enough.

Nora rejoiced in the moments Carl spent with Kaaren. Though few and far between since he was in the fields at dawn and did not return to milk the cows until dark, the little one now met him at the door with a welcome grin. Even though he was so tired he would fall asleep at the table, he took time to listen to Kaaren's chatter and admire her new dress.

Of Peder, he never questioned or mentioned.

One afternoon, Nora moved the rocker and cradle out to the porch so she could sew and enjoy the sun at the same time. For a time, Kaaren played quietly at her feet but soon demanded a song and a story. Nora stuck her needle into the material of the bodice for her new dress and set it in the basket at her feet.

"Here we go." After hoisting Kaaren up onto her lap, Nora picked up the Bible written in English that she had in the same basket and turned to the Gospel of Matthew. Slowly, she read the story of Jesus and the children. Softly, she began singing, "Jesus loves me, this I know." Kaaren joined in and together they finished the chorus.

"More." Kaaren leaned back against Nora's shoulder and Nora closed her eyes. They sang it again. "Yes, Jesus loves me, yes Jesus. . ."

"What are you doing?" Carl's voice cut like a knife.

Nora felt like she had been stabbed. Her eyes flew open to clash with his, limpid pond against glacier. Confusion to fury.

Kaaren stuck her finger in her mouth and whimpered, her chin quivering as she stared from her father to Nora.

"Pa-a-a!" Her wail floated on the breeze spun up by his leaving.

"Shhh." Nora comforted her. "You sit here in my chair and take care of Peder. I will come back."

At Kaaren's nod, Nora rose to her feet and set the little girl back in the chair. Then, she gathered her skirts and ran down the path to the barn.

Carl had the horses backed up on either side of the wagon and shaft and was hooking the traces when she stopped in front of him.

"Why are you angry?" She stumbled over the words, wishing she could use Norwegian instead of English.

He ignored her, continuing the harnessing.

"Carl!" She might as well have been talking to the barn door.

When he lifted a foot to mount the wagon, she placed a hand on his arm. "Carl, what did I do?"

He spun around, reins in his hand. "Do? The Bible. That song. How can you sing and worship a God who kills innocent mothers and children?"

Chapter 11

B ut your son lived!"

Carl stepped forward, towering over her in his fury. "But his mother didn't! She died and he might as well have."

"What are you saying?" She clenched her hands in the sides of her skirt. She would rather be pummeling his chest.

"I'm saying I don't want you teaching my daughter those songs and filling her head with lies about a God who loves her."

"But Jesus—God loves us all. He will help you, if you ask."

"I don't need His kind of help."

"But, Carl." She placed her hand on his arm.

He threw her hand off, the wind of it whistling by her cheek. Leaping up onto the wagon, he flicked the reins. "Ha, boys." Without a look back, he drove down the lane.

Nora stared after him, tears burning behind her eyes. "Oh, God help you, poor, poor man." She bit the knuckles on her right hand, her left pressed against her throat. "Only God can help you. Father, please take away Carl's bitterness. Bring him Your love. Restore his faith. Father, forgive me. I cannot do what he asks."

Dust from the wagon's churning wheels hung in the still air. It smelled like despair.

Nora opened the barn door and wandered inside. Clean floors, harnesses draped over pegs in perfect order—all showed a man who cared about his farm. Outside, the fat cows switched their tails in the shade of the barn, a newly replaced fence post anchored a gate that swung smoothly on oiled hinges. She wandered over to the pigpen. The sow and her piglets lay on a pile of straw under a roof to keep off the hot sun. Carl loved his animals.

On the way up to the house, she thought about him. . .tossing Kaaren in the air to make her laugh. . .of his sitting with the chattering child, answering her myriad questions. Yes, he loved his family. . .the fields, green and growing. . .the rosebush he had brought her. Here was a man with love locked away in his heart, with wounds deep in his soul. Where was the key to that lock? What salve would heal his hurt?

Back in the chair with Kaaren on her lap, she rocked and thought—and prayed.

May flowed into June and Carl continued working from before dawn until long after dark. With the fields planted and up, the cultivating began. Endless hours of riding the metal seat of the cultivator pulled behind two sweating horses, their heads bobbing in time to the plodding of their hooves.

Nora walked everywhere with Peder in the sling and Kaaren clutching her hand or running ahead. One day, they found wild strawberries along a fencerow. She made preserves from the berries and baked biscuits for shortcake.

Carl only grunted when served the treats.

Nora was not sure if the grunt meant "Thank you" or "Give me more." She didn't.

The temper she had prayed so earnestly over for so many years, simmered and, once in a while, spit.

Haying season began. One evening, Carl drove the team up after dark and found Nora milking the cows. Kaaren was playing in the aisle; Peder was sleeping peacefully on a mound of hay.

"I didn't ask you to do this," he said.

Nora continued to squeeze and pull, the milk singing into the bucket. "I know." She kept her forehead against the cow's red flank.

"Take the children up to the house. I will finish."

"Carl Detschman, you are the most stubborn, bullheaded, prideful man I have ever had the misfortune to know." Nora reverted to Norwegian. She did not know enough of the right words in English. She pulled a bit too forcefully and got a mouth-ful of cow's tail.

"Nora."

"No, *you* take Kaaren and your son Peder to the house. Maybe you'll have time to soak your head before I get there." She stripped the last of the milk from each teat and, setting the bucket aside, rose to her feet. "*I* have one more cow to milk."

Carl stepped back before she could trod on his feet.

Nora picked up a clean bucket and her stool and plunked them down beside the next cow. "So-o-o, boss." She settled the bucket between her skirted knees and her head into the cow's flank. With the same easy rhythm, she squeezed and pulled, ringing the milk into the bucket.

She refused to look up when she heard Carl leave. She did not tell him her hands and arms were cramping either. When she peeked over her shoulder, the quilt where Peder had lain was gone.

Nora hid her smile of relief in the warm sweet cow smell, the fragrance of fresh milk foaming in a bucket. Maybe what he needed was to be stood on his ear once in awhile.

So, Nora added the evening milking to her chores. And caring for the gray-and-white barred chickens, as well as the garden and the house.

One day, with the hay cut and cured, Carl wrestled the high racks for hauling hay onto the front and back of the wide wagon bed.

Nora wished for her brothers to come help him. Why didn't he share the haying work with some of his neighbors? The answer came to her immediately. He was too proud to ask for help. And, as Ingeborge had told her in the spring, Norwegians did not always take kindly to superior-acting Germans. That Carl could act supe-rior, she knew for a fact.

"Why do you care?" she asked herself one hot afternoon. She sank into the rocker with a jar of water in her hand. Some she sipped and some she dripped onto a cloth to cool her forehead—she had been hoeing the potatoes.

Down at the barn, Carl had parked the hay wagon under the four, cast-iron prongs that would lift the hay into the steadily filling hayloft. She could see his weariness in the slump of his shoulders. Climb up onto the hay wagon, set the forks, climb down, go around the barn, have the horses pull the rope toward the pile. Trip the prongs and begin all over again. He needed some help.

Nora put Peder in the sling. A jug of water in her one hand, she took Kaaren's small grubby paw in the other. Down to the barn they strolled.

"Hi, Pa." Kaaren announced their presence.

Brownie lay panting under the wagon, his feathery tail fluffing the dirt. Kaaren crawled under with the dog and giggled when he licked her face.

"Here." Nora held out the cool water. Carl wiped his forehead and reached for the drink.

"Thank you." This time she understood his answer.

Carl chugged the drink and, when finished, wiped his mouth with the back of his hand.

"I will help you."

"You would do that?" Carl stared at her over the rim of the jar. Nora nodded.

"Even after the way I've been acting?"

She nodded again. "Just tell me what you want me to do. I've driven horses before at home and I've also helped with gathering the hay." She tipped her head back, the better to study him from under the straw brim.

"But you have the baby."

She patted the sleeping form in her shawl slings. "He's fine. Peder likes being close, being carried like this."

"All right. But you'll tell me when. . .if—" His gaze dropped to the sling and flicked back to her face.

"His name is Peder."

"I know." He sighed deeply. "When Peder needs you, he comes first." They heard a giggle from under the hay wagon and a smile flitted across Carl's face. "Would you please go around the barn and drive the team forward when I tell you to? I'll tell you when to stop, also."

Nora nodded. She leaned over and peered under the wagon. "Come, Kaaren."

Like Mary in the Scriptures, Nora pondered these things in her heart. For a German man to admit he had been wrong was like. . . like. . .

She could not think of anything to compare it with. And he had finally said his son's name—for the first time in a long while.

Thank You, Father. Thank You. Her heart sang.

Dusty, thirsty, and with sunburned cheeks, Nora waved as Carl left for the hay field and his last load of hay. They would hoist it into the hayloft in the morning. Now, she just had the cows to milk and supper to fix. Peder whimpered and twisted in his sling—and a baby to feed, first of all. She turned and trudged up to the house.

"Nora. Nora." The call carried on the evening breeze.

Nora shaded her eyes, staring after the wagon. Carl stood on the front rack, waving his arm and yelling at her.

"What?"

"Leave the cows for me to milk."

She waved back in agreement. "Your pa is a good man," she said to Kaaren in particular and the world in general. The words sounded puny compared to the chorus in her heart.

Each Sunday, Nora felt tempted to beg Carl to take them to church, but each time she remembered his anger at her Bible reading. How she would love to visit with Ingeborge. And hear the organ playing in church, Reverend Moen preaching in Norwegian, and people visiting after the service. On Sundays, she missed home and her family the most.

The first Sunday in August burned so hot even the birds hushed their singing. Nora spread a blanket out in the shade of the cottonwood trees. She sat propped against the tree trunk, her Bible in her lap, fanning herself and singing to Kaaren. Peder lay beside her, entranced by the shifting leaf patterns.

Between songs, Nora eyed the western horizon, praying to see the mounds of black clouds that brought the cooling rain they so desperately needed. Hauling water to her garden used every bit of energy she could find. But, she reminded herself, *Sunday is to be a day of rest, the good Lord said so, Himself.* She turned away from thoughts of Carl cultivating the corn.

When Kaaren's eyelids drooped, Nora took the most recent letter from Norway from her pocket and read the beloved words again. When she closed her eyes, she could hear her mother saying the words she wrote. How far away Norway and the life there seemed now.

Her eyes must have been closed longer than she thought. She jerked awake. No, everything was the same. Kaaren slept, sprawled like a puppet with broken strings. Peder lay on his tummy, cheeks pink from the heat, his breath even and deep.

What bothered her?

She scanned the horizon again. A flat, black band separated the green prairie and the blue sky. Flat, not piled and puffed up like the life-giving clouds. She read her letter again. The black band grew wider.

Go to the house, an inner voice prompted.

"Don't be silly," Nora argued with herself. "The children are sleeping better than they have for days. It's cooler out here than anywhere else. There's nothing to fear."

The black band darkened, spreading now across the entire western horizon.

A grasshopper flew onto her skirt.

Nora brushed it off and bit her lip.

The band, no longer flat, undulated like a blanket settling onto a bed. A fat, green grasshopper crawled over Peder's back. Still asleep, Kaaren brushed one off her face. The action woke her. She sat up, whimpering and rubbing her eyes.

A sound like nothing Nora had ever heard seemed to come from the widening river of black.

A wave of fear brought Nora to her knees, scrambling to gather their belongings. "Kaaren, run to the house." She set the little girl on her feet and pushed her in the general direction.

"No-o-o!" Kaaren wailed and wrapped her fist in Nora's skirt.

Nora clutched Peder to her chest with one arm. With the quilt flung over the other and the basket in her hand, she had no hand for the whining girl. She stared over her shoulder.

The apparition flowed nearer. The sound, like the buzzing of angry bees, filled her ears.

She looked down at her skirt. Three grasshoppers had landed there. She could feel another in her hair. Were they, too, afraid of the approaching menace?

"Kaaren, help me carry the basket." She bumped Kaaren's arm with the handle.

In spite of her blue eyes welling with tears, Kaaren obeyed. She grasped the basket with a chubby hand.

"Now!" Nora forced a smile on her face and a lilt in her voice. "Let's run."

In the past, she dreamed of running and never getting to her destination. Now, it was so. With the baby bouncing in her arm and the basket thumping her thigh with every step, Nora felt like she was running through a quagmire. Instead of coming closer, the house seemed farther away every time she looked up.

After an eternity, they collapsed on the porch. Kaaren held up her arm and giggled at a grasshopper with iridescent wings and bobbing feelers.

"See, Ma. Big bug." She poked him with her finger. Instead of hopping off, he flew away.

Nora looked from Kaaren to the porch posts. Bugs had landed all over, their wings whirring and clicking. They crawled onto her skirt, the quilt, and Kaaren's dress. She brushed several off Peder.

"Ugh." She looked up at the sky now dusky with flying insects. "Kaaren, brush them off and go inside. Now!" Her tone allowed no chance of resistance. She brushed the marauding insects off the baby's things, her skirt, and apron. When the door closed behind them, she grabbed one from Kaaren's shoulder and threw it outside.

She laid Peder on his quilt on the floor and returned to stand at the screen door. Where was Carl? What was happening?

The cows bellowed from the pasture by the barn. As she watched, they stuck their tails straight in the air and the animals charged off across the pasture.

Should she go down and let them into the barn?

She looked out at her rosebush—its stalks writhed like living things. She bit her knuckles to keep from crying out. The bush was buried in gnawing, buzzing creatures.

Clouds of insects turned the day into dusk. Was the sun, too, being eaten alive by the invading hoard?

Her garden!

"Stay here!" She cracked the order and pointed to the quilt. Wide-eyed, Kaaren sat down by the baby. Nora grabbed another quilt off the bed and, clapping the straw hat onto her head, stormed out the door.

She ran to the garden, waving the quilt then, using it like a club, to beat the bugs crawling over her plants. She shook it in the sky and screamed at the avenging hoard, but they kept coming. The crunch of their feeding filled the air. They covered her hat, her arms, her face. She spit out the one that was crawling in her mouth.

Her arms ached from brandishing the quilt. "Fire. I'll burn them out."

She turned to the house. Kerosene, a torch of kerosene, would that work? How to get it burning? Would smoke drive them away? But what would she burn?

Hay! She ran to the barn with her tattered quilt in hand.

Slipping in with the door open only a crack, she spread the quilt on the floor and forked hay onto it. Then gathering up the corners, she half-carried, half-dragged it back to the garden. Her side ached; her legs quivered. She did not dare open her mouth to draw in the deep breaths she so desperately needed—the thought of swallowing a grasshopper made her gag.

She staggered to the house, grabbed a kerosene-filled lamp and the matches, and dashed back outside again. "Stay there, Kaaren," she panted as she closed the door behind her.

She unscrewed the top of the lamp and poured the kerosene on the pile of hay. She scraped the match across the sole of her shoe and tossed the flaming bit of wood into the hay. The fuel caught; smoke rose in tendrils, then billowed up. Grasshoppers fell. But when the fire dimmed, the horde resumed as if nothing had happened.

Carl found her, kneeling in the dirt, now bare of the beans nearly ready to pick and the corn that had been starting to tassle. Rivulets of tears streaked across her skin darkened by smoke and dirt.

He picked her up and gathered her into his arms, brushing a kiss across her cheek.

Nora sobbed against the wall of his chest. "I. . .I tried so hard." She hiccuped between words. "N—nothing stopped them."

"I know. Shhhh, now." He murmured comfort, but Nora was beyond hearing.

"I worked so hard and this flat land—it hates me. My garden gone—my family—no one." She thumped a shaking fist on his chest. "I want to laugh again—and dance—and see my friends. There's nothing left. Not-h-i-n-g."

"I know." Carl picked her up in his arms and carried her back to the house. He brushed the crawling insects off the porch steps and sat with her in his lap.

"Pa?" Kaaren stood inside the door, peeking through the screen.

"You be a good girl and stay there." Carl stroked the hair back from Nora's eyes and laid her head on his shoulder.

"But Ma's crying." Her voice quivered with tears.

"I know. Ma's sad." Carl continued to rock Nora in his arms. "Go see how Peder is."

"Pa, I want my ma-a-a."

Deep in her own fog, Nora heard the cry of her child. She sat up, only then realizing the comfort and strength of the arms that held her. She hiccuped again and wiped her eyes with the edge of her tattered and filthy apron.

Oh, to be able to sink back and let herself float on that sea of calm that follows a cleansing cry. To stay wrapped up in arms so warm and safe. To listen again to the heart that thumped in perfect rhythm beneath her cheek. His two-day growth of beard

119

scratched the tender skin of her cheek. How good it felt.

"M-a-a-a-a!"

Nora stood. When she swayed, Carl caught her around the waist. She looked up into his eyes so close and lost herself in their shimmering blue depths. With a sigh, she leaned her head against his chest again. This was home.

"M-a-a-a."

She could hear the rumble of Carl's answer to his daughter through his shirt. She took another deep breath and stepped back. "Let's go in. She needs us."

With Nora still supported by his arm, they walked up the steps and opened the screen door.

Kaaren hurled herself at their legs.

Carl picked up his daughter and patted her back. Kaaren reached for Nora and wrapped her arms around them both.

"Big bug."

Nora looked up to see Kaaren picking a grasshopper from her father's hair.

"Here, Ma." Kaaren dropped it into Nora's hand and giggled when Nora made a face and threw the insect out the door.

After feeding Peder, Nora took a pan of tepid water into the bedroom, closed the door, and took off her clothes. The water on her skin raised goosebumps, but with each swipe of the cloth, she felt closer to being herself. When she had dried herself and changed into clean clothes, she bundled her dirty ones, tempted to stuff them into the stove and burn them.

She shook her head. All they needed was a good washing. She tied on a clean white apron and, picking up the pan of now-black water, reentered the kitchen.

Carl, too, had washed. Moisture darkened his sun-bleached hair to deep bronze. When he smiled, his teeth gleamed white against the tan of his lower face. That stubborn lock of hair half covered the white line across his forehead left by his hat.

Her fingers itched to brush that lock of hair back into place. Instead, Nora emptied her pan of water into the sink and dipped new water into a pitcher. She unclasped her hair and leaning over the sink, poured the water over her scalp. With the last of the rose-scented soap she had brought with her from home, she washed her hair.

"Let me help." Carl removed the pitcher from her hand and poured the water over her hair to rinse it.

Nora twisted her head from side to side so all the soap could be rinsed away. How wonderful it felt to have someone help her like this. How wonderful to have Carl, stern Carl, rinse her hair. She felt a warmth pool in her middle and spread upward to her heart.

"Thank you." She wrung her hair out and, with the towel she had laid beside her, began drying her waist-length tresses.

"I. . .I think I'll go get started on the milking." Carl backed away. The urge to reach out and touch that rippling mass of gold caught him by surprise. He had only offered to help her. What was wrong with that?

As he brought in the cows, the questions remained in his mind. When he poured their feed, he stared at the flowing grain. Would there be anything left to harvest? What would he feed the livestock this winter? While he had had a good hay crop, hay alone was not enough. The pigs and chickens could not live on hay.

He thought back. The flood of Nora's tears weighed him down until he felt like his shoulders dragged on the floor. Was she really so unhappy here? She had never said so. But why would she? When had he encouraged her to talk with him, other than to learn English?

He picked up his stool and started on the second cow. One bad thing about milking, it gave you too much time to think.

When he had finished and let the cows out again, one resolve shone clear. He had promised to send her back to Norway and that he would do.

He picked up the brimming pails. But, if he paid for her ticket, how could he hire a housekeeper? Where would he find the money to buy grain for his cows, food for his household?

He knew what life was like after the grasshoppers came. They ate everything in sight. Only those vegetables below the surface were saved.

But his potato field was not mature enough to have set potatoes yet.

"God, help me, I don't know what to do." Carl did not realize he had uttered a prayer. He poured the milk into the skimming pans in the cool well house, keeping half a pail out for the house.

He stopped with one foot on the porch steps and looked up at the heavens. Stars peeked out through their windows in the black velvet of the sky. A breeze rattled the bare branches of the cottonwood trees.

He listened carefully. The whirr and crunch of the invading horde was no more.

He walked into the kitchen and set the milk bucket in the sink. "I'll go into town tomorrow and telegraph reservations to New York for your ticket back to Norway."

Chapter 12

But I don't want to go," Nora said.

"I will live up to my word," Carl answered. "When we married I promised you could return to Norway."

Nora could feel her mind running like a crazed thing caught in a maze. "B–but, you have no housekeeper for my. . .the children."

"I will work something out." He turned from her and went to stand at the window.

God, Father God. Please help me. Why does he bring this up now? The prayer continued as she dished the baked beans onto their plates.

The ticking of the clock was the only sound in the silence. She had hurried to put the children to bed. And now she wished they were here to need her. Didn't Carl need her? Who else would love his children, his house, and, yes—his entire farm—like she did?

She nearly dropped the plate of molasses-laden beans. When had love come into her heart?

"Your supper is ready," she called as he stood looking out at the blackness.

Carl sighed as he sat down. He studied the food on the plate before him.

Nora watched him. "Do you want something else?" She jumped up. "I forgot the bread." Returning to the table, she set down a plate of sliced bread and slipped back into her chair. She cast around in her mind for something to say to break the silence.

"The cows. . .they are all right?"

Carl nodded. He scooped a fork of beans and ate them.

"They will still give milk?"

He nodded again. "The grasshoppers didn't bother them, just ate all their feed. Thank God I got the hay in before this happened."

Yes. You must thank God, Nora thought. *When you can thank Him again all will be right with you.* She forced herself to eat. Put the beans on your fork. . .chew and swallow. A bite of bread. . . chew and swallow. Swallowing was the hard part. The boulder, lodged in her throat, made it difficult.

"We'll know more in the daylight. Sometimes, they skip whole fields. I've seen times when one farm would be wiped out and the next one not touched." Carl nodded and finally looked at her, really looked at her. "We'll know more in the morning."

"Please God, let there be something left," Nora prayed on her knees that night. "I am so confused. I did want to go back to Norway. Now, I want to stay here. How do I explain this to him?" She closed her eyes and let the breeze from the window cool her cheeks. One tear slipped from between her eyelids and trickled down her cheek. "Your will, Father. Amen."

Early the next morning, Nora walked to the edge of her garden. She wrapped her arms around her middle and squeezed against the pain that ripped through her. The sun, shining on what used to be her thriving garden, showed not one blade or leaf of green. The black dirt looked like no one had ever planted there. Gray ashes lay where she had tried to burn the marauders out.

The trees, as if caught in the nakedness of winter, raised empty fingers to the sky. The fields lay bare, like her garden.

As she staggered back to the porch, dead bodies of the winged creatures crunched beneath her feet. She sank down onto the steps, the weight of the destruction too heavy to bear.

By her knee, one tough cane was all that remained of her rosebush. Nora reached down with a shaking finger and stroked the stalk, stripped even of thorns. *I never picked one of your blossoms. The third one had just opened. I was waiting for more. So many buds. . .now all are gone.* She buried her face in her knees and let loose the sobs that cramped her chest.

By the time Carl returned from the morning milking, her nose still dripped and her eyes were red. She wiped her nose with a handkerchief and tucked it back into her pocket.

"Breakfast will be ready as soon as you are." When she tried to smile, her lower lip quivered.

"Where's Kaaren and Peder?" Carl glanced around the kitchen.

"Still sleeping. Yesterday must have worn them out."

"Me, too." He poured sour cream over his pancakes and added a spoonful of jam on top. After only one bite, he put his fork down. "I rode out to the fields at dawn. There's nothing left." The words dropped into the silent kitchen and spread like ripples on a smooth lake.

Nora closed her eyes. "What will you do?"

"I'll have to buy grain both for feed and for seed next spring." She waited for him to continue.

Outside on the porch, Brownie scratched at a flea, his leg thumping against the boards.

Carl shook his head. His voice seemed distant, far away like he was talking to someone else. "With no harvest, my savings will go to pay the farm payments. Or, I'll see about another loan." Teeth clenched, he growled. "I hate to borrow money, to be beholding— to anyone."

Silence took over the farm again. One day on a return trip from town, Carl tossed a letter on the table. He shook his head. "Too late."

"What do you mean?" Nora turned from kneading the bread dough.

"A letter from a woman who would like the job of house-keeper. She can even speak English." He poured himself a cup of coffee. "Your reservation is scheduled for the first of October."

Her breath escaped in a hiss, as if someone had punched her in the belly.

Carl tipped back his head and drained the coffee cup. "I heard about a farm that needs hands for the harvest. Can you manage here, if I'm gone a few days?"

"Ja." She took in a deep breath, one that stiffened her back-bone. It was now or never.

"Carl, I want to talk to you." Nora formed the dough into a smooth mound and placed it back into the earthenware bowl to rise. As her fingers performed their usual functions, her mind cast around for the right words.

He started to walk out the door.

"Carl! Sit down." She pointed at the chair. Appalled at her tone, she added a gentle, "Please."

He sat. Back straight as a poker, face about as unbending, he turned to face her. A muscle jumped in his cheek.

Nora swallowed. Why had she said anything? She wound her fingers in her apron.

"I told you I don't want to go back to Norway."

Carl waved his fingers, like brushing off a bug. His look branded her a silly female who did not know her own mind.

"We agreed."

"I know. But. . .but things have changed. You don't have money to spare for my ticket. Peder and Kaaren. . .they. . .they need me." Her heart wanted to cry, *and I care about you*, but, instead, she sat straighter and forced her errant heart to remain still.

"You want me to go back on my word?" Blue eyes drilled ice chips into hers.

"No, no." She shook her head. "You wouldn't be if it is me that changed my mind."

Carl shook his head. "You are so young. How can you know your mind? What is best for you?" He pushed himself to his feet, the matter closed. "I may be gone for as long as a week. You'll have the team in case you need them."

Nora stood at the doorway to watch him swing himself up onto the bare back of the bay gelding. He picked up his sack that he had rested on a fence post, touched a finger to the black hat brim, and turned the horse to trot down the lane.

Tears, pooling in her eyes, made him shimmer and fade in the bright sunlight.

"Where is Pa?" Kaaren asked at the table before eating her mush.

"Gone." Uttering the one word took much of Nora's strength.

Kaaren raised her gaze from her meal to Nora's face. Her bottom lip quivered and tears flooded her eyes. "Pa gone like my ma?" The question ended on a whimper.

"Oh, no, Kaaren. Your pa just went to help another farmer with a harvest. He'll come back soon, very soon."

Every morning, every noon, and again at bedtime, Kaaren posed the question. "Pa's coming now?"

"Soon, little one, soon." Nora hugged and petted both children, tickling Kaaren to make her giggle and tossing Peder in the air to hear his belly laugh. With no garden to care for, she concentrated all her care on the children and the livestock.

She sewed Kaaren two new dresses out of some material she had found tucked away in a drawer. She altered a cotton dress of Anna's that hung in a closet so she would have something cooler to wear. The blue print fabric was on the table, waiting for her to begin cutting.

"You're going to need clothes, too, one of these days," she told Peder one afternoon. He waved chubby fists like he knew exactly what she was saying and agreed wholeheartedly. *They must have saved Kaaren's baby things,* she thought, while holding the bottle for Peder. *But where?*

She searched the house over and finally looked up the stairs. She had only been up there to change the sheets on Carl's bed. With one hand on the rail, she mounted the stairs. Heat, like when she opened her oven door, met her when she opened the door to his room. It was as orderly as his barn. Clothes hung on hooks, good boots were polished and lined up under the black wool suit he had worn the day of the funeral.

She heard Kaaren calling from outside. Leaning over the table in front of the window, she pushed up the sash and stuck her head out.

"I'm up here. Upstairs. What is it?"

Kaaren came running around the corner of the house. "Hi,

127

Ma." She stopped, legs spread apart, and, leaning back to get a good view, waved. Her giggle floated on the still air. "Read now?"

Nora shook her head. "Soon." She drew back in, careful not to bang her head. A piece of paper drifted off the table, so she leaned over to pick it up.

Carl's careful lettering, so familiar to her after the long English lessons, caught her eye. She read, the words leaping off the page and branding her heart.

> *Dear Adolph,*
>
> *I am writing to ask if you and Viola would take care of my children for me. If you could come for them after harvest since I have no one here to feed my animals if I leave. The grasshoppers ate. . .*

The words blurred. How could he?

Baby clothes forgotten, Nora put the paper back onto the table and staggered down the stairs. He really meant to send her back to Norway. What she wanted did not matter. All that counted was his word.

She slumped into the rocker. He did not care for her then, not at all. To him, she was just the housekeeper he had had to marry to save their reputations. "Dear God, what do I do now? I thought he was coming to care for me. But, I was wrong." The heaviness sat on her both inside and out.

The days and nights were so hot their clothes stuck to their bodies. Peder whimpered from a prickly heat rash and even Kaaren drooped like a flower that needed a drink.

The week stretched into ten days. Would Carl never come home?

But when he did ride up on the bay horse, nothing changed. Except now, Nora did not have the animals to care for and, with more time on her hands, she had too many hours to think. She tried to remember the good times with her family, to remind herself that she would be seeing them soon, to think about wading in the stream that rushed and tumbled over the rocks on its way to the

Norwegian sea. Cool water. Laughter—and love again.

"Would you please milk the cows in the morning?" Carl asked one evening. "I'm driving over to the creek bed north of here to cut fence posts. I'll be home before dinner so I can take the butter and cream into town."

Nora looked at him, amazement dropping her jaw. He had not strung so many words together at one time since. . .since the grasshoppers.

"Ja, I can do that."

In the morning, Nora went about her chores with a lighter step. Did Carl's request mean that he was drawing out of his silence? Or that they would go back to talking in the evening?

But dinnertime came and Carl did not appear. Nora pushed the pan of fried chicken off to the side of the stove, along with the gravy and the last of the tiny potatoes she had dug up after the hoppers ate the plants.

She walked around the outside of the house and, shading her eyes, searched the northern horizon. Nothing. At the one o'clock vigil, she saw a hawk floating on the rising air currents. At two, a snake of fear slithered around her middle—Carl never broke his word—something had happened.

Nora ran down to the barn and, after grabbing a bridle off the wall and a can of oats from the nearly empty feed bin, slipped through the gate rails and into the pasture. "Here, boy." She shook the can, calling the gelding. The cows mooed in response. At the sound of rattling oats, the dark bay horse raised his head and trotted toward her.

"Good boy, good." Nora fed him the grain from her palm and slipped the reins around his neck. Holding the reins securely with one hand, she slid the bit between his teeth and the headstall over his ears. "What a good horse." She murmured soothing words, all the while buckling the straps in place and leading him up to the fence.

At the house, she tied his reins to the fence and dashed inside. "Kaaren, bring me Peder's shawl. We're going to find your pa."

How would she mount? By herself it was not a problem. She

had learned early how to leap on a horse. But, what about with Peder and Kaaren. "Father, help me." She took a deep breath and exhaled, letting her shoulders drop and the tension leave. The porch. Surely, the rail was high enough for her to slide onto this animal's back and grab Kaaren the same way.

She led the horse up to the porch, grateful for his docile manner. Someone had trained him well. With Peder's sling locked over one shoulder, she mounted the railing and slung her leg over the horse's back. Her skirts bunched up around her knees, but she and Peder were secure.

"Kaaren, climb up on the rail just like I did." Kaaren stuck a finger in her mouth and hung back.

Nora gritted her teeth. "We'll go find Pa. Good horse." She patted the bay's neck. "See? Climb up now."

Kaaren did like she was told.

Nora leaned over and, with one arm, grabbed the little girl around her waist. With the other, she settled Kaaren's legs across the horse and firmly against her chest.

"Thank You, God. Thank You." Nora dropped a kiss on Kaaren's hair. "Such a good girl. Now, hang on tight to this." She made Kaaren's hands grab onto the horse's mane. "Now, let's go find Pa."

Nora reined the horse around and out of the yard. Once on the prairie, she nudged him to a trot. With the hand that held the reins and guided the horse also anchoring Kaaren, Nora tried with the other hand to keep Peder from bouncing out of his sling. To her surprise, the rough ride did not bother the baby at all.

"Faster, Ma." Kaaren giggled and swung her legs, her hands gripping the coarse black mane.

Nora wanted to kick the animal into a lope, but the thought of all of them being dumped onto the ground made her more cautious. As they settled into the pace, the horse's heavy feet thudded across the soil stripped bare by the grasshoppers. New blades of green promised the return of life.

Ahead, Nora could see the tops of denuded willow trees that lined the creek. What should be a spot of green on the horizon stood naked as the rest of the earth.

Where could he be? The creek curved and rambled for many miles. Her questions kept time with her prayers.

"Carl!" The bouncing gait of the horse kept her voice from carrying like it should. She reined him to a stop and, with both hands bracketing her mouth, called again.

A horse whinnied off to their left.

Nora nudged the bay to a trot again. Ears pricked, he lifted his head and whinnied back at a sound he alone could hear.

Looking ahead, Nora spotted the wagon tracks she had been searching for all along. They led over a hump and down into the flat area bordering the creek.

The horse whinnied again, much closer this time. Nora gave her horse his head and he saw the team before she did. His whinny sounded even louder than back up on the plain.

The team stood patiently, still harnessed to the wagon. The larger gray horse snorted and tossed his head. A few fence posts were in the wagon bed.

But where was Carl?

"Hush." Nora placed her fingers over Kaaren's mouth and strained to hear any noise. Harnesses jingled; horses snorted; a crow cawed his announcement that someone new had entered his territory.

"Carl!" Her voice cracked as she gave his name two syllables. "Ca-rl!"

"Yes."

Had she really heard a sound? The horses pricked their ears in the same direction. She called again.

This time the response came stronger.

She nudged her horse forward, skirting the wagon and angling up the creek bed.

"Carl!" This time she knew she was on the right track. She pushed through the willow thicket, protecting their faces with her bent arms.

He lay on the ground, next to a fallen tree. Even from this distance, she could see his blood-soaked leg.

Chapter 13

Go get the wagon!" he cried.

Nora struggled between the desire to leap down and make sure he was not bleeding to death and the knowledge that what he ordered was imperative—she had to get the wagon. She turned her horse around and headed back the way they had come.

The patient team pricked their ears and whinnied as soon as they saw the bay.

"Kaaren, I'm going to let you down into the wagon, so be ready." Nora nudged the horse right next to the rear of the wagon. "Here we go. Now, slide your leg over his neck, that's right." She spoke in a gentle voice, calm and patient but inside she was screaming—*hurry! Hurry!* "Good. Now hang onto my hand and just slide down."

Kaaren landed on the board floor with a thump. "See, Ma." She grinned up at Nora.

"Ja, good." Nora clutched Peder in his sling with one hand while she leaned forward and swung one leg behind her. Together, they slid to the ground, as if they had been dismounting like this all their lives. She quickly tied the bay's reins to the rear of the wagon and ran to untie the team. Still bearing her heavy burden, she climbed up onto the seat and released the brake.

"Kaaren, come up here and sit down." She pointed to a spot right behind her, still in the wagon bed. As Kaaren, eyes big, stumbled over the posts, Nora settled Peder in her lap.

He squirmed and let out a yowl, clearly unhappy with such rough treatment.

"Good girl." Nora threw a smile over her shoulder and slapped the reins. "Hup now, boys." The team jerked the wagon to a start.

Nora eyed the thicket ahead. No time to find a way around it. "Hang on, Kaaren." She sheltered Peder with her body and forced the team into and through the slapping, tearing branches. She stopped the wagon within inches of Carl.

He lay on the ground, eyes closed, his face chalky white as if all the blood had drained from his body.

"Oh, God, dear God." Her words ran into a litany, Nora not even aware that she was talking out loud. She lifted Peder in his sling over her head and twisted around to lay him beside Kaaren.

"Take care of baby now." She nodded and smiled at the little girl like this was some new game. "I'll get your pa for you." Nora jumped to the ground and knelt by Carl's inert body.

"You came," he said. "I prayed you'd come."

She could hardly hear his voice, weak as it was. "Ja, my love, we are here. Now you must help me."

"Don't. . .worry about. . .bandage."

She bent closer to hear him.

"Used belt. . .for tourniquet. . .stop bleeding."

"Yes, Carl. Now, I'm going to pull you up to a sitting position." She wrapped one arm around his back and grasped his closer arm with her hand. "Now!" She pulled, he pushed.

He bit his lip against the groan.

"Now, put your arm over my shoulders and, together, we lift." This time, he could not suppress the groan.

Nora clamped her teeth together. Sweat popped out on her brow from the strain. But, they were standing.

"Lean on me." This time it was she who groaned as his weight shifted onto her.

Together they took the two steps needed for him to collapse into the bed of the wagon. He pulled himself forward with his arms until his legs were in the wagon, too.

"Pa!" Kaaren had watched all the goings-on with huge eyes. Now, the tears poured out and she threw herself against his chest.

Nora climbed up into the wagon bed. After making sure Carl

was secure, she hefted the squalling Peder in his sling and hauled it back over her head and shoulder. Then, she climbed over the back of the seat, sat down, and slapped the team into motion.

The ride to town lasted an eternity of dust, crying children, jouncing, tears, and Carl's fading in and out. When she finally drove down the main street of Soldall, she had no idea how to find Dr. Harmon. For what seemed like the past 400 miles, she had been praying he would just be there.

"Can you tell me where Dr. Harmon lives?" she yelled to the first person she saw.

The man trotted up to the wagon and peered in. "Oh, heavens. Here, I'll show you." He leaped onto the seat. "Turn right, there, by the blacksmith." He pointed ahead of them. "What happened to him?" He spoke softly so Carl would not hear.

Nora was not sure if Carl was conscious or not. He had not said anything for the last—forever. "He was out at the creek, cutting fence posts. The ax slipped."

"Turn left, here. That's Doc's house and office with the light in the window. I'll help carry your man in." He leaped to the ground before the team came to a full halt. "Harmon!" His yell could be heard clear to Fargo.

A graying man in his shirtsleeves threw open the door. "What'd ya need?"

"Something to carry this man in on. Leg's cut bad."

While the doctor pulled his head back in, Nora climbed back over the seat and laid Peder on the wagon floor. "You care for Peder." She took Kaaren by the hand and sat her beside the baby.

She knelt by Carl's head and put her hand on his chest. Yes, he was still breathing. *Oh, dear Lord. If we've ever needed You, we need You now.*

"All right, ma'am, we'll take him now." Doctor Harmon slid the poles of a stretcher in beside his patient. "Carl!" He turned to look at Nora. "What did he do?"

All the while he was talking, he and the other man lifted Carl onto the stretcher, slid it to the rear of the wagon, and, with one man at each end, lifted the heavy burden. Together, they carried their load up the steps and into the doctor's office.

Nora climbed down and, grabbing Kaaren and Peder, followed the stretcher carriers. She stood in the doorway as they lifted Carl onto a flat, well-padded wooden table.

"Pa, Pa." Kaaren sniffled and cried, hiding her face in Nora's filthy skirt. Peder, worn-out from all the crying, only whimpered now and then.

"Will he. . .can you— ?" The words stuck in Nora's throat. She wanted to throw herself across Carl's chest and howl out her terror, her love, her prayers. She lifted Peder higher in her arms and buried her face in his sling.

"He's alive." Doctor Harmon looked up only long enough to make eye contact with her. "That's all I can say right now."

"Now, dear." A woman's voice came from behind her. "I'm Mrs. Harmon. Why don't you come with me for now? There's nothing you can do here. The doctor will do the best he can."

Nora turned. Lifting her feet to follow the roundly padded woman with the kind voice took all her strength.

"Let me get you a cup of coffee and maybe your little girl would like a glass of milk and a cookie?"

Nora pulled herself back to the moment. "Please, show me the way to Reverend Moen's. Ingeborge will care for my. . .for Kaaren and Peder. Then I will come back."

"If that is what you want. But you are welcome to stay here."

"Thank you."

Mrs. Harmon gave instructions while she walked Nora back out to the wagon. She handed Kaaren to her after Nora had climbed up to the seat. "I'll see you in awhile then?"

Nora nodded. "Thank you." She flicked the reins and the horses broke into a trot.

With a small town like Soldall, the directions were not too complex and she found the parsonage without any trouble. Light beamed from the windows on the ground floor, welcoming her back.

Nora slumped against the board that formed the seat back. Now that Carl was someone else's responsibility, she felt limp, drained of every thread of strength and will. She could feel tears rolling down her cheeks. When had she begun to cry? When had she not been crying?

She stared at the walk from the fence and up the steps to the front door. Could she make it? Would her knees support her?

"God, please." She leaned forward and wrapped the reins around the pole. "You can climb down by yourself, Kaaren. Mary lives here." She pulled herself to her feet. With Peder in one arm, she used the other to brace herself and swung her leg over the wagon side. She stumbled as she landed and the jerk made Peder cry again.

The door opened. Light poured down the walk. "Is anyone— oh no," Reverend Moen's voice deepened. "Nora, what has happened to you? Ingeborge, come quick." As he spoke, he leaped from the steps and wrapped his arm around Nora's shoulders. Ingeborge appeared before her and lifted the whimpering Peder in his sling over Nora's head.

Nora swayed from the lightness of releasing one of her burdens, but John steadied her. They led her inside and sat her in the rocking chair.

"Now, tell me. What has happened?" Ingeborge placed a cup of coffee in Nora's hands and closed the trembling fingers around the warmth. "Drink first."

"Peder. He hasn't been fed for hours."

"Mary, please fix a bottle. John, could you please take the mite in and change him?"

Nora could feel Kaaren attached to her knee.

"Pa's hurt. His leg is bleeding bad."

"He cut himself with an ax cutting down fence posts in the creek bottom. We brought him to Dr. Harmon's." Nora raised her gaze to encounter the sympathy flowing from the face of her friend. "Oh, Ingeborge, he might die. So much blood lost."

"Drink your coffee. John will take you back over there as soon as you have the strength. The children will be just fine here with us."

Her soothing voice and loving hands brought a measure of peace back to Nora. And with it, the strength to pull herself to her feet.

"Mange takk." Nora then went back to the doctor's house and Reverend Moen went with her.

"The doctor is still working with him," Mrs. Harmon said when she met Reverend Moen and Nora at the door. "Why don't you come right in here and have a seat?"

Nora followed her into the parlor and sat down on the chair nearest the door.

"I'll get you each a cup of coffee." Mrs. Harmon bustled out.

"If you don't mind," Reverend Moen leaned over her. "I pray best on my feet and pacing. Will that bother you?"

Nora shook her head. "We need all the prayers we can get."

Several cups of coffee later, Dr. Harmon entered the room. "I've done what I can and I'm sorry to tell you, it don't look good. He's lost a lotta blood. All's I can say is he's in the good Lord's hands now."

"Can I see him?" asked Nora.

"If'n ya want. He's unconscious. Won't know you're there."

"No matter. I want to be with him."

"Just remember, he looks bad." He looked her over. " 'Pears to me you don't look so good yerself. I have an idea. You spend some time with that man of yours and Mrs. Harmon'll heat some water so's you can get cleaned up." He opened the door to a room with a bed. "Here he is."

Nora looked at the white face on the pillow. She stumbled, clamping her teeth against the whirling in her head.

"Grab her." She heard the voice from a great distance.

Arms helped her into a chair and a hand forced her head between her knees. "Easy, now. Just stay that way until the spell passes."

Nora took a deep breath. Her head cleared. Her stomach retreated back to its rightful position.

When she raised her head, she picked up Carl's hand that lay on top of the blankets. She studied his face, every dear line, all the while stroking his hand.

"If we can keep the infection from setting in, every hour he makes it is for the best."

"I'm not leaving him."

"Didn't think you would."

Nora followed Mrs. Harmon's instructions. Get cleaned up,

eat, drink, go back to Carl. There was never any change but she felt needed there.

"We have to keep him drinking, so spoon water into his mouth every fifteen minutes or so." The doctor showed her how. With panic trapped in her throat, she watched until she saw Carl swallow. "That's good." Doctor Harmon left her with a spoon and pitcher of water.

Grateful for something to do, Nora followed orders. Sometime in the wee hours, loving hands covered her with a light blanket. Every time she nodded off, she would wake on the minute to administer the water. With every spoonful, she reminded Carl that she loved him, her words soft and gentle.

People came and went through the next day. At one point, Dr. Harmon sent Nora off to bed, where she slept for several hours before appearing at the door again to resume her post.

In the early morning, Nora had heard the clock strike three o'clock. She jerked fully awake. What was different? Carl? She clasped his hand. Ears straining, she listened to his breathing. Was it slower? Did it hesitate?

"Carl!"

She listened again. A breath. . .a pause. . .a breath. Each slower and fainter.

"Carl! You hear me? Listen to me! You can't die. We need you here. I love you, Carl Detschman!" She gripped his hand. "Don't you die on me!"

She held her breath. *Carl, breathe. God, please, make him breathe.* She waited. The moment stretched to eternity—and back.

Carl took a breath and let it out. And another. And another. Nora wept.

An hour later, when the doctor came to relieve her, he nodded as she told her story. "Right about this time, the body is at its lowest. Lose patients mostly right about now." He clasped Carl's wrist between his thumb and forefinger. "Pulse is stronger." He applied the stethoscope to the man's chest. "Breathing better, too. I'd say he's past the crisis." He stood straight again. "Will you go to bed now?"

Nora shook her head.

"Thought not. I don't want to be doctoring you, too."

About noon, Carl regained consciousness. Nora watched his eyelids flutter. She placed the back of her fingers against his cheek. His eyelids fluttered again and this time he looked at her.

"Ah, Nora, love." A whisper so faint that if she had not been bending close, she might have missed it. His eyes closed again. One corner of his mouth tipped up ever so slightly.

After that, each time he woke he was stronger. Each time he called her "love."

The next day, he raised a hand to stroke her cheek, to brush away an errant tear. "Crying?"

"Tears of joy." She turned her face and kissed the palm of his hand.

That afternoon, Carl drank the good beef broth that Nora spooned into his mouth. When they were finished, he smiled at her. "I have something to tell you."

"Ja?" She leaned on her elbows beside him on the bed.

"When I was so sick?"

She nodded.

"One time, there was a long black tunnel." He paused. "I was going through it to reach a light at the other end. I couldn't wait to get to the light. It kept calling me, but then I heard your voice. I finally reached the light, so. . .so peaceful." He paused again.

Nora watched his face. It glowed like candles were lit inside.

"I wanted to keep on going. . .the love there. Perfect love."

The wonder in his voice, the joy on his face. Nora could feel tears running down her cheeks again.

"But you called to me. You said not to die. You said you loved me."

The touch of his hand on hers, the touch of angel wings.

He smiled. "So I came back." His eyes fluttered closed and he slept.

"Nora?"

She sat up, sleep falling away like the dropping of a stone. Night still darkened the window. "Ja?"

"Will you marry me?"

"We *are* married. Don't you remember?" She smoothed that stubborn lock of hair off his forehead.

"No, I mean a real wedding—in the church. When I was lying there by the creek, I kept praying you would come. I begged God to let me live. A man comes face-to-face with what he's done wrong at a time like that. And you came."

"You said you'd be back for dinner. You always keep your word." She grinned, a teasing grin that made him smile back. "So, I went to see what kept you from your word."

"So, will you?"

"Will I what?"

"Marry me—again?"

"Can we wait until my sister Clara arrives? She should be here any day now."

"We can wait. I want to stand before Reverend Moen on my own two feet."

"And in the church."

"In the church." He wrinkled his brow. "How is Clara coming?"

"Someone sent her a ticket."

"Who?"

Nora shrugged. "I don't know. We'll ask her when she gets here." Silence reigned in the sick room. Carl raised her hand and brought it to his lips. "I broke my word."

"Oh?"

"You won't be going back to Norway."

Nora chuckled. "I tried to tell you that, but you are so stubborn." She laid her head on his chest. "Will our children be bullheaded, like their pa?"

He chuckled into her hair. "Look, my Nora. Out the window."

Feather clouds glowed pink and silver as the returning sun promised a new Dakota dawn for Carl and Nora.

DAKOTA
DREAM

Prologue

To call Jude Weinlander a scoundrel was painting him with the brush of kindness. Bully and cheat were equal approbation. Blond, curly hair, blue eyes, the face of an angel, but within his broad-shouldered physique lodged the soul of Lucifer himself. As with all of his ilk, his degree of impunity increased in direct proportion to the weakness of those he harassed.

He'd been hounding his brother Dag since Jude's first squall while in the cradle.

One night in 1910, when fall first nipped the Red River Valley of North Dakota, Jude and his bunch were slapping cards and slugging whiskey in their favorite haunt, Ole's Saloon.

"An' I'll raise ya two." Jude shoved his money toward the growing pile in the center of the green felt-covered table. He rocked back until his chair teetered on two legs, tapping the top of his cards with one finger. "Come on, Shorty. Make up your mind; we don't got all night."

"Na-a-a, too high for m' blood." Shorty threw down his cards and leaned forward so his shoulder blades stuck out of his shirt like wings, bird wings, definitely not those of angel type.

"Henry?" Jude tossed back the brown liquid in his glass and swiveled around to look for the bartender. He raised his glass. " 'Nother one, Ole. Whyn't ya just leave the bottle?"

"I'll play the next hand." Henry dumped his cards and reached for the bottle the bartender had left. His hand shook, sloshing the liquid over the edges of his glass. His high-pitched giggle belied the broad chest and ample girth.

"Ah-h, you're drunk." Jude fanned his cards again and squinted through the cigar smoke. His chair squalled in protest at the angle it was forced to maintain.

"I'll take that and call you." The dealer laid his cards facedown on the table and pushed his money into the center. He turned his cards. "A flush."

"Hah!" Jude thumped his chair upright and spread his cards on the table. "Full house. Aces high." He reached out and pulled the pile of bills and change over. "Thank you, boys. Sure can use this extra cash. Ya done me a good turn, ya did."

He sucked in on his cigar and blew the smoke toward the ceiling. " 'Nother hand, just to see if'n ya can bet some back?" He stared around at the five men gathered within the circle shed by the hanging gaslight.

"No?" He poured a shot into the glass at his elbow. "Don't say I didn't give ya all a chance." He set the bottle in the middle of the table where his stack of winnings had presided. "Have a little to warm ya on y'r way."

While the others poured and passed the bottle, Jude chuckled to himself. " 'Member I tol ya I had an ide-e?" At their nods he continued. "This'un's a real winner. Dag's gonna be so flummoxed he'll never show his face in Soldall again."

"What'er ya thinkin'?" Shorty leaned forward, his pencil-sharp elbows digging grooves in the green felt.

"We're gonna get him a woman, that's what." Jude waited for their responses. At the men's quizzical looks, he snorted. "What woman would look once at him, let alone twice? See, this here's how we'll do it." They all leaned close, shoulder to shoulder. "We'll send a ticket to a woman in Norway."

"Hey, how you gonna get'er name?"

"Easy, stupid. I jist happened to read the name and address offa that Detschman woman's letter to her baby sister."

"Oh." The men nodded in admiration. Trust Jude to think of something like that.

"Along with that ticket, we'll send a picture of me and a letter from Dag."

"He can't write no letter. He can't even read." Henry thumped a limp fist on the tabletop.

"I know that. But I can write—and read. The letter'll tell her about what a successful man he is—"

"He is that. Dag's the best blacksmith in six counties."

"Don't remind me! An it'll say how handsome—"

The men guffawed and slapped their knees.

"An' she'll expect to fall in love and marry him—" The laughter raised a decibel or two. One chair screeched in protest when its occupant shoved it backwards, laughing fit to split his britches.

"An' Dag'll 'bout die of embarrassment." Jude raised his refilled glass; the others followed suit. "To the end of Dag."

"The end of Dag."

Chapter 1

The way lay long between Norway and America. Clara Johanson tapped the edge of her sister's letter against her teeth as she strode up the last hill before the home farm. While she glanced up at the newly snow-dusted peaks that rose in ever steeper ridges to the east, she failed to appreciate their grandeur this time. All she could think about was America. How would she get to America?

She leaned against a pine tree to catch her breath from the steep climb. Her sister, Nora, had written about how flat North Dakota stretched, about a plague of grasshoppers, two small motherless children, and a silent, German farmer who was stealing her heart away. But she had no money to send a ticket yet.

Clara removed her wool scarf from her head and smoothed her deep honey hair back into its combs. She shook her head and the waves of gold rippled like wheat across her shoulders. Even in the brisk wind off the fjords, moisture dotted her forehead from the climb.

A squirrel chattered in the branches above her.

"Ja, I know, I'm bothering you. But what would you do in my place?" She stared up through the soughing branches to locate her scolding audience.

"Most of my friends are already married but me. . .for me there's no one." Pieces of pinecone dropped around her. She tightened her dark skirts around her knees and sank to the ground softened with pine needles.

"Maybe I should volunteer to the government to be an immigrant bride. You know the Norwegian government is sending

146

marriageable women out to different parts of the world to the men who want families." More cone pieces dropped, one landing on her shoulder. "You don't think I'd make a good wife?"

The squirrel chattered. One answered it from another tree.

Clara caught a flash of red as her comrade leaped from a branch above her to the tree across the track. "Well, I hope you do. See, God, even the squirrels have mates." She shifted her conversation partner without missing a beat. "But I don't. You know I am well-trained to be a wife and mother. Just ask Mor. She started teaching me when I was but a babe."

She thought again of the letter from Nora. Her words spoke of such love between her and Carl Detschman. It hadn't been easy, in fact, Carl had nearly died; but the love shone now from her sister's pen. Oh, to love and be loved like that.

With one fingertip Clara traced a cross in the duff. "I know you have a plan for me. . .for my life. Please let it be in America." She dug the lines deeper. "I'm trying to be patient, really I am." Her sigh lifted and tickled the bows above her. Her prayer rode the sigh to the treetop, begged a ride on the wind, and wafted upward to her Father's ears.

"Uff da!" Dag Weinlander grunted from the force of the kick. "Enough!" He slapped the horse's gray rump with a heavy gloved hand, then wiped the sweat dripping from his brow. He leaned over, grasped the horse's rear off fetlock, and dragged the bent leg between his knees to rest on the platform created by his gripping knees.

"Dag?"

He ignored the familiar voice, instead checking the symmetry of the iron shoe.

A knee-length, split-leather divided apron protected his legs from the hot iron shoe that raised a tendril of burned-hoof smoke when he set the iron against the wall of the horse's hoof. With iron nails clenched between his lips blackened by the forge smoke and his muscles bulging, he raised the hammer and tapped each nail

147

into position. Dag set the shoe and cramped the nails puncturing the outside of the hoof. With the easy strokes of long practice, he rasped each head down and formed the hoof even with the shoe.

With a grunt, he dropped the horse's rear leg and straightened up, one hand pressed against the small of his back. Only one more to go.

"Dag!" A hint of a whine laced the demanding tone.

"Ja?" Dag peered out from the locks straggling over his brow.

"You won't forget?" Dag's younger brother, Jude, leaned against the post.

"Said I'd meet her." Dag picked up the iron flat tongs and shoved the final shoe back into the glowing forge. After a couple of cranks on the blower, the iron glowed red, then white-hot. He set the shoe on edge on the anvil and, with the hammer, pounded more of a curve into the heels. Sparks flew, bright red and orange, against the dimness of the cavernous shop. He dunked the shoe into the water bucket.

"And you'll drive her out to the Detschman farm." This time it was more an order than a question.

"Ja." Dag brushed an intrusive lock of hair from his eyes, using the back of his wrist. Sweat muddied with soot streaked across his cheek.

"Her name's Clara, Clara Johanson." Jude continued propping the center post.

Dag leaned into the ritual with the remaining hoof. The horse snorted and twitched his tail. "Hold 'im."

"Ja. Easy feller." Will, the young helper, gripped the halter more tightly and stroked the horse's arched neck.

The coarse tail hairs snagged on Dag's head and one caught him in the eye. He brushed it away and clamped the hoof more tightly between his knees. The tearing of the injured eye blurred the hoof for a moment or two.

"I'll be goin' on then," said Jude. "You'll take care of Ma?"

Dag nodded, mouth too full of nails to answer. Of course he'd take care of Ma. When hadn't he? Or rather, when had Jude? Surprised at the unaccustomed thoughts, Dag concentrated on finishing off the hoof. The pungent odors of horse manure, cut hooves, horsehide, and smoldering coal all welded together, redolent of blacksmithing. He breathed it in like bellows himself, part and parcel of his life and livelihood.

He rechecked each hoof and, when he straightened his back and looked around, only he and Will remained.

"He left 'bout the time you last answered." Will slipped loose the rope tying the horse to the post. "Seemed in a powerful hurry." He led the horse out the door and toward the livery barn. "You gonna do the other?"

"Ja." Dag heard the two horses whicker to each other, the timeless greeting of friendly horses. Will's voice joined in.

Dag removed his glove and rubbed the back of his neck with fingers so deeply grimed they looked like walnut bark. They matched his neck. He hawked and spit, then kneaded his protesting back muscles with hamlike hands. Outside he could see the daylight dimming.

Will trotted up with the remaining horse and tied it to the hitching post located in the arched doorway of the shingled building.

The train would be in anytime now. Dag stared from the horse to the tree outside. Not enough time. He shook his head. Why'd Jude make such a fuss over his picking up that woman? She could wait till he finished. Johnson's team came first.

He bent to the job at hand.

"You gonna eat first?" Will asked later after stabling the freshly shod horse.

"Nah. You go on."

"I can help you get the buggy ready." Will shifted from one foot to the other.

Dag shook his head. "Go eat."

The train whistle had come and gone long enough for the gaslight above the hotel entrance to be lit before Dag hung his apron on a nail. He shrugged into a black wool jacket, then brushed down his own bay mare. When her coat shone to perfection, he gently laid the harness across her back, careful to smooth every hair under the leather and adjust each snap and buckle. When he backed her into the shafts, it was a contest to see which shown brighter, the horse or the buggy.

He kicked his boots against a post to knock off any clinging mud or manure and stepped into the leather-roofed buggy. Jude had said to take the buggy. Dag shook his head. If that woman had many trunks and such, the wagon would be better.

He picked up the reins and clucked to the mare. The sooner he got this chore done, the better. His stomach rumbled. By the time he drove the nearly one hour out to the Detschman farm and another hour back, his belly'd do more than rumble. He rubbed a hand over a wall of solid flesh. In the dim light he picked a clump of dirt—or manure?—off his pant leg and flicked the matter out of the buggy.

His stomach grumbled again—louder.

He turned the mare in along the weathered train station and stopped beside the raised platform between the hunching building and the ribbon tracks. Two trunks squatted side by side.

With a sound of disgust, Dag levered himself from the buggy. He should have brought the wagon. Now he'd have to make another trip tomorrow.

"*Uff da*," he muttered as he knotted the mare's lead shank around the hitching post. *Let Detschman come in and get 'em. She was his sister-in-law anyway, wasn't she? Why didn't he meet the train? That Jude—what'd he have to do with this whole mess anyway?*

Dag stomped across the wide beaten planks and jerked open the door. It wasn't as if he had nothing else to do. And while Jude said he'd pay for the trip, getting the cash in hand was about as likely as a snowstorm in July.

"*Froken* Johanson." The words died aborning. Dag tried to swallow, but his mouth suddenly felt like a Dakota dust storm. That same storm left grit in his eyes. Was this what being struck by lightning felt like? Lightning didn't usually accompany dust storms.

He stared at the vision that stood before him. Tendrils of deep honey blond hair peeped out from the sides of a feathered black hat. Eyes the blue-green of a hummingbird's back peeked out from the black veil pinned in a swoop across an alabaster forehead. Turned up nose, lips ruby like the hummingbird's throat and smiling as if they'd been friends for years. When she stood, she barely came up to the middle button on his faded and tattered shirt.

Dag tried again to talk. Breathing alone took an effort. Both failed.

"I'm Clara Johanson." Her voice tickled his ears, which responded in a rush of heat.

Dag wet his lips, or tried to.

"And you're. . . ?"

When had the Norwegian language been set to melody? He ordered his gaze to leave her face. To look up at the rafters or down at the floor. Instead, rebellious gaze. It traveled her length, from tip of crushable hat to toe of shiny boots—and back up. Now his ears burned like the forge he'd left behind.

Dag leaned forward and picked up the bag set beside her. He waved his hand toward the door and strode out in silence. He who rarely chose to speak, now couldn't.

He slung her gray-and-black bag into the small space behind the seat and climbed into the buggy.

"What about my trunks?" Clara paused at the edge of the station platform.

"Tomorrow." Dag croaked out the word.

Clara climbed into the buggy and settled her skirts. What a strange man. Maybe he was a bit on the deaf side? She sniffed, her nostrils pinching against the odor. Did he never bathe? Or wash that rat's nest of hair? She tried to ignore the fumes. Thank the good Lord above this wasn't the man in her picture.

She clasped her purse in her lap, wishing the buggy were even a few inches wider. She shifted as far to the side as possible.

"Nice evening, isn't it?" Maybe if she breathed through her mouth it would be easier.

Silence from the man beside her. The harness jingled with the trotting horse.

Clara peered ahead, Ja, like Nora had written, the land certainly was flat. A little bounce of excitement slipped past her mother's orders to act like the woman she now was. . .or would be. The time sequence wasn't exactly clear as to when a person left the exuberance of childhood and entered staid adulthood. She sneaked a glance at the man driving the buggy.

He stared straight ahead. Good. Mayhap he hadn't noticed. If only he hadn't taken so long to come for her. Now it was too dark to see the fields and farms. Off to the right a light from someone's house pinpointed in the darkness.

The mare trotted onward, her puffs of breath a counterpoint to the tattoo of her hooves.

"What did you say your name is?" Her willful stubbornness kicked in. She *would* get him to talk. How could anyone be so rude?

"Have you lived here a long time?" She waited for an answer that didn't come. "Do you know my sister, Nora?" Waiting was getting harder. She wanted to ask him about the handsome man with curly blond hair, the one whose face she'd fallen in love with. The man who sent her a ticket and would be looking forward to claiming her as his wife. But she didn't.

"How far from town do Nora and Carl live?" Pause again. Clara felt like grabbing the man by the ears and turning his face to look at her so he would be forced to answer. "I know you speak Norwegian, I heard you. So I must take it that you are a cruel person at heart who is enjoying my discomfort. Newcomers to America like me must be most entertaining to ignore."

Was that a snort she heard? From the horse? No. Clara ran her tongue over her teeth and tipped her chin a bit higher. "Maybe you just want to hear me prattle away so you can tell all your friends what a simpering fool that new arrival is?"

"Uff da."

Clara nearly clapped her hands in delight. "I agree. No one should be forced to carry on as I have just to get two syllables from her driver."

"Dag. I am Dag Weinlander." How he had fought to ignore

152

her jabs. Dag bit his lip to keep from laughing aloud. What a feisty little thing she was.

"I'm pleased to meet you, Dag Weinlander." Clara settled back against the leather seat. She'd won—the first round. Her forehead wrinkled. What a curious thought. Why should she think there would be other rounds?

Dag focused on the spot up the road between his mare's ears so that his errant gaze wouldn't turn to hers. The tips of his ears still burned or burned again, he couldn't say which.

What did she want from him? He'd been hired to drive her out to her sister's, not entertain her on the way. Once his ears stopped burning, they'd probably drop off from sheer overexertion. No one but Will had talked to him this much since. . .since. . .well, maybe they never had.

The clop of hooves, the jangling of the harness, and the creak of the ironclad wheels sang through the dark.

Clara nibbled her lip. As long as she turned her face slightly to the side, she could breath the crisp night air, unimpeded by the odor of the man next to her. Her nose told her there would be frost before morning.

Ahead, a brass disk peeped its edge above the rim of the earth. As the moon rose, it seemed to fill the eastern horizon with gold.

"Oh-h-h." Her wonder escaped on a sigh. With no mountains or trees to break its symmetry, the moon took possession of the land, rising to float against the black vault of the heavens, bathing the earth in liquid light. Clara forgot the man beside her, her sister in the home awaiting her, and the family she'd left behind. She lost herself in the glory of the harvest moon, the brisk air that kissed her opened lips, and the hush that blanketed all the simple sounds around her. "*Mange takk*, dear God." She whispered, sensing that anything louder might shatter the glory.

A crystal tear slipped down her cheek, testimony to God's nighttime handiwork.

Dag watched the girl beside him. He'd seen a harvest moon before and he'd felt its power and majesty. He'd never seen a woman bathed in moon glow and transfixed by its beauty.

Clara shivered and took a deep breath. She looked around, as if surprised at her reaction. Her glance caught the movement of Dag's head from the corner of her eye. Had he been watching her?

Dag pulled gently on the left rein and turned his mare into the lane leading to the Detschman farm. "We're here."

Clara perched on the edge of the seat, straining to catch the first glimpse of welcoming windows.

Ahead, lighted windows dimmed in the brightness of the moon. While leafless trees shielded the house, the moon reflected off the roof of a large barn, windmill, and various other buildings, all snuggled against the earth's breast.

A dog barked. A horse whinnied from the pasture. The mare lifted her nose and answered.

A door opened, spilling light across the porch and down the steps.

Clara felt the tears gather and clog in her throat. She'd finally reached her sister's new home. Nora's American home. Now they'd be together again.

Before the buggy stopped rocking, Clara leaped from her seat and scrambled down the step to land lightly on the ground. She darted through the gate, up the walk, bounded the two steps while pulling up her long skirt, and threw herself into her older sister's arms.

"Clara, you're here already." Nora hugged her little sister close. "We didn't expect you until tomorrow or the next day."

"I wanted to surprise you." Clara leaned her head against her sister's shoulder. "I have so much to tell you." She wiped away an escaping tear. "I can't believe I'm here, in America, in North Dakota, with you."

Nora hugged her sister once more and then stepped back. "Clara, this is Carl." She took the hand of the man who waited patiently behind her and brought him forward.

"I am pleased to meet you." Carl extended his right hand, the left still clasped by Nora.

Clara nodded, her speech temporarily drowned by the tears she kept swallowing.

"And this is Kaaren." Nora reached behind her to grasp the little girl's hand, hiding in her mother's skirts. "Kaaren, your Auntie Clara from Norway."

Kaaren, finger in her mouth, buried her face in Nora's white apron.

Clara squatted down and looked the little one in the eye. "Oh, my. Now I'm an auntie. And you're my first niece. We're going to have such fun." She stood again.

"And where is that baby boy I've read so much about?"

"Sound asleep and we want him to stay that way. You can cuddle him tomorrow. Come in now."

"Oh, my bags."

"I'll get them." Carl stepped off the porch and headed for the buggy where Dag waited, patiently leaning against the high wheel.

As the sisters turned toward the warmth of the open door, Clara spun back around. "I haven't thanked Dag for bringing me all the way out here."

"Don't worry, Carl will take care of that for you. Have you had anything to eat? I'll make fresh coffee." They passed into the house.

Dag turned down Carl's offer of coffee and food and, after shaking hands, stepped back into the buggy. He touched a finger to his hat brim, turned the mare in a circle to head back out over the land, and clucked her into a trot.

He listened for the familiar night sounds. How faint they seemed after the chatter that had filled his ears. He'd never realized before how quiet the night could be. And how far away his hovel stood. He ignored the temptation to look back at the lighted windows.

Chapter 2

How then did you get the ticket to come?" Nora asked. Carl had put Kaaren to bed and gone upstairs himself after wishing the visitor a good night's rest. Nora and Clara were enjoying a second cup of coffee in the now-quiet and peaceful kitchen.

"I'll tell you. Let me get the letter." Clara slipped from her chair at the kitchen table and crossed the room to rummage in her suitcase. When she returned she held a water-stained envelope in her hand. "Here." She laid it on the table in front of her sister.

Nora studied the front of the envelope. She pulled the kerosene lamp closer so she could read the faded handwriting. After carefully studying it, she looked up. "How did this get so stained?"

"I don't know. It happened before—"

"Before you got it?" Nora's voice squeaked in amazement. She didn't pay attention to the fact that they'd fallen back into their old pattern of finishing one another's thoughts.

Clara nodded.

"Then how—"

"Did I get it?"

Nora nodded this time. Silence but for the clunk of a piece of coal falling in the stove waited while she studied the barely discernible script again. She looked up.

"I know. God must have His hand in this—or else He just gave the postman extra good eyesight."

"*Uff da.*" Nora shook her head again.

"Open it." Clara gave a little bounce on her chair. "Read the letter."

Nora grasped the fragile paper and pulled it from the envelope. After unfolding it, she choked back a laugh. "Was it really this bad?" She scanned the lines and loops of script; most of the ink had run together or faded entirely. She peered closely where the signature should be. "Impossible. All I can read for sure is 'Dear Miss Johanson.' At least I assume that's what the heading says."

"Me, too. But the ticket was plain enough to use—barely— and then there was this." She handed Nora a picture, faded in places, but still clear enough to see. "Isn't he handsome? Just think—that's the man who sent me a ticket. Do you know him?"

Nora studied the picture. She glanced up at her sister and then went back to studying the photograph. "If he's as nice as he is good-looking—"

"I know. I think I'm half in love with him already." Clara plucked the picture from her sister's hand and sighed when she gazed at the face of her mystery man. "Such hair, curly like that. And look, I think if he smiled, he would have a dimple." She touched the paper cheek with her fingertip. "You didn't say. Do you know who he is? I wonder why he didn't meet the train?"

"No, I don't. I mean I've never seen him before, but then there are many people in Soldall that I've never seen. If they don't go to church. . ."

"Surely he must go to church." Clara could feel her heart begin an erratic thump in her chest. "You really don't know him?"

Nora shook her head. She reached for her sister's hands. "No, but mayhap Carl does. Or Ingeborge." She covered both of Clara's hands with her own. "This is surely a mystery, isn't it?" She picked up her coffee cup and sipped.

"Ugh." The face she made accompanied the words. "Cold coffee. Let me warm yours up, too." She started to push back her chair.

"No, not for me." Clara stared at the picture, worrying her bottom lip between her teeth. Should she tell Nora about the little knot of fear that seemed to be cutting off her air? She sucked in a deep breath. A yawn caught it and creaked her jawbone.

"*Uff da.* Here we sit yakking when you just got off the train. I can see you need your bed. We can figure all this out in the morning." Nora tucked a strand of hair behind Clara's ear and caught her own yawn. "You made me yawn, too."

The clock chimed. . .and chimed.

"There, it is ten o'clock already and we've been sitting here for hours. Come. Carl brought Kaaren into my bed so you can have her bedroom. That way you can sleep as long as you want in the morning." Nora rose to her feet and laid a hand on her sister's shoulder. "Not to worry, little sister of my heart. Your man will show up one day and then you can decide if you like him as much as you think."

"Ja, that is the way of it." Clara stood, slipping the letter and picture back in the envelope at the same time. "I just thought you would know him and this would all be cleared up at once." She tapped the edge of the envelope with her finger.

"And tomorrow you can tell me all the news of home—"

"And give you the presents Mor sent and the letters, too. Everyone wrote when they knew I was to come." Clara lifted her chair so it wouldn't creak on the floor and snugged it up against the table.

Nora picked up the carpetbag with one hand and lamp in the other and led the way through the parlor to the back bedroom. She set the lamp on the oak chest of drawers and the bag in front. A rag doll flopped against the pillow covered by a patchwork quilt on the bed.

Clara sank down on the edge of the bed. "It seems like weeks since I've slept in a real bed." She picked up the doll and studied the black button eyes and smiling mouth embroidered in red. "This looks like your handiwork. Remember the one you made for me?"

Nora nodded. "That was my first. And you pulled the eyes off in the first hour. After the second time I had to resew them, I embroidered the eyes, too, in green to match yours."

Clara laughed and gave the doll a squeeze. "You are very good with a needle. All the hardanger lace for your bride's chest. I had a hard time learning to sit still for so long. Mor did her best. Such patience she has."

Nora sat beside her sister. "And your bride's chest? Did you fill it?"

Clara nodded. "But just don't look too close at the stitches. Oh, I forgot. My trunks are still at the station. Mr. Weinlander said Carl would have to come get them since he had only the buggy."

"How did he know to meet you?"

Clara blinked. She looked at her sister. "Why, I don't know. I never thought of it. The stationmaster told me the man from the livery would come for me. I waited quite a time and when he finally came—*uff da*." She wrinkled her nose. "I don't think he's ever heard of a bath, let alone taken one. And rude." She planted her fists on her hips. "Getting him to speak was—"

Nora chuckled. "And did you? Get him to talk?"

"But, naturally." Clara flopped back on the bed, looking at her sister as if she'd doubted the sun would rise.

Nora shook her head. "Dag just doesn't talk to anyone. He says the fewest words possible to complete his business. And that's all."

"Oh." The little word carried a wealth of understanding. Clara chewed the inside of her lower lip. She felt the chuckle dance around the corridors of her mind before bursting forth full-blown; its merry music skipped from bed to window and around the room.

Nora shook her head. "What are you up to now, sister mine. I know that laugh."

Clara smothered her face with the rag doll. "Nora, dear, the man needs help."

"You just think about your mystery man. When you find him, you won't have time to be fixing Mr. Weinlander." She rose to her feet. "Now you sleep as long as you'd like in the morning. I know you're tired from the long journey and the bed will feel good." She reached out a hand to pull her sister to her feet. "Mayhap Carl can drive to town tomorrow for your trunks. And to tell Reverend Moen we can have the wedding Sunday. We were waiting for you, you know."

"But you're already married."

"I know. But that one seems a sham, so we decided to have a real wedding, in the church and with me wearing my *bunad* and *sølje.* And with you to stand up for me once we heard you were coming."

"I am happy for you." Clara patted a hand over her mouth to disguise the yawn. "I'll see you in the morning then."

Nora folded back the covers. "I'll leave this lamp with you." She stopped again in the door frame. "You'll never know how glad I am you are here. Sleep well, God bless."

Clara stifled a yawn again. "*Mange takk,* dear sister." Her eyelids seemed weighted with stones as she removed her clothing and pulled her nightgown over her head. *"Mange takk"* was all she finished of her prayers before sleep winged her away to dream of a curly haired man with broad shoulders and the promise of a dimple in his right cheek when he smiled.

Clara awoke to silence. Where had everyone gone? She lay in the soft feather bed, reviewing the hours spent on the train, back to the ship, and ended up at her parent's home in Norway. Such a distant place. Would she ever see the rest of her family again?

She bit the inside of her lip against the pain of missing them all. "Not all, silly. Nora's around here somewhere. Think how much you've wanted to see her and now you can." She threw back the hand-stitched quilt and sat up cross-legged in the bed. With her elbows propped on her knees, she rested her chin in her hands.

A song trickled through her mind, one learned in the choir at home. She hummed the tune while studying the white fabric stretched across her knees. The words came to her mind: *Oh God, our help in ages past.* "Good thing." She left the tune and turned to prayer, clenching her eyes shut so she wouldn't be distracted by the sun's painting squares on the polished floorboards. "Father God, I know You've always been with me and this journey proved Your faithfulness again. But what about the man who sent for me? Where is he? Who is he? How can I marry him if. . .if. . ." She waited for her thoughts to settle down. "I do so want to be married. I know I make jokes about it but, Father, I need someone to love. . .someone who loves me. I want a home and a family." She paused again. A far off *moooo* blessed her silence. "Is that wrong of me?" No answer floated down from the heavens. None arose from her heart either.

A sigh rose from deep in her heart. It was hard to wait for an answer. She quieted her mind again. The song returned, the pace faster, the notes livelier. Unable to resist the joy she felt rising from somewhere deep inside, she whispered a final "amen" and flung herself back on the pillows.

She stared up at the high ceiling, then wrapped both hands around her shoulders and squeezed. "I, Clara Johanson, am now in America!" She jumped from the bed, danced on the rug, and then got dressed. While the sun was shining in so warmly, the room felt like a cold fall day after a frosty fall night.

The clock bonged nine times as she opened her bedroom door and walked through the parlor toward the kitchen. While the house was empty, the coffeepot steamed gently on the back of the stove.

"Bless you, sister mine." She poured herself a cup and, wrapping both hands around the warmth, basked in the heat of the stove. As her gaze wandered around the kitchen, admiring her sister's handiwork, she stopped at the loaf of bread resting on the counter beside the jam jar and the molded butter on a plate.

She left her place at the stove and stuck a finger in the jam and then into her mouth. "Ummm." She licked all the sticky sweet berry taste off her finger and, after setting down the coffee cup, sliced herself a piece of bread. After burying it in butter and jam, she took the bread and coffee and eased herself down into the smaller of the two rockers in front of the stove.

"Ahhh." Alternately drinking and chewing, she continued her study of the kitchen. The stove had been recently cleaned and its silver trim gleamed in the beam of sun from the window. The ruffled curtains that framed the picture-perfect fall tree in the window above the sink sparked in the same sun. Clara nodded. Yes, her sister was the spotless homemaker their mother had trained her to be . . .always the one to be perfect at what she did.

Clara set the chair to rocking with the tip of her toe. Well, at least her hardanger stitching always outdid her sister's. She sighed and leaned her head against the back of the rocker. It was always hard to measure herself against perfection, yet she loved her older sister as only a younger one could.

"I've missed you so," she whispered to the tune of the clock chiming the hour. She plunked her feet on the floor and pushed herself to her feet. "And I've had enough of this lazing around. Nora, dear one, where are you? And those precious children of yours." She set her cup in the sink, covered the bread, and pushed the coffeepot to the side of the stove.

She lifted her coat from the hook on the rack and stepped outside to a glorious day of sun that warmed her cheeks. A fall-nipped breeze lifted the golden tendrils curling about her face. *Maybe today will be the day,* she thought, *the day my curly haired man will come riding up the lane.* She stared up the empty lane with two lines of hard-packed soil the width of wagon wheels. A line of grass grew in the middle.

"Clara, down here." Nora waved from the low building to the side of the barn.

Shrugging off the dream, Clara waved back and, leaping from the porch, trotted down the path. The windmill creaked its song and, when she looked up, she saw a *V* of geese heading south, adding their wild cries to the plaintive notes of the windmill.

"You can carry the eggs," Nora said, her smile wide and eyes dancing, "or Peder." She motioned to the baby slung in a scarf and riding on her hip.

Kaaren, finger in her mouth, peeked from behind Nora's dark wool skirt. Her coffee-colored hat had tilted slightly to the side, nearly hiding one blue eye.

Clara squatted down, eye level with the shy little girl, and crossed her arms on her knees. "I'm your Auntie Clara, remember?"

Kaaren nodded, her finger stuck firmly in place.

Clara itched to reach out and straighten the hat, but she could remember being the shy one. "Maybe you could show me the cows and horses."

"Pa's cows." The finger left her mouth and pointed off to the barn. "Horses gone."

162

"Shall we go see?" Clara raised back to her feet and extended a hand.

Kaaren studied the hand and then looked up at Nora, as if asking approval. Nora nodded.

Kaaren reached out and slipped her hand in Clara's. When they started off, she hung back. "Ma come, too?"

Nora shook her head, her smile a benediction. She adjusted the baby's sling and picked up the basket of eggs. "You two go on. We'll have coffee when you come up to the house."

"I'll take those." Clara nodded at the egg basket. "After we see the cows."

Nora shook her head and started up the path.

Hand in hand, Clara and Kaaren meandered from the watering trough where the cows stood head to swishing tail, to the pen where the big black-and-white sow came to beg for bits of grass, to the corral where the work team dozed in the sun.

"Your pa is a good farmer," Clara said, admiring the tight fences and healthy-looking livestock.

"Pa's gone to town." The finger went back into the little girl's mouth. Kaaren switched from English to German to Norwegian, depending on whatever word she wanted.

"Let's run." Clara tugged on her hand. Together, the two of them dashed up the path, through the gate, and bounded up the porch steps, Clara lifting her by-now-giggling-charge up the three stairs. She swung the little girl up in her arms and whirled her around before hugging her close and kissing her rosy cheek. "You're good enough to eat." Clara nibbled on the squirming little girl's neck.

Laughing and giggling they entered the house and removed their coats. When Clara picked Kaaren up so she could hang up her wrap, the little girl wrapped one arm around her aunt's neck after placing her coat on the hook.

"I see you've made friends." Nora set a plate of cookies on the table. "Wash your hands while I pour the coffee." She shifted the baby in her arm to the other side. He grinned and waved a chubby hand when Clara chucked him under his double chin.

With each holding a child on her lap, the two sisters dunked their cookies in their coffee and smiled at each other across the checkered red-and-white oilcloth table cover.

"I wasn't sure this would ever happen." Nora's look encompassed the entire scene.

"I know." Clara held her coffee cup steady while Kaaren dunked her cookie, too. "If it hadn't been for that letter, who knows how long it would've been?"

"Surely Carl will know who it is when he comes back. He went in to talk with Reverend Moen about having our wedding on Sunday right after services."

"How will you get ready?"

"There's not so much." A pink tinge brightened her cheeks. "Oh, Clara, he—my Carl—he is such a good man. God is surely good to me."

"And to him. Look how you have cared for his children and—"

"But he had much sadness."

A silence fell and Clara reached out to cover her sister's hand with her own. "But now there will be much happiness. And I am here to make sure this marriage is done right. This time you will wear your *bunad* and sit for a portrait so we can send one home to Mor and Far."

"And maybe soon we will celebrate a wedding for you."

Clara shook her head. "When we find my mystery man. You don't suppose something has happened to him—"

"Like with my Hans, you mean?"

Clara nodded. "To come so far like you did and your man had just died." She shuddered, as if a goose had just walked across her grave. "I don't know how you—" She shuddered again.

"As Mor says, 'We will give God the glory,' ja?"

"Ja, that we will." She rested her chin on the head of the little one against her breast. *And maybe one day, I'll have lambs like these.* Clara kept the thought in her heart. She had to find her man first.

When Carl returned from town, he shook his head over the picture. "No, I don't know this man, but maybe Reverend Moen will. He knows everyone for six townships."

"Or perhaps Ingeborge will?" Nora finished putting the last of the supper on the table. "Let's eat and you can tell all about your trip at the same time."

After bowing their heads for grace, Nora dished up the plates, set them in front of her family and then she sat down.

Carl turned to her, a twinkle in his eyes. "Reverend Moen said he'd be delighted to remarry us on Sunday since the first one didn't seem to take."

"Carl." Nora blushed and pushed at his arm. "You know that's not the reason."

He covered her hand with his. "So you say. And Ingeborge invited us all for dinner afterward."

"Did you ask her what we could bring?"

Carl nodded. "And she said, 'Just yourselves.' This is to be her wedding gift to us." He took a bite of the pork chop smothered in applesauce on his plate. "Oh." He waved his fork for emphasis. "She said you are not to worry about a thing. New brides have too much on their minds already."

Clara watched the byplay between Carl and Nora. The tint creeping up her sister's neck was most becoming. How pleasant it was to watch someone with the love light shining so brightly in their own eyes, they needn't light the lamps. She felt a lump lodge in her throat.

"Auntie Clara."

"Ja, what is it?" She bent over to listen more closely to the whisper.

"Are you going to stay forever?" Kaaren stared up with eyes dark in the lamplight.

Clara felt the lump melt and begin to burn behind her eyelids. This little girl had already lost more than any child should when her mother died. "I don't know how long forever is, but I plan on being around a long, long time." Her whisper seemed to be just what Kaaren needed to hear as the smile that brightened her face more than matched those exchanged by the two other adults at the table.

Kaaren's pigtails bobbed, she nodded so emphatically. "Good."

165

How long is long, Lord? Clara prayed that night after helping tuck Kaaren into bed and cleaning up the kitchen. Nora had set cooked cornmeal into loaf pans to fry for breakfast and started yeast rising for bread baking. How different it was watching her sister do the things their mother had always done. *Am I ready, Father?* Her prayer continued. *I know Your hand has been leading me, but now . . .what has happened?* She shoved the niggling worries down and slammed a door on them. God wouldn't have brought her all the way to America without a purpose in mind. Would He?

But doubting was a sin. . .wasn't it? He did bring her. . . didn't He?

The thought of the man with curly hair flashed across her mind. Along with her mother's admonition, "Handsome is as handsome does." Clara had never understood what that meant.

The man was certainly handsome—wherever he was. Whoever he was. What should she do with the doubts? "Father, forgive me. Help me believe. . .and trust."

Chapter 3

n the name of the Father, and of the Son, and of the Holy
Spirit, I now pronounce you man and wife." Reverend Moen
closed his prayer book and nodded at the two standing before
him. "Carl, you may kiss your bride." In an undertone, only for the
ears of those four closest, he added, "Again."

Clara bit back a giggle. She could tell Carl and Nora had some
ribbing in store for them since they had asked to be married a second time. But the teasing was such fun with the Moens.

The organ struck up the recessional. Clara handed her sister
the white leather Bible with a small spray of gold and rust chrysan-
themums on the top. Nora, clad in her black *skyjørt*, red vest, and
white *forkle*, looked the perfect Norwegian bride even if she wasn't
wearing the formal bridal headdress.

Clara reached up to kiss her sister's cheek. "God bless." She
needed to wipe her eyes, but her handkerchief lay in her bag, wherever that was. How come she always cried at weddings? It wasn't as
if this were a sad occasion. She turned and followed Carl and Nora
down the aisle.

Some members of the congregation had elected to remain to
help wish the newlyweds God's blessing. Clara found herself
searching the faces for a certain curly haired man, but she hadn't
found him by the time they all exited the sanctuary.

She hugged her sister again. "Oh, if only Mor and Far could
have been here." Clara felt herself choke up again on the words.
She wiped a tear from the corner of her eye.

"I know," Nora whispered back, "but at least you were here."

The pastor's wife, Ingeborge Moen, a baby in each arm and

the other children clustered about her like chicks with a hen, herded her brood to the door.

"Here, let me take Peder." Clara reached out for the sleeping baby. She took the quilt-wrapped bundle carefully in her arms and, at the babe's whimper, slipped into the swaying motion common to women everywhere. She watched as Carl and Nora greeted the people around them.

"Such a wonderful story and with a happy ending," Ingeborge sighed at Clara's elbow. "Your sister is a fine woman. She has made Carl to laugh again."

"She never told us much about those early months." Clara patted Peder's back when he began squirming. "We had to read between the lines, more what she didn't say than what she did."

"It wasn't easy. Peder was colicky, Carl wanted her to speak only English, and who was there to teach her and Kaaren, poor mite, who missed her mother so bad. I tell you, those two earned their happiness."

Peder ignored the comforting sway and added his opinion to the discussion. As with all babies, his idea of communication after the first subtle whimpers that had been ignored was a full-throated howl.

"Shush, shush." Clara jiggled harder.

The baby yelled—louder.

Clara looked around the room for the baby's mother. "They've gone into the office to sign the marriage certificate. Come." Ingeborge nodded to the outer door. "Let's take these two young ones home and feed them. And I have a marvelous idea." She picked up the conversation again after they'd corralled the older children running around outside and started down the street.

"Why don't you and the children stay with John and me tonight? Carl and Nora deserve to have a night alone, don't you think?"

"Why. . .why, I'm sure that is a fine idea, but do you have room?"

"Oh, there's always room for one more."

"Ja, but this is three and one of us isn't always the best company." She glanced at the baby whimpering in her arms.

"Did Nora tell you that I helped nurse Peder there for a few days?" Clara shook her head. "So that baby and I were pretty close for a time. We'd love to have him back, and you can see how much Kaaren loves to be with Mary. You can have the same bed Nora used when she first came."

"If Carl and Nora agree, who am I to argue?" Clara now knew what it must be like to be pushed along like a leaf on a spring freshet. How could you turn down a person who made everything look as if you were doing her a favor? And besides, who wouldn't want to be alone the first night? She felt a warmth creep up her neck. At least that's what folks said about newlyweds.

Clara didn't have time to think about the picture she had tucked away in her bag until after she and Ingeborge had kissed the children good night and listened to their prayers.

"What a wonderful day." She sank into one of the rocking chairs in front of the gleaming black-and-silver cookstove.

"Ja, I know those two will be truly happy. And did you see the blush on your sister's neck when we told her about you and the children staying here?" Ingeborge set the chair on its creaking song with the toe of her foot. "Oh, to be so young again and beginning a life together."

Clara felt a tug in the region of her heart. She'd already pinpointed those twinges she'd identified as jealousy. Where was the man who had sent for her?

"I have something to show you." She leaned over and picked up her bag from the floor by the chair. She'd brought it back into the kitchen with her after kissing Kaaren one last time. Surely Ingeborge would know who this curly haired dream man was.

With trembling fingers she opened the mouth of the black leather bag and pulled out the picture. "Here." She extended her hand across the space and handed the picture to Ingeborge. Why did her breath catch in her throat and her stomach feel like cream being tossed in a churn?

Ingeborge smiled her comforting smile and glanced down at

the picture. "Ja, he is a fine looking man." She looked over at Clara with a question in her eyes. "Who is he?"

The churning in her midsection clumped together and fell to her toes. "I thought maybe you would know. This is the man who bought my ticket to America. He thinks he is getting a Norwegian wife, but I've been waiting. He never appears."

"Oh, my." Ingeborge patted Clara's hand where it strangled the wooden arm of the rocker. She studied the portrait again, all the while shaking her head. "Oh, my dear, I wish I had good news for you." She paused. "But maybe John knows this man. I'll go ask him."

Clara leaned her head against the back of the rocker and let her eyes close after Ingeborge left the room. The memory of her mother's voice calmed her rampaging thoughts. Prayer was Mor's answer to anything and everything. *But Mor,* she wanted to plead, *it's been four days and I haven't heard from him.* Like the kiss of butterfly wings, her mother's voice reminded, *Pray for him.*

"That's not so easy," Clara muttered. "I don't know his name or anything about him." She could feel a smile tickle the sides of her mouth. But oh, he was beautiful.

She opened her eyes when she heard Ingeborge in the doorway. What was the look she caught on the woman's face? It had been so fleeting. Was it—no—she didn't get a chance to think about it again.

"John thinks the man looks familiar but. . .ahh. . .he isn't. . . he can't say he knows him either." She stuttered in an uncharacteristic fashion.

Doubts crowded into Clara's mind again. "Is there something wrong? Something you're not telling me?" She leaned forward in the chair, her hands clamped together in her lap. "Ingeborge, what is it?"

"Nothing, nothing at all. We. . .uh, John and I, we'll ask around." She turned to move the coffeepot over the hotter part of the stove. "John said he'll be in for a cup of coffee in a minute and then you can tell him the entire story." She crossed to the cupboard and took down the coffee cups.

Clara commanded that her hands unclench themselves while she took in a deep breath and let it out slowly. There *was* something they weren't telling her. There was. She could sense it.

But later when the three of them had taken their places at the table and munched crisp molasses cookies with their coffee, the feeling left. She told the entire story from the moment she first saw the water-stained and smudged envelope until the present.

"And you haven't seen anyone that looks like this man since you arrived?" Reverend Moen leaned forward in his chair.

"No. And not heard one word. It's as if he fell off the face of the earth." Clara took a sip of now-cool coffee to quell the dryness in her throat. "Each day I think now this will be the time he comes forward but—" She raised her hands, palms up in a gesture of resignation. She looked from the pastor to his wife. "He doesn't come."

Reverend Moen rubbed the bridge of his nose with one long finger. He nodded and looked up at her. "We shall see. We shall see."

That night in bed, Clara listened to the sounds of the house creaking and settling for the night. So far the only men she'd met in this new country had been Carl, Reverend Moen, and that blacksmith who carted her out to the Detschman farm. And none of them looked anything like the man in her picture.

A week later, when the weather dropped below freezing and hovered there even during the day, Carl announced they would begin butchering the next morning. All the young hogs were fattened and ready.

"Dag will be bringing out his scalding tank and helping me dip and scrape. I thought we'd give a side to the Moens." He glanced at Clara sitting at the other end of the table. "You ever raised pigs and butchered them?"

"Of course. Far and the boys did most of the work, but I can grind sausage with the best of them. And headcheese." She nodded her head. "Mor taught us how to season it just right." She looked at Nora for confirmation.

"And the hams." Nora joined her sister in the memory. "But where will we get the hickory for flavor?"

"Don't you worry." Carl patted his wife's shoulder as he rose to go back outside. "We know how to smoke the bacon here in North Dakota, too. You just get all the knives sharpened and the pans ready."

"Selling the meat will surely help buy feed for the winter." Nora cleared the table after he left. "Those grasshoppers ate nearly everything. Clara, I've never seen anything like it. So many they blotted out the sun. Only the root crops lived through it. Thank the good Lord the rains came and the grass grew again so the cows could pasture. And the hay was already in the barn."

Clara shuddered. Insects had never been her favorite friends. "Does that happen often?"

"I hope not."

Clara was still brushing her hair the next morning by lamplight when she heard the dog barking and horse harnesses jingling. She could see her breath in the room, the night had turned so cold. As Carl had said, perfect butchering weather. A twinge of sorrow for the animals about to lose their lives crossed her mind. But at least here she hadn't cared for them for months and played with the babies when they were tiny.

She braided her hair in back and coiled it in a bun at the nape of her neck. Wearing her worst dress covered with a huge apron, she felt ready for the day.

"You remember Dag Weinlander," Carl said when he brought the men in for coffee before beginning. "And this is Will, his helper." Carl introduced two other men. Clara nodded to each, secretly studying each face in case it matched her picture. She didn't bother to look too carefully at the blacksmith. It was obvious he hadn't washed since their first meeting. She wrinkled her nose and tended to pull away when she refilled his coffee cup.

"Mange takk." Dag's deep voice surprised her.

"Ja." She responded automatically. The man could speak. She flinched inwardly. She could just hear her mother scolding her for thinking unkind thoughts about another of God's children. As she passed around the table with the coffeepot, she glanced up to catch him watching her. He ducked his head when he caught her eye.

The same thing happened at dinner. This time Clara could feel the heat rise on her neck. She shrugged off the feeling and headed back to the stove for another bowl of chicken and dumplings. She must be imagining things. But his voice stayed with her, even if the only exchange had been the polite "Thank you" and "You're welcome."

By the time she'd served the fresh fried liver for supper, Clara didn't care if she never saw a pig again. Or smelled the odors of blood and fresh meat. She and Nora had washed all the intestines to ready them for sausage casings and set both the shoulder and hindquarters to soak in brine before they could be smoked. They would have to grind the fat and begin rendering it out for lard the next day. And steam the krub, sausage made of ground potatoes and the fresh blood. They'd serve that for dinner as a special treat.

"Come, little one," Clara lifted Kaaren onto her lap when she and Nora collapsed into the twin rocking chairs. Nora held the bottle for the nearly sleeping baby Peder. "You've been such a good girl today," Clara said as she snuggled the nightgown-clad child close.

"Pa made me a ball."

"Ja. That old pig bladder has a new use now." Clara looked to her sister, glad she didn't have to remind Nora of all the fun they'd had with pig bladders after butchering time. Her return smile said it all.

Kaaren leaned her head against Clara's shoulder. A yawn started with Kaaren and traveled from mouth to mouth to mouth. The little girl giggled as she yawned again. "Mr. Weinlander is a nice man."

Clara stopped rocking and stared down at the little one in her lap with eyes drooping shut. Where had that come from?

"He threw my ball." The words spaced out as sleep over-came her.

What kind of a man is he? Clara thought as she snuggled down in the flannel sheets in her bed a few minutes later. She didn't have time to dwell on it or even say brief prayers before sleep closed her eyes like it had Kaaren's.

"Clara, I can't tell you how grateful I am for all your help," Nora murmured two nights later after they'd collapsed into the rockers again. The children were already in bed and the two sisters were enjoying a last cup of coffee and the quiet of a sleeping house.

"Ja, it's been good." Clara lifted the cup to her lips and inhaled the rich aroma. "How come it was easier at home?"

"More of us and we had Mor to run things." Nora shrugged her shoulders up to her ears and rotated her neck from side to side. "And there were no little ones to help us the last few years."

"That is true." Clara pushed herself to her feet and went to open the oven door. She pulled a pan of browning ground lard for-ward and, with a large spoon, began skimming the melted fat off and pouring it into the bread pans. When she'd dipped all she could, she picked off a piece of the crispy remainder and popped it into her mouth. "We should make cornbread with some of these cracklings tomorrow."

"That sounds good." The yawn nearly cracked Nora's jaw. "Thank you, again." She pushed herself to her feet. "When all this is over, we'll have to start on English lessons for you." She patted a hand over the next yawn. "Good night. Sweet dreams."

Clara was too tired to even picture the curly haired man, let alone dream.

Nora had just pulled the pan of cornbread from the oven the next afternoon when they heard the dog barking.

Clara parted the starched white curtains to see out the win-dow better. "It's Reverend Moen."

"And Ingeborge?"

"No, by himself."

Nora opened the door. "Come in, come in. You're just in time for hot cornbread and coffee."

"Thank you." He turned and shook hands with Carl, who had come from the springhouse. "And thank you for the side of pork." The two men shook hands. "We are truly grateful."

After the flurries of greetings, everyone gathered around the table. Clara cut the cornbread and, after placing the golden squares in bowls, drizzled maple syrup over the tops and passed the treat around the table.

By the time they'd poured the second cups of coffee, most of the news had been shared. Reverend Moen cleared his throat. "While I appreciate the coffee and the visit, I really had a special purpose in coming out here today." He stopped and looked directly at Clara across the table. "We have an older woman in our congregation who is in need of help. . .Mrs. Gudrun Norgaard. Her husband died last winter and lately she hasn't been very well herself. She really needs someone to live with her all the time." He paused.

Clara could hear the kettle hissing on the stove.

"I thought of you, Clara. Would you be willing to move into town and help take care of Mrs. Norgaard?"

Chapter 4

"Does she speak Norwegian?" Clara's voice squeaked on the last word.

Reverend Moen smiled and nodded. "Yes, and English and even some German. Her husband used to be the banker in town and, besides having an abundance of guests, they traveled."

"What will Clara be doing?" Nora asked. When she looked up from studying her coffee cup, the sheen of tears hovered in her eyes.

"She'll be companion, maid, and sometimes help the cook, who is also the housekeeper. Mrs. Norgaard has spent much of her time in bed lately, but the doctor feels someone young and lively will help her regain her strength." Reverend Moen smiled again at Clara. "I think our God provided the perfect person in you."

"But. . .but—" Clara clamped her lips together. *God, why?* she pleaded within her heart and mind. *This isn't what I thought You planned for me. I'm supposed to be getting married and. . .and.* She sent pleading looks to Nora, then Carl, and finally to Reverend Moen.

"How soon do you need to know her decision?" Nora sat up straight in her chair.

"Mrs. Norgaard needs someone immediately since Mrs. Hanson, the cook, has to go home to care for her mother for a time. That was one reason I thought of Clara. I. . .we. . . were hoping you could return to town with me. I'm sure Carl would bring the remainder of your things when they come to church on Sunday."

"Yes, of course." Carl nodded as he spoke. "Nora, you would help her to get ready?"

Just a minute, Clara wanted to pound her fist on the table and make the dishes rattle. *You're deciding my life. I want to make my own decisions.* She bit off the thoughts before they could become full-blown words.

Reverend Moen leaned his elbows on the table and tented his fingertips. The silence in the room was broken only by the mewing of the cat at the door to go out.

Clara knew what an animal in the circus must feel like with everyone staring at it. She scrubbed the front of her teeth with the tip of her tongue.

"I don't want Auntie Clara to leave. I needs her here with me." Kaaren slipped from her mother's lap and ran around the table to cling to Clara's skirt.

Clara bent over and laid her cheek on the little girl's head. "I won't be very far away and I'm sure Mrs. Norgaard would love to have you come visit." Clara felt her stomach drop down around her knees. The decision was made. She'd just said so. She gave Kaaren an extra hug and, planting her hands on the table, pushed herself to her feet. "I'll be ready whenever you need me to be."

"It's not like you'll be across the ocean or some such," Nora reminded them both as she helped Clara gather her things and pack them in the well-worn carpetbag.

"I know." Clara removed her gray Sunday dress from the nail on the wall.

"And maybe by living in town, your young man will find you more easily."

And maybe not, Clara thought as she looked around the room for anything she'd forgotten.

"Just think, you'll be closer to Ingeborge. Why, you could run over to see her anytime you'd like."

Clara hefted the bag and marched out the door. Why did she feel like the red caboose being towed along by the steaming engine whether it wanted to or not? She shook her head at the thought. She had made the final decision—hadn't she?

After one more neck-wrenching hug from Kaaren, Clara allowed Reverend Moen to assist her into his buggy. She waved good-bye as he guided the horse in a circle to turn the buggy around and trot out the lane. When her heart wanted to send a plea heavenward, she stopped it. Right now she didn't want to talk with Him. Miffed was the word that came to mind. Could one be miffed at God? She resolutely closed her ears to the sound of her mother's admonishing voice.

Clara could feel Reverend Moen watching her in between guiding the trotting horse. She let herself relax against the back of the seat as he began whistling. When she recognized the tune, she sneaked a peak at the man beside her. Yes, the courage of "Onward Christian Soldiers" was what she needed right now.

"Why are you worried?" His voice was gentle, like the sun warming her shoulders.

"I. . .I've never cared for someone who is sick before. Or who lives in a grand house." She took in a deep breath and let it out in a sigh.

"You'll do just fine or I wouldn't have asked."

Clara fingered the corner of her picture through the fabric of her bag. Did she dare ask him if he'd remembered who the picture reminded him of? If he'd remembered, wouldn't he have told her? And anyway, if the man hadn't come forward by now, did she really want to know him?

Clara rubbed the spot between her eyebrows where frown lines showed. Her mother said lines like that showed one didn't trust God with everything. But it's hard to trust when things aren't going the way you thought they should. Clara continued listening to the arguing and questioning in her mind.

The raucous call of a crow from a willow by the creek caught her attention. He didn't sound too happy with his life right now, either. He flew off, black wings glistening in the sun.

Up ahead, Clara could see the outskirts of Soldall. The lonely whistle from the westbound train floated back on the breeze. Smoke from the engine smudged the faded blue sky. Clara shivered as the late afternoon breeze warned them of the coming frost. Would she be lonely and cold like the crow and the train?

Reverend Moen turned his horse into the lane of a two-story

square house surrounded by pillared porches. A leaf from one of the two sentinel elm trees floated down as he pulled the animal to a halt amid a rustling of leaves already hiding the ground.

Clara stared at the windows, all curtained or draped. The place was big, like a palace, and beautiful with its white paint and dark shutters. But it certainly needed a bit of life; everything seemed so quiet.

"You ready?" Reverend Moen broke her concentration. "You know, if you really are unhappy here after trying it for a time, we'll find someone else."

Clara nodded. She took in a deep breath and let it out, while stretching her mouth into a smile. She clamped her teeth to stop the quiver in her chin. She squared her shoulders after Reverend Moen helped her alight. Maybe that way she'd feel more like one of those soldiers he'd been whistling about.

The woman who met them at the door must have been born smiling. "Come in, come in." She held open the dark oak door set with fancy cut glass. "I'm Mrs. Hanson and I know you're Clara. Reverend Moen, she's all you said she would be. You just come right on in here and. . ."

Clara felt like she'd been swamped by a wave of words and was being washed out to sea. At the same time, she caught her breath at the richness of the dark woods on the floor and walls, the carved stairs curving off to the left, and the fire crackling and snapping in the fireplace. A real fire, with wood, not the glow of coal.

"I thought a fire would make all of us feel better, so now you just sit down and make yourselves comfortable. Mrs. Norgaard, bless her heart, is taking a nap, she sleeps so poorly at night you know, and she told me to make you feel right to home. Now I have the coffee almost ready and after Reverend Moen brings the rest of your things in, we'll just have a bite."

Clara nodded and did just what she was told. She didn't have to worry about what to say because the woman never took a breath. She felt a bubble of laughter rising like warm yeast down about her middle. All her worry and fears of the housekeeper's not liking her, all gone to waste.

179

And after she met Mrs. Norgaard, Clara's remaining fears took off like the crow they'd seen on the drive in. Even propped by pillows, the frail woman lay dwarfed by the carved, four-poster bed. A lace-trimmed cap covered yellowed gray hair and her eyes mirrored the sorrow she'd lived. The smile that nearly appeared flitted away before it could dimple the sunken cheeks.

"Thank you for coming so quickly."

Clara had to bend close to hear the words. "You are welcome. I hope that I can be of help to you."

"Mrs. Hanson has to leave in the morning, so she'll show you where everything is."

Clara nodded.

Reverend Moen stepped up to the side of the bed. "I must be going now. I'll stop by tomorrow or Ingeborge will."

"Thank you." She sank back against her pillows as if the brief exchange had been too much.

Clara followed the reverend out the door. "Is she really so sick?"

"At heart. And when the heart is heavy, the body gets too tired to continue. She feels she has nothing left to live for and that she'd rather join her husband in heaven."

"But. . .but, how can I help her?"

"Ask our heavenly Father, He'll tell you." Reverend Moen settled his hat back on his head. "Bless you." And with that he shut the door behind himself and went whistling down the walk.

The tune stayed in her mind. But who said she wanted to be a soldier anyway?

Clara trailed her fingers up the splendidly polished banister as she climbed the stairs. Her room was just across the hall from Mrs. Norgaard's, and she paused at the door before turning back to check on her new charge. She tapped lightly and entered the dim room.

The first thing I'd like to do, she thought, *is open those draperies and let the sun shine in. And get her sitting up in the chair in front of the window so she can watch the glorious leaves drifting down.* Did they have squirrels in North Dakota? Surely they must.

"Is there anything I can get for you?" she asked gently.

"No, no thank you."

Clara waited by the bed. The silence matched the dimness of hue.

"You can go settle into your room. I'd like to sleep again."

Clara struggled with the faint order. She'd been hired to care for this poor sick woman. *God, what do You want me to do? How can I help her the best?* She waited, hoping against hope that God wouldn't mess this one up like He had her marrying the young man in the picture.

Instead of God's voice, she heard her mother's. "A merry heart doeth good like a medicine." Clara knew it was a quote from somewhere in the Scriptures, probably Proverbs. How was that supposed to help her?

"I will lift up mine eyes unto the hills, from whence cometh my help." Well, so much for that one, Psalm 121. The last hills she'd seen were just out of New York. Her mind's eye flitted to the mountains of Norway, the glistening peaks, and the granite faces. The wind singing through the pine trees. Now, those were hills worthy of lifting up one's eyes.

"Are you still here?" The faint voice was painted in querulous tones now.

"Yes, ma'am."

"What are you doing?"

"Praying, I think."

"Well, pray then that I may go home soon."

Clara thought of the hills and the strength they always gave her. "No, I think not." She turned around and strode to the tall windows, draped in a dusky rose velvet. With determined hands she pushed back the heavy lengths of fabric and then the sheer cream panels, tying both back with the cords at the sides. After checking the latches, she bent over and pulled up the sash.

"What are you doing? Young woman, ah. . ."

"The name is Clara, Clara Johanson, and I'm letting in what little is left of today's sun and fresh air."

"I. . .I'll freeze. It's November, you know." The voice sounded stronger already.

"Now, why don't I help you over here so you can see out? And while you sit in the chair here, I'll straighten your bed and—"

"No, this is the height of foolishness. I'm ringing for Mrs. Hanson and she'll tell you what I can and cannot do." Mrs. Norgaard leaned over and pulled on a cord beside her bed.

"Good, then she'll help me help you." Clara closed the window again and strode back to the bed. "Why don't we have her bring a tray with coffee and cookies on it at the same time. How do we go about telling her what we want?"

Mrs. Norgaard flopped back against her pillows, her hand pressed to her chest. "We want?" The words ended on a squeak.

"Mrs. Norgaard!" Mrs. Hanson stopped in the doorway. She stared from the windows to Clara and then to the woman in the bed. A smile started, immediately hidden by the clenching of her lips. Her eyes refused to match her mouth and, instead, danced with delight.

"We'd like coffee and maybe something sweet, if you have it." Clara clamped her hands together. Was she understanding Mrs. Hanson right? "But if you could help me move Mrs. Norgaard to the chair first?" She nodded at the dainty upholstered chair by the low table. "We'll turn the chairs so we can watch the trees and the sunset." Clara suited her actions to her words.

"That sounds wonderful." Mrs. Hanson bent over the bed. "Up we go, my dear."

"But, but, I. . .I—" Mrs. Norgaard found herself ensconced in the chair with a blanket over her knees and a shawl around her shoulders before she could so much as fluster.

"A tray will be right up." Mrs. Hanson left the room with a wink to Clara.

"I am so grateful you speak Norwegian," Clara said as she straightened the blanket and tucked it around Mrs. Norgaard's feet. "Now, is there anything I can get for you before I make up the bed?"

The little woman shook her head, her chin set at a pugnacious angle. The lace on her cap fluttered in the motion.

Lord, I sure hope I'm doing the right thing, Clara thought as she pulled off the covers and stripped off the sheets. Only the sounds of her actions rustled the silence of the room. The thought of Reverend Moen's whistling made her smile. What would happen if she began whistling? She knew how. Even though well-brought-up young ladies did not whistle. She sighed. Whistling was out for now.

But the tune wasn't. Her mind fit the words with the melody. "Onward Christian soldiers, marching as to war. . ." Was this really a war going on here? She shook her head. No, only a skirmish—and she knew who the winner would be.

"Where do you keep the clean sheets?"

"In the linen closet. You'll find it on your left in the hall." Mrs. Norgaard shifted in her chair. "Before you do that, could you please bring me that footstool? If it would be no trouble."

Clara did as asked and tucked in the blanket again. "I'll be quick."

"No hurry, I. . .ah, see the sun through the reds and golds of the tree leaves." She snapped her mouth shut as if afraid she'd said too much.

Clara put a clamp on her grin and hurried to finish her chore.

While the coffee time passed quickly, it wasn't because of the inspiring conversation. Mrs. Hanson joined them and, unlike her voluble self of the earlier hours, said very little. Her bright eyes missed nothing however, and her nod clearly expressed approval.

Mrs. Norgaard sipped her coffee and, after taking two bites of cake, crumbled the sliver of pound cake into her napkin. When she leaned her head against the back of her chair and let her eyes droop closed, Clara took pity on her.

"Here, ma'am, let's put you back to bed." She set the cup and saucer on the tray and clasped the older woman's delicate hands. Together, she and Mrs. Hanson helped Mrs. Norgaard back to bed.

She sighed as the covers were smoothed over her. "That did feel good. Thank you."

"I'll let you rest now. Dinner won't be for another hour or so."

Mrs. Hanson paused at the doorway. "Would you like yours up here on a tray, too, or would you come down?"

Clara shrugged in consternation. "What is best?"

"We have much to go over."

"Ja, that is right."

A deep sigh came from the vicinity of the bed.

The two women looked at each other, over at the bed, and then, covering their mouths with their hands, tiptoed out.

"Come down as soon as you've settled yourself in your room." Mrs. Hanson patted Clara's arm. "You'll do real well with her."

Clara opened the door to her room and immediately crossed to the windows to open the draperies. Why did everyone like it so dark in this house? She stood at the window, gazing at the long yard fronted by the street. Two young girls walked by, swinging empty lard pails that had contained their lunch. The sun was slipping downward as if in a hurry to get to bed.

Clara turned from the window and surveyed her new home. A canopied bed piled high with lace pillows and a crocheted spread took her breath away. Never had she slept in anything so grand. A lace-skirted dressing table with a triple mirror reflected the fading sunlight, and, on the opposite wall, a tall armoire stood open to receive her few clothes. Clara sank down on the edge of the bed. All this for her?

She traced the intricate pattern in the spread with one finger. The rose-colored coverlet underneath set the design off to perfection. She glanced up to catch her reflection in the mirror. Was that really Clara Johanson she saw and not some young woman born to all this wealth and beauty? She felt like pinching herself to make sure she wasn't dreaming.

"Speaking of dreaming, girl, you need to go downstairs and learn all you can before tomorrow, when this house and that woman in there all become your responsibility." She spoke sternly, but the girl in the mirror couldn't resist a wink.

By the time she returned to the haven of her room, she'd followed Mrs. Hanson through the entire house, learned where all the food was stored, how to stoke the cellar furnace with coal, the location of all the cleaning supplies, and tried to memorize a list of all Mrs. Norgaard's likes and dislikes. The recipe books were all in English, as were the books in the library. She needn't worry about the laundry or the deep cleaning because Mrs. Hanson expected to be back in a week or two at the most.

"Just keep doing what you started," Mrs. Hanson said as she puffed her way back up the stairs. "I've settled her for the night and she has a bell by her bed to call you with since the bell pull only rings downstairs. If you need anything fixed, we always ask Dag, the blacksmith, and anything else, Reverend Moen will help." She put a finger to her bottom lip. "I can't think of anything else—oh, the doctor is two streets over and one back. We have an account at Lars Mercantile for groceries and what else."

Clara felt like her head was spinning. What in the world had she gotten herself into—correction—what had she been gotten into?

"I'll be leaving right after breakfast, so you get a good night's sleep now." Mrs. Hanson opened the door to Clara's room and, after lighting the lamp by the door, stepped back. "Good night, my dear, and God bless."

"And you." Clara staggered across the room and collapsed on her bed. No wonder people with grand big houses hired others to work for them. The thought of all the dusting to be done made her shudder. She hefted her carpetbag onto the bed and removed her few garments, hanging some in the armoire and laying others in the drawers. She placed her Bible on the stand by her bed next to the lamp and her brushes on the dressing table. By the time she changed into a flannel nightgown and brushed her hair one hundred strokes, she could feel her eyelids drooping. She sank to her knees and leaned her elbows on the spread.

"Father in heaven," she paused, waiting for the right words to come. "Thank You for this day." She paused again. "I guess." She shook her head, her thumbs rubbing into her eyes. "Mor says to thank You for everything and while that doesn't seem to make much sense to me, I know Your word says that also. So thank You for Mrs. Norgaard and my new home and position in this beautiful house." She huffed out her breath. "And thank You that we haven't found my young man yet." She shook her head again. "Forgive me for not being very thankful. Amen." She started to rise and sank back down. "Amen—again."

She blew out the lamp and climbed under the covers. Hands crossed on her chest, she stared at the canopy over her head. She thought back to the way she'd taken over in Mrs. Norgaard's room, ordering her around like that. *Clara, I can't believe that was you,* she told herself. Maybe God had a hand in it after all. She fell asleep with that thought in her mind.

A jangling snatched her back from the deep well of sleep.

Chapter 5

Where was she? The jangling came again. Clara sat up in bed and threw back the covers. Mrs. Norgaard—the bell—was something wrong? She fumbled for the flint to light the candle then slid her feet into waiting slippers. Light in hand, she crossed the room and opened her door. The bell came again.

"Mrs. Norgaard, are you all right?" She knocked and opened the door almost in the same motion. Moonlight streamed in the windows, painting branch shadows on the floor.

"Please, I have to use the chamber pot. I'm afraid I might fall."

"Yes, of course." Clara set the candle and holder down on the table beside the bed, along with the weight of fear she'd shouldered with the bell jangle. Such a simple task and yet so important.

After she had Mrs. Norgaard tucked back in bed, Clara clasped the hand that lay on top of the coverlet. Gently she stroked the papery skin that stretched over bones so light as to be air-filled. "Is there anything else I can do for you?"

"You might sing again. You have a lovely voice—so long since there's been any singing in this house." The words came slowly as if with great effort.

Clara closed her eyes and began to sing, "Beautiful Savior, King of creation, Son of God and Son of man. . ." When she finished the second verse, she picked up her candle and, leaving the door open a crack, made her way back to her own room. With both doors open, she would hear the summons more quickly.

This time when she crawled back into the bed, she, too, felt blessed by the music. She thought of all the years her Mor had

187

sung her children to sleep just like this. Who'd have thought these songs of her childhood would play an important part in her life now?

By the time Mrs. Hanson left for her train in the morning, Clara was feeling like the train had run over her, or at least dragged her down the track. Mrs. Norgaard showed her restlessness by ringing her bell or pulling the cord every few minutes with something she either needed or wanted to tell Mrs. Hanson. The stairs were looking higher and higher with each trip.

"This is a good thing." Mrs. Hanson nodded up the stairs just before she left the house. "Herself is at least taking an interest in life again." She patted Clara's cheek. "I knew the minute I saw you, you'd be just what she needed. Now remember, I'll be back for the laundry and such. You spend as much time with Mrs. Norgaard as she allows." Her eyes twinkled. "Rather as much as you can talk her into."

Clara nodded. "I hope your mother will be well soon." She waved and then leaned her back against the door after closing it. "Because I wish you were back here already."

The bell tinkled from the second door on the right—upstairs.

"Coming." Clara checked her appearance in the long mirror over a carved walnut table in the hall. She smoothed one side back and reset the comb that held her wavy golden hair up and off her face. After fluffing the tendrils of hair that insisted on curling over her forehead and wrinkling her nose at the image in the mirror, she trotted up the stairs.

"Ma'am." Clara stepped to the side of the bed.

Mrs. Norgaard opened her eyes as if the effort were beyond her strength. "Is Mrs. Hanson on her way?"

"Ja and none too soon. It is a good thing we are not too far from the station."

"Could you help me sit up against my pillows?"

"I can do better than that." Clara crossed the room and picked up the oval-backed chair to bring it back by the bed. "Let's get you up in this while I freshen your bed. You must have a wrapper around here somewhere." She checked all the usual places—foot of the bed, coat tree, under the covers—and finally stepped to the carved walnut armoire and opened the doors.

The scent of lavender wafted out. Clara sniffed appreciatively and studied the garments hanging in front of her. Morning dresses, shirtwaists, bombazine skirts, all in rich fabrics and jewel colors. She reached out to stroke the sleeve of a sable fur jacket. Such luxury. Resisting the urge to lay her cheek against the sleek garment, she turned instead to the hooks on the door. Both shawl and wool robe hung there, plain hens among peacocks.

"Here, now." She carried the robe to the bed and smiled down at her charge. "Once you are sitting up, I could brush your hair for you. That was always a treat for me, when my older sister would brush my hair."

Mrs. Norgaard nodded and eased over to the side of the bed. Clara helped her sit upright and snuggled the robe around the thin shoulders. Once situated in the chair, the woman sat up straight, obeying the dictates of a lifetime.

Clara picked up the hairbrush from the dressing table and, after removing the cap and pins, began drawing it through the limp strands. She smiled when she heard a sigh of appreciation. "That does feel good, doesn't it?" She continued the long, even strokes. "Perhaps tomorrow I could wash it for you. Mrs. Hanson said you were about due for a bath. Think how wonderful soaking in the tub would feel." She leaned forward to peek around the woman's shoulder. Mrs. Norgaard's eyes were closed but a slight smile hovered at the corners of her mouth.

Clara felt like she'd just been given a gift. *In for a penny, in for a pound*, she thought, quoting one of her mother's often-used maxims. "I know you've had a great sorrow in your life. Tell me about your husband, Mr. Norgaard. What was he like? How did you meet?"

Clara waited. Maybe she should have kept her mouth shut? *God, please keep me from saying or doing the wrong things. I so want to help.*

"He was such a handsome young man, my Einer. I lived in Minneapolis with my parents and this young man came to work at the bank there. My father owned a store and he frequently sent me to the bank for him since I helped him with the accounts and behind the counter when he needed me."

Clara kept up the soothing motions. "So you met him at the bank?"

"No, I saw him at the bank. But we weren't introduced until church one Sunday." She chuckled softly. "Back then one didn't have the freedom of young folks now. We had to be properly introduced by an outside party. I think he bribed the pastor to introduce us." Only the risp of the brush and gentle breathing disturbed the silence.

"Such a smile he had." She shook her head. "And he was trying to be so proper, to impress my mother and father, you know. They stayed right on either side of me." She tipped her head back so Clara could reach the brow more easily. "Penny novels talked of love at first sight, but I thought they were making that up—until Einer spoke to me." Silence fell again.

Clara peeked around to catch the sight of fat tears rolling down her charge's sunken cheeks. She fashioned the gray strands into a bun and pinned it high on the back of Mrs. Norgaard's head. Then, after placing the brush on the dressing table, she knelt in front of the older woman and covered the trembling thin hands with the warmth of her own.

The tears flowed unchecked. Mrs. Norgaard sat upright, as if her back touching the chair were a mortal sin. Her body remained perfectly still, except for the quivering hands and the coursing tears.

Clara felt like her heart was being torn from her chest. Tears burned at the back of her throat and behind her eyes. *Lord God, have mercy on her. Bring healing for her grief.* She reached into her pocket for a clean handkerchief and gently wiped the tears away.

The clock on the tall dresser struck the hour, eleven chimes. Clara found herself counting them, as if at the end there might be some incident of great import. The last bong faded away.

"I believe I'd like to return to my bed now." Mrs. Norgaard pushed herself upright using the arms of the chair, placed her hand on Clara's arm, and crossed to the bed. Once under the covers, she patted the sides of her hair. "Thank you, child. You were right; that did indeed feel good."

After Clara left the room she wasn't sure if Mrs. Norgaard meant the hair brushing felt good or maybe the talking—and the tears? She hummed the refrain of "Onward Christian Soldiers" all the way down the stairs and into the spotless kitchen. Soon, the whistling teakettle accompanied her.

"What we need in this house is some music," she told the pink geranium hanging in the kitchen window. A black-capped chickadee landed on the tray attached outside the window where Mrs. Hanson left crumbs for the birds. "That's it." Clara spun in place. "A bird to sing. One of those golden canaries like my aunt had. I wonder where you would find one clear out here on the prairie?"

She thought about it as she sliced the bread to toast for dinner. Mrs. Hanson had made a pot of chicken soup before she left, and now it was warming on the monstrous iron stove.

"I'll just have to ask Ingeborge when I can go see her. Nora said Ingeborge knows everything and everyone in Soldall." She cocked her head at the flower in the window. "I think you better learn to talk or, better yet, sing, because if someone comes they will think I am surely losing my mind." The geranium wisely kept silent.

The peal of the doorbell brought Clara rushing downstairs again; she had just taken Mrs. Norgaard her dinner. By the time she reached the door, the thing clanged again.

"*Uff da,*" she muttered. "I'm coming." She reached to open the door. A man, face showing florid around a mustache more salt than pepper, all topped by a mashed down fedora, touted a black bag that gave away his identity without a word. "Doctor?"

"Yes, I'm Dr. Harmon." He took off his hat as he stepped across the threshold. "Mrs. Norgaard asleep?"

"No, I just took her dinner up to her." Clara moved back to give the portly man room to enter the hall. "May I take your coat?" She shut the door and, after helping him remove his black wool coat, hung it on the brass tree next to the hall table.

"Good, then I can talk with you first." He walked into the parlor like he'd been here many times before.

"Ah, would you like some coffee?" At his nod, she added, "And have you eaten? I could bring you some chicken soup."

"That sounds wonderful." Instead of sitting in the parlor, he followed her into the kitchen. "Why don't I join you in here? Make it easier for all." Just then the bell pull sounded. "Ah, herself is callin' you. She wants to know who's here, no doubt. You run up and I'll just pour myself a cup of coffee and make myself to home." He suited his actions to his words and pulled out a chair at the round oak table in the corner.

Clara darted a look over her shoulder to make sure he was all right and climbed the stairs. She made a point of not counting how many times she'd been up and down them already today.

"You've hardly touched your soup," Clara said before her patient could respond. "And here it was nice and hot. Mayhap I should bring you another bowl."

Mrs. Norgaard shook her head. "No, I had a bit. Now, who is it that came? I thought I heard Dr. Harmon's voice."

"That's right. He's going to eat downstairs first, then he'll be up. Or—" Eyes narrowed, Clara studied her patient. "Or, he can eat up here with you." She spun out the door. "I'll be right back." She descended the stairs in a swirl of skirts and indecision. Should she take charge here or not? Would the company make Mrs. Norgaard eat better, maybe smile? Let's see, they could move that table from over by the window and put it up against the bed. Then chairs for her and the doctor.

She smacked one fist into the palm of the other hand. She would turn this into a party yet.

Doc Harmon beamed at her, all the while nodding his head while she shared her plan. Together they set two trays with soup in a rose-sprigged tureen, coffee in a silver server, and buttered toast nestled by a pot of jam. Clara included a plate of sour cream sugar cookies for dessert. Like two conspirators in a crime, they set out.

"Good day, Mrs. Norgaard. We've come to share our dinner with you." He set his tray on the dressing table and crossed the room to bring the round table to the bed. "Now, would you rather have a chair or dangle your feet over the edge of the bed. Clara says you've already been up for a while this morning."

Mrs. Norgaard could hardly get a squeak in edgewise.

Just as they had the furniture all rearranged and Mrs. Norgaard moved to her chair, the doorbell pealed again. Clara dashed down the stairs and pulled up at the door, feeling like she was flying apart.

"Reverend Moen." She stepped back and motioned him inside.

"Good day, Clara. How is Mrs. Norgaard today?"

"Would you like to come up and join us for coffee? Or soup? Dr. Harmon and I were just about to eat."

"Coffee, yeh, soup, *nei takk*," he said as he hung up his coat.

"You go on up. I'll get another cup." Clara dashed off to the kitchen. Talk about having a party.

When she got upstairs, Dr. Harmon had settled his patient in her chair, pulled up two more, and dished up the soup. Clara finished pouring the coffee and asked Reverend Moen to say grace. As the familiar words flowed forth, Clara could feel herself back home in Norway with her family gathered around the dinner table.

At the "Amen," she looked up to see Mrs. Norgaard reach up with a tentative hand to smooth her already sleek hair.

I'm glad I did her hair this morning, Clara thought. *No woman likes to have company when she feels a sight.*

It was quickly obvious that the two men were good friends who liked to give each other a bad time. And as Clara suspected, her patient forgot her lack of hunger and downed both soup and toast.

By the end of the meal, Clara knew all the latest news of Soldall. A young boy had fallen out of a tree at recess over at the school and sprained his wrist. His mother threatened to break his arm if he didn't stay out of trees. Doc had agreed with her.

"That young whippersnapper is an accident waiting to happen, not waiting as the case may be." The doctor snorted after telling his story. "He can get into more mischief."

"Isn't he the one who put a mouse in the new teacher's desk drawer?" Reverend Moen asked.

The doctor nodded. "And the frog in the water pail."

Clara squeezed her lips together. It sounded like they were describing her younger brother. Mor had been afraid Lars wouldn't make it to manhood.

"Well, I must be on my way," Dr. Harmon finally said after pulling out his pocket watch and checking the time. "This has been most enjoyable, Mrs. Norgaard. Thank you for your hospitality. How about if I check you over before I leave?"

"And I, too, must be going. Good day, Mrs. Norgaard." Reverend Moen patted her hand. "This has been a real pleasure."

"Thank you for coming." Mrs. Norgaard let the men assist her to her feet and back to the edge of the bed. "Perhaps next time you come, you could bring your daughter, Mary."

"I'll do that. Clara, here, let me help you take these things downstairs." He picked up the larger of the trays and waited while Clara added the bowls and cups to it. Together, they took the trays back to the kitchen.

"Do you need anything?" the reverend asked as he placed his tray on the kitchen table.

Clara shook her head. "No, wait, I mean yes. Do you know anyone who has a canary?"

"A canary?"

"Yes, for sale." Clara set her tray down. "You see, it is so quiet here, not a sound, so I thought the bird would sing and make Mrs. Norgaard feel happier."

"True." Reverend Moen rubbed the bridge of his nose in the gesture that Clara already knew meant he was thinking. "I'll ask Ingeborge." He walked down the front stairs still chuckling about her wanting a yellow bird to sing.

"I think that's a good idea," Dr. Harmon said when Clara asked him about the canary. "Might be just what the doctor ordered—if he'd thought of it." He shrugged into the coat Clara held for him. "Now don't you worry so much about the house and spend your time with her. I'll see you again in a day or so."

194

Clara leaned against the door after they'd left. She could feel the silence settling back down on the house. The bell tinkled from upstairs.

The next morning she talked Mrs. Norgaard into a bath and hair washing. Each time Clara helped her charge, she asked about Mr. Norgaard and each time Mrs. Norgaard shared a bit more. And each time the tears flowed.

One night after she'd helped Mrs. Norgaard to bed, Clara sat on the edge of the mattress to say good night.

"Don't go." The old woman clutched the hand of the younger. The silence settled around them, close and comforting this time, as if in benediction.

"This is the hardest time," Mrs. Norgaard spoke from the dimness. "When the lights are out and all my memories crowd in, piling on top of each other, pushing and shoving until I can't sleep, can't rest." The silence reigned again. "And when I feel so guilty."

"Guilty?"

"Yes, I should have been able to help him more. If only I'd made him stay home and go to bed when he first felt ill." Clara waited. "And if I'd thrown out those awful, smelly cigars, maybe he wouldn't have had a cough to start with." Her voice floated on the stillness, like a leaf kissing the surface of a pond.

Clara stroked the papery hand that lay in hers. *Father,* she prayed while she waited for the voice to come again, *please bring healing to Mrs. Norgaard. Help her to give up the bad feelings. Help her to want to live.* The thoughts seemed to drift heavenward, like smoke rising from a chimney on a still, winter day.

"Einer insisted on going out to that farm with Dr. Harmon. So many people were sick that the well ones did what they could, chores and such. I was helping Mrs. Moen. She collected extra children and housed them until their parents could care for them again. Ah, me. Maybe I was the one who brought the sickness home." Silence again. "We'll never know."

Clara could hear the tears begin to drown out the woman's voice.

"But he was so sick. I was right here beside him. He'd been

tossing and turning and finally settled down. I. . .I thought he was finally resting, so I dozed off myself. When I woke up. . ."

Clara squeezed her eyes closed, but the tears refused to be swallowed.

"When I woke. . .he was gone." Deep sobs, the kind that come after being forced back too long, shuddered through her frame, shaking the bed.

Clara gathered the straining body into her arms and held her. What could she say, even if she could talk around the tears that rained down her own cheeks?

Mrs. Norgaard reached for the edge of the sheet to wipe her eyes. "I never—" she choked on the words, "I never said good-bye. He was gone and I never said good-bye. Did he know how much I loved him?"

Sobs interrupted her words, making them difficult to understand, but Clara murmured soothing noises, whispering the litany of love she'd learned at her mother's knee.

Eventually, hiccups punctuated the silence, and Clara placed a handkerchief in Mrs. Norgaard's hand. After blowing her nose, the now-spent woman lay back on her pillows. She put her hand back in Clara's. "I'm sorry to get you so wet."

"I'll dry."

"Do you think God will forgive me?"

"For what?"

"For being so angry at Him for taking my Einer." She paused. "For wanting to die."

"All you have to do is ask. Mor says He forgives even before we ask, that's what sending His Son to die for us meant. Forgiveness and love that never dies."

"Your mother is a wise woman." Mrs. Norgaard blew her nose again. Her sigh snagged on a leftover sob.

Clara could feel the yawn that caught Mrs. Norgaard and then sneaked up on Clara. She covered her mouth with her hand but still felt the hinges in her jaw creak with the strain.

"Thank you, my dear." Mrs. Norgaard breathed deeply and patted Clara's hand. "You go on to bed now; I'll be just fine." She yawned again. "In fact, I'm almost asleep already."

"I can sit here for a while. There's no hurry."

Clara was about to rise from the bed, thinking her charge almost asleep, when Mrs. Norgaard said with a catch in her voice, "Would you. . .do you know the Twenty-third Psalm?"

"Ja, I do. We memorized that in Sunday school when we were small."

"Would you say it for me?"

Clara closed her eyes and thought of the shepherd with his flock. "The Lord is my shepherd; I shall not want. He maketh me to lie down in green pastures; he leadeth me beside the still waters. . ." Her voice caught in the part about the valley but grew stronger again as she came to, "And I will dwell in the house of the Lord for ever."

"Amen."

"Ja, Amen." Clara nodded. When she rose a few minutes later, Mrs. Norgaard was breathing the soft and even rhythm of healing sleep.

"Thank You, thank You, thank You." Gratitude poured forth as Clara blew out the lamps and undressed for bed. Even while her mind sang the praises, her body felt like a garment with all the starch washed out. She was asleep almost before her head touched the pillow.

When Clara walked into Mrs. Norgaard's room with the coffee tray in the morning, Mrs. Norgaard was sitting up against her pillows.

"I want you to go over to Reverend Moen's this morning and ask him to come here." Even her voice was stronger. "Tell him I'm ready now."

Whatever for? Clara wondered, but she only nodded, a smile tickling the corners of her mouth.

Chapter 6

She had a feeling this was more like the real Mrs. Norgaard.

The doorbell rang before Clara could finish her duties and get out the door. She answered the chimes, still wiping her hands on her apron.

"Good morning, Clara." Doc Harmon tipped his hat with one hand, the other carrying his black leather bag. "How is our patient this morning?"

"Better, I think." Clara stepped back and motioned him in. "She wants me to go for Reverend Moen."

"Whatever for?" Doc laid his hat on the hall table and brushed a hand over his steel gray hair.

Clara shrugged. "Maybe if you ask her, she'll tell you."

"And maybe she won't. The won't is much more likely." Doc started up the stairs. "Do you by any chance have the coffee hot? I've been out delivering a baby north of town and I could use a pick-me-up."

"Ja, I do. There's bread and some cheese if you'd like." She waited with her hand on the carved ball of the walnut newel post.

"Fine. And after you've brought it up, you can run over to the reverend's. I'll stay and visit that few minutes."

Clara did as asked and, within a few minutes, darted out the front door. It was the first time she'd been out since Reverend Moen brought her here. She drew in a deep breath of air redolent of burning leaves and crisp fall weather. As she kicked her way through the leaves blanketing the ground she looked up through the naked tree branches stretching to the lemony sun in the watery blue sky. If the weather patterns were the same here as in Norway, it felt like a storm hovering on the horizon.

She turned to the left and walked briskly down the packed dirt street. She passed the houses, playing the *I wonder who lives there* game that she and Nora used to play on their way to school. But in Norway it was *I wonder what they're doing there,* since they knew all the inhabitants of their small village.

It was different here. Clara refused to allow the worm of homesickness to dig its way into her beautiful day. She thought back to the night before instead. "The Lord is my shepherd. . . ," she sang the song, the ancient words set to a tune they'd learned in Sunday school. Why was it she always felt better when she began singing? How much easier it was to remember Bible verses when they'd been set to music.

She sang her way up a cross street and down the main street until she saw the white picket fence of the Moen home. When she knocked on the door, the reverend himself answered it, his shirt sleeves rolled up to his elbows.

"Clara, how wonderful to see you. Come in, come in." He stepped back, opening the door wide in welcome.

"What brings you to our house? Ingeborge, we've company."

Clara stopped inside the door. "I can't stay but a minute. Dr. Harmon is with Mrs. Norgaard so I could do what she asked."

"And what is that?"

"She said for you to come now, she was. . .is ready." Clara recited the words, hoping the man in front of her would understand the meaning.

"That's all?" He rubbed the bridge of his nose with one finger, his right hand tucked under his left elbow.

Clara nodded.

"Oh, I'm so glad you are here. Sit down, sit down. John, you haven't taken her coat yet. What is this world coming to?" Ingeborge whirled down the last of the stairs and enveloped Clara in a hug that left no doubt as to her joy. She leaned back and studied the younger woman's face. "You look like caring for Mrs. Norgaard is agreeing with you."

"Ja, it is. Such a beautiful place." Clara patted Grace on the head and squatted down to say hello to little James. "But I must get back."

"The coffee will be ready in a minute."

"Another time, *mange takk*. Reverend, you will be coming?"

Ingeborge looked from one to the other, her eyes bright and dimples ready to leap into view with the least encouragement. "Is Mrs. Norgaard feeling up to visitors?"

"She asked for Reverend Moen."

"She isn't worse, is she?" The dimples dove into hiding.

"*Nei, nei.* I think she's better."

Reverend Moen rolled down his sleeves preparatory to putting on his coat even as they talked. "I shouldn't be long." He removed his hat from the hall stand and, putting it on, went out the door, only to return. "Would you rather stay a few minutes to visit or walk with me?"

"Oh, stay," Ingeborge pleaded.

Clara felt like a length of cloth being pulled at both ends. Duty won over and she smiled her apology. "Another time. Perhaps you and the children could come to call soon. That house is so silent. It needs the sound of children laughing."

"We will." Ingeborge patted Clara's arm. "I'm happy that you like it there. I'm sure Mrs. Hanson is grateful she needn't worry about her charge."

"*Farvel,*" Clara said as she waved good-bye from the steps. She trotted after Reverend Moen, who waited for her at the gate. Halfway down the walk, Clara spun around and darted back to the porch. "Do you know anyone who might have a canary for sale? I think the bird's song would cheer Mrs. Norgaard up. And it would make some music in that still house."

Ingeborge shook her head, her brow wrinkling in thought. "Not now, but I'll ask around. That's a wonderful idea. *Farvel.*" She stood in the doorway, waving until they were up the street.

Reverend Moen set a brisk pace and Clara found herself trotting to keep up with his long strides. When they arrived back at the Norgaard place, they met Dr. Harmon just coming down the stairs.

"I don't know what you've done, my dear, but keep it up, whatever it is." He shrugged into his coat and picked up his hat. "I'll check back in a couple of days. Now, Reverend, don't go messing with my patient."

Clara could tell he was playing by the twinkle in his eye.

"She's on the mend so you can't have her yet," the doctor teased.

"And I'm sure you think your medicine did the trick?" Reverend Moen tried to look serious and failed utterly.

"What else?" The doctor chuckled as he strode out the door, waving, one hand behind him.

"You go on up," Reverend Moen said. Clara took his coat at the same time she heard the summoning bell from upstairs.

"I'll be right back." He grabbed his coat and slipped out the door, hitting the ground running. He turned and jogged backwards. "Don't worry," he called back. "It's good news."

Clara shook her head as she climbed the stairs. What a strange day this was turning out to be.

"Just put the tray over there." Mrs. Norgaard pointed to the table in front of the windows. "We'll wait for Reverend Moen and serve then. Do you think you could brush my hair before he gets back?"

Clara set the tray down and turned to find Mrs. Norgaard sitting on the edge of her bed, slipping her arms into the sleeves of her robe. Clara paused to see what her patient would do next. Mrs. Norgaard belted and tied the sash then looked up.

"Could you please help me to the chair? I know it's easier for you when I'm there." She took Clara's arm and raised herself to her feet. Clara waited while Mrs. Norgaard swayed a bit and then steadied herself. "I'm weak as a kitten." The tone was colored in exasperation.

Clara felt like singing as she brushed the long, gray tresses. What could have brought on the change? Their talk last night? The tears? Her prayers? Probably a combination of all three but whatever—Clara gave God all the glory. Her whispers of "Thank You, thank You" played counterpoint to the melody.

When Reverend Moen returned a few minutes later, he

carried a small leather case along with his Bible. Reverently, he removed an embroidered stole and placed it around his neck. Then he set out his communion supplies.

So that's what she was ready for. Clara tucked the last pin in the coil of hair on the back of Mrs. Norgaard's head.

"I'd like the chairs over by the window, if you please." Mrs. Norgaard looked up at Clara. "Thank you, my dear. That felt wonderful. I believe you have the gift of healing in those hands of yours."

Clara held her hands out in front of her, turning them over and back. Could that be? They looked just like her hands had all her life. No different. She shook her head.

"Here, let me help you while Reverend Moen moves the chairs." After seating Mrs. Norgaard, Clara turned to leave the room.

"No, please stay. I'll feel more like we're in church if it isn't just me." Mrs. Norgaard clutched Clara's hand.

Clara nodded.

But I'm not prepared, she thought. *I haven't time to review my sins. When was the last time I received communion? So long ago.* Clara took one of the chairs and folded her hands in her lap. She breathed deeply, letting all the air out till her shoulders slumped. She closed her eyes.

Reverend Moen began reading. "From chapter one of First John. 'That which was from the beginning. . .God is light and in him is no darkness. . .But if we walk in the light, as he is in the light. . .If we say that we have no sin, we deceive ourselves. . .If we confess our sin, he is faithful and just to forgive us our sins and to cleanse us from all unrighteousness.' Let us be quiet now and confess those sins that stand between us and Him."

Clara thought back over the last weeks. *I confess that I doubted You,* she thought. *I know I have not always come to You first but tried to do things on my own. I doubted that You have a plan for my life and I resented not meeting the man in my picture.* She continued thinking about the things she had done wrong. *Father, forgive me,* she prayed. *I don't want anything to stand between us.*

Reverend Moen flipped to Matthew, chapter twenty-six, in

his Bible and began again, this time with the Last Supper.

At Jesus' words, Clara could feel the tears clogging the back of her throat. "This is my body. . .this is my blood of the new testament, which is shed for many for the remission of sins." When she had finished the communion, she wiped the flowing tears away with the corner of her apron.

Mrs. Norgaard reached over and borrowed the other corner. She sniffed and wiped her tears again with the backs of her fingers. The sigh seemed to come from the depths of a soul released from bondage and now ready to walk in the fullness of God's light and freedom.

"Now remember those words, He not only forgives but cleanses us." Reverend Moen closed his Bible and made the sign of the cross. "The Lord bless you and keep you. The Lord lift up His countenance upon you and give you His peace. Amen."

"Amen." The two women chimed together.

A chorus of angel choirs could not have been richer than the quiet that filled the room and made its home in her heart. Clara recognized peace when she felt it.

Time passed but no one disturbed it until Mrs. Norgaard sighed deeply and raised her head. "Thank you, Reverend Moen. I believe I can go on now. I know that Einer is with our Father and I will be, too, one day, but I guess that day hasn't come yet. Not for me anyway."

She reached over and took Clara's hand. "So we'll just have to get me well again. Right?"

Clara nodded. She covered Mrs. Norgaard's hand with her own. "God willing."

"Oh, I think *He's* been willing all along. It's this stubborn old woman who wanted to go the other way."

After Clara rewarmed the coffee and served, she settled Mrs. Norgaard down for a nap and walked Reverend Moen to the door. "Thank you for a beautiful service."

"All I did was read God's Word. We forget how wonderful and

powerful it is, especially when read aloud. As told in Matthew, chapter eighteen, He meant it when He said, 'For where two or three are gathered together in my name, there am I in the midst of them.' "

Clara leaned her cheek against the edge of the open door. "I felt it. . . His presence. . .I mean. I feel like laughing and crying, both at the same time." She wiped away a tear with her fingertip. "Thank you so much."

"You're most welcome. I felt and feel the same. These moments make all my days worthwhile." He placed his brown felt hat squarely on his head. "God bless."

Clara felt the "God bless" for the rest of the day and through the evening. She felt it when she gave Mrs. Norgaard a back rub.

"Tell me how you came to this country," Mrs. Norgaard asked when she was settled against her pillows again.

Clara leaned back against the chair. As she related the story of the stained letter and the picture of the curly haired man, she could feel a difference. She didn't resent God for "messing things up" as she'd thought before.

"I had to confess being angry today because I thought God wasn't playing fair. I thought I understood He was bringing me to America to be a wife—right away. Even though I didn't know the man, I thought God would make it all right."

"And He didn't?"

"I don't know. No one seems to recognize the picture. No one has come forward to say, 'Where's my wife, the one I bought a ticket for and who never showed up.'" Clara leaned her head back against the frame. "But after today, it isn't so important."

"Well, I shall always be grateful He brought you here, however He did it." Mrs. Norgaard folded her hands across her chest. "I know most of the people around here. Why don't you bring the picture here and show it to me?"

Clara thought about the suggestion. "Would you mind if we waited until morning when the light is better?"

"That would be fine." The quiet settled back. "Would you recite the Twenty-third Psalm again? That is such a comfort."

The words fell into the quiet of the room and the peace of their hearts, spreading like ripples on a pond.

When Clara fell into bed, she could only whisper, "Thank You, *mange takk.*"

She woke to a day filled with the brightness of sun glinting off frost. It glittered on the trees and the frost fronds painted on the edges of the windows.

After breakfast she took her picture in to Mrs. Norgaard. Clara studied the older woman's face as she studied the picture. Clara saw the jaw clench and the cords stand out in Mrs. Norgaard's birdlike neck.

"Clara, please go over to the blacksmith's and bring Dag back with you. I want to talk with him."

"Now?"

"Now!"

Chapter 7

Whatever could she want Dag for?

Mrs. Norgaard peered at Clara over the spectacles perched on her nose. "Well?"

"Yes, ma'am." Clara turned and hustled out of the room. She stripped off her apron and hung it on the hook, at the same time reaching for her gray wool shawl. While her hands went about their chores, her mind worried at the question like a dog with a bone. What would Dag have to do with her picture? She thought again of the taciturn blacksmith. Hopefully he talked to others more than he did her.

She flew down the stairs and out the door, catching her breath at the bit of the breeze. Her nose tingled and began to run as quickly as her feet. While the sun was gorgeous, winter not only nipped her nose but bayed hard on the heels of fall.

Clara paused a moment at the wrought iron gate and raised her face to the sun. Eyes closed, she savored the hint of warmth and freshness of the world outside the silent house. She would have to get outside more, that's all there was to it.

She felt like skipping down the street and, after checking to see no one was watching her, did just that. Back in Norway, she might have been racing Lars over the hills or riding their pony up to the summer hut where they took the cows to pasture in the warm season. Thoughts of home killed all desires for skipping.

What would Mor and Far be doing now? She scrunched up her eyes to think better. What part of the day was it in Norway now? She shook her head, letting the shawl fall back on her shoulders. Home was so far away, like another life. She rolled her lips together and looked up to the sky above. Her prayer winged upward like the steam rising from the rooftops. *Keep them safe*, she prayed, *and let us be together sometime again. Mange takk for this wonderful day and the new friends I am making.*

The picture of Else, her best friend since beginning school, took over her mind. But Else was already married and expecting her first baby.

Clara sighed and turned the corner to the blacksmith's shop. She'd just have to make a new best friend along with the new life in this new country. She glanced up the street to the fields beyond. This new, extremely flat, and amazingly huge country.

She had her smile back in place when she stopped in front of the weathered building, open to the street, with BLACKSMITH in black iron letters across the face. She wrinkled her nose at the distinctive aroma of trimmed horse hoof. A gray horse stood on three legs, its rear fourth clamped between Dag's knees.

"Hello, *froken* Johanson," called Will from his place holding the horse's head.

"Hello, Will." Clara smiled at the lanky lad and waited, expecting Dag to join in the greeting.

The man bending over the shoe, tapped home another nail, set down his hammer, and picked up the crimper.

Clara waited.

"Fine day, isn't it?" Will shifted to the near side of the horse.

"Ja, that it is." Clara looked back to Dag. He finished crimping the nails over, set aside the crimper, and picked up the rasp.

"Can we do something for you?" Will looked from Dag to Clara. He caught her gaze, glanced back at the man bending over the hoof, and shrugged.

Clara felt a little fume begin about her heart region and make its way to her mouth. She clicked her tongue against her teeth. *Had the man no manners at all? After all, it wasn't as if they were strangers.*

Dag eyed the final balance of the hoof and straightened. With a gloved hand he stroked the horse's haunches and made his way around to the other side.

He could feel a burn rising from his chest and up his neck.

What could she possibly want? Was this a social call? Who made social calls to the blacksmith? Mercy, but she was beautiful. The sun setting her hair afire above eyes the green of a newly risen field of wheat. He clamped a lid on his thoughts with the same strength he pounded iron.

He also forbade himself to peek around the horse's rear to see if she were still there. Why couldn't he just say "Hello" like Will did? Such an easy thing—for most people. If he dusted off his shirt and walked over to her, would she smile at him, like she had the boy?

The horse snorted, breaking a silence that stretched like a spider web between two blades of grass.

Clara cleared her throat. Why this urge to yell at him?

Dag rubbed his chin with the back of his pigskin gloves. Just a simple "Hello."

"Tell your master that Mrs. Norgaard would like to see him, if he can find the time." *Or the words,* she wanted to add but nearly drew blood biting her tongue.

"Yes ma'am." Will ducked his head.

Clara spun around, her skirts swirling about her legs. Her steps jarred her knees. Insufferable—rude—crude. Each word matched each stomp.

"Tell Mrs. Norgaard I'll be there as soon as I finish shoeing this horse." The deep voice echoed up the dirt street after her.

Clara straightened her spine and her shawl. "Tell her yourself." Her mutter carried no farther than her shoulder.

Even though she'd smiled at a woman on her way to the store and nodded at a man in a wagon who raised his hat in greeting, Clara smacked her hand against the latch on the gate. The gate flew open, clanging against the fence. The sound jerked her back from casting dire consequences upon the head of the man who couldn't be bothered to be civil.

She carefully closed the gate behind her and switched her stomping to a normal gait while at the same time forcing herself to search the two naked elm trees for squirrels. A crow chastised her from the peak of the second-story dormer.

Clara inhaled a deep breath of the sparkly air, mounted the steps, and, by the time she entered the house, had herself totally under control. After trotting up the stairs, she hung up her shawl, retied her apron, and peeked in on Mrs. Norgaard.

The bed stood empty. Clara opened the door all the way and discovered her employer sitting in a rocker in front of the window. Clara swallowed her amazement.

"Could you please fix my hair before he comes?"

Clara nodded and picked up the brush and pins from the dressing table. As she brushed the long hair, she tried to think of something to say. Should she tell Mrs. Norgaard that Dag had been, well, less than helpful? But then he had said he'd come. She heaved a sigh and continued her ministrations.

"Wouldn't you rather tell me about it?" Mrs. Norgaard leaned into the rhythmic strokes of the brush.

"About what?"

"Whatever upset you. I watched you come through the gate—and up the walk."

"Oh." Clara tucked several hairpins in her mouth—to keep from answering or to be more efficient? She braided the long strands, looped the braid into a figure eight and inserted the pins. That left her with an empty mouth and, after thinking about her trip to the blacksmith's, with an empty smile.

"I—" The bell pealed from the front door.

"Show him up and bring us a coffee tray in about fifteen minutes." Mrs. Norgaard patted Clara's arm. "We'll talk later."

On the way down the stairs, Clara considered. Had that last comment been a threat or a promise? Either way—why did that man have to be so infuriating? Her heels clicked on the stairs, each step reminding her that now it was her place to be polite—or not.

She opened the door, her normal welcoming smile tucked safely away.

Dag stood there, porkpie hat clutched between his hands.

Clara motioned him in and led the way up the stairs. She could feel his eyes burning holes into her back. She held herself rigidly straight, her chin at an angle that brooked no appeal. Only the slight trembling of her fingers as they trailed up the banister revealed the effort it took. If he could be silent, so could she.

Dag knew the way. He'd been to the house often, repairing the stove and installing the pump and piped-in water. The iron fence surrounding the property had been hand-formed in his own shop. He sniffed appreciatively. A fragrance of lavender drifted back from the starchy figure ascending the stairs before him. The rustle of her skirts made him conscious of the trim anatomy, rounded where it should be and slender, especially in the ankles.

He jerked his attention to the hand trailing the banister. That, too, slender, with long fingers, dainty but very capable. How gentle those hands had been with the children on the Detschman farm.

Enough! He focused his gaze on his boots. Dusty, bits of mud, and probably—oh, if only he could go outside, clean them off, and start all over again. If only he could fly back to the smithy and answer the blond angel that had said "Hello" in a way that set his heart to hammering. Hammering louder than the sledge upon steel to sharpen a plowshare.

She pushed open the door and motioned him through. "Mr. Weinlander." He heard the sheet of ice tinkle and crackle around him as he walked through.

"Good morning, Dag." Mrs. Norgaard called from her window seat. "Please, come sit with me while Clara brings us some coffee. And make sure you bring three cups, my dear."

Dag sat, dwarfing the chair with his broad shoulders and tall body. He glanced back in time to see Clara glare daggers at him one more time before she turned and, after closing the door with a definite snap, tap away down the hall. If she'd called him a vile name, he wouldn't have felt it more.

He sighed and turned his attention to his hostess, who gave away her awareness of his turmoil by a gentle smile.

Her words however were, as always, politely correct. After asking about his health, the weather, and the state of the smithy, Mrs. Norgaard leaned forward and picked up a picture from the table. "Please look at this and tell me who you think it is." She handed the stained and faded likeness to him.

Dag studied the curly haired man in the photograph. He looked up, puzzlement wrinkling a brow barely peeping from behind the wild hair. "It is Jude, my brother, as you well know."

Mrs. Norgaard nodded. "Yes, I thought as much."

"But where—" Dag studied the picture again. "Where did you get this?"

"That I'll tell you another time. But for now. . .where is he?"

Dag shook his head, the matted and twisted hair swinging in the force of it. "I don't know. He stopped one day—" Dag wrinkled his brow remembering, "to tell me to take care of Ma. He was going to be gone for a while."

Silence but for the ticking clock filled the room. Mrs. Norgaard waited.

Dag nodded. "He told me to pick up a woman, *froken* Johanson, at the station and take her to the Detschman farm. That is all."

"And you haven't seen him since?"

Dag shook his head again. "Is something wrong?"

Mrs. Norgaard reached for the picture and laid it face down on the table. "No, I think not." She clasped her hands loosely in her lap. The silence returned. "Did he marry that woman over in Hammerston?"

Dag started. Did she know *everything* that went on? "Maybe that's where he went, but he'd have invited Ma to the wedding at least—I think." He twisted the hat in his hands. What was going on here?

Mrs. Norgaard sighed and nodded at the same time, as if she'd come to a decision.

Dag waited, expecting her to either continue the discussion or tell him what to do next. He'd learned long ago that one didn't rush Mrs. Norgaard and that no one in town or the surrounding counties treated him with more care and civility.

Clara entered the room, carrying a tray laden with coffeepot, cups, and a plate of apple cake.

Dag nearly tipped the armless, needlepoint chair as he leaped to his feet to take the tray from her. She relinquished the ebony handles, losing her hands in his for just a moment. She resisted the urge to dust them off on her apron. Funny, a tingle like a spark had gone up her arms. She moved the picture of her man off the table so Dag could set the tray down. What was her picture doing here? Had Mrs. Norgaard shown it to Dag?

Her thoughts chased each other like squirrels in an oak tree. All the while, her hands poured the coffee, and passed it and the cake around with the napkins, before she took her own chair. She glanced up in time to see a look of pleasure cross Dag's face as he chewed and swallowed her cake, then sipped the coffee from a cup nearly hidden in his hand.

"More, Mr. Weinlander?" She offered the cake plate again. And again. Until there were only crumbs. Goodness, had the man never had apple cake?

When the coffeepot, too, was empty, Dag set his plate and cup on the tray and, picking up his hat again, stood to go. *"Mange takk."* He nodded both to the old woman sitting so straight in her chair and the young one rising to escort him out. "Is there anything else, ma'am?"

"No, I think not. Thank you for humoring an old woman and coming so quickly."

When it appeared her attention had turned to the window, Dag bobbed his head and turned toward the door.

Clara, trying to determine what the undercurrents in the room meant, let him get ahead of her. Well, of all the—again her mind found something to blame him for. Didn't he know it was *her* place to show him out? Her shoes tapped out her displeasure on the hardwood floor. How could she go around him? The hall wasn't wide enough. She glared at the back of the man. She'd have to find some new names to call him, the ones she'd used so far were wearing out!

Dag stopped at the head of the stairs. Clara did, too, with her nose in his back. Would he *never* do what she expected?

"Excuse me," she muttered, her head down to hide the blush she could feel flaming up into her face. She passed in front of him and preceded him down the stairs. Right now she could do with one of those fans she'd seen in a lady's book.

When she opened the door for him, she looked not higher than the missing button on his shirt. Wool underwear that might have once been white but had forgotten the experience long before showed through the gap of the shirt. Neither had had a recent acquaintance with a washtub.

Dag paused, as if to say something, then mashed his hat on his head, strode out the door, and down the walk.

Clara watched him stride away. For such a big man, he walked with the grace of. . .she couldn't think of a word. The picture of her father, head and shoulders above most of the Norwegian giants of home, whirling Mor around the dance floor in a spirited polka came to her mind. Ya, Dag moved with that same grace. She corrected the thought—Mr. Weinlander. The bell summoned her from upstairs. She gently closed the door and made her way back up the staircase.

Thoughts of the curious bear of a man wriggled in and out of her mind as she continued with her tasks of the day. What would he look like without that matted rat's nest of a beard? Why wouldn't he talk with her, even to say just the polite formalities? Why had her picture been on the table? Why didn't she just ask Mrs. Norgaard and get her questions answered?

That night as she prepared her charge for bed, Clara could feel the questions welling up and pleading for voice. After blowing out the lamp on the stand, she cleared her throat. Only the light from the hall disturbed the darkness.

"Would you repeat our psalm again?" Mrs. Norgaard derailed Clara's train of thought.

"Ja, that I will." Clara sat down on the edge of the bed and closed her eyes. Her voice gentle, she began. "The Lord is my shepherd, I shall not want. . ." As she continued, the words sank into her heart and mind, reminding her of the promises God wrote for everyone. When she finished, she bowed her head. *Peace and quiet have the same sound,* she thought. *Why is it that words written so long ago have such power to bring peace?*

"Our Father which art in heaven. . ." Mrs. Norgaard's voice with these other ancient words only added to the blanket of comfort. Clara joined her and together they whispered "Amen."

When Clara began to rise, Mrs. Norgaard laid a hand on the younger woman's arm. "Stay with me awhile, if you will. I have a story I want to tell you." The words came softly out of the shadowed bed.

Clara settled herself with her back against the carved walnut foot. She waited.

"It all began a long time ago. A man here in town lost his wife one winter and left him with a small son. He had a hard time of it but eventually found another woman to marry. There has never been a surplus of marriageable females here in the Dakotas, so he felt blessed. The family was fine until the new wife had a baby. All she could think of was her son, and the older boy was pushed aside.

"Now as the lads grew, the younger son was quick to learn. None could resist his laughing eyes and curly hair, least of all his mother. And so he grew to take advantage of his older brother, who was not so quick to learn or glib of tongue.

"When the older was ten, the father died, making his elder son promise to care for his stepmother and half brother. They both treated him cruelly, but he finally left school that, although he was slow, he loved, and he then took an apprenticeship under the local blacksmith. When the blacksmith died, he willed his business to the young man, who had proven to have an amazing aptitude.

"And the younger son? Since his mother spoiled him so terribly, he felt that others should treat him like she did and drifted in with the wrong element of town."

"And of the older brother?" Clara forced the words past the lump clogging her throat.

"He continued to withdraw, caught, I believe, in a web of agonizing shyness, convinced he was not worth more than his family had repeatedly told him. And that was nothing.

"It reminds me of Esau and Jacob." Mrs. Norgaard sighed and a pause deepened. "I don't know, God worked a miracle for those two brothers of so long ago and I pray the same can happen today."

"You've prayed for them?"

"Oh, for years. The elder and I struck up a friendship back when he was a lad and was helping me in my garden. My Einer was much too busy in the bank to dig up the garden and help prune the trees. We never had children. Sometimes I wonder if God didn't trust us enough to take good care of them."

"Oh, no." Clara bit back any more of a response, afraid she would halt the flow of gentle and dreamy words.

"So I made it a habit to acquaint myself with the village children and help where I could. One of my girls attended teachers' school in Fargo and one young man has finished medical school. Dr. Harmon keeps hoping this young man will return to North Dakota where we need doctors so desperately." Silence again.

"I receive letters from others who have married and moved away. They all were so special to me, not that I spoiled them, you know. I just made sure that if they wanted to do more with their lives, they could."

Clara drew a bit of flannel from her pocket and blew her nose. "And the younger brother?"

"I haven't seen him in a long time. Good riddance to bad rubbish, I say, but then I have to remember my Lord's commands and pray forgiveness both for my bad thoughts and his bad actions."

The clock chimed from the top of the six-drawer chest.

"You must go to bed now, my dear. Thank you for listening to an old woman's ramblings."

Clara bent over and brushed a kiss on Mrs. Norgaard's forehead. *"Mange takk."*

"God bless."

I have to help him. Clara lay in bed and stared upward at the canopy she could barely discern. *How can I? What can I do? He won't even talk to me.*

She waited for heavenly inspiration.

The clock chimed the quarter hour.

An owl hooted out in the backyard.

"How, God, how?"

215

Chapter 8

Clara woke with the same thought.

As she hurried through her morning ablutions, she ignored the gray skies without and the gray cloud within. How could someone have mistreated a young boy so? Especially the woman who agreed to be his mother.

And what could be done now?

No wonderful solutions had come to her during the night. Was she expecting too quick an answer to her prayers? She brushed her hair, frustration lending vigor to her brush strokes. Mrs. Norgaard said she'd been praying for years. . .and nothing. The lilt had left Clara's voice when she answered the summoning bell. Along with the snap in her step.

Shortly after dinner, the doorbell pealed. Clara wiped her hands on her apron and hurried down the paneled hall between the kitchen and the front entry. It was probably the doctor needing a cup of coffee during his daily round.

"Ingeborge!" Clara reached out to draw her guest inside and instead found herself enveloped in a hug that immediately made her think of Mor. "Come in, come right on in."

"I hope I'm not intruding. John agreed to stay home with the little ones while they napped and so here I am." Ingeborge unbuttoned her coat and let Clara remove it from her shoulders and hang the heavy black wool on the coat tree.

"I'm afraid Mrs. Norgaard might be asleep. She had a busy morning." She led the way into the parlor. "I'll go see and be right back."

"No, I came to talk with you." Ingeborge took a seat on the

brown velvet sofa and patted the surface beside her. "For, you see, I have an absolutely marvelous idea and I need your help."

"Me?"

"Yes, I am thinking of starting a class to teach English to those Norwegians who just immigrated."

"Like me?" Clara put a hand to her chest.

"Yes." Ingeborge gave a bounce on the slippery sofa.

"Wouldn't you love to be able to speak and read the language of your new country?"

"Ja, for sure that I would." A cloud dimmed the rising excitement in her eyes. "But how could I leave Mrs. Norgaard?"

"I think that can be arranged. I just kept thinking what a struggle Nora had had and I know many others feel cut off because they can't talk easily—"

"That's it!" Clara clasped her hands and buried them in her apron between her knees.

"What? Tell me what?"

"You said anyone who needs help with talking?"

Ingeborge nodded.

Clara turned to face her friend. "Even though he—I mean, they, might have lived around here all their lives."

"I hadn't thought to include someone like that, but, of course." Ingeborge's brow wrinkled in concentration.

"Dag Weinlander." Clara leaned against the back of the sofa. "Ingeborge, you are the answer to my prayers."

"I'm glad to hear that since you aren't making a lick of sense."

"What do you know of Dag Weinlander?"

Ingeborge rolled her eyes upward and pursed her lips. "Not a great deal, I must admit. He doesn't come to church or any of the town socials. Besides, I have never found him to be very friendly when I've met with him anywhere. You know, in a town this size, everyone knows everyone else and all their business, too. But he seems a puzzle." She tilted her head to the side and studied her friend. "I take it you know more?"

Clara told her the story she'd heard from Mrs. Norgaard. At the end of the tale, Ingeborge removed a cambric bit from her bag and dabbed at the corner of her eye. "I had no idea. Oh, the poor, poor man." She paused, staring at the bit of fabric in her fingers. She nodded and looked up at Clara, a smile widening her lips as she spoke. "We'll just have to help him out, won't we?"

That Sunday at church, during the announcements, Reverend Moen invited all those who would like help with their English to meet at the church on Tuesday evening at six-thirty.

Ingeborge looked over the heads of her brood to Clara. Their private smile acknowledged that others would be invited, too.

When Clara returned home, she hung up her coat and tripped lightly up the stairs. The closing hymn kept echoing in her mind so she sang along, "Blest be the tie that binds, our hearts in Christian love. . ."

Mrs. Norgaard waited for her in the chair by the window. "I love to hear you sing and that song is one of my favorites. Maybe I'll soon be able to go to church again. I think I miss the music most of all."

"Ja, these folks, they sing good." She took the other chair. "He did it—Reverend Moen said the English class will begin on Tuesday."

"Good. Then our next step is to invite Dag here for me to tell him about the class. His shop is not open for business today, so the livery is where he'll be. After dinner, if you would, walk over there with a message for me. Do we have any more of your apple cake? He seemed to enjoy that."

"No, but I could put one in to bake while I finish the dinner." Clara stood and barely refrained from skipping out the door.

Down at the livery stable a while later, Will came out at her call, rubbing the dust off his hands as he came. "C'n I help you, *froken* Johanson?" His grin displayed a gap between his front teeth, besides showing his delight at her arrival.

"I hope so. Is Mr. Weinlander here?"

"He's at the forge. You need a horse or sumpin'?"

"No." Clara shook her head, a wistful smile betraying her

desire as she looked to the stalls. "Perhaps someday I'll ride again, but for now, Mrs. Norgaard is asking for Da—Mr. Weinlander to come see her."

"Right away." Will touched a finger to his forehead and trotted back through the barn to the separate building facing the other street. Ringing sounds of hammer on steel announced that Dag was hard at work. The lad returned in a matter of seconds. "Said he'll be right over, soon's he finishes the piece he's working on."

"Thank you." Clara refused to recognize the letdown feeling the answer gave. Had she expected him to walk back with her? She paused a moment. "You know, there's fresh apple cake if you would like to come, too."

Will rubbed his mouth with grimy fingers. "That'd be right fine, Miss, but one of us has to stay here. There's a team comin' back."

"Maybe another time?"

"I'd like that."

Clara quelled the urge to walk slowly in case Dag might overtake her and instead hurried to prepare the tray and make fresh coffee.

Dag was more taciturn than ever, if that were possible, when Clara showed him upstairs. He answered each of her carefully thought-out questions with a grunt or nothing at all. She shook her head as she left the room. Getting him to talk was perhaps going to be more of a challenge than she'd thought.

When Clara reentered the room carrying the coffee tray, it was obvious Dag didn't agree with Mrs. Norgaard. He sat with arms crossed over his chest, his jaw set like a snapping turtle.

"Just think about it, please," Mrs. Norgaard pleaded. "You would find it easier to deal with your customers if you spoke more fluent English."

"I have plenty of business." Hoarfrost shimmered on each word.

"Well." The old woman straightened her shoulders and shot him a look that would have melted steel. "Do what you must. All I ask is you give it some thought. Set that down here." She pointed to the table by her side.

Clara hazarded a glance at Dag after carefully positioning the tray so Mrs. Norgaard could pour. He didn't appear to be melting.

Dag watched her hands as she set down the tray. Each movement flowed with the grace of a half-grown wheat field dancing in the wind. Why should he go to an English class? Resentment chased good sense around in his mind. They talked about speaking, but would the class include reading? He thought wistfully of newspapers and the books that graced the shelf at his mother's house. He could barely decipher Norwegian, let alone English.

Why had he been so slow in school? Maybe he was a dumb dolt like Jude said. Stupid and slow—and ugly as a troll. Yeh, the trolls were big and strong, like him, and ugly.

He heard a voice as from a great distance.

"Mr. Weinlander, your coffee. And would you have some apple cake?" Her voice sang like the birds at courting time.

Two of his favorite aromas, coffee and cinnamon. He sniffed appreciatively and accepted the offered food. *"Mange takk." English, speak English, you dolt! Show her you can. But Clara doesn't talk English,* the other side stated. He felt like his brain had become a battlefield.

"Will seems like such a nice young man."

Answer her! Dag choked on his apple cake. He coughed and took a swig of coffee that only made him cough more. When he could breath again, he leaned back in his chair. Sweat beaded on his forehead. He looked up at Clara, expecting to see condemnation, but all her blue eyes radiated was compassion.

A glance at Mrs. Norgaard left him reeling. Dag staggered to his feet. "I must go." He left the house as if a hound of heaven bayed at his heels.

"Wait! Dag, wait!" He was at the gate before her cries penetrated the voices raging in his brain. He strangled the spires on the gate with shaking hands. He could hear her shoes tapping out her hurry.

"Here." She thrust a napkin into his hand. "I wrapped this for Will since he said he couldn't come with you."

Dag nodded without looking above her hands and fled out the gate.

"What are we going to do?" Clara asked that night as she brushed Mrs. Norgaard's hair in preparation for bed.

"First we pray and then we wait."

Clara sighed. "But—"

"No buts, my child. Our Dag has his own devils to work out and only our Father can do that for him. But you and I. . .well, I think we shall invite both Dag and Will for supper. Wednesday would be a good night, don't you think?"

Clara fell into bed, both restless and relieved. Waiting was so hard, but at least she had someone with which to wait. Dag had no one. Her prayers matched her feelings—confused.

Monday there was a letter for Mrs. Norgaard when Clara went to mail hers to Mor and Far. Clara studied the handwriting. If only she could understand English! On her way back to the house, she went by the blacksmith's and handed Will a note to give Dag. It was an invitation to supper.

"Umm. . .ah—" Will stuttered. He looked from the note to Clara, over his shoulder to Dag working at replacing a wagon wheel rim, and back to the note, his gaze darting like sparks flying from the anvil.

"Is there a problem?" Clara could sense his hesitation even if she couldn't have seen it.

"Ah, no." Will shook his head. "He can't stop what he's doing right now or he'll have to start all over, so I'll give him this when he's done."

"Oh." Clara felt a stab of disappointment. More waiting! "Well, all right then." She turned and walked back to the big house, her shoulders hunched against the bite of the north winds. As the postmaster had said, it looked, felt, and smelled like a snowstorm was on the way.

The note, delivered later by Will and crudely lettered as if the writer had missed more school than he had attended, declined the invitation.

Mrs. Norgaard tapped the folded paper against her hand. "I

have a question for you, Will, and I want an honest answer."

Will shuffled his feet, hat squashed between his two hands. "Yes'um."

"Who wrote this?"

Will wrinkled up his forehead, clicked his tongue, shuffled his feet again, and rendered his hat totally useless. "I did."

"Did Dag see my invitation?"

Will nodded. He rubbed his chin with one index finger.

This time it was Mrs. Norgaard's turn to nod. "Clara, why don't you take the boy down and give him a sandwich and maybe some of that apple cake if there is any left. Good day, young man. I hope to see you again soon."

"Yes'm. Thank you." Will bobbed his head and followed Clara out the door. By the time he'd eaten his fill, hard pellets of snow were dashing themselves against the window. He mashed his hat on his head and trotted down the walk, turned once to wave again, and then picked up his feet to hurry home before he froze.

Clara thought about the discussion upstairs as she cleaned up the kitchen. What was going on? And the letter that came. Would Mrs. Norgaard share that with her as she had the others? And on top of all that, what would be their next sally in the war on Dag Weinlander?

"Tomorrow I think I shall want to go downstairs for dinner."

Clara immediately thought of all the steps. How would they ever manage? While Mrs. Norgaard could now walk around her room, she hadn't left it in. . .in. . .Clara had no idea how long.

"I want you to go to the smithy in the morning, if the weather cooperates, and ask Dag to come to carry me down. If he refused to join us for dinner, why then he can return to carry me back up."

Clara felt a chuckle bubbling up from her midsection. She tried to contain it but failed miserably. "Gladly," she answered when they could both talk again.

"Oh, Clara," Mrs. Norgaard said, as the younger woman was leaving the room for the night. "That letter, it was from Mrs. Hanson. She'll be returning next week."

Clara felt like she'd been struck by a widow maker.

The feeling of doom persisted as she crawled into her bed. If Mrs. Hanson was returning, she could go back to the farm with Carl and Nora. Why didn't the thought please her? Since the move to town, she'd only seen her sister once and that was at church.

But what would she do for a job? And how could she help Dag when she would be so far out in the country? And what about the English classes? *God, are You sure You know what is going on here? How can I thank You when I am so confused? Every time I think I have things under control or at least figured out, something changes. Please help me.*

"Why the long face?" Mrs. Norgaard asked when Clara brought in the breakfast tray. "The sun is shining; we can proceed with our plan."

Clara nodded and poured the coffee. She probably wouldn't be doing this for much longer. She walked over to the windows and drew back the heavy draperies. Sun refracted from the diamonds bedded in the inch of pristine snow covering the yard. How clean and pure everything looked. Snow frosted the black branches of the elm tree and bonneted the wrought iron fence posts. An unconscious sigh lifted her shoulders.

"All right. Out with it. This is a side of Clara I've never seen and I'm not sure I like it." Mrs. Norgaard set her coffee cup down with a snap.

Clara sighed again, this time fully aware of what she was doing. But sighing seemed all she was capable of at the moment. She turned to face her employer. "I just want to say how much I've appreciated working for you and—"

"Clara, what are you saying? Are you going to leave me?" Mrs. Norgaard pushed away the bed tray and made as if to rise.

"Well, the letter from Mrs. Hanson. If she's to come back. . ."

Mrs. Norgaard flopped back against her pillows and patted her chest with one hand. "Oh, my dear, is that all? Why, you silly goose. Did you think I would let you go just because Mrs. Hanson —oh, no, no, no. You have given me life again. I want you as long as you'll stay. Please, come here to me." She held out both hands.

When Clara took them, Mrs. Norgaard drew her young helper down on the bed. "Now, promise me if you are unhappy here, you will tell me."

"But I'm not. I just thought—"

"And that when you have concerns that trouble you, you'll bring them to me so we can work them out."

Clara nodded. The lump in her throat made an answer impossible.

"Good. Now that we have that all taken care of, what shall I wear for my first trip down to the dining room? I must look my best if we are to have company."

When the preparations were all complete, Clara threw on her coat, pinned her hat cockily over one eyebrow, and started out for the blacksmith shop. Her breath puffing out like miniature clouds delighted her as did the squirrel scolding her from the oak tree.

"I thought you'd be hibernating by now," she scolded back. "Go wrap yourself in your bushy tail and stay warm." She leaned over and scooped up a handful of snow, packed it, and fired it at the trunk of a tree, where it splatted perfectly.

I'm staying, I'm staying, thank You, God. Thank You, thank You. "Praise God from whom all blessings flow. . ." Her clear soprano voice rose on the puffs of air and joined the crunch of her boots in an aria of praise.

"To carry her downstairs?" Dag looked at her like she was missing a spoke somewhere.

Clara nodded, determined to keep a straight face. "She can't manage the stairs yet, but she so wants to be free from her bedroom for a change." She carefully injected a note of pleading into the last words. It *was* the truth.

"And then back up."

"After we eat."

"Tell her I will come to carry her down and back up." He slapped one hand into the other. "But no dinner."

Clara nodded. "At twelve then?" She caught Dag's nod as he

224

walked off into the dimness of his shop. He *had* talked to her, at least. She allowed herself one skip on the way back home.

While Dag carried Mrs. Norgaard with a gentleness that belied his huge size, he refused to answer any of Clara's questions or comments. And he didn't stay to eat. The reverse process was no different.

"And tomorrow, Dag?" Mrs. Norgaard settled herself on the edge of the bed.

He nodded.

"Then I thank you. You have no idea what a treat this was. I think Clara's determination to make me live again is paying off, don't you?"

Dag nodded and set off as if that hound were on his heels again.

"I'm off now," Clara said from the bedroom doorway that evening. "You sure you'll be all right alone?"

"Perfectly. You just go and learn as much as you can." Mrs. Norgaard settled her spectacles more firmly on her nose. "I'm just grateful I can enjoy reading again." She waved her hand as if shooing away a fly. "Go on, go on."

Clara danced up the stairs a couple of hours later. She was learning to talk English! She and about fifteen other people. And Ingeborge, what a teacher. Everyone had had such a good time, why the hours passed like. . .like a party. She wrapped her hands around her shoulders and squeezed, at the same time spinning in a circle.

"I take it you had a good time." Mrs. Norgaard laid down her book and removed her gold-rimmed spectacles.

"Ja. . .*nei*. . .yes. Good evening." The English words came haltingly but they came. "And we are to meet on Thursday, also." Clara switched back to Norwegian, having used up her store of new words. "Oh, I am so happy."

Wednesday and Thursday Dag appeared to do the carrying— but not eating.

On Friday, when Clara answered the door, she fought to keep the shock from showing on her face.

Chapter 9

Dag had washed himself—and his clothes.

Clara clamped her teeth together and made sure her cheeks spread in a smile. "Good morning." She hesitated over the words but persevered, determined to use her new language.

Dag nodded and started toward the stairs.

"Ahhh." The word for coat totally left her mind. She reverted to Norwegian.

Dag paused, one foot on the bottom stair. He turned to face her. "Ja. *Mange takk.*" He shrugged out of his black wool, thigh-length coat and handed it to her.

Clara hung it on the tree and stared up the stairs. Even his boots were polished. What she'd give to see the look on Mrs. Norgaard's face! Clara ran up the stairs and down the hall. She burst into the bedroom just as Dag was leaning over to pick up his charge. His broad back hid the diminutive older woman from Clara's sight, but when he turned around, Mrs. Norgaard just smiled like this was an everyday occurrence.

Clara stepped back and let them precede her down the hall. As they passed, Mrs. Norgaard winked at Clara, then continued her conversation with Dag. He even answered her question.

Clara leaned against the door frame and watched them disappear down the stairs. She clapped both hands to her cheeks and felt a shiver of pure delight course through her. She rolled her lips together, straightened her spine, and made her way downstairs.

Dag and Mrs. Norgaard visited in the sitting room while Clara quickly set another place at the table. After bringing in the bread she'd baked just that morning and the stew that had simmered for hours, she crossed the hall to announce the meal.

"No, I'll walk," Mrs. Norgaard insisted when Dag bent down to pick her up. "It's just the stairs I can't manage. Here, let me have your arm to lean on."

Dinner passed with Clara and Mrs. Norgaard carrying the conversation, but Clara could feel Dag's gaze on her from time to time. He answered when asked a direct question, but other than that, he ate in silence. Clara and Mrs. Norgaard made a point to discuss the English class taught by Ingeborge.

"We'll have our coffee in the sitting room," Mrs. Norgaard said after inserting her napkin back into the silver ring by her plate. Dag surreptitiously followed suit and leaped from his place to help her to her feet.

This became the pattern for the next three days until Saturday, when Mrs. Norgaard suggested Dag help her down the stairs, rather than carrying her.

"You're sure?" He stared intently into her eyes.

"Clara's been making me walk around my room morning, noon, and night. You'd think she took lessons from an army sergeant."

"I'm just following doctor's orders," Clara defended herself.

"I know, my dear." Mrs. Norgaard smiled at her. "But you must admit you take your duties seriously."

Dag watched the byplay between the two women, aware as ever of the way they made him feel. Was this the way people really treated each other? He'd never heard or sensed a cross feeling between the two of them. Just a caring that flowed peaceful and smooth like the Red River on its summer journey. And they extended that warmth to him. *Him.* Dag Weinlander. *Why?* Sure, he had a strong back for carrying Mrs. Norgaard down the stairs, but she had always made him feel welcome. Why?

Soon she wouldn't need him anymore. He thought of the gift he'd been carving for her in the evenings in front of the fireplace of his sod hut. Even that would help her need him less. The thought caused another pang in his chest. He kept his fingers from digging at the collar of his shirt.

Instead, he offered the old woman his arm, just like they did downstairs. She clutched his arm with both hands as she took the first step downward. He could feel her shaking. Another step. And another. When they reached the bottom, she gave a sigh of relief. His matched.

He swallowed and rubbed his mouth through the beard with one hand. Together, they marched directly into the dining room. After seating her, he sat down, refusing his body the privilege of slumping in the chair. Helping her downstairs was worse than shoeing ten cantankerous horses in a row.

She let him carry her back up. "We'll see you tomorrow then. Dinner is at one, after Clara returns from church."

He nodded. "Oh, and Dag, please bring Will with you. I'd like to become better acquainted with that lad."

"Yes, ma'am." Dag turned to leave. "And *mange takk*."

"Dag, it is I who should be thanking you."

"Umm." Dag departed on that noncommittal reply.

That night he resanded the apple-wood cane he had fashioned from a gnarled branch and applied a last coat of varnish. The twisted wood gleamed in the firelight as Dag set it aside to dry one last time. Each succeeding coat of varnish had deepened the patina, bringing out the highlights of the grain.

"That's beautiful," Will said from his stool by the fire. "When ya gonna give it to her?"

"Tomorrow, when we go there for dinner."

"We?"

"Ja."

"Who's gonna tend the livery?"

"Me. While you heat water and take a bath."

"A bath! It's the middle of the winter."

"Ja, a bath." Dag ignored his assistant's fussing and put away his varnish and rag.

"I'd druther stay with the horses." Will crammed his hands into his pockets.

"You can, after dinner."

"What if someone needs a horse?"

"He can come back."

Will muttered his way to bed.

Dag remained by the fire, lost for a time in his thoughts. When he realized how many of those thoughts centered around a certain golden-haired angel, he abruptly stood and headed for the cornhusk-filled mattress he called bed.

"Dag, this is beautiful." Mrs. Norgaard rubbed her hands down the satiny finish of the cane. "I knew you were a master with metal, but I had no idea you could create in wood, also." She gripped the handle and, standing, leaned her weight on the cane. "And the perfect height." She looked up at him with a smile crinkling the corners of her eyes. "Tired of carrying me around?"

Dag shook his head. "You're sure it fits? I could make it shorter if you want."

"No, this is perfect." She thumped it on the floor. "Now, shall we join the others downstairs?"

Dinner passed swiftly with Will finding time to answer questions in spite of putting away a prodigious amount of roast beef, mashed potatoes, gravy, and green beans.

"I ain't never had such a fine meal." Will leaned back against his chair.

"We have apple pie. I'd be sorry if you were too full to join us." Mrs. Norgaard smiled as she spoke.

"No'm. I'll find room for that."

Clara stood up to clear the table.

"I'll help you, miss." Will leaped to his feet. He grinned a cheeky grin. "That way I'll have more room for pie."

"Have you thought of joining the English class, Will?" Mrs. Norgaard asked when the coffee was poured and pie handed out.

"Nah. I can talk Norwegian, English, and some German. I don't need no class."

"But can you read English?"

"Pretty good. Pa made sure I went to school till I was eleven. Then we started west." He took a last bite of the pie.

"Where are your folks now?" Clara asked.

"Dead." Will scraped up every last bit of apple from his plate.

Clara wished she'd bit her tongue before asking such a question.

"Then Dag found me and asked if'n I wanted to help him as an apprentice." He licked the tines of his fork.

Mrs. Norgaard motioned Clara to get the boy another piece of pie.

"I told Dag he should go—to that class, you know." He grinned at Clara when she set another slab of dessert in front of him. "Winter's a good time, not so busy. He could go."

Dag felt warmth creeping up from his chest and making his collar even tighter. Kicking the boy from under the table was beginning to seem more and more like a good idea. He'd never seen him so loose-mouthed.

Will looked across at his employer. He grinned again. "Could."

"We'd better get back in case someone needs a horse." Dag accompanied his pronouncement with the shoving back of his chair.

"*Mange takk* for my cane," said Mrs. Norgaard. She rose to her feet. "Perhaps just your arm today, helping me with the stairs." As they made their way slowly upward, she added a thought. "See you tomorrow?"

Dag nodded. "Ja." Was that gratitude for another day's reprieve he felt welling up in his heart? How terrible to wish she weren't getting better so quickly. *Just like a dolt like you,* he chastised himself with each upward step.

Mrs. Norgaard stopped three steps from the top. She put her hand to her heart and leaned against Dag's strength while trying to catch her breath again. When Dag made to lift her, she stopped him. "No, I'll make it. Just weaker than I thought." A pant separated each word.

See what you did? His inner tormentor continued. *You were in such a rush to get back to the barn, you. . .* Dag clenched his teeth. *Won't you ever do things right?*

"Good afternoon," Clara practiced her English as she showed the men out. "See you at class Tuesday." She shut the door before Dag could answer.

Clara scoured the kitchen and polished all the furniture on Monday morning while the bread was rising. Mrs. Hanson would be arriving on the four o'clock train and she didn't want the housekeeper to find one thing not up to snuff. Ham and beans browned in the oven, sending a delicious aroma throughout the house.

Dag sniffed appreciatively when he walked up the newly swept walk. While the sun tried to shine, high gray clouds kept drifting across its warmth. A north wind nipped around the corner of the house and caused Dag to shiver. His hands were still cold from the scrubbing he'd given them in the horse trough. This cleaning up for dinner every day took some doing. He tucked a button back into its hole before ringing the bell. He'd have to buy some new clothes—and soon.

Clara answered the door while wiping her hands on her apron. "Good morning." The English was coming easier since she'd been practicing. "Come in."

Dag nodded and stepped inside, removing his coat as he did so and hanging it up himself. While his nose might be more accustomed to perfumes of horse, coke fire, and steel, he could recognize beeswax, lemon oil, and especially freshly baked bread with ham and beans. This, like every meal he'd enjoyed here, would be good—very good.

"See, I'm stronger every day, thanks to you and Clara," Mrs. Norgaard stopped at the bottom of the stairs. She looked back up. "I didn't think I would ever leave that room again, except to greet my Lord in heaven."

Dag covered the small hand that lay on his arm with his large one. "I'm glad you decided to stay with us."

"As I said, thanks to you and Clara." She released his arm and set out with her back rigid but her weight partly supported by the apple-wood cane clasped in her right hand. "See how well this works? Thank you, my friend."

Dinner indeed lived up to what his nose had promised him. He cleaned his plate and nodded when Clara offered to dish him up some more. "You are a good cook."

His comment caught the women by surprise. He never offered anything except *"Mange takk"* unless spoken to first.

"Why, thank you," Clara answered, heat blossoming in her cheeks. "I. . .I wanted everything perfect for when Mrs. Hanson comes back."

Dag looked around at the gleaming furniture and his healthier friend and nodded. "It is."

Clara felt like she'd been given a medal by the King of Norway. Her heart pitter-pattered in her throat—her very dry throat. She blinked against the surge of moisture that should have been in her throat but instead wanted to slip from her eyes. "Thank you" seemed such an ineffectual response to so great a gift but what else could she do? *"Mange takk,"* she replied.

"Take this to Will," she said as she thrust a package into his hands on his way out the door. "And," she gave him a saucy grin, "see you at class tomorrow night."

Mrs. Hanson clapped a hand to her chest when she saw Mrs. Norgaard sitting in the parlor, her royal blue bombazine skirt topped with a white, lace-tucked shirtwaist. Her mother's cameo glowed from its position pinned to the high collar.

"Well, I declare, what has been going on here while I was off caring for my ma?"

Clara giggled behind her. "We wanted to surprise you."

"Lord love you, that you did." She walked over and stood in front of Mrs. Norgaard. "How'd you get down here?"

"I walked." She touched her cane and beamed at Clara. "With help, of course, but I shan't need that much longer. Doctor's prescription here in Clara has done its marvelous work."

Mrs. Hanson sank down in a facing brown velvet chair. "Then

you won't be needing the likes of me no more."

"Don't be silly. Now you sound like Clara when I told her you were coming home. I need and want you both. So unless you have another idea, that will be the last time we'll talk about such a matter." She thumped her cane for emphasis.

Clara and Mrs. Hanson swapped grins.

Mrs. Norgaard looked from the cane to their happy faces and chuckled herself. "Never thought of a cane as part of a conversation before."

In class that night, the students were practicing their greetings and farewells when the door opened and a big man walked in.

"Can I help you?" Ingeborge asked, then clapped her hands to her cheeks. "Dag Weinlander, is that really you?"

"Ja," he replied, nodding his freshly barbered head and neatly trimmed beard. The wild mass of stringy hair now lay on the cutting floor. Thick sable hair waved back from a broad forehead and ended just above his collar. A wide mouth with smiling lips split the beard that just covered his chin.

Clara noticed every detail. The way his ears lay close to his head and the richness of the waving hair. But what caught her attention the most were his eyes. No longer shrouded by clumpy hair and shaggy brows, eyes the blue of high mountain lakes on a summer's day stared back into hers.

She swallowed. She'd been attacked by dry throat again. "Hello, Dag," she croaked.

That night while Ingeborge was explaining the alphabet, Clara caught herself watching Dag. He didn't participate, but sat observing. He looked so different. From wild man to handsome. She couldn't wait to tell Mrs. Norgaard.

"I've been thinking," Mrs. Norgaard said over breakfast, and after they'd wondered at the change in Dag, "about ways to help you with your English. Now that Mrs. Hanson is back and I'm so much better, your duties will be of a different sort."

Clara stopped with a spoonful of hot cereal halfway to her

mouth. She set the spoon back in the bowl. "What do you mean?"

"I know how hard you are trying with your English lessons, so I have decided we will speak only English in this house. Mrs. Hanson and I agree. We'll help you, prompt you, whatever we can do, but there will be no more Norwegian. What do you think?"

I think I'm going to throw up, Clara thought. She stared from Mrs. Norgaard to Mrs. Hanson and back again. "But, but. . .I—" She licked her lips. One of her favorite Bible verses floated through her mind. "I can do all things through Christ which strengtheneth me." She sucked in a deep breath. Her smile flickered like a candle in a draft and then steadied. "All right." She let her rigid shoulders slump. What on earth had she agreed to?

Thanksgiving passed in a daze for Clara. The English-only rule applied when Dag and Will joined them for the annual feast. Will thought it was great fun, while Dag and Clara sneaked each other commiserating glances.

But Clara never felt persecuted. While discouragement sometimes dogged her, she knew they were all taking great pains to help her learn the language quickly. And it was working. With the daily repetitions, lessons with Mrs. Norgaard morning, afternoon, and evening, and her classes at the church twice a week, Clara could finally communicate.

She practiced on the shopkeepers, people at church, the postmaster. She talked to the woman in the mirror and dreamed of taking her new skill out to the Detschman farm.

All the while she spent learning English, she also prepared for Christmas. She fashioned a cloth baby doll dressed in a baptismal gown for Kaaren and sanded wooden blocks for baby Peder. While memorizing vocabulary words, she worked the hardanger lace for an apron for Nora. Mittens and a stocking hat for Carl could be knitted while she conversed with Mrs. Norgaard.

Her present for Mrs. Norgaard was the main problem. No one had found her a canary yet.

One night Dag walked her home from the church. "Won't you

come in for coffee?" she asked, her English no longer halting on the simple phrases.

"Yes, thank you." While Dag sounded more stilted, he, too, followed the English-only rule.

"Ah, welcome, Dag. Come in, come in." Mrs. Norgaard beckoned from her chair in the sitting room. "You know, I've been thinking—" she began after the coffee was served.

Clara felt her stomach fall down around her knees. Every time she heard "I've been thinking" from Mrs. Norgaard, their world turned upside down.

"I think you should come over every evening when there is no school and join us for extra work on English, both speaking and reading. And you could bring Will. I have a hunch he needs some help and is afraid to ask." She peered over her spectacles. "Or embarrassed. Not everyone is able to finish school, in fact, few are."

Dag stroked his chin. He stared right back at the woman across the room. "Yes."

"That's all?" Clara's voice squeaked on the last word.

"It won't be easy." Mrs. Norgaard continued her observation. "Nothing is."

Clara thought about that bald statement when she lay in bed that night. "Nothing is." Was that the way Dag's entire life had been? She thought to her childhood, to the laughter, the pranks, and even school. For her, learning was easy. Even this learning a whole new language was more time-consuming than hard. But then, look at the people she had helping her.

She snuggled down under the covers. Now Dag would have those same people helping him. Plus her. She'd be glad to help. Would he be able to accept *her* help? She thought of the stubborn look on his face when he read aloud in class. If determination was all it took, Dag had it by the mountainful.

Each night as she said her prayers, she included him. After all, she'd promised to do what she could and if Mrs. Norgaard could pray for Dag all these years, could she do less?

Funny, lately she hadn't been praying for her curly haired husband-to-be. When she thought about it, several weeks had passed with him not even entering her mind. "Please take care of him, wherever he is and whoever he is," she concluded. "Amen."

Several days later when Reverend Moen came to call, Clara stopped him in the hall and, in a low voice, asked him if he'd located a canary yet. At the shake of his head, Clara felt a moment of panic. Christmas was almost here and she'd been so sure she'd have a singing present for her friend.

"I'm sorry," Reverend Moen said.

"Me, too."

That evening Clara asked Dag to come into the kitchen with her while Will was settling down with his books by Mrs. Norgaard in the dining room.

"Do you know anyone who might sell a singing bird?" She paused, trying to remember the word. "A canary. I will give this to Mrs. Norgaard for a Yule present so she has music in her life."

Dag nodded as she finished speaking. "Ja, yes," he caught himself, "I do. My mother raises canaries to keep her company. I will ask her."

Clara stared at him in amazement. "Can you do everything?"

"I will see about this." He reached out with one finger and touched her smiling cheek. When he pulled away as if burned, both he and Clara returned with all speed to the other room.

For the rest of the evening, her cheek felt hot to the touch, as if it had been fire that leaped between them.

The doorbell rang several days later. When Clara opened the door, she saw Will nearly buried under the green needles of a pine tree. "The train brought in a load of Christmas trees and Dag made sure you got the finest." He dragged it inside. "Where do you want it?"

"In the sitting room. We cleared out in front of the window. Mrs. Hanson brought up a bucket of sand from the cellar." Clara felt like a child again, dancing with excitement. She wanted to clap her hands and whirl around the room but instead she helped Will stand the tree up. "Oh, it is just perfect."

"There are more branches for you to decorate with, but I couldn't carry everything at once." Will started to brush the needles off his coat but looked around, guilt flagging his already red cheeks.

"Let me take that for you." Clara helped him shrug out of his coat and took it outside to shake. By the time they had the tree set in the bucket, Mrs. Hanson had brought the decoration box down from the attic.

"I gotta be going." Will stared wistfully at the colorful balls and candle clamps in the box.

"Would you like to help us decorate the tree?" Mrs. Norgaard caught his look and asked.

Will nodded. "But I gotta get back to the stable. Dag needs me."

"That is fine. But both of you be here at six and tonight, instead of class, we'll pop popcorn and decorate the tree."

Joy sparkled in Will's eyes as he darted out of the room, returned to grab his hat and coat, and went plunging out the door. They heard his "Yee-haw" as he leapt off the porch and ran down the walk.

Dag hadn't looked her in the eyes since the night he touched her cheek. Clara frowned at the face in her mirror as she gave her golden hair a final brushing and swooped the sides back and up with her mother-of-pearl combs. What was she to do with him? After all, it was just a *touch*. She caressed the spot with her fingertips. And what was a touch between friends?

Should she mention it tonight while they were decorating the tree? She shook her head. No, better to act as if it never happened. She nodded and tried on a smile. A fingertip touched the place again. He had been so gentle. Like the kiss of a butterfly's wing. Her eyes flew open—wide open—at the word *kiss*. She turned and ran from the room as if chased by. . .by the thought of hugs and kisses—and love.

The evening was an unmitigated disaster as far as Clara was concerned. Dag never once spoke to her. He acted as if she were invisible. Clara lifted her chin higher and teased Will like she did her younger brother at home. She kept everyone laughing with her antics—all but the big man with the somber mountain lake eyes.

The tree, however, became the most beautiful she'd ever seen. Because she couldn't resist any more than a child, Mrs. Norgaard broke tradition and let them light the candles, just for a minute.

"Ohhhh." Their breath, expelled all at once, became a sigh of gratitude for something so lovely. The tree shimmered and sparkled, each glass ball and icicle refracting the candlelight and magnifying the glory.

As they pinched out the flames, the memory lingered, a preview of Christmas to come.

Clara and Mrs. Hanson spent the days baking. *Krumkake, fattigmanns,* and frosted sugar cookies. Clara took one day rising and kneading the sweet dough for *julekake,* the Norwegian Christmas bread, studded with currants and candied fruit and flavored with cardamom. The house smelled heavenly. And each evening, there were new goodies to share with her two fellow students.

Dag rapped on the back door early on December twenty-fourth. He put his finger to his lips when Mrs. Hanson started to greet him.

"Is Clara here?" he whispered.

Mrs. Hanson nodded. "Come in and I'll get her. You want some coffee? Breakfast will be ready soon."

"I have the canary for her for Mrs. Norgaard."

Mrs. Hanson pressed her hands together in delight. "I'll get her."

Dag had returned with a quilt-padded bundle and was unwrapping it when the two women tiptoed into the room.

"How did you keep it warm enough?" Clara asked, reaching to help in the dismantling. At the bottom were several stones, still warm from the oven.

"Ma and I packed him real careful. She says he's one of her best singers."

Just then the bellpull from Mrs. Norgaard's room chimed. They started, like kids caught with their hands in the cookie jar. Mrs. Hanson clapped a hand over her mouth to stop the giggles. "I'll go see what herself wants. If I'm talking with 'er up there, she might not hear you." She turned back at the door, her eyes alight with excitement. "Like we talked, Clara, I think the furnace room is the safest place for him. It's warm and dark so maybe he won't sing."

"Ma says that sometimes when you move them like this, they don't sing for a while." Dag removed the last cloth. A bright gold canary cocked his head and looked the two of them over. He cheeped and hopped down from his perch, then up to the sides of the cage, all the while watching his observers. He cheeped once or twice and then attacked the seeds in his dish.

"He's beautiful." Clara clasped her hands together. "Do you think she'll like him?"

"I'm sure she will." He began folding the quilts. "I brought a bag of seed and Ma says you can sprout some for him in the windowsill. He likes greens sometimes and fresh water."

"How much do I owe you?" Clara couldn't take her eyes from the bit of sunshine hopping around the cage.

"Nothing."

"But, Dag—"

He picked up the cage and turned toward the cellar door. "Maybe we should put a lamp down there with him for a time, just to keep him company."

"But Dag, this is my present to give."

"Just include Ma in it. She was pleased to be able to return a favor."

"And you. Without you I wouldn't have found him." Clara looked up into the face of the man towering over her. Why was it that she felt both safe and. . .and. . .she put her hand on Dag's. "Thank you, my dearest friend." Warmth flowed up her arm and curled in the pit of her stomach.

"Ah, good," Mrs. Hanson said as she reentered the room. "I'll check on the bitty thing every hour or so. This is turning into the best Christmas this house has seen in years. Hurry with that and we'll all eat together. Clara, help Mrs. Norgaard get ready, and Dag, you can bring herself down as soon as she rings."

Clara flew up the stairs to help Mrs. Norgaard with her toilet.

"Who is that downstairs?" the old woman asked.

Feeling caught, Clara stuttered. "D—Dag."

"What did he want so early in the morning?"

"Ah-h-h." Even a little fib was outside Clara's capabilities. She resorted to the ruse her parents always used. "You shouldn't ask questions. Remember, this is Christmas."

"I'm not about to forget with all the secrecy that's been hatching around here." Mrs. Norgaard tried to look stern but failed miserably.

The weather held fine for Christmas Eve, so Clara hoped her sister and her family would be able to attend the service. Dag promised to bring a sleigh so Mrs. Norgaard could attend also. This would be her first time in church since her illness.

"Are you sure going out won't lay you low again?" Mrs. Hanson asked quietly, but Clara heard the exchange.

"No, I am fine in health and thankful for this my new family, since this will be the first Christmas without my Einer."

Clara started. In all the excitement, she hadn't thought about Mrs. Norgaard's feeling sad. No wonder she had been quieter lately.

"But this huge house needs lots of people like this coming and making Christmas right. We need little children here. We must invite the Moens, they have no family in town either."

They were gathered in the hall when the jingle of harness bells announced the arrival of the sleigh. When they stepped out the door, the cold bit their noses and cheeks, but Dag soon had them all swaddled in robes, right up to the tips of their noses.

Once out on the street, Clara looked up to see the stars hanging low and brilliant in a cobalt sky. "Oh, look." She pointed to the north. Aurora borealis, the northern lights, danced on the horizon, flaring reds, blues, and greens in an unending heavenly display.

"Only God could create something so magnificent," Mrs. Norgaard whispered. "And to think He brought them out tonight just for me to see. Only He knows how much I have always loved the northern lights."

When they entered the church, the heavenly chorus from outside seemed to follow them in. Clara found herself sitting between Dag and Will, right behind Nora and her family. Ingeborge turned from her place in the front pew and wiggled her fingers. The old familiar hymns soared to meet the stars and the reading of the Christmas story settled into every heart.

When Dag shifted on the words, "Peace among men with whom He is pleased," Clara slipped her hand into his. He stilled immediately. Wasn't that what friends were for, to help each other out?

She could feel him looking at her. She stared straight ahead, concentrating on the sermon.

As they stood for the final hymn, their hands touched, holding the hymnbook. When she allowed her glance to travel up to his face, he stared back—and smiled.

Silence fell after Reverend Moen pronounced the benediction. A silence deep and full with the promise of Christmas. As they turned to leave when the organ swelled in triumphant joy, Dr. Harmon made his way to Clara's side.

"Clara, I hate to ask this, but I have a sick family with no one to help. Could you come?"

Chapter 10

B
ut my family."

"I know and this is your first Christmas in this land, but I'm afraid if I don't have help, the Ahmundsons won't see another Christmas."

"I could go," Mrs. Hanson volunteered.

"Thank you, but someone younger and stronger could help me more. Besides, Clara seems to have that healing touch."

"I will go." Dag's strong voice came from beside and above her.

"Thank you, Dag. I can use you both."

"We will save the presents until you come back." Mrs. Norgaard patted Clara's arm.

"And the dinner." Mrs. Hanson nodded her head, setting the rose on her hat to bobbing.

Everyone seemed to be making the decision for her. Clara felt trapped. She looked back at the altar, the golden cross shimmered in the candlelight. He, too, was telling her to go.

Clara turned to the doctor. "I am ready." She reached across the pew and hugged Nora and the children.

Carl shook her hand. "We will come for you when you have finished. Then we will all celebrate our Christmas."

"Go ahead like we had decided," Clara whispered to Mrs. Hanson. "I just won't be there to hear its first song."

They dropped off the other passengers and followed Dr. Harmon and his cutter out of town. Only the jingle of bells and harness and the snorting of the horses broke the stillness of the midnight air.

The stench of illness smote them in the face when they opened the door to the farmhouse. They found the mother collapsed on the floor beside the cradle of her dead infant.

Dag fired up the stove as soon as they had the woman in bed beside her delirious husband and soon had warm water so Clara could bathe the sweating bodies.

"Give them as much water as you can get them to drink and keep sponging their bodies to break the fever." Doc glanced at the cradle. "I'll take care of that one later, when we have time. I brought onions to make a poultice, see if we can't help them to breathe easier. Soon's the stuff's cut up and steamed, we can apply it. Mr. Ahmundson needs it the most."

Clara listened with one ear while she moved from bed to bed checking on the five children. Only one was cool to the touch and sleeping normally. "Let's move this one to a bed by himself," she suggested. "He's either had a light case or not sick yet."

Dag tenderly lifted each of the children while Clara changed the filthy beds and bathed the dehydrated bodies. When the littlest girl cried out and thrashed around in her agony, Dag crooned a little song that reached her fevered brain and let her relax. Working together, Dag and Clara were able to accomplish their tasks much more quickly.

The three of them worked through the night and the next day, taking turns sponging hot bodies, forcing water between parched lips, and collapsing on the spare bed when there was a moment. One by one, the children cooled, slept, and awoke. Only the parents suffered on.

Dag took time the next day to check on the livery, while Dr. Harmon looked in on other patients. Clara dragged herself around, caring for the children and keeping the parents as comfortable as possible. At three the next morning, the father passed the crisis and slipped into an easy healing sleep.

"Thank You, Father." Clara dropped down by the bed, resting her head on her hands. "Please" and "Thank You" had been her litanies for the last few days.

Dag returned in the morning with a kettle of soup, another of chicken broth, and clean sheets for the beds. He sent Clara to bed and took over the care again.

When Clara awoke in the afternoon, the mother was tossing from side to side, mumbling and calling for her baby. Mr. Ahmundson slept in a chair by the fire, a towheaded three-year-old asleep on his lap.

"Thank you, miss," he muttered, clutching her hand. "You're an angel for sure, come to save my family. Thank God for ye."

Clara patted his hand and headed back to her post beside the mother.

"She seems quieter when you are here with her." Dag stood to let her have the chair. "Doc said he would be back later tonight. He thinks the crisis will come soon."

Clara could hear Dag in the other room, setting out bowls of hot soup for those well enough to come to the table and feeding those who couldn't. Neighbors had come in to do the chores, she heard him tell Mr. Ahmundson. Clara continued dripping spoonfuls of water between the mother's lips and sponging her heat-ravaged body.

"You go get some sleep," the doctor said when he returned late in the evening. "I'll watch with her now."

Clara shook her head. "I can't." She nodded to where the frail woman clutched her hand. "She needs me."

The candle flickered and died and Doc went into the other room to find another. Clara could feel death hovering in the corner. Prickles chased each other up and down the back of her neck, making her afraid to look in case she should see his face.

"No!" She gritted her teeth. "Father, hear us. Her children need her. Please, come with Your Spirit and breathe life into her body."

The woman's breath grew fainter. The exhalations farther apart.

Clara breathed for her, with her. With each intake she whispered, "Live," and with each sigh, she called on the name of the Father.

Mr. Ahmundson stirred from the chair on the other side of the bed where he had drifted off. Tears ran down his sunken cheeks as he took her other hand and pleaded, "Don't leave us, my Inge. Please come back, we need you so."

"Come on, you must fight to live." Clara wanted to jump to her feet and pound her fists on the wall. Instead, she smoothed the cool cloth over Inge's forehead again and down the sides of her face.

"You must let her go," the doctor said softly.

Clara shook her head. She laid her face down on the woman's hand and let the tears bathe the dry skin. "Go with God, Inge." The woman's hand twitched in hers. Clara could hear a breath, a shuddery breath, and a long pause.

Inge breathed again and then again. Her breathing steadied and a slight smile touched the corners of her mouth.

"She's sleeping. Thank the good Lord, He brought her back." Dr. Harmon gripped Mrs. Ahmundson's shoulder. "She's turned the crisis."

Clara sank down on her knees beside the bed. This time tears of joy helped cool the hand she held. "Thank You, Father, thank You," she repeated over and over. When she looked in the corner, all she saw was a dress hanging on a hook.

The first thing Clara heard when she returned home a couple of days later was the trill of a canary. She followed the song to the sitting room, where Mrs. Norgaard sat in the window reading her letters. Mrs. Hanson occupied another chair, her knitting basket at her feet and turning the heel on a gray wool stocking.

"Child, you're back." Mrs. Norgaard rose to her feet so swiftly, her letters scattered across the floor. "Come, sit down. Mrs. Hanson, the coffee. Are you all right?" Her words ran over each other in her haste.

"Oh, isn't he beautiful?" Clara stopped in front of the cage where the small gold bird with a patch of black on his wing eyed her from a beady eye. She continued over to be enveloped in a hug that left no doubt of her welcome. "And yes, I am fine. Just tired."

"Have you eaten?" Mrs. Hanson joined them, alternating between patting Clara's shoulder and removing her coat and hat.

"Thank you, my dear, for my songster. He woke us on Christmas morning with a trill of joy. Our Savior is born and even the birds rejoice." Mrs. Norgaard leaned toward the cage and made chirping noises. The little bird cocked his head and responded in kind. "I think he would talk if he could."

Mrs. Hanson appeared with a coffee tray and set it on the glass-topped coffee table. "The soup's warming and after you get something filling in you, you're going up for a wash and bed. You look like you haven't slept for a month of Sundays." Mrs. Hanson bustled them both over to the couch and had coffee cups in their hands almost by magic.

"Dag told us how you cared for the Ahmundsons. Dr. Harmon says that without you, he'd have lost half the family."

"I saw death hovering in the corner, black and ugly." Clara shuddered in remembrance. "But God's love drove him back. I don't know, I've heard stories like this but—" She paused. "Inge says she heard us calling her, so she came back. It was so hard to tell her the baby had died. You can't imagine how those poor people lived. Your soup made all the difference." She patted Mrs. Hanson's plump hand after accepting a steaming bowlful herself.

"It was them grasshoppers that did it for the farmers. They ate everything showing above the ground. Vile things." Mrs. Hanson shook her head, her tongue clicking in time.

"What can be done for them?"

"You just get some rest and leave that to us," Mrs. Norgaard said firmly.

Clara slept for two days, only rising for the necessary bodily functions. When she made her way downstairs after dressing after a bath in the hip tub, she heard voices in the sitting room. Following the trail of both masculine and feminine voices, she found all the chairs occupied. When she smiled at the folks gathered, she realized all the leaders of the town were gathered.

"Times are hard all over," the postmaster was saying, "but like you said, Mrs. Norgaard, we got to take care of our own. I got me a deer last week, I can put in that. And a sack of flour. Martha says we got extra spuds, too. Some reason those thievin' 'hoppers missed our place."

Clara felt tears sting behind her eyelids as everyone around the room listed what they could share.

"We'll deliver things on Saturday, then." Dag looked to Reverend Moen for confirmation. "From the church. You and Doc know who needs supplies the worst?"

Reverend Moen nodded. "The ladies'll get together and break the sacks down into smaller pieces so's there's some for everyone."

"We'll take the coal out Friday. You say we have three tons, right?"

"So far." Reverend Moen consulted a list he held in his hand. "We can always use more of everything, so pass the word along. As Christ said, 'Whatever you do for the least of these my brethren, ye do it onto Me.'"

Clara thought to the account at the bank where she had been saving her earnings. It would pay for bags of beans or whatever they needed the most. Were Nora and Carl some of those in need? Wouldn't her sister have said something if they were going hungry?

When she mentioned her concerns later to Mrs. Norgaard, the older woman shook her head. "No, Carl wasn't wiped out like others of the farmers, even though he was stripped."

"How do you know?"

"I own the bank, remember?"

"Oh." Clara chewed on the tip of her finger. "I guess I knew Mr. Norgaard owned the bank, but when he died, I. . ."

"Who else could he leave it to? We have no children and his brother died before he did. I have a good manager and now that I am feeling back to par, I will be more involved." Mrs. Norgaard leaned forward on her cane. "But let me tell you, the men of the town aren't too happy about having a woman at the helm of the bank." They chuckled together.

The belated Christmas celebration was more than Clara ever dreamed possible. The Detschmans sleighed into town and the Moens walked over after church. Dag and Will joined the group and Mrs. Norgaard's wish of children laughing in her house came true.

There were presents for everyone. Toys for the children along with dresses for the girls and pants and shirts for the boys.

"How did she get the right sizes?" Ingeborge asked Clara during the middle of the melee.

"I'll never tell." Clara smiled at her friend.

Ingeborge stroked the heather gray, fine wool shawl she'd found in a package with her name. "I've never had anything so grand."

"You had something to do with all this," Nora said, after snagging Peder back from pulling himself up on the Christmas tree.

Clara just smiled. Never had she shopped and spent money like those last few weeks before Christmas. Since Mrs. Norgaard couldn't manage the streets yet, everything not ordered from a catalog had come home under the steam of either Clara or Mrs. Hanson.

"Thank you, Auntie Clara," Kaaren whispered, leaning against her aunt's knees. "You made my doll good. I call her Clara."

The lump that was never far away took up residence in Clara's throat again. She watched Dag's eyes open wide when Mary Moen handed him another package. When he read the tag, he looked over at Clara, his face inscrutable.

She watched him finger the muffler she had knitted out of wool to match his eyes. Those eyes had an uncharacteristic shine when he looked at her again.

There was one red-wrapped package left. Mary brought it over to Clara. Slowly she opened the box. Inside she found a white leather-bound Bible. When she opened it, the words were all in English. The front fly read, "From your friend, Dag." She raised her gaze to meet his. The shine matched in both pairs of eyes.

By the time everyone had devoured the feast the women had prepared and gathered their presents, dusk crept over the land.

"We must be going," Carl said, rounding up his brood. "Thank you for the wonderful party and all the presents. We will never forget your goodness." He shook Mrs. Norgaard's hand and put the other around the shoulder of his wife. "Who could know when we waved good-bye to Clara what wonderful things would come of it."

Nora hugged her sister. Clara felt like she'd had a piece of home as they embraced. "I'll try to come out more often," Clara whispered in Nora's ear. "I have so much to tell you."

"And the man in the picture?"

Clara shrugged. "Who knows?" *And who cares?* she thought.

The winter months passed quickly with evening classes both at church and at the house. Clara was called to help sick families several times and, each time, she prayed for those ill as much as she cared for their physical needs. Each time she was gone, she looked forward to telling Dag about her experiences upon her return.

One night after she returned from a week of caring for a woman with a newborn, she entered the house to find Dag in his usual seat at the dining room table, splitting his concentration between the book he studied and the page of sums he worked over. Mrs. Norgaard, hand on Will's shoulder, was explaining something to him, and he with his usual grin was making her laugh.

Slowly and quietly, so as not to bother anyone, Clara unwound her muffler and removed her coat. Was that a frown on Dag's broad brow? He concentrated so hard, not wanting to waste a moment now that he'd rediscovered the joy of learning. Her fingers itched to smooth the frown away.

Clara stared at her fingertips. What were they thinking of? She shifted her gaze to the man on the far side of the table. Sensing her attention, he raised his head. A smile broke forth that lighted his eyes and showed the gleam of his teeth.

Clara felt her heart clench in her chest. When it started beating again, the warmth spread clear out to the tips of her fingers and toes.

"Clara, you're home." He bounded to his feet and with him came all the others to welcome her back. When he took her hand in his, she felt a jolt clear up to her shoulder.

The memories kept her awake once she finally found her bed. They were friends, good friends, she and Dag. There was no problem with that—was there? But what if what she felt was more than one would feel for a good friend—a male, good friend, a handsome male, good friend?

But what about the man in the picture? a small voice niggled at the back of her mind. Aren't you supposed to marry him—whoever he is? Wherever he is?

Dag strode home that night, his hands locked behind his back, shoulders hunched. He could still feel the jolt like lightning that coursed up his arm. What was he thinking of? No woman, especially not an angel like Clara, would want to love him. Love, there could be no love in his life. Only worthy men found love, and he, Dag, was the most unworthy of all.

You must not see her again, he ordered himself. But the thought of no more lessons, no more sightings of her smiling face, no more Clara beat him downward like a load of steel on his back. He couldn't do it.

You must! The inexorable voice pounded his brain and heart.

Warm chinook winds melted the snow and, with the kiss of the sun, green blades popped up almost overnight. Clara strolled down the street on her way to the post office and then to the general store. Two men on horseback raised their hats in greeting as they passed her.

Clara felt punched in the stomach. One of them, the one mounted on the striking palomino, was the curly haired man in her picture. She spun around to get a second look and saw him glance back over his shoulder at the same time. It was him. Absolutely.

Forgetting the errands, she picked up her skirt and, once out of sight of the main street, raced toward the house. She stopped to unpin her hat that was flopping in a most decidedly unladylike manner and took off again. When she reached the porch, she clung to the white pillar.

Whew! She patted her pounding chest and tried to catch her breath. What she needed was a race or two up the mountains with her brothers.

"Clara, are you all right? What is wrong?" Mrs. Norgaard crossed the porch and stood in front of the panting girl.

"I'm fine. But. . .but—" Clara sucked in a deep breath and forced herself to stand still. "I saw him!"

"Who?"

"The man in my picture. He just came riding into town. He's here! Right here in Soldall."

"Oh, no." Mrs. Norgaard paled and clutched her cane with both hands.

Chapter 11

He's already married," said Mrs. Norgaard.

"But he can't be. He sent me a ticket to come here, and his picture. Why would he do that if he were already married?" Clara found it difficult to breathe around the boulder sitting on her chest.

"I don't know."

"You know him then?"

Mrs. Norgaard nodded.

Clara swallowed. "You knew who it was when I showed you my picture?"

The old woman nodded again.

"And you didn't tell me."

"No, child. I knew he was no good, and since nothing came of it, I hoped he would never return." Mrs. Norgaard turned back toward the door. "Come, let us sit and talk about this thing."

Clara looked up at the sky. Yes, the sun *was* still shining. Then why did everything seem so dark?

"Nothing has changed, you understand." Mrs. Norgaard continued when they were sitting knee to knee on the couch.

"But it has!"

"No. Now think about this. When you didn't know who he was—"

"I still don't," Clara interrupted.

The older woman ignored her. "When you didn't know who he was, you went right on building a good life for yourself here."

"But I'm not married. I came to America expecting to be married."

251

"Yes, but think of your life in the last several months. Would you not have all that's gone on? You have good friends, you speak English well, you can read the language, you have literally helped keep people alive or brought them back from near death."

"No. Yes. I don't know. Does it have to be one or the other?" Clara fought back the tears that threatened to blind her. Here she'd been so excited and now all was ashes. "I thought maybe he was coming for me."

Mrs. Norgaard shook her head, clucking her tongue in sympathy.

"At least tell me his name, if you know it."

Mrs. Norgaard paused. She lowered her gaze to their clasped hands. "His name is Jude."

"Jude. Jude! As in Judas?" Clara threw herself against the back of the couch. "If that isn't poetic justice. Now I really understand what betrayal means." She looked up to catch a look of consternation cross Mrs. Norgaard's seamed face. "I think I'll go up to my room for a while. Don't call me if a certain young cowboy comes calling."

As she fell across her bed, she let the tears come. All of a sudden her life seemed in pieces when but a short while ago she was glorying in the signs of spring. Betrayed! She'd been betrayed. But what was the purpose behind all this? After all, a ticket from Norway to North Dakota cost a great deal of money.

As her brain functioned again, the tears dried up. Now she vacillated between anger at a man who would do such a thing—to a person he didn't even know—and curiosity. Why? She got up and, sitting down at the dressing table, began brushing her hair. The soothing action always made her think better.

She took out the picture and the stained letter and tried to read the letter again but to no avail. Even knowing the man's name, the faded script made no sense. She studied the smiling mouth and laughing eyes. How could one who looked so. . .so. . . charming, the only word she could come up with, do such a terrible thing?

After washing her face, she made her way back downstairs. She still hadn't finished the errands. Maybe she'd stop by the blacksmith's and talk to Dag for a bit. He always made her feel better.

Clara walked the way to the blacksmith's first. As she drew closer, she heard two men laughing, but neither laugh belonged to Dag or Will. The ring of hammer on metal continued unabated.

Hesitant to interrupt if Dag were conducting business, Clara paused outside the door.

"So ya picked the bitty gal from Norway up at the station like I tol' ya."

"Jude, what are you talking about?" Dag's voice held more than a note of exasperation. He spoke in English.

"Wal, looky here. My brother done learned to talk like ever'-body else whilst I was gone."

Metal whanged on metal.

"So, did she think you was gonna marry her? Only the picture I sent didn't match what she see'd?"

Clara felt her eyes widen. She clamped her teeth on her lip to keep from crying out.

"You are not making any sense. I took Miss Johanson out to the Detschman farm like you asked and that was the end of it."

"But I sent'er a letter, with my picture. Only I signed yer name."

"She'da thought you was to marry her." The second man spoke up for the first time.

Clara listened to the two men laughing hysterically and thumping each other on the back. She could feel Dag's pain, emanating from the building like the tolling of the bell when a fire broke out.

"Jude, just get out of town." His voice sounded flat, beaten.

"You low-down, rotten excuse for a human being." Clara flew around the corner like a banty hen defending her brood from a low-flying chicken hawk. "Anyone who would do such a cruel and spiteful thing to another—least of all his brother. Why you ought to be horsewhipped." She stood toe to toe with the tall man and shook her fist in his face. "You think you're so smart. You don't know what it is to be a man. Even the lizards know more about human decency than you do."

Jude backed away, flapping at her with his hands.

Clara met him, stride for stride. "Dag Weinlander is one of the finest men in the country. And you have the nerve to make fun of him. Why he's worth ten of you. Twenty or forty!"

"Lady, enough. Back away before—"

"Before you what? You take to beating women, too? And children, I suppose. I pity your poor wife. God bless her to put up with the likes of you." She backed him all the way to his horse, which also shied away from the barrage of verbiage.

Jude and his cohort swung aboard their mounts and hightailed it out of there. Jude looked over his shoulder as they fled, as if afraid she might pursue them farther.

"Thank God I didn't marry him!" Clara stamped her foot and dusted her hands together, as if good riddance to bad rubbish. As the dust settled, the enormity of what she had done began to seep into her consciousness.

She turned around to find Dag watching her, the old spirit of unworthiness beating him into the dust.

"That's the way! Miss Johanson, you done good." Will leaped forward to grab her hand.

"Will!" The tone of Dag's voice stopped the youth short. He turned, caught the nod, and, after giving Clara a hint of smile for encouragement, left for the recesses of the livery.

Clara watched the lad go and wished she could do the same. What must Dag think of her? She left off memorizing the shoe and looked up to catch the sorrow in her friend's face.

"Clara, how could you. . . ?"

"How could I what?" She felt the force flow through her again. He believed what his conniving brother had said. After all these months, the old Dag was just waiting to be beaten again—by his brother. "Dag Weinlander, I'm amazed at you! Don't you know what a fine man you are? Everyone in town says so. Mrs. Norgaard thinks of you almost like a son. God made you to walk tall like the man you are. He doesn't make mistakes. God loves you and—" She bit off the words. She put a hand to her mouth. She'd almost said, "And so do I."

"And. . .and He wants you to be happy." She stared up at the face above her, drowning in the eyes of mountain lake blue. Eyes that had once clothed her in warmth but were now rimmed with frost. What had she done?

Clara turned heel and strode swiftly down the street before the tears she fought could win the battle.

Go after her, man! screamed the voice in his head. But Dag stood, as if rooted to the spot like a century-old pine tree. What could he say? What could he do?

Clara, she was magnificent. He rubbed the inside of his cheek with the tip of his tongue. Never had he seen his brother back down and run off like that. Why, he'd been almost afraid to get in the way in case she turned on him. A chuckle tickled his ribs.

He picked up his hammer from beside the smoldering forge, but instead of cranking the blower to heat the coals, he slipped the sledge into its assigned slot on the workbench and sank down on an upturned bucket.

Why didn't he let Jude have it? Why couldn't he think of a thing to say? He scrubbed at his scalp as if to drive the ideas either into his brain or drag them out.

Jude hurt Clara! The thought flared forth in a burst of pure, red rage. His brother tried to make a fool out of the woman he loved. Dag ground his teeth together. Where could he find him? He rose to his feet and began pacing back and forth. What would Jude do? Go home to their mother? Dag shook his head.

Hide out? He nodded. One fist slammed into the palm of the other hand. The rhythm beat with each stride. Where would the dirty dog hide? Step, slap. Would Clara ever speak to him again? Step! Slap! What difference did it make? Who was he that she should care?

He leaned against the support post, barely restraining himself from pounding his head against the wood. *Dolt. Dag the Dolt.* He heard again the jeering voice from his youth. One tear squeezed past the power of his will and trickled down into his perfectly trimmed beard.

When Clara returned to the big house, she dropped the mail

on the hall table and dragged herself up the stairs. Without speaking to anyone, she staggered into her bedroom and slumped on the bed.

Dag, her best friend, would probably never speak to her again. And his brother—oh, she could wring his neck with her bare hands, just like butchering a mean, tough old rooster. But Dag—how could she stay in the same town and not see him? Not talk to him? Not study with him, laugh with him, see the world through his magnificent eyes? Not tend the sick or visit the well?

Her hand over her eyes blotted out the sun streaming in the windows.

When Mrs. Hanson knocked on the door, Clara sent her away with a mumbled excuse. What kind of a woman was she to scream at a total stranger like that? But he—Jude—what a perfect name for him—the betrayer—he had laughed at Dag. Tried to make a fool of him. Treated him like pond scum.

She bit her lip so hard she could taste the blood.

"God, Father, what am I to do?" The tears trickled down the sides of her face and watered her hair.

This must be how a bucket feels coming up from the well, she thought, as she pulled herself hand over hand toward the light. A rapping penetrated her fog. And repeated.

She forced open her eyes. The afternoon sun had dimmed to dusk. The thumping she now recognized as Mrs. Norgaard tapping on the door.

"Clara, dear, let me come in. I know you are in there." She tapped again.

Clara pushed herself up on her elbows. Had she locked the door in her anger? She shook her head. Waves sloshed from side to side within her skull. She groaned and flopped back down.

"Clara, please."

"Come in, it's not locked." She covered her eyes with one arm to still the pounding in her head. She must look a sight. She could barely open her eyes, they were so swollen.

Mrs. Norgaard pushed open the door and swept across the carpet. After studying the form crumpled on the bed, she sat down on the edge. "Is it really as bad as all this?" Her voice floated like dust motes on a warm and caring sunbeam.

Clara nodded. She clamped her fingers against pounding temples.

"I've taken the liberty of asking Mrs. Hanson to make you some sassafras tea. When she comes, I want you to drink it all. Better than laudanum to ease a headache." She sat there, not moving.

Clara lay there, listening to her own breathing and the blood pounding clear to her fingertips.

Even Mrs. Hanson was quiet, tiptoeing in and keeping her voluminous comments to herself. She set the tray down, light as a whisper and, after propping Clara against pillows stacked and fluffed behind her, left the room.

"Here." Mrs. Norgaard handed Clara the cup as soon as the young woman opened her eyes.

Clara took a sip and made a face.

"Drink it, it's good for you." Clara obeyed, her thoughts and feelings in too much of a muddle to resist.

When the pain lines furrowing Clara's forehead relaxed, Mrs. Norgaard settled herself in a chair she'd pulled over to the bed. "Now, my dear, I can't help you unless I know what terrible thing has transpired."

"I'm so ashamed." A sob turned into a hiccup.

"What could you have done to make you so ashamed?"

Clara waited, wishing the woman would disappear on one hand and that she were a mind reader on the other. Then she wouldn't have to tell the entire miserable tale.

"There I was, screaming like a fishwife, right out where all the town could hear."

Bit by bit, Mrs. Norgaard dragged the story from her sorrowing friend.

"And so, Dag will probably never speak to me again," Clara finished the tale on another sigh.

A tap sounded at the door. Upon Mrs. Norgaard's "Yes?" Mrs. Hanson stuck her head in. "There's a young man down here who wants to talk with Clara."

"See, I knew Dag has more sense than you give him credit for."

"No, I don't want to see him. Tell him I'm ill."

"You don't look so good, that's true." Mrs. Hanson withdrew her head and they could hear her thumping down the stairs. Silence settled back in the room.

"You have to see him again."

"I know. But not like this." Clara listened to the silence again. By now, peace had begun its gentle attack on her strident emotions.

"You know what I think?"

"No, what?"

"I think I see God's hand in all of this and He has a marvelous plan still to be worked out. But not all tonight." The older woman rose from her chair. "Would you care for a bit of soup or toast?" When Clara shook her head, Mrs. Norgaard just nodded. "All right then, let's get you into bed. Like the Psalm says, 'Weeping may endure for a night, but joy cometh in the morning.' And we want that morning to come soon."

Even after being tucked in and kissed on the forehead, Clara felt sure she'd never cut off the voices in her head long enough to sleep. But the next thing she knew, the rising sun tinted the curtains creamy gold.

The first thing she thought of was Jude on his fancy palomino, hightailing it out of town. She had to admit, it was funny. Like when the horse kept jumping around. She must have been something when even that big dumb, four-footed beast was scared of her. Anything that would carry Jude around had to be dumb.

She stretched her arms over her head and wriggled her toes. Somewhere a rooster crowed. . .and another answered.

When she thought of Dag, she remembered a dog she'd seen beaten one time. How it crawled away with its tail dragging in the dirt. How all his life this man had been beaten down by his conniving younger brother. The fire simmered in her belly again. What could they do to make Jude crawl like the worm he was? How could they get even?

Chapter 12

I could kill him!"

"Dag, no!" Will shook his master's shoulders. "Wake up, Dag, you're dreaming."

Dag fought his way out of the fog and sat upright. He could feel his brother's throat clenched between them, his hands squeezing, squeezing the life out. "No!"

"It's all right, come on, everything will be all right," Will murmured in the soothing, singsong voice Dag had taught him to use with a skittish horse. "You'll never kill anyone, not even your brother, even if he does deserve it."

"He was going to use Clara to make a fool out of me again." Dag sank down on the crinkly mattress. "Why does he hate me so? All my life I tried to do as my father said, take care of Ma and my brother. All my life. I know I'm dumb, dolt they called me, and big and ugly, but Will, I tried." He sat up and grasped Will by the collar of his shirt.

"No, Dag, no, no, you're not dumb." Will reached for the massive hands of his master and friend.

Dag continued, not even hearing Will's plea. "I quit school so I could go to work and earn some money. They could have farmed, but Ma said the land was too poor. Even when I got my own forge, they called me dumb dolt."

"Dag, listen to me. They're just jealous. And lazy and mean."

"Dumb dolt and now I feel such anger I want to kill my brother. My only brother." Dag rolled his head from side to side. After a time he began again. "And now Clara won't see me. After attacking Jude like that. Humph! No one puts anything over on my Clara. God, can't I do anything right?" He threw himself from his bed and thundered out the door of the soddy.

Dag ran as if pursued by the devil himself. As his bare feet pounded the mud of the road, his mind kept pace. *God, if You are really the God they talk about in church, take me away from here now. They say there's a heaven. It'd sure beat this life on earth.* He slipped in one viscous hole and fell to his knees. When he rose to run again, he caught himself slipping and sliding with fatigue.

The next time he fell, he lay flat out, face down in the mud. He raised his head just enough to breathe. "God," he panted at the heavens, "I give up! You hear me, I give up!" The words ended on a screech.

Dag lay there waiting for a lightning bolt to strike him. When nothing happened, he pushed himself to his knees and then his feet. When he staggered home, chills rocked his body, but he stopped at the windmill and, with one shaking hand, began pumping. After sluicing buckets of clean water and scrubbing with the bar of soap in the scrub bucket, he rinsed again and padded into the soddy. He rubbed himself dry with a coarse towel and fell back in bed. Clean, he finally felt clean. "Father, forgive me," he mumbled as he drifted off to sleep.

The rooster crowing from the farm across the way brought Dag bolt upright in bed. Had it all been a dream? More like a nightmare. He rubbed the top of his head. No, his hair was still damp. He had indeed lain in the mud and been washed clean. But now he felt. . .he felt like crowing as the rooster did. He began singing instead, "Onward Christian soldiers. . ." His rich baritone filled the soddy and escaped out the chimney.

Will stumbled from the other room, rubbing his eyes. Dag singing. . .in the morning? Dag singing. . .at all? "Yip-pee!" He dragged his pants from the end of his bed and staggered after Dag, pulling his pants on as he ran.

"I'll go see him as soon as he gets to the shop." Clara took another turn around her room. "He must open at seven." She glanced at the clock on her chest of drawers for the umpteenth time.

"I'll go see her as soon as it is polite." Dag brushed an imaginary piece of straw off his navy wool pants. He gave his hair another brushing.

They met halfway in the middle.

"I'm sorry," they both said at once. They looked at each other and laughed.

"Have you had breakfast?" Clara asked. At the shake of his head, she took his arm. "Good, Mrs. Hanson makes wonderful pancakes."

"I. . .I—" They both started to talk again at the same time.

"Ladies first." Dag looked down at the silly black feather bobbing almost at his shoulder. What was she doing wearing such a fancy hat this early in the morning?

"All right. Please forgive me for making such a fool of myself yesterday."

"The only one you made a fool of was my brother. Please, accept my apologies for the way he has acted."

"Of course. Now that that's out of the way, I have a plan. How would you like to get even with your brother? Turn the tables on him for a change?"

"And how would we do this?"

"Well, this way." They climbed the stairs to the porch as she talked. "Jude wanted you to feel like a fool when I learned of his treachery, right?" Dag nodded and opened the door for her. "What if he thought we were courting?"

"How could we do that?" He helped her off with her coat.

"The way everyone courts, silly. You could escort me to church, to the social at the schoolhouse, out for drives in your oh-so-shiny buggy. . ."

"It's too muddy to take out the buggy." He hung his own coat up.

"Dag, you know what I meant." Together they entered the dining room laughing.

"Now these are the faces I love to see in the morning," Mrs. Norgaard said as she winked at Mrs. Hanson. "I think you better go flip some more of those pancakes of yours and fry extra bacon.

Dag looks like he could eat a whole ham."

She turned to the two young people. "Sit down, my children, and tell me what brings such smiles to your faces."

"We're going to get even." Clara plunked herself down on her chair. "With Jude. He's been mean to Dag for too long."

A slight frown marred Mrs. Norgaard's forehead. "Get even. You know, God says that is His job."

"I know. But we're going to help Him out." Clara explained the plan, totally seriously and in great detail. "What are you laughing about?"

"I'm not laughing." Mrs. Norgaard swallowed the chortle that belied her words. She sipped her coffee to stifle another giggle. When she had composed her mouth, if not her eyes, she continued. "I think that is a very good plan and you should begin immediately."

Dag looked from his young friend to his old friend and back again. There was something going on here that he could sense but not recognize. But then, how much had he ever tried understanding women in his monastic life anyway? He shrugged the thought away. At least this plan was better than the one he'd dreamed of during the dark hours.

The sun smiled on their plan as they walked through the town that afternoon. Dag recognized one of Jude's cronies standing by the train station so he knew word would get back to his brother. But as he and Clara passed the church, he forgot his brother and remembered the song in his heart when he awoke. That night he walked with her to their English class at the church. Will accompanied them, hands in his pockets, whistling away. When Dag had shared a little of "the plan" with him, the young man nodded solemnly. "That'll get him for sure," was his only comment. But he didn't stop whistling.

When Dag walked Clara home, Will made excuses and went another way.

"But I don't know how to dance." Dag threw his hands up in

the air, hoping to end the discussion.

"But if we are to do this courting right, you must take me to the box social at the schoolhouse on Saturday." Clara sat in the chair in front of the window in the sitting room. Late afternoon sunlight slanted in and set her hair afire.

Dag couldn't take his eyes off the golden threads.

"It's for a good cause. They are trying to earn enough money for a new roof." Clara laid her hands in her lap.

"I'll put the roof on myself," Dag muttered in a voice Clara barely heard.

She wet her lips with the tip of her tongue. "You could learn to dance."

"I suppose you would teach me that, too."

"My box will be the best-tasting and prettiest there."

"Will and I do just fine at home. We aren't starving."

"Maybe Jude will be there. This is a perfect opportunity to—"

"Get even. Yes, I know." Dag dragged his hands over his scalp, mussing the hair he usually kept so carefully brushed. "All right. We will go. But we might leave early."

But they didn't leave early, and even though Jude never made an appearance, Dag and Clara had a wondrous time. Dag was blessed with the natural rhythm and grace sometimes given to big men, and once he learned the patterns of a dance or two, he couldn't get enough. He danced every dance, even those he didn't know.

He danced the waltz with Mrs. Norgaard and the polka with Mrs. Hanson. His feet tapped out the reel with Clara, and they swung past each other on the round and square dances. If he made a mistake, he just laughed along with the others and went on dancing.

Clara sank down on a chair along the wall, next to Mrs. Norgaard. "I'm exhausted." She fanned her hot face with her handkerchief. She watched Dag swing Ingeborge past on another polka.

"I think we are seeing a miracle," Mrs. Norgaard whispered in Clara's ear.

"Dag?"

"Yes, Dag. I thank the good Lord every night for what He is doing with our young man."

"I wish—" Clara fanned herself again.

"What, my dear?"

"Oh, nothing. Would you like some punch?" At Mrs. Norgaard's nod, Clara pushed herself to her feet. What she wished was that Dag was truly her young man and that this courting wasn't just a sham.

"Think yer purty smart, don'cha." Jude strolled into the blacksmith's shop late one afternoon.

Dag ignored him, continuing to forge the point on a pickax.

"Well, she ain't for the likes o' you." Jude spit a glob of tobacco juice into the dirt. "You taken her out to see Ma?"

Dag thrust the heavy steel back into the forge and motioned Will to crank the handle on the blower. The whine of the machine overpowered any conversation. When the iron point glowed red, then white, Dag pulled it out and returned it to the anvil.

"Maybe I shoulda taken that little filly fer m'self after all."

"You have a wife."

"Don't remind me." Jude dug a kerchief out of his back pocket and blew his nose. "We're livin' out at Ma's now. To help her out some'at."

Dag returned the piece of steel to the forge. When he looked up, Jude was gone. Now he'd have to send more food and coal out there. He gritted his teeth and wiped the sweat off his brow with the back of his glove.

Knowing he would have a massive cleaning job afterward, Dag took the surry out on a Sunday morning to drive the household of women to church. Mrs. Norgaard still wasn't strong enough to walk the distance. When spring came to North Dakota, the frozen roads bottomed out with the thaw, but the streets in town weren't quite the morass of the country roads.

After greeting friends, Clara and Dag entered the sanctuary and sat side by side. Sharing the same hymnbook made them smile at each other. Singing together, her soprano blending with his baritone, made them smile.

Reverend Moen took his place behind the carved, white-and-gilt pulpit. He smiled at those before him. "Grace and peace from God our Father and our Lord Jesus Christ."

Clara settled back against the wooden pew. Today she could truly sense both the grace and peace. She felt it warm her from the inside out. She ignored the warmth emanating from the man beside her and concentrated on the sermon.

"Today's gospel is from the fifth chapter of Matthew, verse forty-three and following." He glanced again around the congregation and began reading. "Ye have heard that it hath been said, Thou shalt love thy neighbour, and hate thine enemy. But I say unto you, Love your enemies, bless them that curse you, do good to them that hate you, and pray from them which despitefully use you, and persecute you; That ye may be the children of your Father which is in heaven: for he maketh his sun to rise on the evil and on the good, and sendeth rain on the just and on the unjust."

He closed the Bible and then his eyes. "Father, teach us this day what You would have us to learn. Open our hearts and minds that we might indeed listen unto You. Amen."

The congregation responded with one voice, "Amen."

Clara argued with the verses through the rest of the sermon, only catching random phrases of Reverend Moen's message. *But I have been praying for him, from way back when I first received the letter. And right up until. . .* She tried a different tack. *I don't hate Jude. . .I. . .I'm just angry with him. Furious is more like it. I don't want to do good to him. . .I want to get even. He hurt Dag; there's no love in the way he has treated Dag all these years.* She groaned inwardly. *Yes, persecute would be the perfect word to describe the way Jude and his mother treated Dag.*

"Our Father so often gives us a promise along with the hard commands, for these words are truly a hard order for us to follow."

Clara covered her unladylike snort with a cough.

"Just think, that we may be children of our Father who is in Heaven, but who loved us so much He sent His Son to be persecuted and to die on the cross. . .for you. . .and for me." Reverend Moen leaned forward. There was not a sound from the congregation.

"He forgave each of us. . ." The pause stretched.

Clara's heart felt like it was being pulled in two directions and at any moment, it might rip in two.

The pastor continued, "And so must we forgive. Amen."

Dag kept his shoulders rigid through superhuman efforts. *Forgive! I've been forgiving them all my life. So they hurt me. That wasn't so bad; I got used to it. But now Jude has hurt Clara. Beautiful, innocent Clara, who he hadn't even known. All to play a trick on me, his ugly dolt of a brother. That I can't forgive!*

"As you were forgiven." The words chased each other through his mind and around his heart, stabbing him as they ran.

Am I really a child of God? He looked up at the shiny gold cross in front of the picture of Jesus tending his sheep. Dag stifled a groan that tore from his innermost hidden place.

"He died on the cross. . .for you. . .and for me."

For me. For Dag Weinlander. Dag swallowed hard against the moisture rising in his throat and blinding his eyes. He blinked furiously.

"Our closing hymn for today is number 360, 'My Jesus, I Love Thee.' "

As the organ wheezed into the opening bars of the song, Clara and Dag stood along with the congregation. The words poured forth. "My Jesus, I love thee, I know thou art mine. For thee all the folly of sin I resign. . ."

Dag quit singing. He bit his lip and let the words and music roll over him, bathing him in the healing Christ promised. He whispered along with the final line. "If ever I love thee, my Jesus 'tis now."

Clara struggled to reach the high notes—and gave up. Singing was impossible from a throat clogged with tears. Why did Reverend Moen choose such a sermon for today? Had someone told him about their game? Who would? And was it *really* a game? Was getting even ever a game?

Neither Dag nor Clara spoke a word on the ride home, until they arrived at the big house, and then it was only a polite good-bye.

The doorbell announced a visitor just as the grandfather's clock bonged six times.

"Come right on in," Mrs. Hanson said. "You're just in time for supper."

"No, I mean, no, thank you. I'd just like a few minutes with Clara, if I may." Dag gripped his hat in his hands. This would be the hardest thing he'd ever done.

When Clara came to the door, he stared into her eyes, then dropped his gaze to the floor. "Could you come out for a moment, please?"

She nodded, reached behind her for the shawl on the coat tree, and stepped outside, her gaze never leaving his face. "What is it, Dag. What's wrong?"

Her soft voice tore his heart from his chest. "I. . .we. . .that is, I cannot play our courting game any longer." He took a deep breath. "And I cannot see you anymore." He turned and stepped off the porch, his long strides eating up the distance to the fence.

"Dag, what is it?"

He kept on walking.

Clara chewed on her knuckle for one brief moment and flew down the walk after him. When he didn't stop at her calling his name, she grabbed his coat when she caught up with him.

"Now, tell me what this is all about." She put all the force she could into her words.

"*Nei*, no. Just let it be."

"Dag, you can't run away from me now. Not now or anytime." Clara grasped his lapels with shaking hands. "You can't leave because I love you and you love me, if you'd just open your eyes. If you can't see it, maybe I should take one of your hammers and smack you over the head with it till you get some sense."

"You love me?" His voice squeaked.

Clara stepped back. She tipped her head slightly to the side and glared up at him. "I said so, didn't I?"

Dag grabbed her around the waist with both hands and whirled them both around. "She loves me!" he yelled to the robin who fluttered out of his nighttime perch at all the commotion.

He set her down just long enough to wrap both arms around her and lifted her for the kiss he'd dreamed of during the long winter nights.

Clara wrapped her arms around his neck and kissed him back. When they drew apart to breathe, she traced one slim fingertip across his full bottom lip. "I like kissing a man with a beard," she whispered and placed her lips on his again. "But only if that man is you." Her breathy voice tickled the soft hairs around his mouth.

Slowly, he set her down, never letting her move from the circle of his arms. "I feel like Jacob who stole the birthright," he confessed.

"No, you have it backwards. You're the older. Your brother has spent most of his life trying to steal the birthright from you. But now you know how much you are worth. And nothing, no one, can take that or me from you."

"Clara, my heart, I love you." There, he'd said the words. He couldn't remember ever uttering them before. Such simple words. He thought back to this morning. He had said them before. Today, in church. Only it was a different love song, "My Jesus, I love thee, I know thou art mine." He looked deep into Clara's eyes, searching her soul. "My Clara, I love thee, I know thou art mine." And thus he gave her his heart.

Epilogue

Clara rocked gently in the chair on the wide front porch. She could hear the canary singing from Mrs. Norgaard's room up above. He serenaded them from the first rays of sunlight until the golden ball sank in the west.

On the flagpole attached to the house, she could hear the Norwegian flag fluttering in the breeze. The seventeenth of May, Norwegian Independence Day and Clara and Dag's one-year anniversary.

She leaned her head against the back of the seat and closed her eyes. What a day that had been. No, to be exact, the celebration had begun the week before that, when Mrs. Norgaard called her and Dag into the sitting room one evening.

After they took their places on the brown velvet couch, a gentle silence permeated the room.

"I have something for you," she said, her face serious but her eyes sending messages of warmth and love. "I've put off telling you this because I don't want you to be burdened by an old woman's silliness."

"What is it?" Clara felt alarm leaping in her heart. Was something wrong with her friend? Something she'd not told them?

Mrs. Norgaard leaned forward and handed them an envelope. When Clara looked up in consternation, the old woman just nodded.

Dag slit the envelope open and removed a parchment sheet. Together, he and Clara read the formal words.

Clara felt her mouth fall open. She stared from the letter to Mrs. Norgaard and back to the paper in Dag's hands. "You mean, you—?" She couldn't get the rest of the words out.

"Yes, the house is yours, but only if you truly want it."

"Want it? How could you doubt something so wonderful?"

"But that means you will be burdened with me until the good Lord calls me home."

"No, not a burden." Dag shook his head. "You have given me a life." He clasped Clara's hand in his own. "And a wife, and now a home."

"Then I believe we have made a fair trade, for without Clara, I would not be here to rejoice with you." Mrs. Norgaard blinked rapidly, matching the motions of the two on the settee.

Clara crossed the small space and dropped to her knees in front of her mentor. "Thank you, from the bottom of my heart."

Mrs. Norgaard stroked back the tendrils of silky hair that framed Clara's face. "I have one more favor to ask."

"What? Anything."

"Just fill these rooms with laughing children as soon as you can, so I can enjoy them, too."

Clara, dreaming in the rocker, stroked her rounded belly. Little Lars or Lisa seemed in a mighty big hurry to make an entrance—or else the baby was practicing broad jumps.

She sighed. And the wedding had been magnificent. Her in her *bunad* and Nora in hers. Now neither of them would fit into their black skirts or sparkling aprons. Their babies would be born close together.

Dag had stood before the congregation after the pronouncement of man and wife. "I have something I'd like to say," he announced. He glanced at Reverend Moen for permission. At the preacher's nod, Dag continued. "Most of you knew me long before Clara came to Soldall. You brought your plowshares to be sharpened and your horses to be shod. But I was not one to talk and share the latest news."

A ripple of laughter spread across the congregation.

"But you saw me then and you see me now. What happened to me was God's miracle. He took a bitter, beaten man and poured love into his heart, that love that Christ talks about. God used a young woman to bring life to many of us in this town and then He gave her to me. Can you doubt God's great love? If He could love me, He can love anyone."

There wasn't a dry eye in the place.

Clara straightened from her idyll on the porch. The familiar whistle announced the arrival of her beloved whistler. She watched through the breaks in the newly leafed trees for glimpses of his head as he strode the street for home. She rubbed her back again.

Dag took the porch steps in one bound. "Have you been resting like you were told?" he asked, his smile causing her heart to leap in response.

"I have. Resting and remembering." She laid her cheek against the back of his hand.

"Remembering?"

"Oh, about the wedding and the months before that." She kissed a spot on his hand that had gotten too close to the heat.

Dag sank down on the floor beside her, one arm propped on a raised knee. "I have a confession to make."

Clara's eyebrows traveled upward.

"Your present didn't come in on the train."

Clara rubbed her back again and this time squirmed a bit in the seat. "I think yours might be coming sooner than we expected."

Dag turned in time to catch a grimace marring the serenity of her forehead. "Are you all right?" A tinge of panic touched his voice.

"I'm fine. Or I will be after a few more hours." She stroked her fingers through the coffee-hued hair that waved back so richly from his face. She'd come to Dakota to find her dream and now they were living it.

DAKOTA
DUSK

Chapter 1

"Ma, how would you like it if I moved back home?" Jude Weinlander dropped a kiss on his mother's cheek. "I know things ain't been goin' good for you. I. . .you. . . ah. . .the farm needs some work done, bad."

"You would do that?" Tall, iron-stiff Augusta turned from the black iron cookstove and waved a wooden spoon in the air. Shock and heat painted her face bright red.

"Well. . .uh. . .I'm kinda between jobs right now, so's Melissa, and I could stay around for a time, until you get someone to help you again, that is." Jude stuttered over the words while raking a hand through the dark blond curls that fell over his forehead in a charming tangle. He leaned his six-foot frame against the kitchen counter. The smile that had broken half of the female hearts west of the Mississippi and north of the Missouri erased the unaccustomed worry lines from his forehead and relit the flame in his clear, sky blue eyes.

Augusta left off stirring her pot of stew on the stove and sank into a chair at the square oak table, scarred and scuffed by years of hard use. She stared across the room at her son, a gleam of moisture evident in her faded blue eyes, eyes that had once matched those of the young man before her. "Have you spoken with Dag?" She pushed a strand of steel gray hair back into the bun at the base of her neck.

"Nah, why should I?" Jude pulled his rear away from the counter, snagged a chair out with his foot, and joined her at the table.

"He has been helping me out some with beans and flour and coffee and such," she said.

"Don't you keep the hens and cow no more?"

"Ja, sure, but the 'hoppers took the garden and I had no one to do the hay, so they got that, too." Augusta stared out the window. "Not been easy the last couple of years. My hired man quit this spring, you know. Sometime after you left town." She pushed herself to her feet as if the cares of the world were pounding her into the sod. "You want another cup of coffee?"

Jude nodded. "Things'll be easier now, Ma. You'll see." He accepted the chipped mug she offered him.

"Why?" Her tone sharpened. "You got some new scheme up your sleeve?"

"Not yet. Come on, Ma, I left off the cards and such. I aim to help you put this place back together. Dag ain't the only one in this family can take care of his ma." He patted her work-worn hand where it lay on the table. "You'll see."

"It'll be mighty fine having you home again." She sipped from her cup. "Where'd you leave Melissa?"

"She's at her ma's. Said I'd come first and make sure us coming here was all right."

"Son, this is your home. You're always welcome here."

"Not like some other places, huh?"

"You in some kind of trouble?" Augusta peered at him, as if delving behind the smile in his eyes to see if he was fooling her. When Jude employed this smile, the very angels would hand over their halos; its candlepower wasn't wasted on his mother. "Nah, Ma, come on. I just want to help you, that's all."

"I thank you, Son. I most surely do." Augusta straightened her shoulders. "Well, I'd best be gettin' at the chores. You want to milk old Betsy while I feed the hens? Then you can dig those spuds that made it through the 'hoppers."

"I. . .ah. . .I thought maybe I'd go for Melissa this morning. She don't take too well to staying with her ma. They don't get along much."

"Oh?" Augusta caught herself before her shoulders slumped, but barely.

"Don't get me wrong, Ma. I'll milk first." Jude held up a

placating hand. He rose to his feet as if anxious to be at his work. "You still keep the bucket out in the well house?"

After the chores were finished, Jude hitched up the old horse to the ancient wagon and, leaving his saddle horse in the pasture, drove out of the yard. He watched the dust spurt up from beneath the horse's hooves and caught the caw of a crow, but otherwise the fall day stretched empty before him.

I've got to get some money, get some money. The thoughts kept time with the jangle of the harness and the *clumph, clumph* of the hooves in the dust. "Ya suppose there's a game going tonight in Soldall?" he asked the world at large.

The crow circled overhead and cawed an answer.

"If only I didn't have to get Mellie. Sometimes women are more trouble than they're worth." He shook his head. *And this one ain't been worth much for some time.*

If only the baby had lived. Then he'd been one up on Dag. The first grandson, now that would have made his ma proud. But now that Dag was married, he'd probably have a whole houseful of kids.

Jude groaned and shook his hand at the persistent crow. Another trick on his brother gone sour. What a shock it had been to see the new Dag Weinlander—clean-shaven, neatly trimmed hair, decent clothes. Jude looked down at the new hole in the knee of his trousers. The cloth was so weak, it split when he knelt down to milk the cow this morning.

"It ain't fair. My brother, the dolt himself, has a thriving business, a beautiful wife, and that grand house of his. It just ain't fair, I tell ya." The old bay horse flicked its ears and kept up a nodding trot.

By the time Jude had driven onto the lane to his mother-in-law's farm, he had worked himself into a temper. The prosperous look of the farm did nothing to improve his mood. The look she gave him when she let him in the house could have curdled milk.

"Get your stuff. We gotta get back so's I can help Ma."

"I. . .I'm ready." Melissa dragged a scruffy carpetbag from

277

another room. The effort made her catch her breath on a sob as she pushed a limp strand of dingy hair back from her face. "You hungry?"

"You got it ready?"

"No, but it'd just take a minute. I could slice you some bread and—"

"All right, just quit jawing and do it." Jude kept his gaze from wandering to his mother-in-law, but he could feel her glare stabbing him in the back.

Melissa scuttled over to the cupboard and, after slicing the bread and meat, put them together with butter. Then she poured coffee into a canning jar and, after a quick nod in her mother's direction, went to pick up her satchel. Bread and coffee in her hands, she looked from the carpetbag to her husband and back again.

Jude started for the door. At his mother-in-law's "Harumph," he snorted in disgust and whirled back to pick up the carpetbag. The glare he shot at Melissa made her sob again.

The trip home passed without a word. When Jude cast withering glances at Melissa, she studied her hands or the goldenrod nodding in the evening breeze along the side of the dusty road.

That night in bed, Melissa whimpered in her sleep. When she began to cough, Jude jerked the sheet over him and rolled over in bed. "Can't ya do something about that?" he snarled. "I need my sleep."

When Melissa returned to the bed, the smell of camphor floated around her like a mist. Jude sat up, glared at her in the moonlight, and, after punching his pillow, flopped on his other side. What he wouldn't do for a drink.

In the morning, Jude drove his mother and wife into town for church. After dropping them off, he aimed the horse toward the saloon at the other end of town.

He tied the animal to the hitching rack in front of the

flat-fronted building and, after checking the locked door, walked around the back.

"Smitty, hey, Smitty. Open up," Jude called softly as he rapped on the door. The saloon wouldn't open until noon, but by then he should be back at the church to pick up the womenfolk.

"What now?" A rough voice called down from the flung-open window above.

"Hey, Smitty. How ya doin'?" Jude pushed the hat back on his head and grinned up at his friend.

"Well, well. If it ain't Jude come back to town. 'How ya doing' is right. Where you been?" The bartender leaned his elbows on the windowsill.

"Here and there. How about a bottle? I gotta get back and pick up the womenfolk after church or I'd stay for a game or two. How things been, anyhow?"

"Good, good. But not the same without you around. Sure you can't stay for a time or so?" A grin split the man's leathery face. He polished the top of his shiny pate with a cupped hand.

"Not this time, but I ain't gone for good. I'm helpin' my ma out some, you know how it is when they gets older. So I'll be around now and then." Jude shifted from one foot to the other. "What about that bottle or you gonna jaw all day?"

Smitty pulled his head back so fast he banged his head on the window.

Jude laughed and slapped his knee. "Better be more careful with my bottle. I got a thirst 'bout as wide as the Red in full flood." He grinned as he realized it was good to be back in Soldall. Now, if he could just figure a way to get rid of the womenfolk. His fingers itched for the cards the way his throat did for that first swallow of good, solid whiskey.

The door of the saloon swung open in front of him. "Come on in then, you old buzzard." Smitty scratched himself and headed for the front of the saloon. "You heard about your brother?" He continued without waiting for an answer. "After he married that pretty little thing you brought over for him, they moved into the house with Mrs. Norgaard. In fact, as I heard it, the old lady deeded them two the house. Jude, you wouldn't recognize—you seen Dag yet?"

"Now, why would I want to see him? You think I been pining away for the sight of my brother or something?" Jude clapped his hat down on the counter and hung his rear over a bar stool.

"Nah. I just thought I should bring you up to date, so's you're not too surprised or something." Smitty slapped a bottle down on the bar. "That'll be four bits."

"Ah. . .I. . .uh. . .how about I pay for this later? I'm kinda short of cash right now."

Smitty paused for a moment. "You know, I—" He paused. "All right. Just this once. For old-time's sake."

Jude swung off the stool. "Thanks. If nothing else, I'll pay first hand I win." He raised a hand in farewell and headed out the door.

Once seated in the wagon, he broke the seal of the bottle and, lifting the bottle high, poured a generous slug down his gullet. He sighed and wiped his mouth with the back of his hand. It had been much too long between drinks.

He recapped the bottle and set it down in the back in between the burlap bags on the wagon bed. Now, after a stop at the mercantile for a store of tobacco, he'd head back for the church.

"Jude," the store owner said, slapping his hands on the counter before him and leaning across it. "If'n you ain't a sight for sore eyes. Gunna join us for a game tonight? I still gotta get that hunnert dollars back from the last round."

"Soon, soon. Anything new been happening whilst I been gone?"

"You seen Dag? Man, we sure done him a favor, bringing that pretty little gal over from Norway for him."

Jude felt a rage begin a slow burn down about his gut. If he heard about his wonderful brother one more time, he'd smash someone for sure. "Cut the jawing. You got any tobacco? And a couple of cigars. Better add some cheese, coffee, and some of those cinnamon twists. My ma always had a hankering for cinnamon twists." He stared around the well-stocked store as he waited for his order. Cracker and pickle barrels fronted the wooden counter. Boxes of the new dry cereal called cornflakes lined the shelves above the tins of spices. Rakes, hoes, and pitchforks hung from hooks above the boxes of boots and shoes. Kitchenwares filled one aisle and farm implements another.

One of these days, when his ship came in, Jude knew he would come in here and just buy whatever he needed. No more of this putting it on the slip and heming and hawing back and forth over what he could buy. Why, he needed new boots and—he stared down at the split leather on his ancient boots. All he really needed was one good night at the card table. One good night and he'd be back up on top again.

"Here ya go." Adam set the sack up on the counter. "Need anything else?"

"Not for now. Put that on my mother's tab for now. I'll settle up with you later."

"I don't know, Jude. Dag, he's mighty particular what goes on the bill, now that he's payin' it." He glanced up in time to catch the thundercloud racing across Jude's face. "But I'm sure this time'll be okay."

If I hear the name Dag one more time, I'll. . .I'll. . . Jude clamped a lid on his thoughts. He could put up with anything for a time. And what were the chances he'd be seeing his brother anyway? Dag surely didn't bring that highfalutin' wife of his out to the farm, and he sure didn't show up at the saloon to deal a hand or two.

He paused as he swung up into the wagon. Unless Dag had changed in those ways, too. Jude shook his head. Nah, no chance. He dug in the sack for the tobacco and, after stretching open the pouch, dug out a pinch and placed it between his lip and gum. Now that, that was mighty fine. A swallow of good whiskey and a chaw of tobacco. Now, if only he could add a card game to that, the day would be perfect.

He spat a brown gob of tobacco juice into the dirt as he drove the horse and wagon past the Norgaard house. So this is where his brother lived now. He's come up some since the soddie out on the plain. He spat again. Surely, there must be some way to bother his brother again. Some way that wouldn't backfire this time.

When he got to the church he ignored his mother's comments

after handing her and Melissa up into the wagon. How could he get even? He jumped when he heard his mother mention Dag and Clara.

"They're what?" The question popped out before he had time to organize his thoughts.

"Dag and Clara are coming out to visit this afternoon. I told them I'd bake a cake, but she insisted they'd bring supper. Sure will be nice to have a treat again."

Jude dug down in the sack at his feet. "I got you a treat, something you always liked." He pulled out the cinnamon twists. "See, I think of you plenty."

"Why, thank you, you thoughtful boy," Augusta simpered in a totally uncharacteristic manner. She took a candy stick from the sack and passed the packet back to Melissa, who huddled on the wagon bed.

"No, thank you," she mumbled.

No, thank you, Jude mimicked in his mind. *Why can't I say no, thank you to Dag coming out? Why does he have to show up? All I heard about today was how great Dag is doing. Him and that wonderful wife of his.* Jude could feel the anger stirring again in his gut. The fire flickered and flamed as if doused by kerosene. He snapped the horse's reins and stamped his foot against the footrest.

All his life, Dag this and Dag that. And now his brother had a wife that all the town praised while his wife mewled from the back of the wagon. The flames flared higher.

The horse broke into a trot. Augusta clutched the side of the wooden bench. Jude heard a whimper from behind him. Even his mother had gone against him. Here she was, glad they were coming because they brought a good supper. He sucked the juice out of his chaw and spat it off the side of the wagon. It'd be a long time before he sat down to eat with his brother.

When they reached the farm, Jude leaped from the wagon, helped the womenfolk down, and trotted the horse down to the barn. He secreted his bottle down into the grain bin. Now he could take a swig when he needed one and no one would be the wiser.

As soon as the dog barked a welcome for Dag and Clara, Jude slipped out the back door, telling his mother he was off to do the chores.

"You be ready for supper in about an hour?" she asked as the door slammed behind Jude's hurrying form. He lurked behind the corner until he heard the visitors go inside the house.

The internal muttering continued while he threw grain to the chickens and walked out in the pasture to round up the milk cow. Usually she waited patiently beside the barn. But today everything was going wrong, even the cow. When he finally found her, laying down in a slight dip in the sparsely grassed field, chewing her cud, he hurried her up to the barn. Udder swinging, she trotted to the barn door and stopped. The look she shot him from over one shoulder would have rebuked a more tenderhearted man.

As Jude swung open the door, he slapped her on the rump. When he slammed the wooden stanchion bar in place, it pinched her neck. She lowed in protest.

Jude stomped off to the well house for the milk bucket. A slight smile lifted the corners of his mouth when he dug the grain out of the bin. His bottle lay snug in the bin, covered by the golden oats. His mouth watered at the thought. He brushed the grain away and lifted the bottle, sloshing the liquid inside. Did he dare? He shoved it back into its nest. Not now. . .not with Dag on the prowl.

As he milked the cow, its milk streamed into the bucket, the *swish, swish* a music all its own. The milking song covered the sound of the door opening.

"Hello."

At the sound of his brother's voice, Jude jerked on the cow's teats. Before he could recover, the cow planted her foot squarely in the bucket and her tail whipped him across the eyes.

Jude leaped to his feet, milk running down his pant legs. "Did ya have to scare a body to death, creeping up thata way? Look what you made me do." He turned on his brother, fury transforming his handsome face to a mask of hatred.

"I'm sorry I startled you." Dag, his white shirt glistening in the dimness of the barn, crossed his arms over his chest. "But you and I need to talk and this is the only way I could see how to do so without the women around."

"I don't need to talk with you." Jude dumped the milk in a pan for the cats and, after rinsing the bucket out, returned to his stool. " 'Sides, I gotta finish here."

"I'll make this short and sweet. Ma says you have come home to help her out. We both know she needs help here since the last hired man quit. She can't manage all alone."

"I know. That's why I'm here." Jude returned to the squeeze and pull of milking.

"But the truth of the matter is that I've been bringing her supplies and paying her bills at the stores in town."

"So, you want a medal or somethin'?" Jude pushed his head harder against the cow's flank.

"No, I just don't want to see your tobacco on the tab. And I don't want to hear you're in town gambling and drinking. That would break Ma's heart, she's so glad to have you home again. So the rules are: no drinking, no gambling, and you buy your own tobacco and cigars."

"Who do you think you are, coming here and trying to tell me what to do with my life?" Jude stripped the last drops of milk from the cow's udder and shoved himself to his feet.

"I'm your brother, your older brother, and right now you need to join us for supper. Clara and Ma have it on the table. I'd like you to meet my wife since you had such a hand in bringing her to me. I never had a chance to thank you for that, you know." He offered his hand in gratitude.

Jude pushed aside the extended hand and, after releasing the cow, stalked off to the well house.

While the meal was indeed tasty, as Augusta had promised, Jude squirmed whenever he looked across the table to the woman who smiled so lovingly at his brother. Her laugh, her intense blue eyes, the golden hair waving down her back, the way she charmed his mother—they all irritated him. Especially when he glanced at the washed-out woman sitting beside him.

And the look of Dag himself. Had that man really been hiding under the dirt and stench of the blacksmith? And the way he talked. Why, one would think Dag had been to school for years. And Jude knew for sure that that hadn't been the case.

The apple pie Jude was eating was turning into prairie straw in his mouth. Jude shoved away from the table, mumbling that he had something he had to do. He didn't return to the house until everyone else had gone to bed.

The next few days did nothing to alleviate the anger festering in Jude's heart. A coyote raided the chicken house and killed three of their best laying hens. Every time Jude tried to fix something, he needed a new part or another piece of lumber or fencing wire. Only his secret friend buried in the grain bin consoled him.

One day the sun scorched the earth, ignoring the fact that fall was supposedly on the way. The sun burned down on Jude's head as he dug the few remaining potatoes and dumped them in the cellar. The cow came into estrus and broke through the fence to go visit the neighbor's bull, so he not only had to bring her back but had to repair the fence. All day his temper broiled along with the heat devils whirling away over the prairie.

Supper that day was a silent affair. Even Augusta relaxed her steel spine to sit down on the rear porch and fan herself with her apron.

"You'd think this was July rather than September," she said as she wiped the beads of moisture from her upper lip.

Jude merely grunted. The thought of his bottle down in the barn made his mouth prickle.

"Think I'll go on up to bed." Melissa stood in the doorway wiping her hands on her apron.

"Think I'll go on into town." Jude spit a gob of tobacco juice off the porch onto the hard-packed earth.

"What for?" Augusta jerked awake from her slight doze.

"Just to talk to the fellas at the mercantile. Find out where we can get some cheap grain. Not much left out in the barn."

"You won't go near the sa—" Melissa cut off her question at the fierce look Jude fired at her.

"You can go to the store tomorrow." Augusta drew herself up in the rocking chair. "It will be closed before you get there. The only place open in Soldall at this hour is the saloon." Her voice brooked no argument.

"If I say I go now, I'll go—"

This time it was the mother's look that stopped the son.

Jude jerked open the screen door, shoved past his wife, knocking her against the counter, and stormed into the sitting room. He dug a cigar out of the humidor and stomped back into the kitchen to light it in the embers of the stove.

But instead of leaving by the back door, he returned to the sitting room. After kicking the hassock into place in front of the brown velvet chair, he flung himself into the chair and propped his boots on the hassock. The puffs on his cigar sent spirals of smoke drifting to the high ceiling.

Who does she think she is to tell me what to do like that? His thought kept time with the billows of smoke. *A man should be able to do what he wants in his own house.* He shifted his dusty boots on the hassock, deliberately ignoring the tiny voice that reminded him of the household rules. No smoking in the house and no feet on the furniture. The only time the room was ever used was when company came.

Tonight Jude considered himself company. He ignored Melissa's quiet "Good night" and refused to respond when his mother started to say something. As the smoke cloud darkened around him, she snorted and made her way upstairs. A lesser woman might have marked her displeasure with heavy feet but not Augusta. Her feelings seemed to float back and freeze the room.

Jude called his mother every name he could think of and then created a few new ones, all in the regions of his mind, of course. When he finished with her, he started on Melissa. Why was he, of all men, so abused?

Sounds ceased from above except for the rhythmic snoring that indicated that his mother had fallen sound asleep. Jude listened carefully. Only the song of his bottle could be heard in the stillness of his mind.

Jude set his cigar on the edge of the small table beside the chair. If he hurried out, he could be back before anyone were the wiser.

The evening breeze that had felt so refreshing on the porch had increased to a wind, raising dust and dancing devils across the empty fields. The harvest moon shone down, lighting the path to the barn like midday.

Jude swung open the barn door and followed his nose to the grain bin. Practice made finding the bottle easy in spite of the darkness that encircled him like a comforting blanket. Out here, no one would try to tell him to remove his feet from the hassock. That's what footstools were for—resting feet. And chairs for bodies, especially tired bodies like his. His mind kept up the litany of complaints as he jerked the cork out with his teeth, dropped it in his hand, and raised the cool bottle to his lips. The first swallow was all he'd dreamed of.

Jude started to replace the cork, but a glance in the direction of the house and those interfering females made him take another.

After a couple more swigs, he edged his way over to the ladder to the haymow and, clutching his bottle to his chest, clamored up. He snuggled his backside down into the pile of hay and leaned back, exhaling a sigh at the silence and the comfort. No one would look for him here.

Soon his head fell back, the empty bottle slipped from relaxed fingers, and gentle puffings deepened into snores.

"What's—" Jude struggled up from the bowels of his sleep. What was the dog barking about at this time of night? He blinked, trying to decide where he was. After rubbing a hand across eyes filled with grit, he looked up to see gold lights dancing on the walls and ceiling above him. Was it morning already? He stumbled to his feet. His mother would rip him limb from limb if she thought he spent the night drinking in the barn.

"Shut up, you stupid dog," he muttered as he fumbled for the ladder. "You'll wake the whole world if you haven't already."

When Jude stepped from the barn, his heart stopped in his chest. "Oh, no!"

Flames flickered within the downstairs windows of the house, smoke spiraling upward from the open windows.

Jude raced for the back door. His heart pounded in his chest. His mind pleaded for the God he so often profaned to help him get the women out. Surely the barking dog had awakened them, too.

"Ma! Melissa!" His screams rent the air. The wind tossed the sound away, creating instead its own monster song of roaring flames and crashing timbers.

Jude jerked open the door and, arm over his nose and mouth, stumbled through the smoke and heat, searching for the staircase.

Chapter 2

The heat beat Jude back. The dog leaped beside him, barking furiously at the flames. Jude choked and coughed, gagging for air as he leaned forward, nearly toppling to the ground. When he got his breath, he stumbled to the rain barrel at the corner of the house, soaked his shirt in the water, and wrapped the wet cloth around his face. After grabbing a deep breath, he charged through the back door.

The fire wasn't burning as furiously here as he made his way to the stairs. He couldn't call, saving every breath for the ordeal ahead. But the raging flames beat him out again. As his mind dimmed with the heat and smoke, he turned back. He never noticed the pieces of burning wood peppering his back or the heat searing his lungs. His final cry of "Ma" went no farther than his lips as he collapsed on the ground outside.

"Here he is!" the man yelled. "Jude's alive, I think."

"Ma, Melissa." Jude croaked.

"It's gone. All gone." The man draped a wet cloth over Jude's back and offered him a sip of water.

"Gone?" Jude tried to raise his head. Instead he collapsed into oblivion.

"Dag, I think he's coming around."

Jude heard the feminine voice from somewhere down in the chasm where he preferred to remain. At least down there, he didn't hurt so cruelly. His back, his head, his arms—all on fire. He twisted his face to the side. What was he lying on?

"Drink." He forced the word through lips that felt coated with some kind of grease. His throat spasmed around the single word.

"Here." A glass tube appeared between his lips and he sucked greedily.

Where am I? What's happened? The thoughts chased through his mind like the flames had—the flames—the house—Ma and Melissa. The memories seared his mind like the flames had seared his back. A groan tore from his heart and forced its way out his throat.

"Easy now." The voice belonged to his brother, Dag.

"Ma?"

"Send Mrs. Hanson for the doctor." Dag seemed to be talking from far away.

"Ma." Jude put all his energy into the request.

"Easy now, Jude. There's nothing more you can do. You're at my house and burned terribly. It's a miracle you're still alive."

Jude digested the words. But what about his mother and Melissa? Had they gotten out? He could hear the roar of the flames, the dog barking. Were there screams? He tried to remember.

"How about another drink?" The tube appeared again.

Jude drank gratefully. The cool water slipped down like the elixir of life itself. He fought the pain and the fog trying to blanket his mind. "Ma!"

"She's gone, Jude. Both of them."

The simple words sent him spinning back into oblivion. Pain and searing agony brought him back.

The tube appeared and, as before, he drank, sucking in the life-giving moisture. He tried to figure out what he was lying on, but the effort was too great. Instead, he let himself slip back to that no-man's-land. The pursuing flames of his nightmares hurt far less than the thought of Ma and Melissa dying in the fire.

"How do you think it started?"

Jude heard the voice and fought against the pull back to reality. How did he think it started? How would he know? He'd been out in the barn, slugging down his nightly antidote for living.

"Maybe a lamp?" This voice rang with feminine sweetness.

"We may never know. It was an accident pure and simple." The gruff voice belonged to a stranger. Who was it?

"Thank you for coming, Doctor."

Ah, that's who it was. He'd heard the voice before, sometime during the long, long night.

"You take care of yourself now, too, you hear?" Footsteps faded along with the voice.

While Jude kept his eyes closed, he couldn't shut off his mind. Ma was always so careful. She always banked the stove. Only used candles in an emergency. How did the fire start? Had there been a lightning storm? He tried to shrug his shoulders to relieve the itching. Instead, he bit his lip against the fiery pain.

"Drink." He swallowed and forced his voice to obey the command to speak louder. "Drink, please." The tube appeared at his lips again and he sucked greedily.

"Jude, we have to get some nourishment into you so I'm going to give you some broth by the tube now. Can you manage that?"

Jude knew Clara's voice by now. He nodded.

This time the drink was warm and tasted of beef and onion.

"How long since the fire?" Jude raised his head and turned to the side so he could see. This laying on his stomach was getting hard to handle.

"A week." Dag sat down on the floor in front of his brother so they could look each other in the face. "How are you feeling?"

"Guess I'll live."

"We were afraid you were gone, too, there for a time." Dag crossed his legs and leaned against the wall. "Dr. Harmon says it's a miracle you made it."

"He the one who rigged this bed?"

"No, I did." Dag ducked his head in the old habit of humility. "When he said you couldn't lie on your back and you looked like you'd smother on your stomach, I built this. Clara padded it with quilts."

"I allus knew you could make whatever was needed." Jude's voice took on a dreamy quality. It was like looking through a telescope backwards. "Pa said you was one clever boy, even when you was a kid."

"What?"

"That's why I teased you so much."

"Jude, you're talking through your head. Or are you delirious again?" Dag shook his head with a snort.

"Nah. I hated you sometimes. . .most of the time, you know."

Jude let his mind float down the telescope. The pain met him halfway down. He slipped off without answering Dag's last question. How would he know how the fire started?

Just before the blackness claimed him completely, he saw the cigar, smoking on the table in his mother's sitting room. His cigar! The one he'd left when he headed for the barn. The pain now searing his heart made the pain from his back seem like a hangnail.

When Jude awoke he wished he were dead. Why didn't they let him die? He wasn't worth keeping alive. He clenched his teeth and arched his back. The pain drenched him and nothing could erase the agony in his mind. His carelessness killed both Ma and Melissa. How could he live? Why bother?

"Jude, what is it? The pain is worse?" Clara knelt in front of him. "Can I get you something?"

Jude shook his head. He couldn't tell her. How could he tell anyone?

"Here. I made you some chicken broth this time. Doc says you can have whatever you can swallow. But I know that position makes eating difficult."

Her caring words drove the nail deeper. He didn't deserve anyone taking care of him like this. He clenched his teeth against the tube she held to his mouth. *God, please let me die.* He felt like roaring at whatever it was had kept him alive and let them die.

"Jude, you have to eat." Dag took his place against the wall. "It's been two days now and you haven't taken even a sip of water. What is it?"

Jude left the land of the screaming voices and raised his head to look at his brother. Couldn't he tell? Wasn't it written across his forehead—MURDERER—in giant red letters.

Jude took a wet cloth and wiped his brother's face. "Doc says you can get up tomorrow if you are strong enough. He says if we don't get you moving, you'll lose all the muscle tone in your back."

Jude clenched his teeth. All right, tomorrow he'd get up. The sooner he got better, the sooner he could leave. Since he wasn't dying this way, he could take care of the matter better when he could ride away. He took the offered drink and grunted his thanks.

From then on Jude gritted his teeth against the pain and forced himself to down all the fluids and nourishment he could stand. He did exactly as the doctor ordered, all except the laudanum. He refused to let his mind dwell in that no-man's-land that the drug brought with it. He didn't deserve the release.

He still couldn't lie on his back, so he slept on the slotted bed Dag had devised, where his head fit into a brace and looked straight down. In that position, Jude found he didn't have to look at anyone unless he wanted to. And he didn't so choose.

One afternoon when he was lying there, he heard Clara, the doctor, and Dag speaking in the other room while they thought he was sleeping.

"But he was doing so much better. I can't understand the change," Clara said.

"Ja, it's not like Jude to be so silent." Dag's voice sounded weary.

"He's been through a lot. Sometimes accidents like this completely change a person." Doc paused before continuing. "Thought for a while there when he quit eating and drinking we was gonna lose him after all."

Ah, if only it were that easy, Jude thought. *After all the meanness I've bothered my brother with all these years, I couldn't quit and die on him in his own home. How can the man treat me with such love and gentleness when all these years...* His mind drifted back, picking out the instances of his cruelty and he winced.

If his mother's ideas of the Maker's judgments were true, he'd not be standing in line for angel's wings, that's for sure. He had to get well enough to get out of here soon. The thought of being a continued burden ate at him like a canker. He studied the healing burns on the back of his hand and arm; his back they said was worse. The angry red welts glistened under the healing salve Mrs. Hanson kept forcing him to apply. At least now when she spread it on his back, he could stand the touch. Soon, he would be able to wear a shirt and then he could leave.

The thoughts of the bustling housekeeper seemed to bring her to him.

"Time for more cold cloths and medicine," Mrs. Hanson said. Her cheery voice could change in an instant if he didn't respond. He'd learned that the hard way. He knew he was only here on sufferance. While she tolerated him, he could tell from her eyes she wouldn't hesitate to toss him out.

He turned his head when he heard a cane tapping along with a much lighter step and entering his room. Mrs. Norgaard leaned on her cane, but he couldn't raise his head far enough to see her face.

"If we move that chair over by the wall," Mrs. Norgaard said, "I shall be able to converse with our patient more easily." Mrs. Hanson huffed but did her employer's bidding, and Mrs. Norgaard settled herself into her chair in her normal pose, back ramrod straight and never touching the back of the chair.

Silence descended on the room as she studied the man on his stomach. Jude studied the spot on the floor immediately below his face.

Why doesn't she say something? Why don't I say something? The thoughts tiptoed around his mind, fearful the woman in the chair could read them. Jude cleared his throat. Why was she here? Had she come to see him before, when he was unconscious? Had he said anything to her he shouldn't have?

He could feel her eyes drilling into the top of his head. The regrowing hair tingled in response. This was as bad as being called before the class back when he was in school.

Did she suspect the fire had been his fault? That a cigar, the one he'd been warned to not smoke in the house, burned his wife and mother to death. He felt the twisting between his mind, heart, and gut. If she knew, surely she would have thrown him out long ago.

He could stand it no longer. He raised his head, refusing to flinch when the wrinkling skin of his neck and upper back sent pain rippling and stabbing. It wasn't judgment he saw in her eyes. No, they were the eyes of love. Compassion flowed from her to him as if they were bound by golden cords.

He could feel tears burn at the back of his eyes. Tears! *Grown men don't cry.* The order failed to stem the flow. Jude sniffed as quietly and subtly as possible. He blinked not only once but several times, but still one fat tear managed to escape and drip off the end of his nose.

Why didn't she say something? Who turned on the furnace? The room seemed to have heated up twenty degrees or so.

Still, the silence stretched. . .and stretched. But Jude was the one who felt like he was being pulled apart, limb from limb.

"I want to thank—" he cleared his throat and started again. "Thank you for. . .aah. . .having me here. . .in your house."

"This is no longer my home. It now belongs to Dag and Clara."

"Oh." Then the rumors were true.

"They've become my family."

Silence settled in again. Why in the world did he feel like crying?

Jude gritted his teeth. When that didn't help, he bit his bottom lip. Even the taste of blood failed. One didn't yell at a lady. His mother had drilled that into him from the time he was little, but that didn't prevent him from screaming in his head. His body, the fire, the tears, the pain, the heat, the—he ran out of things to scream about.

"It will do no good." The words crept past the damaging words and shut him right down.

"Huh?" He threw his head up as far as possible. "Oh—" He stopped abruptly, but the grimace said more than he intended.

"All the anger you harbor. It will only cause you more pain."

Jude shook his head. If she only knew. The silence seeped in again.

How could she sit so still? He felt his fingers twitch. . .then his toes. He felt like twitching all over. Itching. . .twitching. . . Oh, how he could use a drink!

"When you can accept our forgiveness, it will always be here. Dag and Clara can live no other way and neither can I. Always remember that." She rose to her feet and walked to the door. "Remember, too, that Christ died so we might live forgiven. We all might live so. Good evening, Jude." Her footsteps echoed faintly down the hall.

In the morning he was gone.

Chapter 3

G et outa here before I. . .I—"

"Before you what?" The voice held a trace of a leer
that she was sure matched the face hidden in the dimness. "There's no one to hear you. Ma and Pa are gone for the
night, remember?"

Rebekka Stenesrude swallowed to dislodge the fear clogging
her throat. She could feel the perspiration running down her back
under the flannel nightgown. Why hadn't she gone to stay in town
when she learned that Mr. and Mrs. Strand were going to be gone?
She listened carefully, waiting for the man—if you could call him
that—to move again so she could determine where he was standing. Why, oh why, had she drawn the heavy draperies? If only the
moonlight were lighting the room. But then he could see her more
clearly, too.

A devilish chuckle echoed from the darkened corner. The
sound caused the hairs on the back of her neck to stand at attention. Why hadn't she been more alert? She'd noticed his smiles
and secret glances, but fighting off advances of young men had
never been a problem as there'd never been any to fight off or
even brush away.

Her antennae strained to sense the attacking man. What could
she do? She felt carefully behind herself, seeking something with
which to strike her attacker. Her fingers closed over the handle of
the heavy pitcher on the commode.

"You can't run fast enough to get away and if you scream, well,
who's gonna hear you?"

The voice sent shivers rippling up her back again, but at least now she knew which way the attack would come from. She took a deep breath in an attempt to slow her thundering heart and then flexed her fingers so she could grip the handle more firmly.

Suddenly, he came with a rush, shoving her against the commode. She swung with all her might. The pitcher crashed against him. Both the man and the shards struck the bare floor at the same time.

The scream died in her throat. She leaped for the door, expecting him to follow, but only silence and her tortured breathing filled the room. Was he dead?

Rebekka grabbed her clothes off the hooks on the wall and ran down the stairs. When she paused to listen, she heard a groan. Relieved in one way but furious that she hadn't permanently silenced the oaf, she darted out the door. "Please, God, let a horse be in the barn." The muttered prayer matched the rhythm of her pounding feet.

In the darkness of the barn, she ripped a bridle off the wall and, with outstretched hands to guide her, made her way to the horse stalls. "Thank You, Lord." She took in a deep breath so she wouldn't panic the horse in the stall. Murmuring gentle words, she shuffled carefully to the animal's head and slipped the bridle on over the halter. Each action seemed to take an hour as she fumbled in the darkness. After untying the slipknot, she backed the animal out of the stall. Then, after retrieving her clothes from where she'd laid them on a bar by the door of the stall, she led the animal outside.

A roar of pain and anger could be heard clear from the house to the barn as Rebekka led the horse over to the edge of the watering trough, stepped up, and swung herself astride the horse, her nightgown and housecoat bunched up around her knees.

Adolph Strand crashed the screen door against the wall and staggered out on the porch, clutching his head.

Rebekka dug her heels into the horse's ribs and galloped down the lane. Where would she go in the middle of the night? Thank God Mr. and Mrs. Strand were driving the team and there was no way Adolph could follow her.

A mile or so from the farm, she pulled her horse down to a jog. A full moon directly overhead bathed the land in silver and each leaf and blade of grass shimmered with the heavy dew. A sleepy bird called from somewhere, perhaps the brilliant light of the moon confusing his inner clock. Rebekka drew in a deep breath, the aroma of a steaming horse mingling with some night-blooming flower.

"What a shame not to enjoy a night so marvelous as this." She tipped her head back, luxuriating in the feeling, but shivered again at the thought of what had nearly happened to her. Stirred by the breeze and the night scents, she inhaled again. If only she could keep riding forever.

Rebekka shook her head and made an unladylike snort, matching that of the horse she rode. Forever would be a long time, and she had school in the morning. No matter what had happened tonight, all twenty-one of her students would greet her in the morning with bright and shiny faces. And the schoolmarm must be above reproach. Not riding around the country in the moonlight—in her nightgown and housecoat.

She shuddered again at the thought of how close she'd come to losing that purity required of schoolmarms. That. . .that, she couldn't think of a name vile enough. But to whom could she talk? Who would believe her? She clamped her lips together.

Willowford had been her home now for two years and surely, in that time, the parents of her students must trust her. They must—she shook her head. But they could never be told. The Strand family had lived in the area for twenty years or more, and it would be her word against theirs.

She lifted her face to the moon, staring beyond the silver disk to the star-studded midnight expanse of the heavens. "Father God, what do I do? Where can I go? Your word says You look out for widows and orphans. How about an old-maid schoolmarm?"

She waited, her body relaxed and swaying with the moving horse. Would the stars sing for her, bringing the message she needed? She pulled the horse to a halt to listen better. *Moses had his burning bush,* she thought. *How will God talk with me?*

A bird twittered in the brush in the ditch. A breeze lifted the horse's mane and billowed her nightgown and housecoat. She smoothed them down and dropped her chin to her chest. How silly she was being. God didn't talk to people on earth anymore. Did He?

She nudged the horse into a slow jog; its tapping hooves drowned out the night music. A picture of the Widow Sampson's boxy white boardinghouse came into her mind. Maybe she could at least stay there until she spoke with Mr. Larson, the school superintendent for the district.

"One thing sure," she promised the trotting horse, "I won't go back to the Strands', no matter what anyone says. I'll be on that train for. . .for anywhere first." The horse's ears flicked back and forth, and he snorted as if in perfect agreement.

When they entered the darkened town, she slowed the animal to a walk. Music echoed from the saloon and bright light formed a square clear out to the middle of the street. Rebekka edged the horse to the other side of the packed-dirt street and nudged him back into a trot. She couldn't be seen in dishabille like this and still live and teach in Willowford.

After following the picket fence around to the back of the widow's boardinghouse, Rebecca slid off the horse and onto the ground. She tied her mount to the rail and opened the gate. Rebekka froze as the screech of the hinges echoed loud enough to wake the sleepers halfway down the block.

Then, a dog barked on the other side of the street and her horse rubbed his chin on the picket, sending his bit ajingling.

Rebekka tiptoed up the walk, her hand at her throat. She paused again when the first step squeaked beneath her bare foot. How could she rouse the Widow Sampson without waking all her boarders?

She tapped lightly on the back door. When nothing happened, she tapped again more firmly. "Please, please," she whispered to the heavens. But, instead of a welcome from within, she heard someone making his way down the street, singing, if one could call it that, a barroom ditty.

Rebekka formed a fist and raised her hand. She paused just before banging as a disgruntled voice came from within the house.

"Just hold on ta your britches. I'll be there soon's I can." Other grumbles followed, along with the slap of carpet slippers on a wooden floor. "Who's there?" The words were matched by the door's opening just enough for a mobcapped woman to peek around the door.

"Widow Sampson."

"Why, if'n it ain't the schoolmarm. Miss Stenesrude, what are you doing here this time of night—and in your nightclothes? You're not needing a nurse, are you?" When Rebekka shook her head, the door opened all the way. "Get yourself in here before you catch your death."

"Thank you, I. . .I can explain." Rebekka looked over her shoulder to where her horse tossed his head and tried to reach the tips of the grass growing along the fence. She clutched her spare clothes to her body and then handed them to the older woman. "But first I better see to the horse. Do you have a place I can put him for the night?"

Widow Sampson accepted the clothing and pursed her lips. "Why, I s'pose you can put him in the shed there. We're a mite low on coal right now, so there should be room. He your horse?"

"No. I'll explain as soon as I return." Rebekka started down the steps and turned back. "Have you a rope or something I can tie him with?"

"Uh, just a minute." The older woman shut the door.

A shiver attacked Rebekka now that the danger was nearly past. She could hear the singing coming nearer. Did the man have to come down this street? What if he lived in the next house? Rebekka wrapped her arms around her shoulders to quell more of the bone-rattling quakes.

The door reopened and Widow Sampson stepped out on the porch. "Here you go. Think you can see well enough or should I bring a lantern?"

They both paused in response to the off-key serenade. "Oh,

that man! He would choose tonight to drink himself silly. How Emma puts up with that, why, I'll never know. You get into the shed and keep that horse quiet until Elmer goes on by. Of course he wouldn't remember if he saw you or not, but best not to take any more chances." She handed Rebekka the coiled rope as she talked and shooed her toward the waiting animal.

Rebekka gladly did as Mrs. Sampson said, keeping her hand over the horse's nostrils when it was inclined to nicker at the man weaving his way past them. As soon as the fellow turned into his own gate and stumbled up the stairs to his house and through the door, she stripped off the bridle and knotted the rope, both into the halter and around a post. "I'll feed you in the morning," she whispered. After a quick hug and pat in total gratitude, she hurried back to the house.

In the meantime, Widow Sampson had lit a lamp and seated herself at the oilcloth-covered table, where she'd set a plate of sugar cookies and two glasses of buttermilk. "Here, I thought some refreshment might be in order since I think your tale may take more than a moment or two." She gestured to the chair.

Rebekka sank into it gratefully. Another shiver shook her frame as she wrapped her feet and legs around each other for warmth. "Thank you for letting me in." She clamped her teeth against a shiver.

"My, my, child, you've gone and caught your death." The widow pushed herself to her feet. "I'll be right back. You need something to warm you right now." Her carpet slippers slipslapped into a bedroom just behind the kitchen.

Rebekka waited. She could hear the squeak of a chest lid raising and Mrs. Sampson digging around for something. In a minute the woman returned, her cheeks bright red from the effort and her white lawn mobcap set slightly off to the right, giving her the look of a merry elf. "Here ya be," she said as she draped a blanket around Rebekka's shoulders and handed her a pair of hand-knit woolen socks. "These oughta warm you up."

Rebekka leaned forward to slip the socks over her freezing toes. She wasn't sure if her last shudder was from the cold that seemed to penetrate her clear to the bone or if it was the residual fear with the same knifing intensity. How close she'd come to the brink of losing her life the way she knew it. "Thank You, Lord, thank You." Her words kept pace with the carved clock standing sentinel at the door to the dining room.

She drained the last of the buttermilk and set the glass down carefully so as not to disturb the silence. When she looked up, Mrs. Sampson smiled and reached over to pat the younger woman's hand.

"Ja, you are safe here, now. You know you can tell me what happened and it will go no farther than these very walls."

Rebekka nodded. Did she want to tell? She could feel the flush of embarrassment flaming in her cheeks. What words could she use? What really had happened? She chewed on the inside of her right cheek and clutched the blanket closer around her.

"Our Lord says confession is good for the soul and that don't mean only what we done wrong. Now, I know for certain you wouldn't be here in the middle of the night in your nightclothes if something powerful terrible hadn't happened." She studied the face of the young woman before her. "And I know, too, you weren't to be at fault. Not intentionally anyhows."

Rebekka struggled to talk past the chunk of prairie dirt clogging her throat. Dirt, that's what it was all right. What he was. She swallowed again. "I. . ."

"Take your time, dear, we're in no hurry."

"I'd gone to bed. This is my month out at the Strands', you know, and Mr. and Mrs. are gone to her sister's for a few days." Tears burned at the back of her eyes and down her throat. She squeezed her eyes against the burning and rolled her lips together.

At the feel of the other woman's hand on her own, the tears and fears burst forth and Rebekka laid her head on her arms, the sobs shaking her shoulders. "He. . .he came at me." Great gulping sobs punctuated her words. She wiped her face on the blanket and tried to sniff the flow back again, but failed miserably.

Mrs. Sampson let her guest cry. She patted the younger woman's arm, her "there, there nows" a descant to the guttural sobs. As an occasional sniff replaced the storm, the widow pushed herself to her feet and crossed to the stove to dip a cloth in the warm water of the reservoir on the back of the iron-and-chrome behemoth.

"Here." She handed the cloth to Rebekka. "Now wash your face and hands while I get you a glass of water. Then we'll talk, if you feel up to it."

Rebekka nodded and did as told. How wonderful it felt to be taken care of, like her mother had done back in the good years before—she slammed the door in her mind that had opened just a crack. *Stay with the here and now; no good looking back.*

The chair creaked as Widow Sampson sat back down. She had set two glasses of water on the table. "I could start up the stove and make coffee," she said as she pushed one glass over to Rebekka, "but the noise might wake up my boarders and that wouldn't be very kind."

"I. . .I never thought, I mean—I thought you'd have room for another. Are your rooms full, then?" Rebekka's heart took up that erratic thumping again. What would she do if. . . ?

"Now, now, just don't you worry yourself none. I got a room for you. Why, Mr. Prescott moved out just two days ago. I cleaned it all right nice again, so you can see, it's just waiting for you. Nice corner room it is, too."

Rebekka inhaled a sigh of pure relief. At least something was going right. She wiggled her feet in the wool socks, scooting them back and forth on the floor and then wrapping them together under the chair. She brushed an errant tear from the corner of her eye. Why had this happened to her?

"Well, as I started to say," and the words drifted off as her mind returned to the farmhouse. She clamped her jaw against the fury she could feel exploding in her chest. "He attacked me! That. . .that—" She couldn't think of any words bad enough. "And he thought I was funny. He was laughing. Until he rushed me and I hit him."

"You hit him?"

"With the pitcher from the commode. When he crashed to

the floor, I grabbed my clothes and ran out the door." She continued with her story, not leaving out any details.

"Well, I never."

"I never either. And now I don't know what to do. Can I please
stay here until I talk with Mr. Larson, the superintendent? I. . .I can
pay." She could feel her mouth drop open. "At least, I can if I can
get my things from their house. But I have money in the bank, too,
. . .some." She raised her gaze from studying her clenched fists.

"Now, don't you worry. Why, when we tell Lars what happened, he'll go out there personally and whip that young pup.
Surely the sheriff could do something about this."

"No!"

"No?"

"Don't you see, I can't tell anyone. If this story gets around, I'll
lose my position. Teachers are fired for a lot less reason than this."

"But it wasn't your fault." The words exploded from the
widow's lips. She caught herself. "I know. I know. The snickers. The
men will all get together and say you enticed him. That's what
Adolph'll tell anyone who asks."

"I know. And those who don't. What can I do?"

"Let me think on this, child. You go on and get a good night's
sleep and we'll let the good Lord tell us what to do. He never
makes mistakes." The older woman sighed and shook her head.

"You. . .you believe me, don't you?" Rebekka pushed her cuti-
cle back with a trembling finger. She looked up to see Mrs.
Sampson smiling at her.

"Yes. Have no doubts in your mind about me. And God, who
knows your heart, will work this out. God has a plan in mind, you
can be sure of that."

"I know. . .I think." Rebekka caught herself on a yawn. She
pushed herself to her feet. "And you. . .you won't tell anyone?
Not ever?"

"Come along, my dear. That question don't even bear an
answer." Mrs. Sampson picked up the kerosene lamp and led the
way up the stairs. She opened the second door on the right. "The
bed's all made up. I'll bring up warm water in the morning, but

usually my guests come downstairs for their own. Breakfast will be at seven, prompt. Mrs. Knutson has to open her shop at eight." She set the lamp down on the five-drawer oak dresser and dug a spill from the drawer to light the room's lamp from the one she brought in.

Rebekka stared around in delight as the warm glow of the kerosene lamp brought to life the rainbow colors in the log cabin patchwork quilt on the spindle bed. A hand-crocheted doily kept the matching pitcher and bowl from scratching the top of the commode; a braided rag rug lay by the bed, ready to keep feet off the cold floor on a winter morning.

"Oh, this is beautiful." She looked around to find brass hooks on the back of the door and hung up her dress.

"I have an armoire in the storage room that I could bring in here for you to hang up your clothes. If you decide to stay, that is." She chuckled at the sight of the younger woman trying to disguise another yawn. "You go on to sleep now. Nothing can hurt you here." She picked up her lamp and closed the door behind her with a quiet click.

Rebekka felt the bottom of her night dress and realized it was damp. But, she had nothing else in which to sleep. She'd just pulled back the covers when she heard a tap on the door. "Yes?"

Mrs. Sampson peaked through the crack in the door and held out a faded flannel nightgown. "Here, yours is still damp, I'm sure. Don't want to take a chance on you coming down with something."

"Thank you." Rebekka crossed the room and accepted the offering. "You are so kind."

"Ja, well you need some kindness right now." She harrumphed her way back out the door.

"Oh, Lord above, what am I going to do?" Rebekka either prayed or pleaded, she wasn't sure which, after she snuggled down under the crisp sheets. If she told Mr. Larson exactly what had happened, would he believe her or throw her out? If she didn't tell him, how would she explain the need to leave the Strand farm before the school year was up? Where would she go? She allowed her gaze to drift around the peaceful room, where the moon cast bright spots upon the waxed floor and the sheer curtains fluttered in the night breeze. She gulped back a leftover sob. Resolutely, she climbed from the bed and knelt on the rug.

"Heavenly Father, I have to leave this in Your hands. I don't know what to do. I thank You for sending Your angels to protect me." She shuddered again at the memory. "Please, if it be Your will, I would be pleased to stay in Willowford. Thank You again. Amen." She rose to her feet and slipped back into the cooling bed. The idea of closing her eyes and letting the memories surge back was about as frightening as the actual event.

She rubbed her cold feet together and then snuggled them up into the folds of the nightgown. Warmth stole around her, rich and comforting, like the sense of peace that crept along into her heart. On a gentle sigh, her eyelids drifted closed. When they fluttered open one last time, she smiled at the thought. There were two smiling angels sitting at the foot of her bed. What a wondrous dream.

She greeted the morning cockcrow with a catlike stretch, starting with her arms and working down clear to her toes. "Thank You, Father," she breathed at the thought of the restful sleep she'd had—no nightmares. . .no memories. She sat straight up. But what about the angels? She chuckled as she left the bed and went to stand in front of the window.

Dawn had bowed out, giving way to sunrise and the glorious birdsongs greeting the new day. The aromas of freshly turned earth and the green shoots sprouting up to meet the sun drifted in on a teasing breeze.

A tap at the door caught her attention. "Just your warm water, dear." The cheery voice brought a smile to Rebekka's face.

"Come in, Mrs. Sampson." Rebekka hurried across the floor to open the door. "Thank you so much." She stepped back to let the bustling housekeeper in.

"And how did you sleep? Was the bed all right?" She set the pitcher in the bowl on the oak stand and placed the towel draped over her arm beside the bowl. "There's soap there. I made it myself. I add rose petals for the fragrance." She peered into her guest's face. "You look rested, in spite of all you went through." She patted Rebekka's arm. "Breakfast in half an hour." And out the door she went.

Rebekka clapped her mouth closed, sure now that she understood how one felt after being whirled around in one of the summer tornadoes. Then she took her white blouse and dark skirt down from their hook and shook them to dislodge both horsehair and wrinkles. After laying them across the bed, she poured water into the bowl. As she picked up the soap, she inhaled its faint fragrance. What a luxury after the lye soap she'd been forced to use on the Strand farm.

After washing, Rebekka stared from her nightgown to her skirt and blouse, then to her feet. She had no underthings and no shoes. How could she call on Mr. Larson like this?

She combed her fingers through her hair and wished for the brush and comb sitting on her dresser at the farm. All of her things. She had to retrieve them, but how?

Teeth clenched against the surging anger, she pulled the nightgown back over her head and picked up the white blouse. Noticing smudges on the front and sleeves, she took the garment over to the washstand and applied the soap and water and some hard scrubbing to remove the stains. She dried the blouse as much as possible and smoothed the damp surface with her fingers. All the while doing this, she brooded over the injustice of it all.

It wasn't her fault! But if it wasn't, why did she feel so guilty? Why did she feel like she should wash again and keep on scrubbing?

She shoved her arms into the sleeves and buttoned the pearl buttons, then put on her walnut brown serge skirt. Standing in front of the mirror, she finger-combed her hair again and braided it, clamping the end with her fingertips until she could ask Mrs. Sampson for some pins.

As she made her way down the stairs, she could hear two women's voices coming from the kitchen. A canary trilled when they laughed, adding his music to the homey scene. Rebekka paused in the doorway.

The round table was now set for three, a pot with bobbing pink cabbage roses set between the cut-glass salt and pepper shakers and a gleaming golden mold of butter.

The gold-and-black canary hopped about his cage in the front of the window, pipping his song as if he were responsible for the coming of the new day.

Rebekka cleared her throat. "Ah, good morning."

"Oh, there you are." Widow Sampson turned from stirring her kettle on the gleaming black stove. "Mrs. Knutson, you know Rebekka Stenesrude, the schoolmarm, don't you?"

A diminutive woman, as slim as Widow Sampson was round, nodded and smiled at the same time. "Of course. I. . .ah—" She ducked her chin and made as if to sit down then paused from fussing with the chair. "If there's anything you need. . ."

Rebekka tore her gaze from the other boarder to stare helplessly at Mrs. Sampson. When the older woman barely shook her head, Rebekka breathed again. Thankfully, she hadn't told the secret.

"I mean, Alma said you had to leave your things. Whatever I have that you can use, you are welcome to it." Her voice faded into a whisper. "I don't want to be presumptuous. . .or anything."

Rebekka felt like circling the table and wrapping the bitty bird of a woman in her arms. Instead, she clamped her fingers over the back of the chair in front of her. "Thank you." She picked up the end of her braid. "You wouldn't by any chance have extra hairpins, would you?"

"Oh, yes." A bright smile lighting her face, the little woman darted out the door and up the stairs.

"Never worry, your secret is safe with me, but I had to tell her something." Mrs. Sampson placed a filled bowl of oatmeal at each place. "I have a plan. We'll talk when she leaves for her shop."

Abigail Knutson returned and placed pins and a comb and brush by Rebekka's place. "There, and now, let's eat. I mustn't be late."

After grace, the three women chatted happily while eating their biscuits and jam besides the oatmeal and coffee. Rebekka

309

wiped her mouth with the napkin she'd spread on her lap and tucked it back into the carved wooden napkin ring. "Thank you. I haven't enjoyed breakfast like this in a long time." She raised a hand and shook her head when Mrs. Sampson tried to refill the coffee cup.

Mrs. Knutson left immediately after placing her breakfast things in the sink. "Now you remember, if I can help with anything, you be sure to tell me."

Rebekka nodded and rose to take her things to the sink, also.

"Now." Mrs. Sampson sat back down after the front door closed. She lifted her coffee cup to her mouth and, after a sip, she pointed to the other chair. "Sit down and I'll tell you my plan."

Chapter 4

Well, what do we do?" Rebekka asked.

Mrs. Sampson took another sip of her coffee and smiled at Rebekka over the rim. "First of all, we take a buggy out to the Strand farm, return the horse, and pick up your things."

"But what about Adolph?"

"By the time we get out there, he should be out in the fields with spring planting. When did you say Mr. and Mrs. Strand are coming back?"

"Tomorrow, Sunday, on the evening train. And you're right. Adolph is behind in his work, so he'll be pushing hard." Rebekka raised stricken eyes to her benefactress. "I don't ever want to see him again."

"I know, my dear." Mrs. Sampson patted Rebekka's hands, clenched on the tablecloth. "That's the beauty of my idea. This way you can return the horse. Adolph is such that he'd probably turn you in for stealing the animal."

"Oh, no. He wouldn't." Rebekka shoved herself to her feet with such fury, the chair rocked behind her. She stormed across the kitchen and back. "Yes, he would. Let's go. I need my shoes and other things so I can go talk with Mr. Larson."

"And I'll be right behind you. You won't get any resistance from him with me along. I know a thing or two about what's going on in this town that just might come in handy right about now."

Rebekka whirled from her pacing and stopped at Mrs. Sampson's side. "You are a jewel among thousands. I can't wait to begin."

"Well, you wash up those dishes while I go get a team at the livery. Then we'll be on our way." Mrs. Sampson paused at the door. "And Rebekka, remember, I'm behind you all the way."

The young woman tried to smile through the film that suddenly covered her eyes but sniffed instead.

The drive out to the Strand farm passed quickly as the two women used the time to get to know each other better. Instead of a wagon, they rode in the comfort of a well-sprung buggy with a flashy chestnut horse trotting between the shafts. The horse that had brought Rebekka to town kept pace behind the buggy, shaking its head now and again at the lead rope.

As they drew nearer, Rebekka slipped into silence. The sight of the house in the distance sent terror coursing from her toes to the top of her head and back down again at breakneck speed. She could feel the fear gnawing at her stomach. What if he was up at the house? She couldn't even bear to use his name.

Mrs. Sampson kept the reins in one hand and used the other to pat Rebekka on the knee. "Now, now. This'll be all over in just a few minutes. There's no need to be afraid. I just know our Father will make this go easy."

Rebekka couldn't force an answer from her dry throat if her life depended upon it.

But for the creaking of the windmill above the well house, the farm lay silent in the sunshine. Rebekka watched the windows carefully to see if the dog's barking brought anyone to peer out. As soon as the dog realized that Rebekka rode in the buggy, he yipped and leaped in apology. *At least the dog likes me,* Rebekka thought, bringing a smile to her quivering lips.

Liking you is just the problem, her inner voice remonstrated with her other thoughts. *If he hadn't liked you so much.* . . .Rebekka turned to Mrs. Sampson. "Why don't we pull up at the barn and I'll take the horse inside. Then we can go to the house."

Ten minutes later they were out the door and trotting back down the lane. Rebekka allowed herself both a prayer and a sigh of relief. With her personal items stuffed into a carpetbag and her school things in a box she found on the back porch, she dared breathe in a breath of freedom.

"Maybe I should have left them a letter or something." She looked over her shoulder at the slumbering farm.

"You can always mail them one." Mrs. Sampson flicked the reins over the chestnut's back and he picked up the pace.

"I know what I'd like to tell them."

"Ja, I know."

"I just wish there were some way to. . .to. . ."

"Get even?"

"No, I mean, yes." Rebekka paused and drew in a deep breath. "I mean, there should be some way to punish him for what he did and to keep him from doing so again."

"I learned a long time ago that the best revenge is letting God handle the situation. There's a verse, 'Vengeance is mine. . .saith the Lord,' and since He sees more than we do, I'd kinda rather let Him dole out the punishment."

Rebekka thought awhile on the widow's words. "But it seems He takes so long to go about it."

"That's true." Widow Sampson flicked the reins again. "Git up there now. We got plenty important business to tend to."

Widow Sampson looped the reins around the whip pole and descended to the ground in time to lift the box out of the back of the buggy. After tying the horse, the women made their way into the boardinghouse and carried Rebekka's things upstairs to her room.

Rebekka felt herself smiling at the curtains billowing in the fresh breeze. *I already think of this as my room,* she thought in amazement. After two years of moving from home to home, she hadn't thought of any place as her own in a long time.

Mrs. Sampson bustled back out of the room and left Rebekka to redress and redo her hair. Staring in the mirror, Rebekka let her mind wander. Not since she was little had she had a room of her own. After her father started drowning his sorrows in the bottle at the local saloon, she and her mother had been moved from pillar to post with never a place to call their own. And rarely a moment's peace.

But at one time, she'd had a room with a quilt and rug and bright white curtains and a picture of Jesus on the wall. Jesus with the lambs. Rebekka laid her brush back on the dresser. Back at her grandmother's house, she'd had a real home. Back in her grandmother's house, life had been altogether different.

She wound the braid into a scroll at the base of her skull and pushed in the pins to secure it. After dampening a finger, she smoothed back the tendrils about her face that resisted confinement. Now she must present herself to Mr. Larson as her true self. *The old-maid schoolteacher who couldn't*—she amended the thought, *wouldn't—stay with the Strands any longer.* And she wouldn't, nay, couldn't tell him why.

The two women climbed back up in the buggy with nary a word between them. Mrs. Sampson slapped the reins over the horse's back and clucked him forward. They turned right on Main Street and trotted past the mercantile, the Lutheran church, and the doctor's dispensary. Mr. Larson lived up on the bluff overlooking the Missouri River. The horse dug in its feet to gain footing on the grade.

"He should be home for dinner about now. Good a time as any to be the bearer of good news."

"Good news?"

"Ja, you're still here." Mrs. Sampson tightened the reins and tied them around the whipstock as soon as the horse stopped. "And you're only asking for a permanent place to live. Not too big a request, considering."

"But. . .but, I can't tell him what really happened."

"No need. Just tell him what you want." She climbed down from the buggy and tied the horse to the rail fence. An apple tree in full bloom filled the air with the fragrance of spring and spread protective arms over the rope swing hung from its branch. A rag doll leaned against the trunk as if comforted by the support.

Rebekka paused at the picket gate. Two of the Larson children attended her school and she knew there were two more at home. How could she talk to the father with his children around?

Mrs. Sampson took Rebekka's arm and led her up to the steps. "Don't be afraid. You have nothing to fear."

Ja, sure. Rebekka felt like ripping her arm from the firm clasp and running back down the road. What would she say if he asked her why? She'd never learned to lie. It was a sin, remember. Her mother had sent her to bed without any supper when she told just a little white fib. What would she say?

She tucked a stray wisp of hair back into the severe coil and squared her shoulders. After one last glance at the woman beside her, Rebekka raised her hand and tapped on the door.

The door opened and Mrs. Larson greeted them with a wide smile. "Come in, come in. Why, if I'd knowed you were coming, we could have set another two places at the table for dinner." She wiped her hands on her skirt-length white apron and gestured them toward the sitting room. "Can I get you some coffee? We'll be having dessert in just a minute. Lars, look who's here, Miss Stenesrude and Widow Sampson."

After exchanging a conspiratorial glance, Rebekka and Mrs. Sampson followed their hostess. Nothing had changed. Give Mrs. Larson a moment and look out. When she started talking it took stronger hearts than theirs to stop her.

She bustled them into sitting on the horsehair sofa in the sitting room and met herself going out again.

"I. . .I need to talk with Mr. Larson," Rebekka called to the retreating back. The woman bustled on.

"Whew," Mrs. Sampson drew the back of her hand across her forehead as if to wipe away a flood of perspiration. She leaned back against the stiff sofa and turned to warm Rebekka with a smile. "Can't say as I ever am prepared when I see Elmira after a time. She talks faster than a tornado spins." She kept her voice to a whisper.

Rebekka clamped her bottom lip between her teeth and forced herself to sit perfectly erect, her feet primly together, her shoulders back and chin high. That was the only way to keep from turning into a mound of mush. Surely this couldn't be worse than facing a class of twenty brand-new students, ranging in age from five to fifteen. She bit her lip. Yes, it could. What if she had to lie? Why, oh, why couldn't Adolph keep his hands and lascivious thoughts to himself? Only with sternest self-control did she keep herself from shuddering.

Mr. Lars Larson sported the sunburned face and pure white forehead of a man who spent his days in the blazing Dakota sunshine. No ruler could have drawn a more perfect line than the one his hatband had done, dividing his face. He wore the sober look of a proper Norwegian upon learning that women were calling upon him in his professional capacity as school superintendent.

"Now, what can I do for you ladies?" he asked after all the proper greetings were exchanged.

A movement at the door caught Rebekka's attention. Two shining faces with smiles fit to crack a rock, peered around the corner. The girl, braids pulling her hair into some semblance of order, waved and then hid her giggle behind her hands.

"Come, children, say hello to your teacher and then go about your chores." Mr. Larson shot an apologetic glance at the women sitting on his sofa and beckoned the children. Two smaller replicas tagged behind the boy and girl who were her students.

"Hello, Inga and Ernie." Rebekka reached out her hands to clasp those of the towheaded children and draw them to her side. "Maybe you could introduce me to your brother and sister."

"This is Mary and Johnny. They're twins." Inga took over as the oldest.

"They're babies. They don't go to school like us big kids." Ernie puffed out his skinny chest, visible under the straps of his faded overalls.

The two little ones clung to the chair where their father sat. When Rebekka greeted them, they each stuck one finger in their mouths and ducked their heads in perfect unison.

"They always do everything the same." Ernie turned his serious blue-eyed gaze on his teacher. "Ma says that's 'cause they was borned at the same time."

Rebekka nodded. She dredged up every bit of schoolmarm control to keep from ordering the children out to play so the adults could talk.

Mr. Larson must have sensed her feelings for he patted the twins on the bottom of their matching overalls and sent them out of the room. "Inga, Ernie, enough now. You go help your ma."

The children filed out of the room, sending smiles over their shoulders.

Mr. Larson turned as they left. "And Inga, close the door behind you."

Rebekka breathed a sigh of relief at his consideration. All of a sudden, the coming interview didn't seem quite as frightening. Surely a man as considerate of his children as this would be sympathetic to her plight.

"Now, you want to talk with me. How can I help you?" He looked from Rebekka to Mrs. Sampson and back.

The silence deepened as the discomfort level in the room rose. Rebekka looked toward Mrs. Sampson and received a nod of encouragement. "I. . .I—" She pictured herself in front of a classroom of students and took a deep breath. "I cannot remain at the Strands' any longer. The situation there is totally untenable and I must have another place to live." The words gained strength and purpose as they followed one another, starting at a stagger and ending in a march.

Mr. Larson leaned back in his chair, rubbing the line of demarcation between summer and winter on his forehead. "Well, you know, we've always done things for the schoolteacher this way. He or she, you in this case, moves from home to home throughout the school year. We excuse those folks who absolutely can't afford to feed the teacher or who don't have room for one."

"I know." Rebekka lifted her chin a mite higher.

"What else can we do? Now, if you were married, you'd be living in your husband's house and then there wouldn't be no problem."

Rebekka bit her lip on a retort to that nugget of information.

"Just what's the problem with finishing out your stay at the Strands'?"

Rebekka refused to cringe at the blunt question. Instead, she looked Mr. Larson straight in the face and answered, "I'd rather not say." Now she knew what a witness must feel like in court.

Out of the corner of her eye Rebekka could see Mrs. Sampson straighten herself, an act that reminded her of a hen all fluffed up and ready to attack anyone who disturbs her chicks.

Mr. Larson raised a hand. "Please don't think I'm not concerned about this. I am only trying to get to the bottom of a problem."

Mrs. Sampson cleared her throat.

Rebekka felt a burst of strength, as if she were inhaling confidence. "We have worked together now for the good of Willowford's children for nearly two years. Wouldn't you agree that it's been a productive two years, Mr. Larson?"

"Well, of course."

"Wouldn't you like to continue the progress that we've made?" Without giving him time for a response, she sailed on. "At this time, we have all the school-age children in the district enrolled in school and two of our eldest are preparing for college. Now, wouldn't you say those are major accomplishments?"

"Yes, I—"

Mrs. Sampson leaned back just a trifle.

"I would be sorry to see the education of Willowford's children suffer even the smallest of disruptions, wouldn't you?" Rebekka asked.

Mr. Larson nodded.

"I hear there's a shortage of teachers coming out of Normal School the last couple of years." Mrs. Sampson nodded sagely. "The folks of Willowford do appreciate having a trained teacher over in the schoolhouse." While unspoken, her "for a change" rang through the quiet of the room.

Mr. Larson rubbed his forehead again. "Now, look. This is the way we've always done it. And it's worked. Now, why should we change?"

"Remember that incident one night last summer?" Mrs. Sampson tossed the question out, casually, as if she were pitching a pebble into a pond.

Mr. Larson's lower face matched his forehead. He closed his eyes. "Oh, my."

"Now, the ways I see it, Miss Stenesrude would be much closer to the school, were she to live in my house. Beings we're just across the creek from the schoolhouse."

"But we have no money."

"And that way she could go over on cold mornings to start the stove earlier. Keep Willowford's children warmer, you might say."

Only a groan rose from the other chair.

"You can be sure I would do my part for the children of my community and give you a real good rate. In fact, it might be that Miss Stenesrude would be willing to help me out some, to help pay her expenses, you know."

Mr. Larson leaned forward. "I'd have to clear this with the rest of the school board, you realize."

"Like you did the well?" Mrs. Sampson smiled, but the whisper penetrated to the bone.

"I take it this would be agreeable to you?" Mr. Larson turned to Rebekka. At her nod, he continued. "When would you like me to go with you to pick up your things at Strands'?"

"We've already done that," Mrs. Sampson said, "I know you won't regret this, Lars. You've made a wise decision and the fewer people who know about this, the better. Don't you agree?"

Mr. Larson mumbled something as he pushed himself to his feet. "Let me see what is keeping Elmira with that coffee."

Rebekka breathed a sigh of pure relief. She hadn't had to lie. But on the way home, she was surely going to ask Mrs. Sampson what had happened last summer.

By Monday morning Rebekka felt like she'd lived at the widow's boardinghouse all her life. While she'd had a nightmare on Saturday night, Sunday night she slept through and woke up to face the new day with joy and a sense of adventure.

Rebekka felt a smile tug at the corners of her mouth as she lay in bed relishing the peace and loveliness surrounding her. While dancing in the early morning breeze, the sheer curtains struggled against the ties that looped them back. When she planted her feet on the braided rug, she resisted the urge to dance along with the curtains. Stretching her arms over her head to banish the last yawn, she crossed to the window and knelt to place her crossed arms on the sill.

"This is the day that the Lord hath made, I will rejoice and be glad in it." Her verse was certainly easier to live up to today than it had been in the days past. "Thank You, Father, for bringing me here to live. It's been so long since I felt like I had a real home. What would it be like to have a home of my own?" She thought of the Larsons, their fine home on the hill, and their towheaded brood. Would she ever have a home like that? Was there a man out there somewhere who would invite her to share his home? Who would love her with the kind of love Christ talked about? Whom she would love the same way?

A robin pipped his early morning love song to the heavens from the tree in the corner of the backyard. Rebekka searched the branches until she saw him, his red breast puffed out and beak open wide. "Hope you find her, Mr. Robin," she whispered. "Everyone needs that perfect mate." She swallowed the lost feeling that crept over her and pushed herself to her feet.

"How silly, mooning around like that." She scolded herself all the way through her morning wash and even while brushing her hair. Long, wavy strands that shaded from wren brown to deep sienna snapped in the electricity from her brush, creating a cloud about her head that reached halfway down her back.

She smiled at the heart-shaped face in the mirror. What would it be like to wear her hair free but for two combs to catch it back from her face? She laughed at the sight of her hands trying to harness all that wildness. What was the matter with her this morning? She wet the brush and slicked the unruly strands straight back and into their usual braid and the braid into its coil at the base of her head.

She checked the mirror again. There now, the schoolmarm was back in control where she should be. The old-maid schoolmarm who would always teach other peoples' children to the best of her ability.

She quickly made up her bed and, picking up the slop jar, made her way downstairs for breakfast.

The feeling of anticipation returned as she crossed the bridge that spanned Bryde Creek. The creek flowed full and brown, swelled with runoff from the spring rains. At the sound of her feet tapping on the planks, Rebekka gave a little skip and four quick heel smacks to add to the stream's spring song. Soon the summer would be here and what would she do then?

She continued the thought. Eight more days of school and then the big picnic. Everyone was already having trouble studying and the older boys had left weeks earlier to help with spring planting. Other years she had returned to stay with her mother in Minnesota, but since her mother died, she had no family—no immediate family that is. Somewhere she might have relatives on her father's side, but no one knew for sure. Her mother had a sister somewhere, but they had lost touch through the years of her father's dragging them from pillar to post and back again.

"And that's what being married gets you," she warned the creek. "So stay the way you are." Her heels clicked a rhythm of their own as she headed on toward the schoolhouse. She looked around to see if anyone had heard or seen her—talking to the creek no less. Surely they'd think she'd been addled by the sun or something. Definitely not a good example for a teacher to set.

She looked over her shoulder, a grin peeking out around her admonishments. So was the creek male or female and was it really single? Or would you call it a marriage when two creeks flowed together and then into the river? She shook her head. Maybe she had been addled by something. Or maybe she'd been around her pupils too long. Those were the kinds of questions she encouraged from them.

She'd written the instructions for the first lesson of the day on the blackboard before some pupils arrived giggling at the door. Rebekka put all thoughts of her own questions out of her mind and concentrated on her pupils. She checked the small watch she wore pinned to her plain white blouse. Ten minutes until school began.

"Mith Thtenthrude," a small charmer with two missing front teeth lisped. "Our cat had kittenth."

Rebekka squatted down to be on eye level. "How many did she have?"

Emily wrinkled her forehead and began raising fingers until she showed four on one hand and one on the other. "Five."

"Very good. Is she taking good care of them?"

"Yeth. Thee had them in Bernie'th bed." She clapped her hands over her mouth to stifle the giggle. Her blue eyes sparkled, and when Rebekka laughed with her, they both looked back to see Bernie plunking his lunch pail down on his desk. Emily whispered between her fingers. "Bernie wath mad."

Rebekka rose to her feet and checked her watch again. "Bernie, would you be so kind as to ring the warning bell?"

Bernie nodded his pleasure and scampered out to the cloakroom, where the heavy rope hung from the bell tower. As the bell pealed its warning across the town, she could hear the children shouting and laughing as they ran toward the school.

Yes, this would be another high-spirited day and there was so much she wished to teach them before the end of the year. She waited for them at the door as they lined up, boys on one side and girls on the other, starting with the youngest in front and ending with the oldest. The boys' line was regrettably short since all those over twelve were helping their fathers in the fields.

"Bernie, the final bell." She waited while the tones rang out again. It was precisely eight o'clock. "Elizabeth, will you lead the morning prayer?" At the girl's nod, Rebekka opened the Bible she carried. "Today we will read from Psalm Twenty-three. 'The Lord is my shepherd; I shall not want.' Now, let us repeat that together." All the voices raised in unison at the familiar verse. At Rebekka's nod, Elizabeth bowed her head and waited for the shuffling to cease. Her musical voice joined with the bird choruses from the trees planted on each side of the school.

"Father in Heaven, we thank Thee for this day. Thank Thee that we can go to school and learn so many things. Please help us to do our best." Elizabeth paused, then finished swiftly. "And let everyone come to the picnic. Amen."

Rebekka rolled her lips together to keep from smiling. She and every child there knew Elizabeth was hoping that James Johnson would be in attendance. Elizabeth and James had been making eyes at each other for the last year.

"Thorlief, will you lead the flag salute?" At his answering grin, she turned and led her charges into the schoolroom.

When all the feet ceased shuffling, the boy's voice began, "I pledge allegiance to the flag. . ." At the finish, they all took their seats and folded their hands on their desktops.

Rebekka sat down at the piano and sounded the opening chords for "America the Beautiful." As the voices rose in song, she felt shivers run down her back. The children sang so wonderfully.

After the singing, she walked to the front of the room. "Today we'll start with reading. Take out your books, please."

By the end of the day, Rebekka felt like she'd been whipped through the eye of a hurricane—twice. After the last child departed, she had yet to sweep the floor and wash the blackboards. These were all chores the older boys did when they were in attendance, so she missed their presence doubly. She also needed to work on her lesson plans for the rest of the week.

When she finally closed the schoolhouse door, she sank down on the steps and wrapped her arms around her knees. At least she didn't have to walk two miles home again like she had done for the last month. And other places had been farther. She breathed in deeply of the soft air, content to be right where she was at that very moment.

Rebekka was as ready as her pupils were for the school picnic.

They'd planned games and contests for every age group from the three-year-old race to the horseshoe pitching for the older men, with the school board providing awards. Everyone in town and the surrounding area was invited.

That Saturday dawned with a thundershower, but by ten o'clock, the sun shone brightly and folks began to gather. Trestle tables had been set out and they groaned under the array of food brought by the women.

Rebekka stood on the steps and surveyed the colorful crowd. If numbers were any indication, this would be the very best school picnic that Willowford had ever seen. Only one cloud floated on her horizon—would Adolph Strand have the gall to appear? She checked every wagon and buckboard that drove up and tied up in the grove down by the creek.

"Anything else you need?" Mr. Larson appeared at her side.

"No, nothing. Just enjoying the excitement. The children have been looking forward to this day nearly as much as Christmas." Rebekka returned a wave from a newly arrived family. "Thank you for the prizes you brought. And also for the extra gifts. It means so much to the little ones to be part of the school program."

"Well, you met my two. They'd be crushed if everyone got something and not them, so I brought plenty. We'll save the leftovers for next year." He picked a stalk of grass and nibbled on the succulent stem. "Ah," he muttered as he chewed the stalk and spit out the tough section. "Umm," he started as he studied the toe of his dusty boot.

"Yes?"

He looked up at the tops of the trees bordering the creek. "There. . .ah. . .been any problems, I mean anyone hanging around or anything?"

Rebekka could recognize the flush creeping up Mr. Larson's neck because it matched the one on her own. "No, no problem. And thank you for your concern." She bent down to answer a question from one of her young students, grateful for the distraction.

When she stood up again, Mr. Larson was striding across the schoolyard. *Bless you*, she thought. *You really care and yet it is so hard for you to show it.*

By late afternoon parents were loading tired and even some sleeping children into the wagons, gathering up their things, and heading home to do evening chores. If the enthusiasm of those departing meant anything, the picnic had indeed been the success Rebekka dreamed.

Now it was time to close the school for the summer. Since several of the women had already helped clean while the children were running three-legged and sack races, the building had the smell and sound of summer slumber. The last remaining pupils policed the yard, cleaning up every scrap of paper, and then charged off to their homes.

"Bye, Miss Stenesrude. See you in the fall. Have a good summer." The calls went back and forth. Mr. Larson locked the door for the final time and pocketed the key.

"What are you figuring to do this summer?" he asked as they stopped at the rail fence bounding the schoolyard.

"I don't rightly know, besides helping Mrs. Sampson, that is." She looked up at him with a smile. "But I'm sure the good Lord knows. He promised to provide."

"Ja, that's right." He tipped his hat. "Be seein' you then." He started off, then turned. "You want a ride back to town?"

"No, thank you. I like the walk." She waved him off and, after picking up her bag loaded with books and papers, ambled toward the boardinghouse. When she paused on the bridge and looked down, the creek had retreated to its summertime ramblings, burbling over stones and babbling around tree roots. The song it sang seemed to promise good things ahead.

Even though she was tired from the rigorous day, Rebekka found herself smiling with the stream and singing its song on her way home.

"There's a letter for you," Mrs. Sampson called when Rebekka walked in the door.

Chapter 5

Next stop, Willowford." The conductor called.

Next stop, home, thought Rebekka as she stared out the window, trying to catch a glimpse of a familiar landmark. Two months was a long time to have been gone. She leaned her head back against the seat and thought of all that had happened since she had opened the letter. . .the letter from her grandmother, her father's mother.

She still couldn't believe how they had found her. And now she had family. She, who had no one, suddenly had a grandmother, an aunt, three cousins, and various other in-laws and almost in-laws. People in Minneapolis certainly did live differently than her friends in Willowford. Why, she'd never seen the contraptions called horseless carriages, electric lights, and indoor privies. Granted, she'd read about those things in newspapers, but now she'd seen them with her own eyes.

She brought herself back to the present and peered out the window, checking if she could see the Missouri yet. Instead she saw smoke.

Smoke across the prairie, as far as she could see! Prairie fire! Fire between here and Willowford. Which way was the wind blowing? Would the train be trapped? The thoughts raced through her mind like flames driven before a gale-force wind.

"No worry, folks," the conductor announced in his sonorous voice. "The wind is coming from the east, blowing due west, so we're in no danger."

Unless the wind changes, Rebekka let her thoughts drift to the cataclysm on the prairie. While the train slowed down, she leaned forward, as if she could encourage it to forge ahead. What was happening in Willowford? There was nothing to stop the fire between here and there. She'd seen the Willowford Volunteer Fire Department practice. Had they put their skills to use?

As the train covered the remaining miles, the prairie on each side of the tracks lay charred and blackened. Some fence posts still smoldered, and here and there a haystack sent tendrils of smoke skyward. Farm buildings off to the north lay in an oasis of green where the farmer had set a backfire to save his home. Plowed firebreaks kept the rampaging inferno from gobbling up another farm. A third lay in smoking ruins.

"They was some good, the soddies like I lived in as a child," one of the passengers said. "Prairie fire burnt right on over us. All we had to eat that year was potatoes. Good thing the livestock lived in a soddie barn, too. I'll never forget us runnin' to herd the cows and chickens inside."

Rebekka shuddered. But people didn't live in soddies anymore, usually.

Smoking piles of animal dung dotted a pasture. She hated to look in case there were also dead animals lying around, but so far she didn't see any.

The train whistle sent its haunting call ahead of them. Rebekka leaned her forehead against the grimy window. The feeling of relief at the sight of buildings still standing caused a lump to rise in her throat. But where was the creek, the trees that lived along its bank? And that smoking ruin she could barely see for the tears streaming down her cheeks. The schoolhouse lay in smoldering rubble.

Her schoolhouse. All the books for which they'd saved and scrimped. The flag, the bell. . .had she left any of her personal things in the desk? She thought of the shelves of books donated for a library someday. All gone.

She drew a handkerchief from her bag and wiped her eyes. As the train crossed the railroad bridge over the creek, she understood why it was hard to see from a distance. The men had cut the trees to use the creek as a firebreak. The trunks and limbs not under

327

water still smoldered. The men of the town leaned on shovels or tossed dirt on stubborn patches. Black with soot, they stared at the train, their weariness evident in the drooped shoulders and slack-jawed faces.

Rebekka blew her nose. She couldn't cry anymore now. At least they'd saved the town. They could rebuild the school. But until then, where would they meet? The church? School was due to start in three short weeks. What would they use for books?

Her mind raced ahead as she stepped down on the station platform and thanked the conductor for his assistance. Had anyone been injured? Guilt stabbed her as all she thought about was her school. Buildings could be rebuilt, but what if someone had died or was severely burned? Were the children all right?

She set off down the street to Widow Sampson's boarding-house. Men congregated at the saloon where the owner had rolled out a keg and was handing out free beer.

"Miss Stenesrude, Miss Stenesrude." A young boy, blackened and unrecognizable, came running across the dusty street. "Did ya see? The schoolhouse burnt right down."

"Yes, I saw. Is everyone all right?"

"Ja, just some burns from blowing stuff. And everybody's coughing. You never had nothing hurt like breathing smoke. Pa says we'll prob'ly start school in the church until they can build a new school."

"Thank you, Kenny." Rebekka felt relieved she'd finally figured out who her bearer of bad tidings was.

"Can I help you with your bag?" The boy fell in step beside her. "I'm plenty strong."

With a flash of trepidation, Rebekka relinquished her bag to the boy's sooty hand. How would she get the soot off the handle? She pushed the thought back as unchristian. Her "Thank you" sounded more fervent because of her doubts.

"Ah, my dear, I am so glad you are returned and safe through all this." Mrs. Sampson wiped her hands on her apron and grasped one of Rebekka's in both of hers. "How was your family? Ain't it awful about the school? But thank the good Lord, He spared the town. They was all ready to send the women and children to the other side of the river by boats and the ferry, but we was fightin' the fire right alongside the men."

Rebekka felt a stab of guilt. She should have been here helping. "Were they able to save anything from the school?"

Mrs. Sampson just shook her head. "And no one's been out to the farmers yet to see how they fared. We just came home and washed up. My hair's still damp." She patted the coronet of braids she wore.

"Have you had any new boarders?" Rebekka asked from halfway up the stairs.

"Nah, your room is still the same one. You make yourself ta home and I'll have the coffee ready shortly. Mrs. Knutson went over to her shop to check and make sure everything is all right there. We'll have supper soon's I can set things out. If you still would like to help me, we need to wash everything down tomorrow to get rid of the soot. Like spring cleaning all over again. I closed up the rooms afore I left to help on the fire line, so this house ain't bad as some."

Rebekka shuddered. The smell of smoke permeated everything inside and out, and the odor made her eyes water. What they needed now was a good rain to wash things clean again.

That night she fell asleep with her windows wide open and the breeze trying to blow away the fire's residue. How good it felt to be home, in spite of the fire. But what would she do about school?

In the morning the three women were aproned and wearing kerchiefs tied over their heads to protect their hair as they dragged the rugs out to the line for a good beating, washed and hung out the curtains, and scrubbed down every surface in the house. Since she was the tallest, Rebekka stood on a stool to wash the outsides of the windows.

"Good afternoon, Miss Stenesrude," Mr. Larson called as he opened the picket gate and strode up the walk. "Seems everyone in town is doing the same thing today. Scrubbing and counting our blessings. Good to see you back."

"Good to be back. Although I wasn't too excited about my

welcome." She climbed down from her stool and wiped her hands on her apron. "What can I do for you?"

"Could you come to a school board meeting tonight at the church at seven?"

"Of course."

"Good. I have two more members to call on. I'll see you then." He turned and strode back to his horse. "See you tonight."

The meeting that night had one item on the agenda. How would they get the money to rebuild the schoolhouse?

Within a week the bank had loaned the school district enough money to begin the building. Rebekka spent a good part of every day driving the buggy to the outlying farms to invite the people to a school raising.

"You mean like a barn raising?" one woman asked.

"Just like that." Rebekka nodded. "Plan on the second Saturday in September. Most people will be done harvesting by then, so we'll make it into a school building and end of harvest celebration. If enough people turn out, we should be able to frame the walls and put on the roof by Sunday night."

"Count on us."

Rebekka missed only one farm and that was intentional. As she drove by the Strands', she kept her eyes straight ahead. But ignoring the goosebumps chasing each other up and down her back wasn't as easy as looking the other way. Why did she feel that the whole situation wasn't resolved yet? She hadn't even heard hide nor hair of Adolph. She tried to put a lid on her worry box. "Remember, you ninny, that God says He watches over us like a hen with her chicks. And you know how fierce that little hen can be." The horse flicked his ears at her voice.

The lumber came in on the train, and the townspeople hauled it in their wagons to the school site. Rebekka walked among the stacked lumber piles, inhaling the scent of freshly milled timbers and siding. Wooden kegs of nails, crates of window glass, and the sawhorses belonging to Lars Larson lay in readiness. The flat river rocks used for support under posts and beams had been measured and placed in the proper positions.

Off to the side, the cast-iron bell salvaged from the burned building rested, cleaned and repainted and ready to lift into the new tower. Rebekka stopped at the bell and tapped it with the toe of her boot. A hollow thunk made her smile. Like everyone or everything, the bell needed to be hung in the right position to make music. "Soon," she promised the inert object. "Soon you'll be calling the children to school again." She turned in place, taking in all the supplies, ready for the morning. All that was needed were the people.

The hammering and sawing started about the time the first rooster crowed in Willowford. Rebekka bounded out of bed and rushed through her morning toilet as if she were afraid she might miss out on something. Downstairs, Mrs. Sampson was already taking three apple pies out of the oven.

"How can we find room on the table?" Rebekka moved bowls of food around to make room for the steaming pans. "You trying to feed all the builders yourself?"

"Nah. Just doing my share."

Rebekka dished herself a bowl of oatmeal from the kettle on the back of the stove. "You'd be up there nailing if they'd let you."

"Ja, I would. But since they'd drum an old woman like me. . ." Rebekka gave a decidedly unladylike snort. Mrs. Sampson gave her a look and then continued, "Off the roof, I want to make sure the workers come back the next day to finish the job. Our children need that school."

"And I need my job." Rebekka poured a dollop of molasses on her cereal, then some milk, and sat down to eat. "But what are we going to do for books and desks? The library? Oh, and our piano?"

"Won't the insurance cover some of that?"

"I hope. But it all depends on how much the rebuilding costs. I sent a letter to the state teacher's association requesting their help and Mr. Larson contacted the State Board of Education. But all that takes time."

"We used to have the parents pay for their children's books.

So there still might be books in peoples' homes that can be used. If you tell everyone to bring any books they have at home, you'll have something to start with." Mrs. Sampson lifted the full tea-kettle off the stove and filled the dishpan in the cast-iron sink.

"Thanks. I'll start passing the word today. Do you have some-one to help carry all this over to the schoolyard?"

"I'm picking up the wagon at the livery at ten. Then Mrs. Knutson and I'll go around to some of the other houses to help them. I'm bringing my washtubs for the lemonade."

Jude Weinlander let his horse drink from the river's edge. He leaned his forearms on the saddle horn and stared upriver. The town lay shimmering in the September heat, and even from this distance he could hear the pounding of hammers.

He stared across the blackened prairie, where shoots of green could be seen poking up through the ashes toward the sun-light. Drying goldenrod nodded in the breeze across the river, where leaves already sported the tinges of fall. But on this side, all lay desolate.

When his horse, Prince, raised its head, ears pricked toward the sound of building, Jude nudged the animal forward. "That's the way we'll head then." He spoke for the first time since he mounted up, just before sunrise. The horse flicked his ears as if truly interested in what was being said. "Hope you know what you're doing." The horse snorted and broke into a trot. When he raised his head and whinnied, a horse answered from the town ahead.

Jude sat on his horse at the edge of the beehive of activity. Floor joists and flooring were already in place and different groups were framing up the walls. The north wall stood while men nailed the plate in place. Hammers pounding, saws buzzing, people laughing and swapping stories, children running and laughing along a creek where the willows had been cut for the firebreak—it looked more like a party than a building site.

Across the creek, Jude could see the town. He strained to read the sign on the train station—WILLOWFORD. He shrugged. Good a place as any. Maybe they could use another hand on the building.

He watched the busy scene to determine who was in charge. A tall man, fedora pulled low on his forehead, seemed to be answering questions and keeping his laborers busy. Jude stepped from his horse and tipped his hat back before searching in his saddlebags for hammer and pigskin gloves. Before leaving his mount, he loosened the saddle cinch and wrapped the reins around a willow stump.

Two barefoot, overalls-clad youngsters charged by him, their speed outclassed only by the volume of their shouts.

"Need anything to drink?" A tall woman dressed in a white blouse and ankle-length serge skirt moved from helper to helper offering drinks from a bucket on her arm.

"You got something stronger than that lemonade?" One of the sweating hammer wielders asked.

"Now, you know better than that." The woman grinned, changing her face from plain to pretty. Auburn highlights glinted from hair imprisoned in a coil of braids at the back of her head. Springy tendrils of hair framed her heart-shaped face in spite of her determined efforts to tuck them back into their prison.

As if feeling his gaze, she turned and stared straight at him. With one hand she brushed back a lock of hair before going on to the next man to offer him a drink.

He watched the way she moved about the yard, her long-legged stride, free of feminine artifice. Funny, he hadn't noticed something like the way she moved, since, well, since. . . He clamped a lid on the memories of his other life. Nothing mattered now but the next job. . .the next town. . .the next meal. And maybe working here for a few hours would at least give him that.

He kept his eye on the man in charge, following him around the corner of the building before getting his attention. "Ah, sir."

The man waved at a man nailing boards in place on a wall frame and then strode over to answer another's question.

Jude paused by a man busily sawing boards laid across the sawhorses. "Who is the man in charge here?" he asked.

"Ah, that'd be Lars Larson, the man getting a drink from the schoolmarm."

"Thanks." Jude tipped his hat and, stepping across a couple of beams, made his way around the building. So that's who she was, the schoolmarm. "Mr. Larson." He walked closer. "Mr. Larson."

Lars Larson turned from a laughing comment exchanged with the tall woman Jude had noticed before. "Ja?" At the sight of a stranger, he offered his hand. "I'm Lars Larson. What can I do for you?"

"I wondered if maybe you could use another hand." Jude concentrated on keeping his gaze from swinging to the woman. He forced himself to look Mr. Larson in the eye instead.

"You know how to use a hammer?"

Jude nodded, his mouth set in a firm line.

"I can't pay you. This is a community project. The school burnt in a prairie fire a few weeks ago." Mr. Larson studied the man in front of him. "But there'll be plenty of food, if'n that appeals to you."

Jude nodded. "That'll be fine."

"You go on and join that crew on the front wall."

Jude tipped his hat to Mr. Larson and then to the woman standing off to the side with a slight smile on her face. "Ma'am." He turned and pulled on his gloves while crossing the schoolyard.

As he reached the men raising the wall, he drew his hammer from its place in his belt in the back on the right side.

"Who is he?" Rebekka stared after the man. She turned to Mr. Larson, who shrugged.

"Just a drifter, I imagine. At least he'll get a good feed for his labors." Mr. Larson took another sip from the dipper and wiped his mouth with the back of his hand. "Thank you, Miss Stenesrude. That lemonade tastes mighty fine."

He didn't even say his name and I heard everything they said. Rebekka allowed her thoughts to drift as she continued around the building with the lemonade bucket. Again she saw and felt the shock of his gaze. Did she know him from somewhere else? She tried to think. No, she'd remember someone with a gaze so summer-sky blue. Eyes so blue they seemed to pierce like shards of ice on a winter day. Now why did she think of winter? Today when the sun was so hot that she'd had to wipe her face with a handkerchief twice already.

She returned to the washtub to refill her bucket and she felt it again. How could the gaze from a man she'd never even met before send shivers up and down her spine?

Rebekka handed her half-full bucket to her oldest pupil, reminding her to stay out of the way of the men while they worked, and then she went over to help the women setting up the tables for dinner. From the looks of the groaning boards, no one would go hungry. In fact, there'd be plenty left for supper, too. That way those that didn't have animals to care for could work through until dark.

"Who was that man talking with you and Lars?" Mrs. Sampson paused in the act of cutting her pies.

"I have no idea." Rebekka felt the urge to look over her shoulder again. If she did, she was sure she would see him watching her. "He didn't give his name, just said he knew how to use a hammer."

"Well, he wasn't just blowing smoke. I been watching him. You mark my words, he's used that hammer plenty. Has an air of mystery about him, wouldn't you say? Or maybe it's sadness."

"I wouldn't say at all. I don't know the man and probably never will." Rebekka turned to her friend. "You sure have strange ideas. He's just a drifter."

"I wouldn't be too sure."

Just then someone came up to ask Rebekka a question, so she had no more time to pursue the discussion. But something niggled at her just the same. Who was he?

At the stroke of noon Rebekka rang the triangle, calling everyone to eat. The Reverend Haugen came down off the ladder where he'd been nailing on the upper plate and, after wiping his face on a bright red kerchief, bowed his head. "We thank Thee, O Lord, for the gifts Thou hast given us, for the food the women have prepared, for the progress on our building, and for the protection Thee offers us all. Hear our prayer and now give us strength to continue through the day before us." At the universal "Amen," he raised his hands. "Let's eat."

The men formed two lines and moved down the length of the laden tables, loading their plates as they went. Another row of tables had benches on each side ready for the men to slide first one foot and then the other under the table and sit down. As soon as the men had filled their plates, the women and children did the same.

Rebekka had switched from carrying lemonade to carrying coffee and made her way down the table with a huge pot. At her "Coffee?" the seated men held up the mug from on the table in front of them.

"There's more lemonade, too," she said as she poured coffee and offered praises for jobs well done.

"Coffee?" she said again, stopping just before the stranger.

He turned without a word and held up his cup.

Rebekka felt her hand shake as she poured the dark brew. When the cup was full, she raised her gaze to see the man studying her over the rim of the cup. He lifted the steaming mug and, after one swallow, turned and set the cup down. Without a word, smile, thank you, or by your leave, he resumed eating.

Rebekka paused as if giving him a chance to remedy his bad manners. But when he continued to fork potato salad into his mouth without another glance, she stepped to the next man at the table.

"Coffee?" Now her voice shook, too. She cleared her throat and took a tighter grip on the pot holders with which she held the pot. Of all the. . .

She stayed away from him after that—far away—and did the slow burn. What an ingrate. Had his mother not taught him common decency? No manners? Everyone was taught to at least say "Thank you." Weren't they?

Obviously not. She stopped after her last round with the water bucket and gazed up at the new schoolhouse.

As the sun was setting, the men on the roof were nailing the last rafter in place.

"That's it for tonight," Mr. Larson called. "We'll start again at first light. Reverend Haugen has agreed to lead the worship service tomorrow right here so those who want can attend without much of a loss of time. We can use the good Lord's blessing." He waved toward the tables, set now with plates of sandwiches and the left-overs from dinner. "Now, come and help yourselves. These women would be mighty hurt if anyone left here hungry."

Rebekka kneaded the aching muscles of her lower back with her fists. If she had to carry one more coffeepot she was sure her shoulders would come loose from their sockets. She could hear others groaning, too, but everyone laughed off the pains and dug into the food.

Jude pounded in the last nail and, after sticking his hammer back into its usual place, he climbed down the ladder. He pulled off his gloves and tucked them into his back pocket, then crossed to where the men were washing their hands and faces in a row of buckets of water lined up on a bench.

He tipped his hat back and, sloshing water up in cupped hands, he washed his face first, then hands, and finally his arms up to his rolled-back sleeves. He could feel someone watching him but, when he turned around, no one seemed to be paying him any attention. Then why that creepy crawly sensation up his spine? He lifted his hat and ran damp fingers through the waves trapped beneath the hatband. The slash of silver that began at his upper temple on the left side caught a glint from the setting sun.

The glint caught Rebekka's gaze, in spite of her efforts to not look at the man. What was wrong with her? She'd never in her life paid so much attention to one man, and a drifter at that.

After the crowd finished eating, they slowly left the school grounds and headed for their homes. Lars Larson sat down beside Jude on the bench and leaned his elbows on the table. "You sure got a way with that hammer of yours. Been building long?"

Jude shook his head. "Nope, just the last year or so."

"You from these parts?"

"No." Jude cut and levered another bite of pie into his mouth.

"You plannin' on coming back tomorrow?"

"If nobody minds."

"You got a place to stay?" Mr. Larson leaned on his elbows.

"Down by the river'll do."

"You're welcome to my barn. You can put your horse out in the pasture and leave him there long as you want." Mr. Larson swiveled around like he was getting ready to leave. "What'd you say your name was?"

"Jude Weinlander. And I appreciate the offer." Jude accepted a cup of coffee from the woman pouring and thanked her. Then he turned back to Mr. Larson. "Just where is your barn?"

Mr. Larson pointed out his house on the knoll on the other side of Willowford and pushed himself to his feet. "See you in the morning then and thanks for your work on the school today."

Jude nodded. He watched as the man gathered his family into a wagon and drove off. He slapped at a mosquito buzzing around his head and sipped his coffee. This was a good town, he could tell already. The townsfolk made even drifters feel welcome, at least this one who could nail up a wall with the best of them.

He turned and studied the bare bones of the new school. Siding covered most of two walls, the rafters were ready for the nailers, and two men had been splitting cedar shakes to finish the roof. Tomorrow would make a big difference if as many people turned out as today. He inhaled air redolent of freshly sawed wood. Even the ache in his back only added to the contentment. He started to reach in his pocket for a cigar but remembered he didn't even have a nickel to buy one. He'd have to find a paying job pretty soon.

Bedded down on soft hay that night, he thought back again to the day. Glints of auburn off a tall woman's hair and a laugh that floated like music on the air brought a smile to a face that had found little reason to smile in a long while.

Stretched out on her bed after helping Mrs. Sampson boil potatoes and eggs for salad again the next day, Rebekka thought over the day. She'd never realized how friendly and caring the people of

Willowford were. All those who pitched in to raise the new school building and not a cross word heard all day. She deliberately kept her mind away from the stranger with the black hat and the slash of silver in his hair. He didn't look old enough to be going gray already.

She rolled over and thumped her pillow. Who was he? Where had he come from? She could ask Mr. Larson tomorrow. Sure, just go up and say, "Mr. Larson, I saw you talking with that stranger. Tell me his life history." Even the thought of such outrageous actions sent the heat flaming up her neck.

If she waited long enough, Mrs. Sampson would find out plenty. If she had the patience to wait. A mighty big word, "if." Would he be back tomorrow?

Chapter 6

Y ou think he'll be back today?" Rebekka asked.
"Who'll be back?" Mrs. Sampson removed a pot of baked beans from the oven.

"You know. The stranger," said Rebekka while carefully spreading frosting on the chocolate layer cake in front of her. She leaned over to make sure frosting covered every spot; that way she didn't have to look up at Mrs. Sampson or Mrs. Knutson. She wondered if they noticed the flush she could feel creeping up her neck.

"Need more eggs for that potato salad?" asked Mrs. Sampson, crossing over to taste the mixture in the bowl.

"No, I don't think so." Mrs. Knutson pushed her friend's fingers away from the food. "And yes to you, Rebekka. I heard him tell Lars that he'll be back."

"Oh."

"Why?" Both women stared at Rebekka as she scraped the bowl for the last bits of frosting.

"I. . .ummm. . .well, it would be a shame to lose a good carpenter like him."

"How do you know that?"

"What?"

"That he's a good carpenter." Mrs. Sampson flashed a grin at her longtime boarder.

"Anyone could see that." Rebekka flipped new curls into the top of the cake.

"Anyone who was watching, that is." The two widows turned to focus totally on Rebekka.

Rebekka wished she had never started this discussion. She

340

kept her gaze on the cake, but her flaming cheeks refused to cool. *One would think you're interested,* she chided herself. *You know better than that. He, whoever he is, is just a drifter, a man passing through. Be grateful he helped on the school and let it go at that.*

She mentally shrugged off the thoughts and, with a grin tugging at the corners of her mouth, asked, "Either of you catch his name?"

The three of them were still laughing as they loaded the wagon to bring the food over to the schoolyard.

They arrived just in time for the church service. Reverend Haugen stood in front of the impromptu altar and raised his hands for silence. People found places to sit on the benches, the remaining stacks of lumber, or the ground. A hush fell, broken only by a bird's song.

"This is the day that the Lord hath made," Reverend Haugen began the service.

"Let us rejoice and be glad in it," the scattered congregation responded.

"Let us pray." The Reverend bowed his head and waited for the rustling to cease. "Lord God, bless us this day as we worship Thee and bless the fruits of our labors. Open our hearts to hear Thy word. Amen." He raised his head and looked over the people gathered. "Today we'll sing the songs we know best since we chose not to bring the hymnals. Let's start with 'Beautiful Savior.' " As his rich baritone rang out the opening notes, everyone joined in.

Rebekka felt the sun warm on her back while a playful breeze tickled the strands of hair that refused to be bound into the coil at her neck. As she sang the familiar words, she let her gaze roam around the gathering. Her pupils, their families, the townsfolk, some who came to church regularly, and some who didn't. She kept her eyebrows from rising when she recognized the saloon owner and exchanged a wink with Mrs. Sampson when they both noticed two of the older youths making calf eyes at each other.

I wish we could worship outside like this every Sunday, Rebekka thought, *at least as long as the weather is nice. Seems to me people feel closer somehow. Maybe it's because we're all working* _together on something truly important._

As the Reverend read, Rebekka forced herself to concentrate. "From 1 John, chapter four, 'Beloved, let us love one another: for love is of God. . .'"

Here, today, her thoughts continued with a mind of their own. _It is easy to love one another._ A black cloud of remembrance dulled her joy. Well, maybe not everyone.

When they raised their voices in the final hymn, she allowed herself a glance around the group again. Now, why was it that the sun seemed to shine brighter when she saw the stranger, leaning against the corner of the schoolhouse?

And why was her neck warm when she caught a grinning Mrs. Sampson watching her?

By the end of the day, the building looked complete—from the outside. A roof, windows glinting in the dying sun, and the door hung above three steps, all there but the bell hanging in the tower.

"Looks pretty good, if I do say so myself." Lars Larson joined her in staring up at the men coming down from nailing the cap along the roof's peak. "Sure is farther along than I thought possible."

"Just goes to show what a determined group of people can do when they set their minds to it. When do you plan to rehang the bell?" Rebekka turned to watch two children playing tag under the ladders. When their mothers called them away, she looked up at Mr. Larson.

"Soon's we're done with supper. Thought we'd use that as a good way to finish the day."

"Wonderful."

"Excuse me, Miss Stenesrude, I need to talk to Jude before he gets away," Mr. Larson said as he left her side to stride across the yard to where the man in black, as Rebekka called him in her mind, was leaving the yard.

"At least now I know part of his name," Rebekka said to no one in particular.

"Here, how about pouring coffee?" Mrs. Sampson handed her the heavy pot. "And it's Weinlander."

Rebekka took the pot and scurried off. There it was, that blush that crept up her neck. She'd never flushed so much in her whole life as these last two days. What in the world was wrong with her?

"Weinlander, wait up."

Jude turned at the calling of his name, and he watched as Lars Larson caught up with him.

"You're staying for supper, aren't you? That's the least we can do after all your fine work. I think you're a good part of the reason we got so much done."

"Ja, I'll stay. I was just going over to look at the creek. Pity you had to cut down all the trees along it." Jude tipped his hat back.

"It was that or lose the town. You know, with that fire and all, there's lots of building needs doing before the snow flies. Might you be interested in staying on and working for me?" Mr. Larson caught his suspenders with his thumbs. "I know how good you are. You could run one crew and me another."

Jude lifted his hat and ran his fingers through his hair before using both hands to place his hat back in place. He looked off to the horizon on the other side of town. When he nodded and said, "Guess I could," Mr. Larson let out his breath as if he'd been holding it. "Guess I could."

"You could probably get a room at Mrs. Sampson's boarding-house. I heard she has a vacancy."

"Well, I better—"

"If it's a case of money, I could give you an advance, and since you're working for me, I know she'll let you pay the rest later. The food's good there, too."

Jude thought of the beans and no coffee he'd subsisted on for the past week. One morning he'd even borrowed a cup of milk from a cow in the barn where he'd slept. When he'd gone to look at the creek, he'd been hoping to see fish. Fried fish had sounded mighty tasty. And how long had it been since he'd slept in a real bed?

He looked back to the waiting man. "All right. But if you don't mind, I'd as soon sleep in your hay barn till it gets colder."

Mr. Larson grabbed his new employee's hand and shook it. "Good. That's Mrs. Sampson over there, the lady with the white hair and white apron who's been overseeing the food serving. Just tell her I sent you." Before Jude could walk off, Mr Larson put a hand on Jude's arm and dropped his voice, "I'll just pay the room for now."

Jude nodded his thanks. He'd pretty much used up his store of words in the last two days. Everyone had been so nice to him. If they only knew who he really was. The thought caused the two slashes between his eyebrows to deepen. If they only knew, they'd never speak to him again. They'd just run him out of town.

He joined the last of the laborers at the wash bench and, after sluicing down, took a seat on the benches by the laden tables. While some folks had left to attend their evening chores, many more laughed and joked around the tables. Jude listened to the jokes as the two young men beside him flirted with all the young women bringing refills of potato salad, fried chicken, sliced ham, and baked beans down the row.

Mrs. Sampson brought him a piece of apple pie and sat down beside him. "Lars told me you need a room?" She spoke in a low voice, only for his ears. "By the way, I'm Widow Sampson with the boardinghouse."

"Glad to meet you." Jude picked up his fork. "You make this pie?"

She shook her head. "That chocolate cake is my doing. Yesterday I noticed you seem a mite partial to apple pie, so I snagged you a piece before it was all gone."

"Thank you. I'm sure the chocolate cake is good, too," Jude said as he cut off a bite of pie and lifted it to his mouth.

"I have a proposition for you. I need some things done around my place that you could fix if you had a mind to. You could work off some of the board if you'd be so inclined."

Jude turned and looked at the cheery woman beside him. "But you don't know me."

"I know what I see."

Jude wanted to ask her what it was she saw but instead took another bite of pie.

"Well?"

"I'd be so inclined," he nodded. "And thank you."

"It's the big white house off Main Street on Sampson Street."

Jude turned and looked at her. "Sampson Street?"

"Mr. Sampson was well liked by the founding fathers." The twinkle in her eyes invited him to smile back.

Jude scooped up the last bite of pie as he said, "I have a horse."

"I know. I have a fenced pasture behind the house and a shed that could be called a small barn. You can get feed and hay at the livery after you get back on your feet."

Jude swung one leg over the bench so he could face her.

"Why are you doing this?"

Without flinching and looking away, Widow Sampson met his gaze and said, "I don't really know. It just seems what I am supposed to do." The two stared at each other, both measuring and weighing the person in front of them. "Is there anything else I should know about you?"

"Not that I can think of," Jude answered without batting an eye. Inside his head he finished, *If you only knew.*

"Then we'll see you back at the house when you've finished here. You can bring your horse tonight or pick him up tomorrow." Mrs. Sampson rose to her feet. "Stay here. I think I see a piece of chocolate cake with your name on it."

They sure got chummy fast, Rebekka thought as she carefully avoided looking at Jude and Mrs. Sampson. She absolutely refused to let herself amble over to see what was happening.

"All right, folks, let's gather 'round. The pulley is installed for the bell. All you children, Miss Stenesrude, come over here. It'll be your job to pull the rope that will raise the bell." Lars Larson waved his arms to encourage the children to make a line by the rope lying on the ground.

"Miss Stenesrude, you take the end. John, Elizabeth, you bigger kids, start right here." Mr. Larson handed them the heavy rope. "You little ones, line up on both sides. Now, when I count to three, you'll all pull together, understand?"

Children came from every corner, laughing and giggling as they grabbed the rope.

Rebekka looked up on the roof where two men sat on the edge of the tower, ready to secure the bell when it reached its new home. One waved at her.

"We're ready when you are," he called.

"Mith Thtenthrude, can I be by you?" Emily Gordon pleaded with her round blue eyes.

Rebekka stepped back and shared her rope with the little one. "Of course. Now you be ready to pull."

"One," Mr. Larson's voice rang out. Silence fell. "Two." Giggles erupted along the rope line.

"Stop shoving me!" a small boy demanded.

"Get off my foot!" yelled someone else.

"Three! Now, pull steady, don't jerk. You want the bell to rise nice and easy." Mr. Larson walked along with his pulling team as the rope stretched from the tower clear to the ground and along the caterpillar of pullers.

"Good, good!" A man inside of the building who was guiding the bell called. "Easy now."

The line of children snaked back, each one carefully pulling on his section of rope. Rebekka watched as the older ones looked out for the younger and they all worked together to raise the bell.

"There it is!" The cry rang out as the top of the bell cleared the ledge. The two men waved. The line stopped.

"Ith almotht up," the lisper beamed up at Rebekka.

"Sure is. You did a good job." Rebekka leaned down and laid a fingertip on the little one's button nose.

"Don't drop your rope," the charmer cautioned.

Rebekka nodded solemnly. "I won't." She raised her gaze to the bell tower as one of the men called out.

"Easy now. Only an inch at a time."

The children stared up at him, waiting for the signal and then barely moving back. The bell inched upward.

"That's it." The two men secured the bell and raised their

hands for the cheer. "Okay now, on three. Pull the rope for the bell to ring. One, two, three!"

The children pulled; the bell rang out, the *bong, bong* sounding joyous and richer for the cleaning. They pulled again and the bell sang for them all.

"Yeth," the little one said, clapping her hands and turning to Rebekka, who lifted the child into her arms. Together they and all the crowd clapped and cheered.

Reverend Haugen walked up the schoolhouse steps and turned to face the gathered people. "A fitting end to a wonderful day. Let us bow our heads and thank the Lord for watching over us." He waited for the rustlings to cease and bowed his head. "Dear Lord, we dedicate this building to Thee. Be with our children who learn here and the teacher that teaches them. We thank Thee for keeping us all safe and in Thy care. Now, please give us safe travel and good rest. Amen."

Rebekka shook hands and wished everyone good night, thanking them for their efforts. As the last wagon was loaded and left, she and Widow Sampson folded tablecloths and picked up the stray napkins.

"What a day," Rebekka said as she rubbed the small of her back with her fists. "Mr. Larson said we would be able to open school next Monday. They'll be finishing the inside of the building this week." She turned to catch a secret smile that Widow Sampson tried to hide. "All right. What's that for?"

"You'll see." The older woman packed the last box into the wagon. "Are you riding with me or walking?" she asked as she climbed up on the seat of the wagon.

"I'm coming," said Rebekka as she stepped up and pulled herself onto the wagon seat. When the horse started off, she looked over her shoulder to the schoolhouse, gleaming faintly in the dusk.

"Thank You, Lord," she whispered.

"What's that?"

"Just happy, that's all."

"That's enough."

"You want me to take the horse back?" Rebekka asked when

they pulled to a halt at the boardinghouse.

"That would be nice, dear. Then I can get these things put away. When you get back I have something to tell you." The Widow Sampson stepped to the ground and tied the horse to the fence. Together, the two women unloaded the wagon, carrying baskets and tubs to the back porch.

"I wouldn't mind if you told me now." Rebekka paused before returning to the horse.

"Just hurry back. I hate to see you out after dark."

Rebekka hummed along with the horse's *clip-clop, clip-clop* trot back to the livery. Since no one answered her call, she tied the horse to the hitching post in front and swung off back to the widow's house. As she walked the quiet streets, lights glowed from windows, a dog barked, and another answered. Since it was Sunday night, the saloon was closed and dark.

But there were plenty of lights at Widow Sampson's boardinghouse and Rebekka looked across the yard in surprise. She'd have thought Mrs. Knutson would have gone up to her room and Mrs. Sampson would be finishing up in the kitchen. The gate creaked as she opened it; a horse nickered from somewhere out in the pasture.

Rebekka froze. Who's horse was out there? Had an animal gotten loose and found its way to their pasture? She locked the gate behind her and strode up the walk. Surely she wouldn't have to take a strange animal back tonight.

At the sound of voices, she paused on the back porch. One voice was a man's. Perhaps someone had come for his horse. She breathed a sigh of relief, opened the back door, and crossed through the pantry to the kitchen.

"What?" she said as she saw the stranger, sitting perfectly at ease at the table in Mrs. Sampson's kitchen.

"Rebekka Stenesrude, I'd like you to meet our new boarder, Jude Weinlander." Mrs. Sampson shot Rebekka a look of apology.

"Miss Stenesrude." Jude rose to his feet and tipped his head in the time-honored greeting of male to female.

"Mr. Weinlander." Rebekka knew her manners. What she

didn't understand was how one man's eyes could look so. . .so. . .sad wasn't nearly strong enough. Not blank, not dead, just filled with deep-down, soul-searching sorrow. Whatever had happened in his life to bring that darkness to eyes that should have sparkled like the sun, dappling a Minnesota lake in the summer?

Again the slash of silver in his dark blond hair caught her attention. Did he ever smile? What would it take to make a smile light his eyes and crease his face? *Silly,* she chided herself. *He's a drifter. He'll be here and gone before you know it.*

"Mr. Weinlander will be working for Lars," Mrs. Sampson said as she reached for the coffeepot on the stove. "Would you like a cup before you retire?"

Rebekka shook her head. "No, thanks. I think I'll go on up." The usual camaraderie seemed to have fled the kitchen. Would things ever be the same?

Jude watched her leave the room, her back straight, her head high. He wondered how she could hold her head so straight with that thick braided coil at her neck. It looked heavy enough to tip her all the way over. Tonight she wasn't smiling. In fact, the temperature had dropped ten degrees in the room when they'd been introduced. But he'd seen her smile at the children today. And all the others helping at the school. She had a wonderful, heart-catching smile when she allowed it out to play. Must have something to do with being a schoolmarm.

He picked up the cup of coffee set before him and sipped. No matter. He wouldn't be here long enough to get to know her anyway.

Mrs. Sampson sat down across from him and, with a sigh, stretched her shoulders and leaned back in the chair. "This has certainly been a busy two days. Glad we don't have doings like this too often."

Jude set his cup down and ran a calloused fingertip around the edge of the mug. He could feel a war going on inside him. Why in the world did he have this desire to tell the woman across from him his life's story? Surely if she knew, she would send him packing in an instant. He cleared his throat. He could hear footsteps overhead.

That must be Rebekka's room. Why in the world was he thinking of her as Rebekka? Miss Stenesrude.

He took another swallow of coffee. "I need to tell you some things."

Mrs. Sampson studied him across the top of her cup. "Not if you don't want to, you don't."

Jude pulled at the collar of his shirt. "It's been awhile since I told anyone—in fact, I never have." *Why do you want to do this?* his mind cautioned. *What is there about this woman that invites you to tell all?* He looked across the table into the most compassionate eyes he'd ever seen.

"You don't need to do this."

"Ja, I guess I do." He took a deep breath and began. "I been a no-good all my life, deviling my older brother and making life miserable for my wife and mother. But I can't make my wife and my mother sad anymore because they are dead and it's all my fault." He continued with his story without a break. "And now you know. So if you want me to leave, I'll understand."

"Do you play an instrument?"

The question surprised him. "What?"

"I asked if you played an instrument."

"I know what you said. I heard you." He stared at the woman across the table. Her smile warmed him clear down to his ankles. He shook his head, feeling a laugh starting down in his middle. "Yes, I play, if you call a mouth organ an instrument."

"Good. That means we'll have nearly an orchestra right here. Miss Stenesrude plays the organ and piano, Mrs. Knutson the fiddle, and I do a fair-to-middlin' job on the gutbucket. . .banjo some, too. I think we'll have some real high times, come winter." She pushed herself to her feet. "More coffee?"

Jude shook his head. "No, thanks." He stared at the woman who had just given him his life back. "Is that all you have to say?"

She poured her coffee and turned to look at him. "No. There'll be no smoking or drinking or playing cards in my house!" Then her eyebrows raised in question.

"Of course not."

"And it's high time you understand that God forgives us when we ask. . .and even before. You need to plug into that. Breakfast is at seven, earlier if you need, I make your dinner bucket, and supper is served at six o'clock sharp. You needn't worry that I'll tell tales on you. Your life is safe with me." She walked over to the sink and set her cup into the dishpan. "I'll show you to your room." She picked up the kerosene lamp and led the way up the stairs.

Rebekka heard them come up the stairs. What on earth had they been talking about all this while? She turned over and thumped her pillow. She missed sitting in the kitchen discussing the day with Widow Sampson. Why had he come along and ruined everything? Now this house that had felt like home felt more like just a place to live.

Chapter 7

Everywhere Rebekka went, Jude was there.

"Howdy, Miss Stenesrude," said Johnny J., her oldest pupil, as he waved at her from his painting ladder when she approached the school on Monday morning. "Sure is looking good, wouldn't you say?"

"I certainly would." Rebekka stopped to admire the sparkling white paint. "You're doing a fine job." She opened the door to find Jude nailing up the thin boards and the chicken wire for the plasterers who were coming next. "Mr. Weinlander," she said as she tipped her head in acknowledgment.

"Miss Stenesrude." Jude continued nailing, the hammer ringing in perfect rhythm.

Now he was here, ruining her joy in the new building. How could anyone else be happy when he stared out at them with such sad eyes? She slanted a peek in his direction. There was no indication he cared whether she was in the room or not; he just continued with his work.

Rebekka paced the room, picturing the blackboards for the wall, where her desk would go, and if she would change the configuration of the children's desks. She'd seen a school building with movable desks, and since the school was also used as the town's meeting hall, theater, and dance hall, movable desks would be a decided advantage.

She took a paper and pencil from her bag and began a list of supplies, including the changes she would like to make. But where could they get the money? She'd have to talk with Mr. Larson to see if there was any left from the bank loan. As she paced, she tapped the pencil end against her teeth.

When finished, she put the things back in her bag and walked toward the door. "Good day, Mr. Weinlander." She kept her voice cool and terribly proper.

"Ummm." The hammering continued without a break.

As she stalked the path homeward, she fumed at the snub. Didn't he even have the grace to be polite?

After having talked with Mr. Larson and called on two families who had recently moved to the area, she walked into the boardinghouse and found him sitting at the table drinking a cup of coffee.

"Supper in half an hour," Mrs. Sampson said as she turned from the pot she was stirring on the stove and smiled at Rebekka. "There's a letter for you on the entry table. And a box arrived. Must be books, it's so heavy. Jonathan brought it over from the train station."

"Wonderful. Thank you." Rebekka crossed through the kitchen and went out without looking that man in the face. Two could play at his game. She stopped at the oak secretary to pick up scissors and knelt by the box. As she cut the strings, she read the address.

"Who are they from?" Mrs. Sampson followed her into the sitting room.

"A school in Fargo." Rebekka folded back the top of the box and peered inside. "Arithmetic, history, reading," she said as she shuffled through the books, setting them outside the box as she dug deeper. "What a gift. This gives me at least something to start with." She opened a letter taped to the inside of the box top.

She read aloud, "Dear Teacher, We are sorry these aren't brand-new, but we planned on sending these to the Indian Reservation after we received new textbooks. Please send them on when you are finished with them. Please accept our sympathy on the burning of your school." Rebekka looked up to Mrs. Sampson. "Isn't that wonderful?"

Jude, who was standing behind Mrs. Sampson, saw Rebekka's shining eyes and felt like a mule had kicked him in the gut. Why, she wasn't plain at all, like he'd first thought. When she smiled like that, her eyes could teach the sun something about shining. And all it took was a box of hand-me-down books for her school, no less.

Jude turned and left the two women talking. He needed to wash before supper anyway. As he pumped a bucket of water at the outside well, he thought back to the school in Soldall. They had plenty of books. There was even a library in town, at the school, of course. And Mrs. Norgaard had a whole room full of books.

But was he ready to write to them? He sluiced water over his head and shoulders and scrubbed with the bar of homemade soap left on the bench beside the bucket. As he rinsed again, he shook his head. "How can I ask them for something when they've already given me so much? And all I ever did for them was cause trouble."

But this wasn't asking for something for himself, his argument continued. Rebekka's, Miss Stenesrude's—he even caught himself correcting his thoughts—happiness wasn't for herself either. What she needed was books and supplies for her school so she could teach the kids who would be coming to her. Cute kids like the little girl with the lisp. . .and the two young lovebirds.

Jude dried himself with the towel Mrs. Sampson had hung on a nail above the wash bench. He would write the letter tonight. It was for the children of Willowford, after all.

After repacking her box of books, Rebekka sat down in the sitting room to read the letter from her aunt. What a joy it was to have family again. She who had felt alone for so long. She smiled at the news that one of her cousins was getting married, a second was increasing her family, and her grandmother wished Rebekka could come for another visit soon.

Rebekka tucked the letter back into its envelope. Maybe she could go see them for Christmas. What would it be like to spend Christmas with people who were her real family, not only friends, but related? Her mother said they'd had Christmas with her mother and father, back when Rebekka was little, but Rebekka couldn't remember them. Most of her memories were not worth dragging out.

"I'll carry that over to the school for you on Friday," Jude said as he stopped in the arched doorway. "Should be done with the walls by then."

Rebekka started. She hadn't heard him walk across the floor. "Why. . .why, thank you." She looked up in time to catch a fleeting glimpse of something lighten his eyes. No, she'd been mistaken. . . only the dark remained. But she couldn't pull her gaze away. Such deep, dark eyes. All she could call it was sadness.

"Supper's ready," Mrs. Sampson called from the kitchen.

Rebekka let the conversation between the two widows flow around her, answering only when asked a question. She concentrated fully on each bite, but if someone had asked her what she was eating, she couldn't have said. She didn't dare look up for Jude sat right across the round oak table from her, and she knew for certain that if she looked into his eyes again, she would blush enough to light up the room.

"Please pass the bread." His voice, deep and rich like maple syrup flowing over steaming pancakes in the morning, played bass to the women's soprano.

At the sudden silence, Rebekka looked up. "Oh." She passed the bread plate that had been sitting directly in front of her. But she didn't look across the table. No, sirree. She only looked to Mrs. Knutson, who sat on her right and who passed the plate to Jude.

But his hand caught Rebekka's eye. . .tanned, long, blunt fingers. She forced her gaze back to her plate. What was the matter with her?

When she finally escaped to her room, Rebekka gave herself a good talking to. She tried to sit down at the table beside the window to write her letter but instead ended up pacing the floor. *You ninny. You are the schoolteacher, remember? You can't talk to anyone. You have a respected position in this town and that man is only a drifter. Besides that, he doesn't care a bit for you and you don't want him to.*

She kept her shoulders back and her spine straight. When she felt she'd said and heard enough, she sat herself back down in the chair and took out paper and pen and uncapped the inkwell. She dipped the pen and began, "Dear Aunt Sofie. . ."

Her mind floated down the stairs and into the sitting room, where she could hear Mrs. Sampson and Mrs. Knutson and Mr. Weinlander talking. A black blot spread across the white paper. *"Uff da."* Here she was the schoolteacher, who was supposed to teach penmanship, and she'd blotted the paper.

Only women's laughter drifted up the stairway. Did that man have a personal law against laughing?

Rebekka took another sheet of paper from her packet and began to write again but stopped when she heard the stairs creak under a heavier tread.

Then she stared down at the newly spreading black smear and wrinkled the page, dropping it next to its mate in the wastebasket by the table. Now she'd not only not finished the letter, but she had wasted two sheets of paper. And paper costs money.

After asking for paper and a pen, Jude climbed the stairs to his room. He sat down at the table by the window and after uncapping the ink, wrote in a bold, firm hand to his brother, Dag. He pictured his brother reading the letter aloud at the supper table in the big house in Soldall. They would all be sitting at the long oak table in the dining room—Dag, Clara, Mrs. Norgaard, and Mrs. Hanson, who would be jumping up to serve. Gaslight from the chandelier above the table would bring a brilliance to the room, impossible with kerosene lamps like the one sitting on the edge of the table.

The house was grand, for certain. And his brother had grown into the grandness himself, changing from the shy, filthy blacksmith to one of the leading businessmen of the town, even though he was still the blacksmith. Jude chewed on the end of the pen. Where was the anger and jealousy he'd felt all these years? There was Dag with all the trappings Jude had dreamed of and here he was, a drifter in a town far from anywhere, and he. . . he didn't hate anymore. Had it, too, been burned away?

He finished the letter and addressed the envelope. He'd pick up a stamp and. . . .he shook his head. He couldn't even buy a stamp until payday. How could he ask for one more thing from Mrs. Sampson? He put the envelope aside. He'd mail it next week.

As he closed his eyes in bed, his mind flitted back to the sitting room and Rebekka. He gave up. He couldn't call her Miss Stenesrude in his mind any longer. Rebekka, kneeling in front of the box of books. Rebekka, with such joy and delight, he'd almost smiled at her. Almost—until he caught himself.

He turned over and folded the pillow under his head. He'd ask for a stamp in the morning. After all, it was only three days until payday.

By the end of the week, Rebekka had collected two more boxes of books from people in the community. On Friday, while she sorted her papers and books into the desk the doctor in town had loaned the school, she heard a team draw up by the school.

"Hello, Miss Stenesrude," a male voice paged her from outside. Rebekka pushed back her chair and crossed to the window. Jonathan Ingmar, the stationmaster, tied his team to the hitching post planted to the side of the schoolhouse and walked to the rear of his wagon. A flat, wooden crate lay in the wagon bed.

"I'll be right there to help you," Rebekka told him from the open window then dashed out the door and around the corner. But Jude got there first, and the two men were lifting the crate out by the time she arrived.

"That must be the blackboard. I can't believe it got here so quickly." Rebekka walked beside them, ready to lend a hand if the tall, skinny crate leaned too far to the side. The two men carried it to the front of the room and set it on the floor, leaning against the desk.

"I'll get my hammer," Jude said as he strode across the room and out the door.

"I need to get home to my dinner," Mr. Ingmar said. "You need anything else, Miss Stenesrude?"

"No, Mr. Ingmar, and thank you so much for delivering this."

"No trouble. I brought my team in for a shoeing this morning." He cast a glance out the door. "You're sure you're all right with. . . ?"

Rebekka caught his meaning. "Nothing to worry about. Mr.

Weinlander and the others are finishing up the school building. Mr. Larson went on home and—" She felt like she was blathering. "So, thank you again." She walked him out to his wagon and waved him off.

When she reentered the school, she heard the screech of nails being pulled. Jude picked up the top section of the crate and put it off to the side as she reached him.

"Brand-new. Can you beat that? I'll be the first person to write on the new blackboard." Rebekka squatted down and ran her fingers over the dusty black surface. When she looked up at Jude, she thought she caught a smile. . .almost. At least his right cheek had pulled back a mite. She was sure it had. She smiled in return—just in case.

"If you give me a hand, we can lift it out right now or wait until the others return."

"Let's do it now. I can't wait to see it on the wall." She paused. "Shouldn't the wall be painted first?"

"We can take it down again. Might not get at the painting until a cold snap anyway."

"All right." Together they lifted the blackboard out and stood it against the wall. "It's heavy."

Jude removed his yellow measuring stick and unfolded it to measure the height and length of the blackboard. Then he measured down from the ceiling and marked on the plastered wall. Lightly tapping with his hammer, he located the studs and drove home the nails needed to hold the heavy blackboard.

Rebekka watched as he accomplished each task with an economy of movement and the sureness that comes with practice and pride in his work. She wanted to offer to help but had no idea how.

"Ready?" He shoved his hammer back into his belt and leaned over to pick up the blackboard. "This'll be heavy."

"I know." Rebekka prepared herself and, with one eye on Jude and the other on the blackboard, hoisted it up and set the back of the frame over the line of nail heads. When it was in place, she gave the oak frame a pat and turned to smile at Jude.

"Thank you. Oh, that's wonderful." With a swirl of her skirts, she spun back and stroked her hand down the frame again.

The smile she gave him lit up the room. . .and his heart. Jude felt like clutching his chest. What could one do with a smile like that but treasure it and keep it safe? Keep it to take out again on a cold winter's night and warm himself when he was far away down the road.

"You're welcome." He forced the words past a lump in his throat.

When she turned back, he had his usual expression in place. But he could literally feel his face cracking.

He picked up the pieces of the crate. "If you need anything else, just holler." Crate pieces on his shoulder, he strode out the door.

Rebekka watched him go. Funny, but for a minute there he had seemed almost friendly. She finished up her work and dusted off her hands. Tomorrow the men were slated to build the desks. They'd be crude until later on in the winter, Mr. Larson had told her, when finishing work would be done. Right now he had a house and barn to frame and enclose before the snow fell since both of them had burned in the prairie fire.

Rebekka closed the door and set off for home. She could hear the hammers and saws at work behind her. The men were finishing the privies and the coal shed.

On Monday morning, she arrived at the school early, too excited to eat breakfast. When she opened the door, the fragrance of new wood greeted her and she stopped just to look around. The American flag hung from its stick in one front corner, a globe donated by the mercantile dominated the other. While the children's desks and benches were still unpainted wood, they at least had places at which they could sit and write. Her desk appeared to be the only real piece of furniture in the room.

She left the outside door to the cloakroom open and walked softly to the front of the room. After laying her satchel on the desk, she turned to face the benches. "Please, Father," Rebekka whispered, "bless this year and all of us who come here to learn and to teach. We ask Thy special protection on this place so that all who come here may be safe and feel wanted. Fill me with wisdom and love for all my children. I thank Thee in Jesus' precious name. Amen."

When she opened her eyes she thought she saw a shadow crossing the door. Had someone been there? Immediately she heard two male voices in the schoolyard—Jude's and Mr. Larson's. By the time Rebekka walked to the window and looked out, Mr. Larson was climbing back into his wagon to drive away.

He looked up and caught her wave. "Have a good day, Miss Stenesrude," he called and waved again at her. "Thank you." At his bidding the horse trotted out to the dirt road and turned left, away from town.

Rebekka checked the time on her brooch watch—seven-thirty. Still half an hour until school started. She wandered to the window overlooking the back of the school. Jude stood on a ladder, nailing the shingles onto the roof of the boys' privy; the girls' was already finished. Hat pushed back on his forehead, shirt sleeves rolled back to his elbows, he laid a shingle, nailed it in place, and laid down the other, all with a rhythm born of long practice.

She'd never enjoyed watching a man work before, in fact, she'd never much watched a man do anything. A child's laughter drew her away from the window and back to her desk. The day was truly beginning. . .a whole new year was beginning.

"Miss Stenesrude, see the books I brought." Yes, school had begun.

"That's wonderful." Rebekka walked across the room to stand at the door. Buggies and wagons brought children from the farms farther out; those from town walked across the bridge or ran up the lane. Two tied their horses in the shed.

"John, will you ring the bell?" She checked her watch—five minutes to eight—right on time.

The *bong-bong, bong-bong* rang out across the schoolyard, over the river, and out to town. The children cheered, their voices loud and high with delight. At eight o'clock they were lined up in two lines for the final bell. Rebekka turned and led her charges into their new schoolhouse. Elizabeth led the pledge of allegiance, another child recited a Bible verse, Rebekka led the prayer, and the day was begun.

As Rebekka assigned places at the bench/desks, she collected all the books that the children brought, carefully writing the family's name in each book so they could be returned when finished.

She introduced three new pupils, children of the recent arrivals to the area. All the while concentrating on the children and the beginning of the day, she kept one ear on the hammering coming from outside the building.

"Now I know it will be hard to concentrate with all the noise around us, but I expect you to pay attention just like you always have."

All the children nodded. "Yes, ma'am."

"Now, we all know we are short of supplies, so we will share books. I expect those of you in the fourth grade and above to help with the younger ones."

"Yes, ma'am."

Giggles erupted from a smart comment from the left side of the room, and Rebekka nailed the guilty one with a stern look. "Andrew, would you like to say that so we all can hear?"

A dark-haired boy with faded overalls rose to his feet. "No, ma'am."

"Then we'll hear no more such outbursts?"

"Yes, ma'am. I mean, no, ma'am." He shuffled his feet and looked up at her from under indecently long, dark eyelashes.

Rebekka shook her head and then checked her watch—ten o'clock. "There will be a twenty-minute recess. When you all come back in, I expect you to pay attention. And keep out of the way of the men working."

"Yes, ma'am."

"Excused." The horde leaped to its feet and turned to pound out the door when Rebekka raised her voice. "Order!" The pupils walked sedately to the door, but once through it, broke into shouts of laughter.

Rebekka sank down into her chair. Why did she feel like it

should be time for school to be out rather than only morning recess? *It's just the first day*, she reminded herself. *Every year's first day is just like this—except for the pounding and sawing going on outside.*

As her usual habit, she started reading a book to the entire school the last half hour of the day. "We're going to read one of Mark Twain's lesser-known stories to start this year. It's called *A Connecticut Yankee in King Arthur's Court*. Have any of you read it?" When they all shook their heads, she opened the book and started to read.

Her voice floated over the enraptured children and out the windows to the ears of the man working on a window frame. Jude paused in his measuring. He'd read the story way back when he was in school, but no one with such a musical voice had ever read to him. Schools, they were a'changin', that was for sure.

That night at the supper table, Mrs. Sampson and Mrs. Knutson kept asking questions until Rebekka related her entire day. The only thing she failed to mention was her awareness of a certain carpenter working outside the building.

When she fell into bed that night, she didn't even have to roll over before being sound asleep.

"Was there a rainstorm during the night?" she asked at the breakfast table in the morning.

"Thunder, lightning, the works. You mean you slept right through it all?" Mrs. Sampson set the bowls of oatmeal before each of her boarders.

"I guess so. I'm not sure I even remember crawling into bed." When she glanced for a second time at the empty chair across from her, Mrs. Sampson chimed in.

"Mr. Weinlander ate at six. Said he needed to get a head start on the day, what with so much to do and all. That man, he's a real hard worker, he is."

"Oh," Rebekka said as she sprinkled brown sugar on her cereal and then poured milk over the top. She hadn't really wanted to know where he was, had she?

By Thursday things were settling into a pattern at school. Everyone seemed to ignore the nailing outside and was reading, writing, and working their arithmetic on the no-longer-brand-new blackboard.

After the last child ran out the door that day, she swept the room, washed the blackboard, and settled at her desk to correct some essays she'd assigned during the day. She chuckled as she read one child's highlight of her summer. She'd fallen in a patch of poison ivy on a picnic and spent days soaking in oatmeal baths. "Now I know what poison ivy looks like," she wrote at the end. "And it's not pretty."

Rebekka turned to the next paper and checked the pile of those remaining. She had six or seven papers to go when she heard someone walking up the three stairs to the cloakroom. She raised her head, ready to answer any question one of the workmen would have.

The man paused in the door. Shivers started at her toes and shuddered their way to the top of her head. The last time she'd seen him, he'd been out cold, knocked unconscious by the pitcher she had slammed against his head.

Chapter 8

Thought I'd find you here 'bout now." Adolph's voice wore the sneer she'd heard hissed through the night of months before.

"Will you please leave?" Glacier frost couldn't have been colder.

"Now, don't act thata way. You know we got unfinished business, you and me." He swaggered down the center row, between the benches.

"If you don't leave, I'll—"

"You'll what?" He placed his hands flat on the desktop and leaned toward her.

It was all Rebekka could do to keep from gagging. He'd borrowed his swagger from a bottle down at the saloon, just like that night he attacked her.

"Get out!" She hissed from between clenched teeth. When he leaned closer, she raised her voice, putting all the authority she'd ever learned into the words. "Get out! Don't you ever come near me again!"

Her command ended on a shriek as his hand snaked out and grabbed her by the neck to pull her into a kiss.

Rebekka screamed again and flailed at him with her fists. Suddenly, there was nothing there to hit. Adolph, with Jude's strong hands at neck and seat, was tap-dancing back down the aisle, and then Jude flung him out the door.

Rebekka could hear the thud when he hit the ground.

"And if you ever come near her again, this is only a taste of what you'll get, you hear?" Jude was yelling.

"I'll get you!" Adolph said as he clambered aboard his horse and rode away.

Jude turned and strode back into the schoolroom. Rebekka met him halfway down the aisle, her eyes wild and tears streaking down her cheeks. When he opened his arms, she threw herself into them. Her braid tumbled down her back and sobs shook her frame.

"Easy now, easy." Jude held her close, murmuring words of comfort, in spite of the hard line of his jaw. By all the saints, he'd felt like killing the young fool. "Did he hurt you?"

Rebekka shook her head and burrowed closer to his shoulder. "I got. . .*hiccup*. . .away last time, too."

"Last time?" Now Jude was sure he'd go after the fool.

When Rebekka finally quit sobbing and calmed down, Jude felt reluctant to let her go. When she pulled back and dug in her sleeve cuff for a handkerchief, he stepped back. "Are you all right now?"

"I. . .I think so." She blew her nose and mopped her eyes.

"Did he hurt you?"

"Do you mean physically or emotionally?"

"Either."

"Or my pride?"

"That, too."

Rebekka took in a deep breath and let it out. "All three."

"That brute!"

"No, no. He just pulled my hair and jerked my neck. He didn't really injure me physically. But why should any man think he can treat a woman that way and get away with it?"

"Did you tell the sheriff last time?"

Rebekka gave him the same look she gave a pupil who'd repeatedly made a dumb statement. Then she studied the knuckle on her right thumb. "I couldn't tell anyone he'd attacked me. He said he'd tell them I en—" she choked on the words, "I enticed him. That I was asking for it. And even if no one believed him, my name would be dragged through the mud and no respecting school system would hire me."

Jude tried to think of an answer to refute her statements but he couldn't. She was right.

"It's the liquor that does it. It's always the liquor." Rebekka shook her head. When she realized her hair was hanging down her back, she reached up to coil it again.

Jude stepped back farther and tightened his jaw. If she only knew. How many times had he teased a woman? How many times had he taken kisses rather than asking? How many times had he been drunk and had no idea the next day of what he'd done?

"I need to finish up outside. Will you wait and let me walk you home? That way we know he won't bother you again."

Rebekka fought a battle with herself, but it never showed on her face. Yes, she wanted to walk home with him. No, she didn't want to come to depend on a man, especially this man who would one of these days be going on down the road. No, she didn't want Adolph to attack her again. Yes, she'd. . .

"I'll be here correcting papers whenever you are ready."

She had to force herself to concentrate on the essays. Whenever she thought of the close call, she started to shake all over. She'd never felt so vulnerable in her own school before. The more she thought about it, the more furious she became. Anger at Adolph, at the liquor, at the men who serve liquor, at those who drink it, smoldered deep within her.

The walk home with Jude passed in silence, both of them caught up in anger at the same situation but from different angles. Jude plotted ways to take care of the young Mr. Strand. Rebekka dreamed of destroying the saloon.

"I'll be ready to leave when you are in the morning." Jude laid a hand on her arm to stop her at the gate to the boardinghouse yard. He continued before she could quit sputtering. "I know you hate having to accept my help but, please, think of the children. If you let me walk you over and back, you'll always be there for them."

"But I. . .I have to go early to start the stove once the cold weather hits."

"I could do that."

"And shovel the steps off and—"

"Some of those things you could ask the older boys to do."

"I do, but they come from so far and have to get home to do their chores. Mr. Weinlander—"

"Jude. I think after what we've been through, you could call me by my given name."

"Jude, then. I really can't ask this of you."

"You aren't. I'm offering." He leaned over to unlatch the gate. "And Miss Stenesrude—"

"Rebekka."

He said her name, as if tasting it on his tongue. "Rebekka, at least try it my way for the next week or so. If Mr. Larson needs me on another job, we'll discuss this. All right?"

Rebekka nodded. "All right. And thank you. I—"

"That's enough. You go on in, I have to wash up."

Rebekka stepped through the gate he held open and walked on up the back steps and into the kitchen.

"Child, what happened to you?" Mrs. Sampson dropped her long-handled spoon and crossed the room to stand in front of Rebekka. Gently, she grasped Rebekka's chin and turned it to the right. "You have bruise marks on your neck. And your hair is down. What happened?"

Rebekka sank down into a chair at the table and poured her story into the widow's sympathetic ear. "I thought Jude was going to kill him there for a minute, but he threw him out the door instead. Thank God he was there or. . .or—" Rebekka closed her eyes against the horror of it.

Mrs. Sampson set a cup of coffee in front of the younger woman. "Here." She dumped two spoonfuls of sugar in it and stirred. "Drink this. You'll feel better."

That evening they all gathered in the sitting room as if in unspoken agreement that no one wanted to be alone. Rebekka sat down at the piano and lifted the keyboard cover. She ran her fingers lightly across the keys, letting the notes seep in to relax the fear and anger from the afternoon. As she drifted into a Chopin sonata, she could feel the tension drain out of her shoulders. Closing her eyes, she let her mind float, feeling the beauty of each measure. Her hands continued to work their magic as she flowed into "Beautiful Savior" and then to "Sweet Hour of Prayer."

Jude watched her from the wing chair in the corner. Lamplight glowed in the auburn highlights of her hair, now slicked back into its tight restriction. Her lashes lay like dark veils on the high rise of her cheeks. The music drew them together, wrapping them in a magic net. But she didn't know that, and he wasn't about to tell her. What would it be like to have a woman like her in his life? He took the idea out and toyed with it, all the while watching the straight back of the woman on the piano stool, swaying in time with the music. But he put it away. He didn't deserve a woman like Rebekka. He didn't deserve any happiness at all. He had killed it long before.

"Why don't you go get your harmonica?" Mrs. Sampson leaned across the intricately carved table between their chairs and whispered so as not to disturb the player. "Mrs. Knutson will get her fiddle and I'll get my banjo. Let's see how we all sound together."

The three left the room at the same time.

Rebekka opened her eyes, finally aware of the near-trance she'd been in. Music did that for her. "Hey, did I play so badly you have to leave?"

"You know better than that." Mrs. Sampson turned at the newel post on the landing. "We're just going to join you. No sense you having all the playing fun."

The two women tuned their strings to the piano while Jude practiced a few trills on the mouth organ. Rebekka spun the stool around, a wide smile replacing the former somberness. "So, what'll we start with?"

"You know 'Turkey in the Straw?' " Mrs. Sampson strummed an opening chord then looked at Jude. When he nodded, she strummed again and away they went. The lively music had all their feet tapping. They played on with each of them calling out tunes.

"That's enough," Mrs. Sampson said, laying her banjo down. "I haven't played for so long, my fingers are near to bleeding."

"Me, too." Mrs. Knutson agreed as she blew on the end of her fingers on her left hand. "These strings are murder. We'll just have to do this more often." She laid her fiddle back into it's case. "I haven't had so much fun since. . .since I don't know when."

Rebekka closed the keyboard cover. "You would have thought we've been playing together forever. There won't be a shortage of musicians for the dances this winter."

"How about a cup of coffee? And there's still some of that pie left, Jude, in case you're interested."

Jude stuck his mouth organ into his shirt pocket. "Never could turn down a piece of pie." He stood and stretched his hands above his head. "Lead me to it."

When Rebekka said her prayers that night, she had an extra thank you for the music played in the sitting room. What had started out as a way to let go of the anger from the afternoon turned into a party. "Father, that was such fun. And I think Jude even smiled a time or two. Shame I had my back to them. I'd like to see him laugh some time. Thank You he was there to. . .to. . ." The anger swelled up unbidden, tasting bitter on her tongue, and she couldn't say the words. She rested her forehead on her clasped hands on the edge of the bed. The hard floor beneath the rug made her knees ache.

"What can I do about Adolph, so he doesn't attack anyone else?" The remembered smell of liquor on his breath made her gag. She waited for more words to come, but she saw only black. "Please help me. In Jesus' name. Amen." She shivered in the breeze lifting the curtains at her window. The bite to it made her think of frost and fall.

She pushed herself to her feet and slipped beneath the covers. This night she was grateful for the quilt to pull over the sheet and blanket.

In the morning, Jude was already gone by the time Rebekka had finished dressing and had entered the kitchen for breakfast.

"He said to wait for him; he'd be back to walk you over." Mrs.

Sampson turned the bacon with a long fork. "How many eggs you want this morning? I thought to make you a fried egg sandwich for your dinner."

"Two, I guess," Rebekka answered as she pulled out her chair. "And that sounds fine." She sat down and placed her napkin on her lap. "But he doesn't need to do that. I'll be just fine."

"Don't think it'll do you any good to argue. Seems like when he makes up his mind about something, he don't let nothing get in his way." Mrs. Sampson set Rebekka's plate in front of her along with two pieces of toasted bread. She poured herself a cup of coffee and sat down. "That was some fine playing last night, if I do say so myself."

"You can say that again." Rebekka spread ruby-red choke-cherry jelly on her bread. "Do you think—" She didn't have time to finish her question as the sound of male feet on the back porch cut her off.

"You about ready?" Jude took off his hat as he entered the room.

"You don't have to do this, you know," Rebekka said after swallowing the food in her mouth.

"I know. Finish your breakfast. I'm due for a cup of coffee anyway." He crossed to the cupboard and took out a cup, filled it, and sat down at the table. "Any of that pie left?"

"You know you finished the last piece last night. Will molasses cookies do?"

"Ja, sure." He leaned back in his chair.

Was it just her imagination or had he winked at Mrs. Sampson? Rebekka finished her eggs and wiped her mouth with her napkin. "I'll be right back down."

The walk to the school passed without conversation. Every time Rebekka tried to think of something to say, she thought it sounded silly. Since when did she have trouble thinking of topics to talk about?

"Thank you," she said as she started up the steps.

"Don't leave until I'm ready this afternoon."

Rebekka sucked in a breath, ready to lambaste him for giving her an order, but he was already off around the corner of the building before she could come up with the appropriate words.

The walk home passed without words also. He tipped his hat at the gate and turned back to the school. "Tell Mrs. Sampson I'll be here at six."

Tell her yourself, was what Rebekka wanted to say. Instead, she blustered into the kitchen and did as he asked. Guilt at taking up his work time kept her quiet.

But he doesn't have to do that, she argued with herself, her heels tapping out her ire on the stairs to her room. *But you did feel safer, didn't you?* The other side of her argument won.

By the end of the week, Jude and Rebekka had progressed to discussing the day's events on their way home from school. He asked her how the children were doing and, by the time she told him, they were already at the boardinghouse's gate.

"You read real well," he said as he tipped his hat and then strode back to the school.

Rebekka watched him go. Now what had he meant by that? She thought to the open schoolhouse windows. He must have been listening to the story she read at the end of the day. She felt the heat begin at her collar and creep upward. What an unusual man.

On Monday, James Olson returned to school and by Wednesday the other three older boys joined the row in the back of the room. Harvest had finished early due to the extra long hot weather.

On Friday, Jude announced that he was finished with the outside work on the school and would be moving on to the barn Mr. Larson was building for Ed Jameson. They hoped to have both the house and barn usable by the time winter set in.

"I've asked John Johnson to walk with you." Jude tipped his hat and turned away as usual. "He'll be here at seven-thirty Monday morning. He'll also walk you home in the evening."

Rebekka fumed as she strode up the walk. He could at least have asked her instead of telling her. But now that darkness was coming earlier, she knew she'd be grateful for the escort. She could have asked one of the older children herself. *But would you have?* the voice from within asked her. No, she had to admit, she wouldn't have.

Saturday, she saw Adolph Strand at the mercantile and the look he flashed her spelled pure hatred. Rebekka ordered her hands to stop trembling but it did no good. She left without purchasing the writing paper for which she'd come.

That night, the nightmare returned for the first time since the incident at the school. Hands grabbing for her. . .foul breath. . .the smell of liquor gagging her. . .eyes so filled with hate she felt like she'd been stabbed. . .a voice screaming. She sat straight up in bed, her heart pounding enough to jump out of her chest.

The room lay dark around her. Without the friendly moon to light it, all the shadows seemed to hover, strangling her every breath. Rebekka coughed, the sound chasing the shadows back to their corners. She drew in three deep breaths and let them out, feeling her heart slow back down and take up its normal pace again.

She lay down against the pillows and created in her mind the picture of Jesus the shepherd, carrying one of the sheep. "Jesus. Jesus. Jesus." She repeated the name aloud until she could feel the warmth creeping back into her bones. The name faded into whispers and silence as she drifted off to sleep.

When she arrived at the schoolhouse on Monday morning, the new heating stove resided in its place of glory, all shiny black and chrome. After the frost of the last few evenings, the heat would be welcome in the mornings.

"I think we should have a celebration on Saturday night the week after this," she announced at the close of school. "We'll celebrate both the new school building and the end of harvest. What do you think?"

"Will it be a dance?" one of the older girls asked.

"Of course. But I've been thinking. What if we have a box social first to help pay for the new desks?"

As the cheers erupted, Rebekka raised her hands for quiet. "You all make sure to tell your parents, now. I'll post a sign down at the mercantile and tell everyone I see. We'll have a real party."

"When will our desks be finished?" one of the younger children asked.

"Not until after they can't work outside anymore. Maybe we'll have them done for Christmas. I think Mr. Weinlander will be doing them."

"I saw some desks in the Sears catalog. They was real nice."

"Were, Elmer, were nice."

"That's what I said, they's nice."

"All right everyone, let's have a grammer review right now." Groans resounded back to her. "I am, past tense, now."

"I was." The class answered back.

"She or he?"

"Was." One "were" was sounded from over by the window.

"They?"

"Were."

"Now do you understand, Elmer?" He nodded. "Let's all repeat it together." The declension echoed from all their throats. Rebekka smiled. "Class dismissed."

At supper that night Rebekka announced her plans. "And I think we could provide some of the music for dancing. This way the same musicians won't have to play all night and not get to dance."

"I'd like that. We need to find another piano player, too," Mrs. Sampson said, passing the bowl of stew around once more.

"We won't have to worry about that. The school piano burned in the fire, remember?" Rebekka dished herself out a small helping. "And I hate to borrow the church organ. Every time we move it, it gets wheezier."

"Organ music just doesn't do for dancing like a piano anyway. We'll do without. There are enough fiddles, guitars, and such," Mrs. Knutson said, setting the bowl down in front of Jude. "Help yourself, young man. You need plenty of fueling for the work you're doing." She patted his arm. "I been hearing mighty good things about you."

Jude looked at her with a raised eyebrow.

"Mrs. Jameson was in today to order a new winter coat since hers burned in the fire. She says the barn's about done and you've started framing the house. This time she'll finally have two more bedrooms. And for their brood, that'll make a big difference."

Jude nodded. "They need more room all right. They've been living in tents since the fire." He helped himself to another of Mrs. Sampson's rolls. "That Jameson has two fine sons. Not afraid of work, let me tell you."

Rebekka listened as the conversation flowed around her. Each night the four of them talked together more, with Jude taking part rather than sitting silently, watching them with those sorrowful eyes. While she hadn't seen him smile yet, at least there was animation in his face. What would his laugh be like? Rich like his voice?

". . .don't you think?" Mrs. Sampson waved her hand in front of Rebekka's face. "Hello, there."

"What? Oh, I guess I was off gathering wool somewhere." Rebekka shook her head. "What did you say?"

Mrs. Sampson grinned a knowing grin. "I asked if you thought we could have this party without any liquor being served?"

Rebekka looked up to find Jude watching her, as if aware her thoughts were of him. She swallowed. She could feel the warmth start below her neck and work its way up. One would think an old-maid schoolmarm like her would be past the blushing stage.

"I certainly hope so." She folded her napkin and slipped it back into its ring by her plate. "In fact, I shall make sure everyone knows that that is the rule." Now she even sounded like an old-maid schoolmarm.

"The men won't like that much." Jude pushed his plate back and leaned his elbows on the table. "And if you want to make money for the school, you want plenty of men there to buy dinner boxes."

"Surely, they can do without for one party." Rebekka leaned her elbows on the table, directly across from him. She could actually feel the steel setting into her jaw.

"Now, now." Mrs. Sampson stood and began clearing the plates. "Anyone for spice cake? I made it this afternoon from a new recipe I got from Isabel down at the post office."

Jude leaned back, breaking eye contact with Rebekka. "Make mine a big piece, please. My mother used to make the best spice cake."

Rebekka felt her jaw drop. The steel melted. This was the first time he had ever mentioned family. She stood and helped Mrs. Sampson clear the table. When she looked a question at her friend, the older woman just nodded.

"Here, you can pass these around." She handed Rebekka the dessert plates. "I'll pour the coffee."

But when Rebekka went to bed that night, she couldn't get over the idea that all men thought there should be booze at every social event, and when it wasn't served, they brought their own. She thought of an article she'd read in a newspaper. Maybe prohibition would be a good idea. The suffragettes were marching both for the end of liquor and the beginning of the women's vote. What would happen in Willowford if the women got together and made their views known?

Friday afternoon the school received its first cleaning by all of the pupils and their teacher. They washed windows, swept and cleaned all the building debris out of the schoolyard, and cleared an area outside for dancing. Since it would be a harvest moon and if it wasn't too cold, the dancing would be outside.

Rebekka lifted her face to the late afternoon sun. Indian summer brought its own kind of warmth—crisp nights, cottonwood and willow leaves turning autumn yellow, the few maples and elms splashed with russet and gold and all the shades in between. But the days called to her, inviting her out to enjoy the last warm slanting rays of sun, yet with a tang that sang of coming cold.

"Mith Thtenthrude." Emily tugged on her skirts. "Look what I brung you." She handed Rebekka three nodding black-eyed Susans she'd found in the ditch.

"Thank you. I'll put these in water on my desk. They're just right for the party." The little girl smiled, her grin stretching rounded cheeks until her entire face glowed at the compliment. Rebekka squatted down and wrapped Emily in a hug.

Jude saw the two of them, towhead to mahogany head, as he rode his horse back from the Jameson farm. The slanting sun lit the tableau with a golden light, catching him right in his heart.

He pulled on the reins, bringing his mount to a halt, and crossed his arms on the saddle horn. But the moment disappeared as Rebekka rose to her feet and patted the little one on the shoulder. Emily ran off and the teacher looked up to see the rider on the black horse. She waved and turned back to the schoolhouse.

"All right, everyone, I think we're finished. Would you rather leave early or hear another chapter of *Connecticut Yankee?*"

"Read to us. Read to us."

"Everyone find a place to sit, then. I'll get the book and be right back." She turned and entered the schoolhouse, returning in a minute with the book. As she took her place on the top step, children clustered around her like she was a hen with too many chicks.

Jude dismounted and walked his horse into the schoolyard. He folded his legs and sat Indian fashion on the ground, just like the children who turned and welcomed him with smiles as if this were an everyday event.

Rebekka caught her breath. She hadn't expected an adult to join her audience—especially this particular adult. She found her place and began reading. At first her tongue stumbled over the words, but, as she got into the story, she forgot Jude and read to entertain her children.

The night of the party the harvest moon climbed over the edge of the earth and into the sky, huge and golden. While the breeze carried a nip, the warmth of the earth rose to help spread fog veils in the hollows. Laughing people greeted each other as they walked, rode, or drove their wagons and buggies into the schoolyard. When the yard filled, they pulled up along the road.

Rebekka watched as it seemed the entire county turned out for the box social. The tables inside groaned under the fancy boxes, ready to be auctioned off to the highest bidder. Every woman, young and old, had prepared her box in secret, yet hoping a certain someone would buy the right one so they could enjoy the meal together.

She'd brought her box in her bag so no one would see which was hers. Wrapped in blue-and-white checked gingham with a bright red bow, it lay underneath several others. Wouldn't it be something if Jude bought her box? She watched the door, but that certain man hadn't come through it yet.

Lars Larson had volunteered to be the auctioneer for the evening, so when it looked like most of the people had arrived, he stepped to the door to announce the start of the bidding. Everyone crammed into the school building, and even with all the windows and the door wide open, the temperature rose like a thermometer stuck in hot water.

"All right folks, let's start with this little beauty here." He held up a red box with a blue ribbon, ran it past his nose, and declared, "Whoever gets this box will have some good eatin'." He held it high. "Now, what am I bid? Remember folks, this is all for a good cause. Our children need new equipment to go with their new schoolhouse."

The stack of decorated boxes dwindled as the basket of coins filled. Rebekka kept one eye on the table and the other on the door. When Jude finally walked in, she breathed a sigh of relief. When he bid on another box, she felt a stab of. . . She considered the feeling. It couldn't be jealousy, could it? She shook her head.

"Something wrong?" Mrs. Sampson asked from beside her.

"Oh, no, no. I just remembered something."

"Jude arrived."

"I know."

Mrs. Sampson chuckled. Her box went on the block next and Jude bid on it. The price rose all the way to a dollar before he dropped out and Ed Johnson from the mercantile claimed his dinner partner.

Mrs. Sampson fluttered her hand as she left with her partner and the box.

The three remaining boxes looked lonely on the tables that had been so full. Two looked almost the same, both had blue-and-white gingham but one sported a blue bow, the other a red.

Mr. Larson waved his hands over them and picked up Rebekka's. "Now, what am I bid for this lovely creation? I know there are some of you out there without a supper partner. Let's make these last boxes count."

Rebekka kept her eyes straight ahead. She didn't dare look back at the man in the full-sleeved white shirt and dark pants. Without his fedora, his hair gleamed deep gold in the light given off by the myriad of flickering kerosene lamps set around the room. The silver streak caught the light and. . .she refused to look again.

"I'm bid one dollar. Who'll make it one and a quarter?" Mr. Larson continued with the singsong chant of a born auctioneer. "One—there, one and a half."

Rebekka wanted to see who was bidding, but she daren't even look. When she heard two dollars, she swallowed—hard.

Jude's voice rang out, "Two and a half."

Down in her middle, Rebekka felt a little shiver begin. Had someone told him which was her box? She looked to the back where Mrs. Sampson shook her head.

"Three dollars," young Johnson sang out.

"Too rich for my blood." Jude bowed to the younger bidder.

Rebekka felt her heart bounce somewhere down about her toes, but she made sure a smile showed on her face as she stepped forward.

John looked from her to the young woman standing beside her, and Rebekka could see the consternation on his face.

"Why he thought he was bidding on Elizabeth's box." Rebekka looked back to Jude, who shrugged and bid two-fifty on the other gingham box. As he came forward to claim his partner for the supper, he offered Elizabeth his hand. The two young people tried to look happy, but their smiles, even to those who knew them, were forced.

"Well, now," Mr. Larson slammed his hammer down. "It

appears to me we had a slight mixup with the boxes. I thought no one was supposed to know which was which."

"Obviously they didn't," a jocular voice called from the back. "But fair's fair. You go with the partner who paid for your box."

"Easy for you to say, Jameson," Jude called back. "You peeked." Laughter floated around the room.

"I have a suggestion," Jude gathered the three of them together. "Why don't we all go outside and eat together? That way we'll all get extra helpings."

The two young people grinned at each other and at Jude. Rebekka's shiver changed to a warm spot. What a thoughtful thing for him to do.

On the other hand, it would have been nice to share a box, just the two of them. *Don't be silly,* she scolded herself. *Put a smile on your face and have a good time.* "Let's go," she said as she picked up one box and handed it to John while Jude lifted the other. "I'm starved. And if we don't hurry, the dancing will start before we're finished."

She followed Jude out the door. Barn lanterns hung from poles around an open area cleared for dancing. She stopped so quickly, Elizabeth ran into the back of her. "A piano," she said, staring at the wagon off to the side. It's load—a piano. "Where did it come from?" She looked from Jude to the wagon and back.

"Well, Nels over at the saloon wanted to give something to the party, so a bunch of men loaded it up and drove it out here," Jude said.

Rebekka stopped like she'd been slugged. "From the saloon? I certainly hope that's all he donated for the night's entertainment."

"Now, Rebekka. Don't look a gift horse in the mouth. You wanted a piano, you got one. Now, come on, let's eat."

Rebekka looked around for John and Elizabeth.

"I thought they'd rather be alone. I remember what it was like to be young and in love," Jude shrugged. "So arrest me, I gave them the right box."

The warm spot in her middle melted and flowed out to her fingers and her toes.

The box could have been packed with sawdust for all the attention Rebekka paid to it. What she really wanted was to make Jude laugh. But, a smile would do.

Jude did a respectable job of demolishing the contents, all the while exchanging remarks with Rebekka about the evening, the people present, and the amount of money earned. What he wanted to say, he couldn't, and a sincere "Thank you" had to suffice. He just wanted her to keep laughing. The rich contralto joy that flowed through the music of her laugh, warmed him clear down to the icy spot that hadn't melted in two years.

He watched a dimple come and go on the right side of her wide mouth. He didn't, no, couldn't deserve her. Slowly, carefully, he drew his cloak of guilt back around him and shut her out.

Rebekka watched him pull back. There would be no smile this night. What had happened to him that. . . ?

"Time for the music to start," Mrs. Sampson announced, appearing out of the circle of light. "You two ready?"

Rebekka nodded. At least this way she could contribute something to the evening herself. And she didn't want to dance anyway. Earlier she'd been looking forward to whirling around the packed-dirt dance floor. But in her dream Jude had been her partner. Something told her for sure that wouldn't happen now.

They played jigs, reels, and hoedowns, sprinkled with waltzes and a square dance or two. They'd just swung into a Virginia reel when a gunshot split the air.

Chapter 9

Rebekka crashed the chords.

"Call the doctor!" The shout came from behind the schoolhouse.

"What's going on? What's happened?" someone screamed.

Pandemonium broke loose with children crying, men shouting, the sound of a fight, fists thudding on flesh. A crash, the sound of a table or some such shattering under the force of a falling body.

Rebekka sprung to her feet and jumped down from the wagon. Lars Larson grabbed her arm. "Get back up there and start playing again. We'll do a square dance, 'Texas Star.' I'll call."

Rebekka, torn between going to see what was happening and listening to the wisdom of Mr. Larson, nodded. She accepted Jude's hand to pull her back up on the wagon bed. After sitting back down on the piano stool, she looked over the heads of the teeming crowd. The doctor with his black bag in hand disappeared behind the building.

"Please God, protect my school. Please don't let them break up what we've worked so hard to replace," she murmured under her breath as she sounded the opening chords. Then, aghast at her concern for the school and not the men involved, she amended her prayer. "And please take care of those who are hurting."

But if they've been drinking. . . She didn't finish the thought, trying instead to think back over the evening. Had men been sneaking out back for a snort or two? She couldn't be sure. She'd been too busy playing and helping all the dancers have a good time.

"We can do this," Mrs. Sampson said over the twang of her banjo. "Jude, you take the melody."

Mr. Larson joined them in the wagon bed. "All right folks, form your squares. Partners ready?"

At their assent, he swung into the call. "Alamen left with your right hand. . ."

Rebekka followed the words, her mind anywhere but on the tune. At least her fingers knew what to do.

"Now, bow to your partner. . ."

What was happening behind the school?

The dance whirled to a close. Applause followed the final chord and Mr. Larson raised his voice again. "Last waltz, folks. Find that special partner for the last waltz." He turned to the musicians. "Choose what you will. I'll go see what's happening and be right back."

Mrs. Sampson took the lead. At her nod, they joined in and played through the tune. After the applause, Mr. Larson again took over.

"That's it and thank you all for coming. Remember to take your lantern or you won't have anything to light your barn with in the morning. Thank you for supporting our school." He waved his arm and the musicians swung into "Good night, ladies, good night, gentlemen. . ."

Rebekka sang along with the others. At the close, she shut the cover over the keyboard and spun the top of the stool around. "Now, Mr. Larson, what happened back there?"

"A couple of young bucks got into it. Nothing serious."

"And the shot fired?"

"Just a flesh wound. Doc took care of it. Now, now, I know what you're thinking. We couldn't search everyone who came tonight. Yes, they brought booze with them. And yes, they'd been drinking."

Rebekka clamped her jaw shut. She could feel the sparks shooting right off her hair she was so furious. If she said anything, it would be too much. Men and their booze. Couldn't they live without it?

Jude watched her burn. The fire flashing from her eyes threatened to scorch anyone and anything in its path. In his other life, he would have been right back there, carousing with the drinkers, making a joke out of anyone who tried to force them to stop.

Now he was on the other side. Now he wanted a life not dependent upon booze to have a good time. He'd been having a great time this evening and he'd felt a part of a group bent on making other people have a good time. But what had it cost to change him?

He hitched the livery team to the wagon and turned around in the schoolyard. "Ladies," he pulled up even with the two widows and Rebekka. "Can I give you a ride home?"

Without looking at him, the three boosted themselves up onto the back of the wagon bed and sat with their feet hanging over the edge. He could barely hear their discussion over the groaning of the wagon wheels under the weight of the piano, but he knew he didn't really want to know what they were saying.

He stopped at the gate to the boardinghouse and let them off. Their "Thanks" came in unison, but no smiles accompanied the word. Instead, they continued their discussion on up the walk and into the house. Jude flicked the reins and the horses walked on. After telling Nels thanks for the loan of the piano, he left the loaded wagon in front of the saloon and trotted the team back to the livery.

While he had a gentle hand on the reins, he kept a tight hand on his thoughts. Too many memories clamored to come forward and be recognized.

Playing the organ in church the next morning kept Rebekka's mind occupied because she had to read the music. When her fingers faltered, she commanded them to find the right keys. When her feet failed to pump the correct pedal, she ordered them on. But the Scripture, the sermon, and the prayers went right over her head.

She'd seen Jude saddle his horse and ride out first thing this morning. Where was he going? He couldn't be working on Sunday because Mr. Larson felt strongly about honoring the Sabbath. He and his family lined the second pew on the right. Didn't the man believe in going to church? It wasn't like other towns where the pastor had just the one church. Willowford had church only every other Sunday because they were part of a two-point parish. Reverend Haugen lived in St. John, where the other church was located, and he traveled to Willowford.

Right now, she would have liked to travel someplace. Anyplace would do, just away. What were they going to do? She played the closing hymn and continued with a postlude. How could they get the women together? Other than sewing or quilting bees, the women let the men lead. And look where it had gotten them—someone shot in a fight at a fund-raiser and party for the schoolchildren.

She pushed in all the stops on the organ and tucked the sheet music inside the bench. She really needed to practice more if she was to be the church organist, but right now she didn't even want to be that. Why hadn't God taken better care of the evening? After all, she'd asked Him to.

By Monday morning a plan had begun to form in Rebekka's mind.

"You look like the cat that ate the cream," Mrs. Sampson commented when Rebekka sat down at the breakfast table.

"I'll tell you about it when I finish thinking it through," Rebekka promised.

A blustery wind buffeted her and her escort all the way to the school. *At least winter held off until after our party,* she thought as they crossed the bridge. Dry leaves blew before them, the trees denuded by the storm that had sprung up during the night. Rebekka shivered and walked faster.

"We have to get the stove started and the room warmed before the children get here." She looked up to the gray clouds scudding across the sky. "It could even snow."

"My pa says winter's come. He had to break up ice on the stock tank this morning," John said, his nose matching the red of his stocking cap.

Rebekka looked up again. The roof of the schoolhouse caught her attention. Smoke rose from the chimney and blew away on the wind. When they opened the door, warmth flowed outside and invited them in.

Rebekka hung her coat in the cloakroom. "Were you already here?" she asked.

John shook his head. "I bet Jude—ah, Mr. Weinlander, did this."

Rebekka nodded. He'd said he'd take care of the fire in the mornings. A little nettle of guilt stung her mind. And here she'd been downright rude to the man ever since the dance. And all because he was a man. He'd had nothing to do with the fight or the drinking. All he'd done was be male.

She rubbed her hands together over the warmth of the stove. Now she had time to work on her lesson plan. Christmas would be here before they knew it, and what should they do for a pageant this year? But who wanted to have another celebration anyway?

Snowflakes drifted down like lace doilies when Rebekka and John left the schoolhouse that afternoon. Huge, wet flakes clung to their clothes and even their eyelashes.

"You hurry on home," she said as she turned into the street along the boardinghouse. "And thank you for all your help, John. You have no idea how much I appreciate it."

"I don't mind. And thanks for the book." He raised a hand in farewell, his treasured book tucked under his jacket so it wouldn't get wet.

Rebekka nodded. The extra time with John was paying off in more ways than one. He'd become a reader for sure, if she had anything to say about it. And his requesting to borrow a book was certainly a step in the right direction.

She shook the snow off her coat and hat, unwinding the scarf around her neck as she kicked off her boots at the doorsill. After hanging her things up on the back porch, she walked into the kitchen, redolent with the aromas of baking chicken and its dressing. Her stomach growled in anticipation.

"And hello to you, too," Mrs. Sampson said with a laugh at Rebekka's consternation.

"Pardon me." The young woman laughed along with her friend. "Mrs. Knutson home yet?"

"No, and neither is Jude." She peered out the window.

"Looks like it's coming down harder."

"Good thing they got the roof on the Jameson house," Rebekka remarked as she went to the sink and washed her hands. When she got the dishes out of the glass-faced cupboard to set the table, they heard boots being kicked against the doorstop on the back porch.

"Well, at least Mrs. Knutson is home safe."

The sparrowlike woman flitted in, still brushing snow from her hair. "Even my hat didn't suffice," she said as she smoothed her hair back up into the pompadour that crowned her head, adding an inch or two more to her meager height. "What a day! Seemed everyone in the county needed something before the snow fell. As if they haven't known it was coming for weeks now." She set her bag of tatting in the dining room. "Three dress orders for Isabel. I think she must be planning a trip or something."

While they discussed the happenings of the day, Rebekka divided her attention between the conversation and the back door where, to her relief, she again heard the thump of boots on the step.

"Good, Jude's here, and supper's ready soon as he gets a chance to wash up. Bet he's near froze after that long ride in. I don't doubt they stay out there during the week if the weather stays bad."

"Sorry I'm late," Jude called as he hung up his things. He stopped at the stove to rub his hands in the rising heat. "Brrrr. When winter comes around here, it doesn't just pretend. This is the real thing. Evenin' everybody."

Heat poured into the room when Mrs. Sampson opened the oven door to remove the roasting pan. Jude leaned over and inhaled the rich aroma of baked chicken. "Now, that alone is worth the cold ride. Gimme five minutes, all right?" He opened the lid on the reservoir and dipped hot water into the pitcher waiting on the counter. Pitcher in hand, he left the kitchen.

"Oh, Rebekka. I almost forgot. There's a letter for you on the hall table," Mrs. Sampson said, brushing back a lock of hair with the back of her hand.

"Thanks," Rebekka said, then went to get it. Compared to the kitchen, the rest of the house felt chilly; perhaps the coal furnace needed stoking. She picked up her letter and ambled back to the warm kitchen. Sitting down at her place, she slashed the envelope with her dinner knife and started reading, mumbling softly. "Dear Rebekka," her aunt wrote in a firm hand. "We are all fine here, but I thought I'd better get our invitation out early. We would love to have you come for Christmas and stay until after the New Year. Grandma especially asked me to invite you."

Rebekka raised her gaze to find Mrs. Sampson watching her.

"Is everything all right?" She set the platter of sliced roast chicken on the table.

"They want me to come for Christmas." Rebekka felt a lump form in her throat. She hadn't celebrated a holiday with family in ten years.

"Are you going?" Mrs. Knutson brought the stuffing bowl.

"I don't know."

"Going where?" Jude entered the kitchen in his stockinged feet so no one had heard him coming.

"To Minneapolis. . .for Christmas with my family."

"Sounds wonderful." He pulled out his chair and sat down. "When will you leave?"

But I don't want to leave this family either, Rebekka thought as she looked around the table at the dear faces, these people who were becoming so much more than just friends. This was her family, too. "I don't know." She folded the letter and replaced it into the envelope. *Please ask me to stay here.* She bit her tongue to keep the words from tumbling out. What in the world was she thinking? Of course she wanted to spend Christmas with her relatives, really she did.

But when she went to bed that night, she wondered whom she was trying to convince. Especially since they'd had another musical evening.

She was prepared to wake up to a dark and blustery day, but

instead, the rising sun reflected off the crystallized world out-side. The elm tree outside the window wore frosting branches and the spirea bushes laid down under their pristine blanket. By the time she and John followed the already-made tracks across the bridge, the sun was glinting off the snow, hurting their eyes. Rebekka looked thoughtfully at a drift off to the side. She hadn't made snow angels for a long time. Perhaps they could do that during recess.

That afternoon, the stationmaster delivered three boxes to the school. "You boys come on and help me," Jonathan Ingmar said as he lugged one box in and set it down by the stove, where everyone was gathered to eat their dinner. Two of the big boys followed him out the door and returned with two more boxes that they set down by the first.

"Who are they from? What are they? Can we open them now?"

The questions flew fast and furious.

Rebekka retrieved her scissors from a desk drawer and handed them to one of the newer children. "Go ahead, cut the twine."

His grin didn't need an interpretation. As he cut the strings binding the boxes, the other children ripped off the wrapping.

"Go ahead." Rebekka answered the question before it could be asked. "The address was for Willowford School. Just save me the return address so we know who we must thank."

As the children peeled back the carton flaps, a letter lay right on top. Emily handed it to her teacher. "Thith ith for you."

Rebekka read the perfect script. It was addressed to Jude Weinlander. She tucked it into her pocket to deliver tonight.

"More books. Look. *Tom Sawyer, Huckleberry Finn.* A whole set of encyclopedias, *McGuffey's Readers.* . .ten of them." The children piled them out on the floor. "Who sent them, Miss Stenesrude?"

"I don't know," she answered. "But I'll find out."

"Chalk, pencils, paper, even glue." The children sat back in delight. "And colored paper." Down in the bottom of the third box lay three sets of watercolor paints. One of the older girls picked one up reverently.

"I've always wanted to paint," she whispered as she traced a gentle finger over the brightly colored squares.

"And now you shall," Rebekka said, rising to her feet. "Why don't you pack all that back in the boxes for now? As soon as we have shelves, we can put them out."

That evening, when Jude saw the letter, a shutter closed across his face. Rebekka watched it happen. One moment he looked at her with interest, the next he was gone. He stuffed the letter into his shirt pocket and continued with his meal.

Rebekka left it alone until they'd finished supper. When he asked to be excused, she followed him to the base of the stairs. "To whom shall I send the thank you letters? The children are so thrilled with the supplies and would like to thank the sender."

"I'll give you the address in the morning," Jude said then climbed the stairs without another look back. The curve of his shoulders, though, spoke volumes to the woman watching him. She put her hand to her heart; the ache there pulsed for the pain of the man for whom she cared so deeply. Was it the love one has for the wounded or some kind of deeper love? Rebekka wished she knew.

Up in his room, Jude read the entire letter for the third time. While Mrs. Norgaard penned most of it, there were personally written messages from Dag and Clara, pleading for him to come home to Soldall. They missed him, prayed for him, and were thankful he'd finally written.

Mrs. Norgaard asked if there was anything else the school needed. She volunteered to collect more books and send them on, but Jude would have to let her know.

Jude put the paper down on his desk. She was a sly one, that Mrs. Norgaard. Here she made it impossible for him not to respond. The school needed so much and the thought of a piano flitted through his mind. No, that was a want, not a need. The children sang like larks anyway, with or without a musical instrument to lead them.

He walked to the window and peered out. Much of the snow had already melted. When they finished up out at the Jamesons' he could go home. Mr. Larson hadn't mentioned any other jobs. He listened to the music float up from the sitting room.

"Come home, come home, all who are weary, come ho-o-o-me." The words of the age-old hymn, sung in harmony by the three women downstairs, tugged at his heart. Home, where was home anymore?

In the morning he left the address for Rebekka and told Mrs. Sampson he would be gone for a while. They would be staying at the Jamesons' to finish up as quickly as possible.

When he mounted his horse in the early dawn and rode down the street, he felt a compulsion to look over his shoulder at the two-storied, slightly Victorian house, smoke rising straight up from the chimney in the still air. If anywhere was home at this time in his life, that was it. Was Rebekka up yet? Was this home because Rebekka lived and played and sang there? He already missed the evenings at the boardinghouse and he wasn't even out of town yet.

The week seemed to drag its feet, like those who plowed through the mud that followed the snow. Early mornings the ground crackled beneath their feet as John and Rebekka broke through the frost cover. But by afternoon, the mud clung to their feet—gumbo they called it. Usually North Dakota soil turned to gumbo only in the spring.

At school one afternoon Rebekka opened the *Old Farmer's Almanac* and read the prediction. This was to be an unusually cold winter, with plenty of snow and blizzards, and an early spring with an excess of rain. *Wonderful,* Rebekka thought. Her pupils would go stir-crazy for sure. Could be this would be a winter when they had to close down during the worst weather. Last year had been mild, so they only missed a week in January.

She rapped on her desk for attention. "Children, finish what you are working on and we'll take time to talk about the Christmas pageant. We'll plan it together, so come up with good ideas."

When she dismissed them that Friday, the pageant's planning was well under way. But she still hadn't answered her letter. Would she go to Minneapolis for Christmas?

Even though the three women didn't overwork themselves, that Saturday equaled three normal ones in the amount of things they had accomplished. Rebekka had just gone to bed when she heard shots ring out. She threw on her wrapper and ran down the stairs.

"Sounds like it's coming from the saloon," Mrs. Sampson said as she opened the front door so they could hear better. Shouts, another gunshot. "That one was the sheriff's shotgun." Mrs. Sampson clutched her wrapper more tightly around her.

The sound of running feet announced the emissary before he arrived at the boardinghouse. "Doc says come quick," he panted. "He needs a nurse."

Mrs. Sampson whirled back into the house to grab her boots and coat. "What happened?" she asked as she shoved her feet into the ice cold rubber.

"Two men down. There was a fight, somethin' awful." He grabbed her arm and hustled her down the walk.

Rebekka closed the door and leaned her forehead against the stained wood. The booze won again.

Chapter 10

Mrs. Sampson dragged herself in the door at seven o'clock the next morning.

"What happened?" Rebekka leaped up from the table where she and Mrs. Knutson had gathered for coffee. Neither claimed to have slept a wink. She poured Mrs. Sampson a cup of coffee, while Mrs. Knutson took her friend's coat and hat and hung them up.

With the three of them around the table, Mrs. Sampson took a sip of her coffee and rubbed her tired, red eyes. "It was terrible. One man I didn't know was already dead. Shot through the heart. Two more were injured. One we patched up and sent home. The other, Ole Johnson, Doc worked over all night. But it wasn't enough. He died an hour ago."

"But Ole Johnson has four children at home. Two of them are in my school." Rebekka swallowed the tears that already burned the back of her throat. Those poor babies. What would Ethel, their mother, do now? The family was dirt-poor already.

"I know. We did the best we could. He was shot in the gut. Couldn't stop the bleeding." Mrs. Sampson spoke in the monotone of weariness and despair. "Two men died tonight because two others got in a fight. Ole wasn't fighting. He caught a stray bullet."

"But he was drinking at the saloon when he should have been home with his family. They don't have enough money for food and clothes, but he can spend the night drinking at the saloon." Rebekka felt the fury burn out her tears. "When will they learn?"

"Never," Mrs. Knutson said quietly. "Some men never learn."

Rebekka looked up at her. "You, too?"

The other woman sat straighter in her chair. "My Claude froze one night in a snowbank coming back from the saloon. He said he had a right to have some fun once in awhile, and drinking and playing cards with the men was his idea of the best time."

Rebekka reached across the table and clasped the widow's hand. "For me, it was my father."

"Well, something should be done. More and more I think that closing down the saloons and stills is a good idea. Make booze illegal, that's what." Mrs. Sampson rubbed her upper arms with work-worn hands. "I hate the stuff."

"I hate what it does to people." Rebekka rose to her feet to begin making breakfast. She fetched the frying pan and the eggs from the pantry and the side pork from the safe out on the porch.

"You don't have to do that. Give me a minute to rest and I'll be fine." Mrs. Sampson started to rise, but Mrs. Knutson laid her hands on her friend's shoulders, gently pushing her back in her chair.

"Let us. You've already done your share for today."

"Thank you, both. Thought I'd go out to see Ethel this morning and help with washing the body and readying him for burying." Mrs. Sampson shook her head. "What kind of a Christmas are those poor folks goin' to have now?"

"The funeral will be tomorrow?" Mrs. Knutson sliced the bread and set two slices in the rack over the coals.

"I'm sure, since that's when the reverend will be here. Otherwise he'd have to make another trip." She yawned fit to crack her jaw. "Think I'll take a little lie down before I go."

The three went about the duties of women everywhere who reach out to their sisters in grief. Rebekka fried sausage for scalloped potatoes while Mrs. Knutson baked a cake. When the food was ready, Mrs. Sampson got out a bar of her special soap and several towels. Her box of mercy complete, she walked out to the horse and buggy Rebekka had fetched from the livery.

"We'll take care of things here, don't you worry." Rebekka helped tuck a rug around the widow's knees. "Give her our

393

thoughts and prayers and hug the children for us."

"Will do." Mrs. Sampson flapped the reins and the horse trotted down the street.

The next day after church, the congregation remained for the funeral service. Reverend Haugen said all the proper words but Rebekka had a difficult time sitting still and listening. During the prayers she gripped the back of the pew in front of her to keep from leaping to her feet. This man's death wasn't God's will. If he'd stayed home where he belonged he'd still be singing with the rest of them, rather than leaving his wife to weep and his children to sob for their father. She bit her tongue to keep from shouting the words aloud.

"Dust to dust," the reverend intoned the words at the cemetery. But after Ethel Johnson and her oldest son each tossed a handful of dirt on the pine box, she straightened her shoulders and turned to the other mourners.

"Please, do something about this evil in our town. Good men can't be safe when the booze takes over. Do something before other tragedies happen." She wiped her eyes. "Please. Do something."

Rebekka clamped her hands together. The idea that planted itself in her mind after the fight at the box social had matured. Like wheat nodding in the field, the plan was ready for harvest.

"Tell every woman in town that we will be meeting at the church tonight at six o'clock. If we hurry, we can catch some of the farm wives also."

Quickly, the word spread. When anyone asked a question, the answer rang the same—just be there.

That night Rebekka stood at the front of the pews watching as the women filed in. She closed the doors when it looked like every woman in town and the surrounding area had arrived. After taking her place again at the front of the room, she raised her hands for silence.

"I know you are all wondering why we called this meeting, but after the sad afternoon and Ethel's, Mrs. Johnson's, plea, I think you can guess what we are about."

Gaining courage from all the nods and assents, Rebekka continued. "Many of us have suffered because our men drink. If I polled the room, I'm sure you all have stories to tell. My father was the drinker that ruined my young life. My mother died, I think, of a broken heart. He died because his body couldn't handle any more liquor." She continued with her story and finished with, "I never told anyone this before because I was too ashamed. I thought other people would look down on me because my father had been the town drunk, one of them anyway. And wherever we went." Rebekka looked out over the heads of the women gathered. "Now is the time to do something about this problem in Willowford."

Silence lasted but for a moment when a woman in the back rose to her feet and started clapping. Others joined her, and soon all of the women were on their feet, clapping. The applause soon became as one pair of hands, the steady beat from the heart of each woman.

Rebekka nodded and smiled. When she raised her hands again, the women fell still. "I have a plan. You want to hear it?"

The answer came as one voice. "Yes!" The women took their seats.

"We start with the legal process by talking with Sheriff Jordan. We'll ask him to close the saloon."

"He won't do nothin'. He's a man." The comment came from the back of the room; laughter greeted the sally.

Rebekka went on to outline steps two, three, and four of her plan. The women applauded again. "Now remember, this plan is our secret. The good Lord sees in secret, but the men won't."

"Unless someone blabs," a woman off to the right called out.

Mrs. Sampson rose to her feet, stretched herself as tall as she could, and ordered, "No one will blab." She stared around the room, daring someone to argue.

Nobody said a word.

"Now, who will call on the sheriff with me?" Rebekka asked after the silence stretched to give anyone a chance to comment.

Three hands went up. Mrs. Johnson from the mercantile,

Mrs. Sampson, and, Rebekka caught her breath in surprise, Mrs. Larson. "Good. We will let you all know what happens. And if that fails—"

"Like we know it will," another voice interrupted.

"We'll see you all on Friday night. You know where."

The women stood as one and filed out into the night.

The next afternoon after school, the four women met at the boardinghouse. "Ready?" Mrs. Sampson looked at each of them directly. For a change Mrs. Larson didn't have much to say.

"Who wants to do the talking?" Rebekka asked.

"Let me start." Mrs. Sampson pulled her red knitted hat down over her ears. "I have plenty I want to say to him—and all the men."

As they entered the sheriff's office, Sheriff Jordan pushed his chair back and rose to his feet. "Well, hello, ladies." Steam rose from the coffee cup at his left. "What can I do for you?"

Rebekka clamped her lips together at the syrup dripping from his voice. He surely wouldn't be so sweet when they finished with him.

The women took up their places as if assigned. One on each side of the desk and Mrs. Sampson in front.

"Sorry I don't have enough chairs to go around. I wasn't expecting company," he said, his smile faltering slightly at the corners.

"We want to talk about the shooting on Saturday night."

"Now you know I can't discuss a case like that. I have the two men in lockup who accidentally did the shooting. Or rather who are accused of the crime."

"And when their lawyers post bail, they'll be out on the road again." Mrs. Sampson leaned her arms on the desk.

"Well, ja. That's the way our legal system works. Everyone is innocent until proved guilty. We'll have a trial and—"

"And the most they'll get is manslaughter because, after all, it was only a fight and no one meant to do any harm."

"Well, now, Alma—"

"Mrs. Sampson."

He looked at her for a moment and tightened his jaw. "Mrs. Sampson, that's for the judge and jury to decide."

"A jury of all men."

"Now you know the laws, Al. . .Mrs. Sampson." The sheriff leaned on his straight arms, towering above the woman across the desk. "Now, what can I do for you ladies?" He cut the end of each word like a sharp cleaver through chicken bones.

"You can close down the saloon so there won't be any more such 'accidents.' "

"Now you know I can't do that. The Willowford Saloon is a reputable business. Nels pays his taxes just like everyone else. Why, he even loaned out his piano for the school party. . .out of the goodness of his heart. You know that, Miss Stenesrude." He shook his head. "What you're asking, I just can't do that."

"In spite of all the fightings and killings caused by the liquor served there?"

"Now, that was an accident, I told you—"

"That leaves us no alternative but to deal with this ourselves. Good day, Sheriff. Ladies?" Mrs. Sampson turned and strode out the door, the three other women following like soldiers behind their general.

Evenings, the three women at the boardinghouse plotted and planned. During the day, other women were seen coming and going. While all their errands looked legitimate, the boardinghouse hadn't seen such activity in years.

It's a good thing Jude isn't here, Rebekka thought one night as she finished her prayers and crawled between the icy cold sheets. *He'd have tried to stop us for sure.* But oh, when she thought of it, how she missed him. They hadn't had a musical night since he had left.

Friday night at eight o'clock the women gathered at the church. Whispers sounded loud in the dark, as they huddled together both to keep warm and to receive their instructions one last time. Axes, hatchets, and a buggy whip or two were drawn from satchels and from under coats.

"Now, remember," Rebekka spoke in a low, but carrying voice. "Be careful you don't hurt yourself and do not do the men harm. Just the saloon."

"All right. May God be with us." She raised her voice in the old marching hymn. "Onward Christian soldiers, marching as to war. . ." Fifty women, young and old, marched out of the dark church and formed a line, four abreast, to sing their way down the street.

They sang their way the three blocks to the saloon, up the wide wooden stairs with their feet in perfect rhythm, stomped across the wooden porch and through the double doors, now closed against the winter's cold.

They sang as they laid the whips about, driving the men from their gaming tables like cattle in a drive. They sang while they smashed all the bottles lining the glass shelves behind the bar and chased the few diehards with their axes. The third verse swelled while they made kindling of the tables and chairs. "Forward into battle. . ." The words sung from fifty throats could be heard above the crashing, the smashing, and the yelps as men ran out the door.

The shotgun roared as Sheriff Jordan slammed the doors open.

Rebekka and her platoon of ten lined up behind the carved walnut bar with a marble top and, on "Three," they all shoved, tipping the entire bar over on its side. The front was already splintered by the swinging axes.

"That's enough!" Sheriff Jordan roared, loud as his gun.

"Onward Christian soldiers, marching as to war. . ." The women swung into the chorus and, shouldering their axes, marched out the door.

"Just keep on marching right to the jail," the sheriff boomed his order. He stood to the side as the marchers left, eyes straight ahead like good soldiers. "Oh, no. Ann, Mary, what are you doing here?" His wife and seventeen-year-old daughter faced forward and marched with their sisters.

The singing women turned right into the jail and marched

in. Those who couldn't force their way through the door marched in place and sang in time on the porch and in the street. Their marching and singing kept them warm, in spite of the night wind that growled across the plains, promising snow and cold to freeze one's bones.

"Let me through. Excuse me. Sheriff!" Nels pushed his way into the packed jail. When he finally made it to the sheriff's desk, he leaned on his arms, panting and glaring like a mean hound who'd just been whupped.

"I. . .want. . .to file charges. These women destroyed—" His voice rose to a shriek. He took a deep breath and started again in a lower key. "These women destroyed my saloon. The only thing left in one piece is the piano." His voice rose again. He heaved and puffed, trying to get his breath again.

"I know, Nels. I was there, remember?" Sheriff Jordan stood at his desk.

"Well, you didn't come quick enough. They broke everything—"

"I know, except the piano." The sheriff raised his voice to be heard over the singing. "Cut it out. Quiet!"

The women sang on, their faces forward, looking neither to the right nor the left.

"Alma!"

"Mrs. Sampson." Her voice cut through the air like the buggy whip she'd used earlier.

"I want to press charges." Nels thumped his fist on the table. "Put them all behind bars. Look what they did to my saloon." He thumped again.

Sheriff Jordan swung around, his fists clenched. "Just get outside right now, Nels, before I throw you in the clink. I got fifty women here to deal with and I ain't got enough jail cells for ten. You got any better suggestions, you just tell me now or leave. I'll talk with you later."

"Well, I never!" The saloon owner looked around the room until he was impaled on Mrs. Sampson's glare. "I'll be back." He pushed his way out of the room, no "Please" or "Excuse me" left in his gullet.

Mrs. Sampson and Sheriff Jordan faced each other over the desk again, like a replay of the Monday before.

The women kept on singing.

Out of the corner of her eye, Rebekka watched the standoff, careful to keep on singing even though her throat felt raw like a ground-up piece of meat. She tried to keep a grin from cracking her face. The orders had been to keep a straight face and keep on singing. She tried to hear what they said but, short of moving out of her place, she couldn't distinguish the words.

Their faces said plenty however. Glare for glare they stared and stormed like two bears over a kill.

Sheriff Jordan threw his arms up in the air. "All right, ladies, about face. Go on home. And stay there!" His roar matched the shotgun that he used for crowd control.

The singing stopped.

"And what are you going to do about the saloon?" Mrs. Sampson cut through the silence.

"I don't know."

The women turned as one and marched out the door. Out on the street, they let themselves smile for the first time.

Rebekka watched them head for their homes. *But what will they face when they get there?* The thought wiped the smile from her face.

"Don't you worry none about us," Mrs. Jordan said in a low voice, as if having read Rebecca's thoughts. "We know how to handle these men of ours, most of us anyway."

Chapter 11

Nels won't be rebuilding."

"What? You mean that?" Rebekka asked as she dropped her satchel on the table. "How did you hear?"

"Sheriff Jordan came by to say there are no charges being filed. Gave me a lecture on civil disobedience, however." Mrs. Sampson spread the frosting on a chocolate layer cake in front of her. "Said if he'd had a bigger force, he'd a'clapped us all in jail until we rotted." She turned the cake, her eyes twinkling above the smile that came and went. "But he'da needed a bigger hoosegow, too."

"But what will Nels do about the saloon?" asked Rebekka as she dipped a finger in the bowl and licked off the frosting.

"Well, the building wasn't his, he rents it, so I 'spect he'll build a place somewhere on the outside of town." She checked the cake to make sure she hadn't missed any spots.

"Then we failed." Rebekka felt her shoulders slump.

"No. We stood up for what we believed and now the men of this county know their women can accomplish something when they all get together. But unless prohibition goes through, there'll always be places men can drink and play cards. You gotta remember, some women like to join them."

In mid-November, the setting sun was slanting across the snowdrifts when Jude was returning to the boardinghouse. As he rode past the school, he wished it were earlier so he could have given Rebekka a ride home or at least walked with her. The snow in the schoolyard had been trampled by many feet, a circle for "Run,

Goose, Run" packed by the game players.

Just past the school he saw three angels formed in the snow, one large and two small. "Who do you think made those?" he asked the only live creature around, his horse. The black gelding tossed his head and snorted. Jude shook his head. Here he was, the man who'd rather not talk with anyone and now he was so starved for conversation, he even talked with a horse.

"It's all her fault, you know." Prince nodded then tugged on the bit. Home lay just across the wooden bridge. "What am I to do?" Prince lifted his tired feet a bit higher. He pulled at the bit again, his ears pricked toward the town ahead.

The horse's feet thudded across the bridge. Beneath, the creek lay frozen, drifted snow filling the creek bed nearly to the tops of the banks. Snow muffled the *clop, clop* of the hooves on the timbers.

The stillness of the schoolyard and winter silence of the creek made the jangle of the bit ring loud on the crisp air. Somewhere ahead a door slammed. Smoke curled up from chimneys and lighted windows beckoned a traveler home.

Prince turned on Sampson Street and broke into a trot. "I have to tell her, don't I?" Prince shook his head and picked up the pace.

Before he headed up the walk to the house, Jude led the horse into the barn, threw in some hay, and dumped a pan of oats in the manger. By the time he hit the back porch, he was nearly running. He leaped up the steps and kicked snow off his boots. His coat caught the hook along with his hat, and his saddlebags hit the floor. He pulled off his boots at the jack and padded to the door to the kitchen. Heavenly smells assailed his nostrils, and the sounds from inside said supper wasn't yet on the table.

As he opened the door, he knew why he was so excited—he was home! Rebekka jumped up from grading her papers at the table and took a step toward him, her smile wide as the sun on a summer day.

"Welcome home, stranger." Mrs. Sampson spun around and gave him a hug.

Jude stopped as if he'd been struck.

Mrs. Sampson patted his cheeks with both her hands. "Does

you good, boy. You need more affection in your life. Just want you to know how much we've missed you." He looked over her shoulder to Rebekka.

What he wouldn't give to have her in his arms instead. He returned the older woman's hug and squeezed Mrs. Knutson's hand. When he straightened, his gaze refused to leave Rebekka's. The two looked deep into the other's eyes, all the while separated by five feet of kitchen floor and a lifetime of sorrows and fears, hopes and dreams.

"Hello, Rebekka," his voice cracked.

"I. . .we're glad you're back." She clamped her fingers around the back of the chair so she wouldn't throw herself in his arms. Why could Mrs. Sampson hug him? What would happen if she just walked across the canyon separating them and into his arms? What would he do? What would she do?

"I hear you're a prohibition rabble-rouser."

"Oh." She mentally shook herself. A grin broke loose and shattered her reserve. "It was nothing. We just busted up a saloon and almost got thrown into prison. All fifty of us, all women."

"Way I heard it, there were axes flying and whips and over a hundred yelling and screaming womenfolk, driving the poor men of Willowford right out into the cold of night."

Rebekka threw back her head and laughed, a contagious sound that invited everyone to join in. "So that's how the story has grown." She looked to the two widows who were chuckling along with her. But when her gaze returned to Jude, her breath stopped.

He was smiling. A real smile that banished the sadness from his eyes and crinkled the corners. "You women are some piece of work." Even his teeth showed.

It was all she could do not to fling herself across the space. He smiled! Jude, the sad, not only spoke a longer piece than she'd heard from him yet, but his smile. . .

"Supper's on the table soon's you wash up." Mrs. Sampson plunked a pitcher of hot water in front of Jude. "Your room's been closed up, so it'll be a mite chilly, but leave the door and the register open and it'll be warm in no time."

"Thanks." Jude walked back out into the back entry, picked up his saddlebags and then the pitcher on his way back through the kitchen. "You musta known I was coming." He nodded at the cake on the counter.

"If I'da knowed you was coming, I'da baked you an apple pie." Mrs. Sampson turned to finish the gravy she was stirring on the stove.

Rebekka heard a ghost of a chuckle float back from the dining room. A smile and a chuckle all on the same day? Would wonders never cease?

That night after filling Jude in on all that had gone on in his absence, they broke out the instruments and played all the tunes they could think of.

"How 'bout another piece of cake with our coffee?" Mrs. Sampson asked as she put away her gutbucket. "This sure has been mighty pleasurable."

Rebekka closed the cover on the keyboard. "I'd love some." She spun around on the stool and caught herself falling into the deepest blue eyes she'd ever seen. Clear, warm, like a lake on a summer's day.

"Me, too." Jude reached for her hand and pulled her to her feet. "Rebekka, we need to talk."

"Cake's on." Mrs. Knutson stopped in the doorway arch.

"Oh, excuse me. . .I mean. . ."

"We're coming." The mood lay in tatters at their feet.

As Christmas drew nearer, the days seemed to move in double time. Rebekka, like many others, ordered many of her Christmas gifts from the Sears catalog, at least those she didn't make herself. As the packages arrived on the train, she wrapped them and placed those for her family in a trunk. She'd take them with her when she boarded the train for Minneapolis the day after the pageant.

At school, preparations for the pageant progressed on schedule. One night Rebekka asked Jude if he would help make the sets for the Christmas play.

"Of course. When would you like the help?"

"Would tomorrow be all right? John and two of the other boys need some carpentering help and then the painters can go to work."

"Sounds like a major production."

"Oh, it is, and the children wrote most of it themselves. They even composed two songs to use." She sat down at the piano and played through both tunes, singing the words along with the melody. "See, aren't they wonderful?"

Jude nodded. *Yes, you are,* he thought. *Wonderful and beautiful and. . .* He closed his thoughts off like shutting the damper on a stove. And not for him. When he told her what he'd done, she'd close down that wonderful smile and turn away, afraid to be with a man who had killed his wife.

The day before the pageant, the blizzard struck. It howled across the plains and the Missouri for three days, burying everything in drifts ten feet tall and twice as wide. Then it shoveled up the drifts and tossed them in the air, blowing with a fury unstopped by humans or their flimsy houses.

No one ventured out. The trains stopped in the nearest town. Only the furious wind, driving the snow before it, lived on the prairie.

On Christmas day, the world awoke to silence. Silence so deep it hurt the ears to hear it. While bitter cold captured the drifted snow and froze it into mountains and ridges, the sun reflected off the glittering expanses to blind anyone who ventured forth.

"Are you sorry you couldn't visit your grandmother?" Jude asked as he and Rebekka stood at the kitchen window. They could see the rope connecting house and barn that lay partially buried beneath the frozen crust. Jude had followed it to go out and feed Prince during the storm.

"I'm more sorry about the pageant. The children worked so hard and, for some of them, the presents at school might have been the only ones they received."

"You can always put it on in January."

"We will. It's just that they were so excited. You lose some of that with delaying," Rebekka sighed and turned from the window. She couldn't tell him she'd been glad to see the blizzard that stopped the trains. She wouldn't want to be guilty of wishing anything as awful as that storm on the farmers and townsfolk alike, let alone all of God's other creatures.

After dinner, they gathered in the sitting room around the piano to sing all the carols they knew and then some over again. Mrs. Knutson brought out her Bible and read the Christmas story from the Gospel of Luke.

Rebekka heard herself saying the so-familiar words along with the reader. "And in those days. . ." Into the hush of the afternoon, the story carried the same message as it has all through the ages. A Babe was born, the shepherds and angels rejoiced. When Mrs. Knutson closed her Bible, they all sat in silence for a time.

"I love the part where 'Mary kept all these things, and pondered them in her heart.'" Rebekka leaned her head against the high back of the wing chair.

"I wonder about the innkeeper. Here I have a boardinghouse. What would I have done if I was full up and a young couple came, asking for a room?" Mrs. Sampson rubbed under one eye. "It's so easy to sit here and say 'Shame,' but what would I have done?"

"Knowing you, you'd have moved them right into the sitting room and helped deliver the baby yourself," Mrs. Knutson said, smiling at her dear friend. "You've never been able to turn anyone away."

"Thank you. I always said God gave me this big house for a reason."

Jude listened to the exchange, agreeing wholeheartedly. She could have turned him away but she didn't. "I think about the shepherds who believed what the angels said and right away went looking for the Baby. Shepherds are a mighty tough audience. But then, I guess if the whole sky starts singing and you see a multitude of angels, that oughta convince anyone."

What about you? Rebekka thought, trying to listen to what he was saying between the lines. *Will it take the entire heavenly choir to convince you that God loves you no matter what?* Love, what a wonderful word. She turned it around in her mind, looking at it from all angles. She loved her teaching and her students, playing the piano, singing. She loved the sun on her face and the breeze in her hair. She loved Jude. Wait a minute! Sure, she loved Jude like a friend and brother in Christ.

But Mr. Larson was a brother in that way also and walking with him didn't set her toes to tingling. Her toes and all other parts inside and out. Sheriff Jordan's smile didn't make her go mushy in her middle.

She used the conversation flowing around her to watch the man who set her heart afire. While he rarely smiled, she knew what it did for his face now. And his voice, that deep, melodic way he had of talking, as if he thought out each word in advance so as to use the best one. She hadn't planned to feel this way about any man. Was this her Christmas gift from the Lord of Hosts?

"I have something for each of you." Mrs. Sampson rose to her feet. "It's not much but, well, what would Christmas be without presents?"

Each of them went to their rooms and returned with wrapped gifts. Rebekka handed hers around and sat back in the wing chair to open her presents. A lace collar made by Mrs. Knutson, a warm muffler with matching hat and mittens in a warm rust color that set the roses blooming in her cheeks from Mrs. Sampson, and the third box, she hesitated to open. She looked up to catch Jude watching her, the smile lurking at the corners of his mouth.

She unwrapped the parcel. Inside knelt a hand-carved wooden angel, her arms spread as if to welcome the world. The feathers on her wings, carved in intricate detail, invited the caress of a fingertip.

Rebekka struggled against the tears clogging her throat and burning her eyes. "She's. . .she's just beautiful." She looked up to see Jude watching her. Was that love she saw glowing in his eyes? Could she feel the way she did and not have him return the feelings?

"My, my, son, I didn't know you could carve like that." Mrs.

Sampson shook her head. "You're a real artist."

"I didn't know, either. Out there at the Jamesons', old Grandpa spent his evenings whittlin' so I asked him to show me. That little angel was hiding in a hunk of cherrywood, just waiting to come out."

"Thank you. I've never had such a perfect present." Rebekka traced the grain of the draped gown. "She's so beautiful."

Like you, Jude thought but didn't say. He had no right to say such things, but he couldn't stop thinking them.

Mrs. Sampson opened a set of eight napkin rings of rich walnut and Mrs. Knutson two spools for her lacemaking.

Jude opened his presents as if he couldn't believe anyone would give him something. The red muffler from Mrs. Knutson he wrapped around his neck, the gray wool socks from Mrs. Sampson he promised to wear the next day, and the final package he held in his lap. His fingers had a life of their own as they untied the silvery bow and carefully pulled apart the paper. The mouth organ lay in a bed of tissue, gleaming as the light hit the chrome-and-brass trim. He picked it out of the nest and put it to his mouth. Long, sweet notes hung on the air, each a part of another, as he played "Silent Night."

Rebekka could feel the shepherds quaking and the glories streaming down. The room, her heart, seemed full of the glories of Christmas.

"Thank you." His words blended with the notes hanging in the room as if loathe to part. Other words hung on the air between the two young people, unspoken words but feelings deep enough to withstand the not telling.

After the new year, Rebekka started reading *The Pilgrim's Progress,* since the storms continued unabated and everyone was virtually housebound. One night they remained in the sitting room after the reading when Mrs. Sampson asked what they thought the story meant.

"Nothing," Jude said, looking up from his carving. "It's just a fine story, that's all."

"No, it's an allegory." Rebekka kept her finger in the place. "And all allegories have a meaning." Jude just shook his head.

"This is the story of all of us who fail and fall," Mrs. Sampson said with certainty. "It shows how God always comes to meet us. He picks up his fallen children, dusts us off, and sets us on the right path again. We can never be so bad that He gives up on us." Jude snorted, the shake of his head nearly negligible.

"It's true." Mrs. Knutson joined the discussion. "All we have to do is ask for forgiveness and He gives it. That's why Jesus died, for our sins."

"Well, it's a good story." Jude held the piece of wood he worked with up to the light. "A real fine story."

"Remember that God even forgave Paul after he helped kill Christians, made him into a real leader in the church and for all of us." Mrs. Sampson laid her knitting in her lap. "I'm just grateful that He did it, that's all, or I wouldn't be here."

Jude looked up at her in surprise. Surely a woman such as she had done nothing serious enough to think about leaving life?

But when he climbed the stairs that night, he couldn't shake the thought. Would God really forgive all that he'd done wrong?

Chapter 12

School resumed in mid-February. Rebekka stood before her pupils. "Welcome back and let's pray that's the last of the bad weather."

"Whenth the pageant?" Emily raised her hand from the front row. Her feet could now touch the floor as she sat so straight in her new desk.

"How about the first of March? That will give us two weeks to prepare." The children cheered and fell to their lessons with a vengeance so they could have time to practice.

The pageant went off without a hitch. The curtain pulled back when it was supposed to, no one forgot their parts, and, at the end, the audience cheered for five minutes. But Jude's smile was the best accolade Rebekka could have wished for.

One morning Rebekka awoke to the music of dripping icicles. The chinook blew in during the night and was turning the snow to mush as rapidly as it could. The snow seemed to disappear almost overnight.

But when the rains came in torrents, the town began to worry. The Missouri was still frozen, there hadn't been time for the ice to melt, and now, with all the rain, there could be trouble.

Rebekka grumbled on her way to school one morning. First the prairie fire, then the blizzards and the terrible cold, now rains that seemed to be reenacting the forty days and forty nights of Genesis. Bryde Creek rushed under the bridge but just barely. Another six inches and the bridge to the school would be impassible.

How was she supposed to prepare her students for the examinations when they hadn't been in school for half of the year?

Saturday, a watery sun peeped through the clouds. Sunday, Jude rode Prince out over the prairie rather than take up Rebekka's invitation to join them in church. When he rode past the church, he heard the congregation singing; he pulled Prince to a halt.

"Throw out the lifeline, throw out the lifeline, someone is drifting awa-a-y. . ." The words poured out of the cracks and crevices of the country church as if sung for his ears alone. He nudged his mount into a trot. Maybe next time the pastor was in town, he'd go with Rebekka. Couldn't hurt.

Monday, the rains returned, drenching the land and running off the ground still frozen under the mud.

Some of her students had stayed home and, by one o'clock, Rebekka toyed with the idea of sending everyone home. But she hated to make them walk in the downpour. Perhaps it would stop by the time school was to let out.

She could feel the tension in the room, the children sneaking peeks at the windows just like she was. "All right, that's enough." She rose to her feet and headed for the piano that had been donated at Christmastime. "We can take an hour out and call this getting ready for the last day of school's concert."

The children cheered and gathered around her, the little ones in front and the taller in the back. They ran through some drills with Rebekka striking chords up a half each time. The "la, la, la, la, la, la, las" rang clear to the rafters. When she swung into "She'll Be Comin' 'Round the Mountain When She Comes," everyone laughed and joined in all the funny sounds.

Their "toot toot" stopped in midsound. Rebekka listened. Who was hollering? What was that roar? It sounded like three freight trains bearing down on them.

She leaped to her feet and ran to the windows facing south. In horror she saw gray water surging between them and the town. Waves rolled before chunks of ice, tearing at the banks and already climbing up to the schoolhouse steps. Out in the main channel of the Missouri, trees ripped past, tumbling in the flash flood that rose by inches each minute.

How would she get the children out?

411

"Everyone, over here. John, you get the jump ropes from the cloakroom. Everyone, grab your coats. And let us pray. "Father God, please help us. Amen."

She checked the windows on the north. A rise just beyond them was their only chance. Could the big ones help get the little ones there?

"Rebekka, Rebekka!" A male voice sounded from outside. "Help me open the door." Water that had begun seeping under the door, gushed in when it opened.

"Jude!" Rebekka had never been so glad to see anyone in her life.

"Okay, children, follow the instructions exactly!" Rebekka lined them up, little ones held by the bigger.

"Okay, kids, we have ropes out here and men to help you. Come on out. John, you stay there to help Miss Stenesrude." He grabbed Emily around the waist and handed her off to the next in line, the water lapping at his hips.

Rebekka kept her voice calm, even though she was screaming inside. "That's right. Next." One by one, the children were passed the long distance between the school and the rise.

The water covered the floor. Rebekka could feel a rocking motion, as if she were standing on the deck of a ship. The men stood in waist-deep water.

Rebekka didn't dare look at Jude for fear he'd see the panic in her eyes. "Thank You, God. Okay, John, you go now."

"You, too. Here, take my hand."

"Get out of here!" Jude yelled this time.

Rebekka felt the building shift again. Like a grand ship on her maiden voyage, the school slipped from its pilings and tipped forward.

"Jude!" Rebekka couldn't tell if she screamed or just thought it.

"Rebekka!" Jude pulled himself up into the cloakroom. "I have the rope. We have to swim for it." He grabbed her around the waist and flung them both into the swirling river.

Rebekka clung to his neck, trying to keep her head above the freezing water.

Jude's face had the gray cast of one who was cold beyond endurance.

She found the rope with one hand and kept her other around his rib cage.

"Hang on, my dearest," Jude said. "We're almost there."

Three men waded out in the water and pulled the two ashore.

Rebekka had never been so cold in her life. Her teeth chattered like castanets and she fell into the arms that held out blankets. "Jude, where's Jude?"

"Over there," someone answered. "We're trying to get him warmed. He's been in that freezing water longer than anyone."

"The children?" She could hardly force the words past her clacking teeth.

"Cold, but all right."

"Willowford?" She felt herself slipping into a gray place where she would sleep the pain in her feet away. She thought she heard a voice but could no longer answer. Peace and oblivion.

When she woke up, the lamp reminded her of sunrise. She opened her eyes and looked around. She lay in her room at the boarding-house. Had the flood been a dream?

"Here, drink this," Mrs. Sampson ordered as she held a cup to Rebekka's lips.

Rebekka sipped, then pushed herself to a sitting position. "I'm fine. Where's Jude?"

"Sleeping in his room. He has some frostbite on his feet, but he'll be okay."

"What about the flood?"

"Like all flash floods, as soon as they crest, they're gone. The Missouri is plenty high and still flooding, but the town is safe again." Mrs. Sampson turned at the sound of another voice. "There's that man again. He'da been in here hours ago if I'da let him."

"Jude?" Rebekka felt her cheeks widen. She could no longer keep the grin from busting forth. "How's the school?"

"Fine, or so they tell me." Jude stood in the door. "Just off it's pinnings and downstream about two hundred yards. We built it good and sturdy. Should last a hundred years or so." He stared at the woman propped against the pillows. He'd come close to losing her and he'd never told her how much he loved her.

He gave the two widows a look that sent them laughing from the room. When he sat down on the bed, he took Rebekka's hand in his. "I asked God to save us."

"And He did."

"I can't ask you to marry me until I go home and make things right with my family."

"Marry you?"

"And I need to explain what happened in my life." He stroked the tender skin on the back of her hand.

"Jude."

"I know God forgives me now. I—"

"Jude." She placed her fingers gently against his lips.

He raised his gaze from her hand to her face.

"I have one question." She studied the lines of his beloved face.

"What?"

"Do you love me?" She could feel the lump threatening to cut off her breathing.

"What kind of a question is that? Of course, I love you. What do you think I've been saying? But you have to know everything—"

"Then, yes." She reached for his strength, that formidable strength that had saved her and the children from the flood's waters. "I already know all the important things. What happened before has nothing to do with us." When he wrapped his arms around her, she snuggled into his chest. As she raised her face to look up at him, she caught a sheen in his eyes.

"That hymn you sang a while ago—'Throw out the life-line. . .'"

Rebekka nodded.

"Well, seems we needed one right bad and there it was." He kissed her eyes. "But I'm home now." He found her lips. "I almost lost you," he muttered into the side of her neck.

"I'm glad I found you," Rebekka answered.

The kiss they shared was all she'd dreamed of and feared never to experience. Together, they looked out the window to watch the sun sink into the horizon. Dusk settled into the room, bringing the peace of evening. But Rebekka knew. And now Jude knew, too. For every dusk there is a sunrise, and together they would face anything that came their way. They and the Savior who promised a bright new morning after the end of a long hard day.

DAKOTA DESTINY

Chapter 1

"Mary's home! Mary's home!" Daniel, the youngest of the Moen brood, left off swinging on the gate to the picket fence and leaped up the porch steps to the door. "Mother, did you hear me?"

"Only me and half the town. Must you yell so?" Ingeborg Moen made her way down the steep stairs and bustled over to the door. "Did you see her or was it the little bird that told you?"

"I saw—" A gloved hand clamped gently over his mouth.

"Hello, Mother." Mary stood in the doorway. At seventeen, she had shed the little girl and donned the young woman. Golden hair fell in curls down her back, held back from her oval face with a whalebone clasp, high on the back of her head. Eyes the blue of a Dakota summer sky still shone with the direct look that made students in her Sunday school classes squirm, much as her younger siblings had for years.

There was something about Mary that not only commanded attention but also made one look again. Was it the straightness of her carriage fostered by years of Mrs. Norgaard insisting the girls of Soldall walk and stand tall no matter what their height? Or the firmness of her chin that bespoke of a will of her own? Or was it the twinkle that hid under long, dark lashes and flirted with the dimple in her right cheek whenever she was trying not to laugh—which was often?

Ingeborg gathered her eldest chick in her arms and hugged her as if they'd been apart for years instead of months. "Oh, my dear, I have missed you so. The house, nay, even the town, is not the same without my Mary." She set the young woman a bit away and studied the girl's eyes. "How have you been, really? Has the school been hard for you? And the train trip home—all went well?"

"Mother, how can I answer so many questions at once? This has been a most marvelous year, and when I finish this time next spring, I will be able to teach school anywhere in North Dakota. Isn't that the most, the most—" Mary threw herself back in her mother's arms. "Oh, much as I love school, I have missed you all sorely."

Daniel thumped her valise on the waxed wooden floor. "Did you bring anything for all of us?"

"Of course I did, and how come you're not in school?" She hugged her ten-year-old brother. "You're not sick, are you? You don't look it."

He pulled away, already at the age of being embarrassed by being hugged in public. "Naw, not much anyway."

Mary looked a question at her mother. This, the baby in the family, had suffered many ailments in his short life. He seemed to catch anything that visited the school or the neighboring children, and with him it always lasted longer and took more of a toll.

"He'll be going back tomorrow." A shadow passed over Ingeborg's placid features. She lived by the creed that God loved His children and would always protect them. She'd taught that belief to her children all their lives, both she and the Reverend John, her husband. But sometimes in the dead of night when this one of her brood was near death's door, her faith had been tried—and wavered. But such doubts never lingered longer than the rise of the new day, for she believed implicitly in the mansions Jesus had gone to prepare.

Mary sniffed once and then again. "You baked apple pies."

"The last of the barrel. I'd been saving them for you, hoping they would last."

"I helped peel."

Mary stroked Daniel's pale cheek. "And I bet you are the best apple peeler in Soldall. Now, let me put my things away and we will sample some of Mother's crust cookies, or did you eat them all?"

He shook his head so hard, the white blond hair swung across his forehead. "I didn't."

Mary headed for the stairs. "And you, my dear Mor, will fill me in on all the happenings of town and country since your last letter."

"Will came by yesterday." Daniel struggled up the steps with the heavy valise.

"He did, eh?" Mary looked up to catch a nod from her mother. A trill of pleasure rippled up Mary's back. *Will, soon I will see Will again. And we will have an entire summer to find out how deep our friendship really goes.*

She turned back to her little brother. "Here, let's do that together. That bag is so burdened with books, no wonder we can't lift it." Mary settled her hand next to Daniel's on the leather grip, and together they lugged it up the steep stairs—Mary laughing and teasing her little brother all the way. They set the case down, and with a sigh of happiness, Mary looked around the room she'd known all her life.

The first nine-patch quilt she'd made with her mother covered the bed, and the rag rug on the floor had warmed her feet since she was ten. Stiffly starched white Priscilla curtains crossed over the south-facing windows, and an oak commode held the same rose-trimmed pitcher and bowl given her by her bestamor, her mother's mother. The ceiling still slanted the same, its rose wallpaper now fading in places.

Daniel stood silently, intuitive as ever of his eldest sister's feelings. When she finished looking around, he grinned up at her. "Didja see anything new?"

Mary looked again. The kerosene lamp still sat on the corner of her dresser. As soon as she unpacked, the brush and hand mirror would go back in place. She looked down at her brother. "What's up, Danny boy?"

He looked at the ceiling directly above her head. She followed his gaze and her mouth fell open. "Electric lights. Far put in the electricity."

"The church board voted."

Since they lived in the parsonage, all improvements were at the whim and financial possibilities of the Soldall Lutheran Church. They'd all grown up under that edict.

Mary reached up and pushed the button on the bare bulb hanging from a cord. Light flooded the room. "Now I can read in bed at night." She spun in place, arms outstretched as if to embrace the entire world, or at least her home and family. She swooped Daniel up and hugged him tight. *He is so thin*, she thought. *Has he been worse than mother told me?* He hugged her back and whispered in her ear. "I've missed you so."

"And me you, Bug. Let's go down and have some of that apple pie, if Mor will cut it before dinner." His childhood nickname slipped out; she hadn't called him that in years, but today, today was a time for remembering. Who knew what a magical day like today would bring?

Mary and Daniel, hand in hand, were halfway down the stairs when the front door opened again and the Reverend John Moen entered, removing his well-used black fedora as he came. Mary put her finger to her lips, and she and Daniel froze in place.

"So, Mother, what's the news? Ummmm, something surely smells good."

As he walked toward the kitchen, Mary and Daniel tiptoed down the stairs.

"Apple pie? For me?"

"Get your fingers out of the crust." The laughter in Ingeborg's voice could be heard by the two creeping nearer.

Mary silently mouthed, *one, two, three,* and she and Daniel burst around the corner. "Surprise!"

"Land sakes alive, look who's here!" John grabbed his chest in mock shock. "Mary, come home at last." He spread his arms and Mary stepped into them, forcing herself to regain some sort of decorum. "Lord love you, girl, but I was beginning to think you were never coming home." He hugged her close and rested his cheek on smooth golden hair. "When did you go and get so grown up?"

Mary blinked against the tears burning the backs of her eyes.

Her father had aged in the months she'd been gone. Deep lines bracketed his mouth, and the few strands of gray at his temples had multiplied. She stepped back, the better to see his dear face. "I'm never too grown up to come home to my family. Even though I've been so busy I hardly have time to turn around, I've missed you all so much."

"Come now, we can visit as we eat. Daniel, John, go wash your hands. Mary, put this in the center of the table, please." Ingeborg handed her daughter a plate of warm rolls, fresh from the oven. Setting a platter with a roast surrounded by potatoes next to her place, Ingeborg checked to make sure everything was to her liking.

"Mother, you've gone to such trouble. I'll be around here for months." Mary clasped her hand over the back of the chair that had always been hers. "Oh, it feels so good to be home." She counted the places set and looked over at her mother. "Who else is coming?"

"You'll know soon enough." A knock at the door brightened Mor's eyes. "Go answer that while I bring on the coffee."

Mary gave her a puzzled look and went to do as bid.

"Hello, Mary." Will Dunfey's carrot hair had turned to a deep auburn that made his blue eyes even bluer. The smile on his face looked fit to crack the square jaw that he could set with a stubbornness like a bear trap. His shoulders now filled out a blue chambray shirt, open at the neck and with sleeves buttoned at strong wrists.

"Will!" Mary warred with the desire to throw herself into his arms. Instead she stepped back and beckoned him in. He took her hand as he passed, and a shiver went up her arm and straight to her heart. When he took her other hand and turned her to face him, the two shivers met and the delicious collision could be felt clear to her toes.

"So you're finally home." Had his voice deepened in the last months or was her memory faulty?

"Yes." *Say something intelligent, you ninny. This is only Will, you remember him, your best friend?*

"Invite him to the table, Daughter." The gentle prompting came from her mother.

"Oh, I'm sorry." She unlocked her gaze from the deep blue pools of his eyes and, finally coming to herself, gestured him toward the table. "I believe Mother invited you for dinner."

Will winked at her, nearly undoing her again, and dropping her hands, crossed the room to shake hands with her father. After greeting the Reverend and Mrs. Moen, he took the place next to Mary's as if he'd been there many times.

The thought of that set Mary to wondering. When she started to pull out her chair, Will leaped to his feet to assist her. Mary stared at him. *What in the world?* She seated herself with a murmured "thank you" and a questioning look over her shoulder. Where had Will, the playmate hero, gone, and when had this exciting man taken his place?

Dinner passed in a blur of laughter, good food, and the kind of visiting that said this was not an unusual occurrence. Daniel treated Will much like his bigger brothers, and Ingeborg scolded the young man like one of her own.

Mary caught up on the news of Soldall as seen through the loving eyes of her father, the slightly acerbic gaze of her mother, and the humorous observations of Will, who saw things from the point of view of the blacksmith and livery, where he worked for Dag Weinlander.

"The doctor was the latest one," Will was saying. "I'm going to have to go to mechanic's school if this drive to buy automobiles continues. You know, at first Dag thought they were a fad, but now that Mrs. Norgaard owns one and expects him to drive her everywhere, he thinks they're the best."

"Mrs. Norgaard bought an automobile?" Mary dropped her fork. "At her age?"

"Now dear, seventy isn't so old when one is in good health." Ingeborg began stacking the dishes.

"She says she has too much to do to get old," John said with a chuckle. "When I think back to how close she was to dying after her husband died. . .if it hadn't been for Clara, she would have given up for sure."

"That seems so long ago. I remember the classes we had at her house to learn to speak better English. Mrs. Norgaard was determined all the girls would grow up to be proper young ladies, whether we wanted to or not."

"She took me in hand. If it hadn't been for her and Dag, I would have gotten on the next train and kept on heading west." Will smiled in remembrance. "I thought sure once or twice she was going to whack me with that cane of hers."

"Did she really—whack anyone, that is?" Daniel's eyes grew round.

"Not that I know of, but for one so tiny, she sure can put the fear of God into you."

"Ja, and everyone in town has been blessed by her good heart at one time or another." John held up his coffee cup. "Any more, my dear?"

Ingeborg got to her feet. "I'll bring the dessert. You stay right there, Mary."

"Thanks to her that I am at school." Mary got up anyway and took the remainder of the plates into the kitchen.

"And that the church has a new furnace."

"And the school, too," Daniel added.

"Is Mr. Johnston happy here?" Mary had a dream buried deep in her heart of teaching in the Soldall school, but that could only happen if the current teacher moved elsewhere.

"Very much so. His wife is president of the Ladies' Aid, such a worker." Ingeborg returned with the apple pie. "I'd hate for them to leave. Their going would leave a real hole in the congregation."

Mary nodded. So much for her dream. Surely there would be a school near Soldall available next year.

They all enjoyed the pie and coffee, with Will taking the second piece Ingeborg pushed at him. He waved away the third offering.

"Mother, you are the best pie maker in the entire world." Mary licked her fork for the last bit of pie juice. She looked sideways at Will, but he seemed lost in thoughts of his own. Was something wrong?

When she looked at her father at the foot of the table, a look that matched Will's hovered about his eyes. What was going on?

"I better get back to the church. I have a young couple coming by for marriage counseling." John pushed his chair back. "You want to walk with me, Son?"

"Sure." Daniel leaped to his feet.

"I better be getting back to work, too," Will said with a sigh. "Thank you for such a wonderful meal, Mrs. Moen. I will remember these get-togethers for all time."

"Thank you, Will. Mary, why don't you walk Will to the gate? I'll do the cleaning up here." Ingeborg smiled, but the light didn't quite reach her eyes.

A goose just walked over my grave, Mary thought as she sensed something further amiss.

She locked her fingers behind her back as Will ushered her out the door. An intelligent word wouldn't come to her mind for the life of her.

"So, did you enjoy the last half of school?" Will leaned against the turned post on the porch.

"I loved most every minute of it. I had to study hard, but I knew that." Mary adopted the other post and turned to face him, her back against the warm surface.

Will held his hat in his hands, one finger outlining the brim. When he looked up at her, the sadness that had lurked in the background leaped forward. "Mary, there is so much I wanted to say, have wanted to say for years, and now—" He looked up at the sky as if asking for guidance.

"Will, I know something is wrong. What is it?"

He sat down on the step and gestured for her to do the same. "First of all, I have to know. Do you love me as I love you—with the kind of love between a man and a woman, not the kind between friends and kids?"

Mary clasped her hands around her skirted knees. All the dreaming of this time, and here it was: no preparation, just boom. "Will, I have always loved you." Her voice came softly but surely.

"I mean as more than friends."

"Will Dunfey, understand me." She turned so she faced him.

"I love you. I always have, and I always will."

"I had hoped to ask you to marry me." He laid a calloused hand over hers.

"Had hoped?" She could feel a knot tightening in her breast.

"I thought by the time you graduated I would perhaps own part of the business or one of my own so I could support you."

"Will, you are scaring me." Mary laid her hand over his.

Will looked up at her, his eyes crying for understanding. "I signed up last week."

"Signed up?"

"Enlisted in the U.S. Army to fight against the Germans. They say this is the war to end all wars and they need strong young men."

Mary felt a small part of her die at his words.

Chapter 2

O h, Will, you can't leave!" The cry escaped before Mary could trap it.

He studied the hat in his hands. "You know I don't want to."

"Then don't." Mary clasped her hands together, her fingers winding themselves together as if they had a mind of their own. "I. . .I just got home."

"I know." He looked up at her, his eyes filled with love and longing. "But they need men like me to stop the Huns. I couldn't say no. You wouldn't really want me to."

Yes, I would. I want you here. I've been looking forward to this summer for months. It made the hard times bearable. But she wouldn't say those words, couldn't say them. No one had ever accused Mary Moen of being selfish. "Of course not." Now she studied her hands. If she looked at him, he would see the lie in her eyes.

A bee buzzed by and landed on the lilac that had yet to open its blossoms.

Will cleared his throat. "I. . .I want you to know that I love you. I've wanted to tell you that for years, and I promised I would wait until we—" His voice broke. He sighed. "Aw, Mary, this isn't the way I dreamed it at all." He crossed the narrow gap separating them and took her hands in his. "I want to marry you, but that will have to wait until I come back. No, that's not what I wanted to say at all." He dropped her hands and leaned against the post above her. "What I mean is—"

"I don't care what you mean, Will, darling. I will be here

waiting for you, so you keep that in your mind. I will write to you every day and mail the letters once a week, if I can wait that long." She grasped the front of his shirt with both hands. "And you will come back to me, Mr. Will Dunfey. You will come back." She lifted her face to his for the kiss she had dreamed of in the many lonely nights away at school.

His lips felt warm and soft and unbearably sweet. She could feel the tears pooling at the back of her throat. *Dear God, please bring him home again. Watch over him for me.*

"We will all be praying for you," she murmured against his mouth. "I love you. Don't you ever forget that."

"I won't." He kissed her again. When he stepped back, he clasped her shoulders in his strong hands. "I'll see you tonight?"

She nodded. "Come for supper."

She watched him leap off the porch and trot down the walk to the gate. When the gate swung shut, the squeal of it grated on Mary's ears. It sounded like an animal in pain. Maybe it was her.

"Did he say when he was leaving?" Ingeborg asked when Mary finally returned to the kitchen.

Mary shook her head. "And I forgot to ask." She slapped the palms of her hands on the counter. "It's. . .it's just not fair."

"Much of life isn't."

"But why should our young men go fight a war in Europe?" She raised a hand. "I know, Mother. I read the newspapers, too. Some want us to be at the front and some want us to pretend it's not there. I just never thought we would be affected so soon. Are others of our boys already signed up, too?"

Ingeborg shook her head. "Not that I know of."

"Then why Will?"

"Now that he has, others will follow. He's always been a leader of the young men—you know that."

"But I had such dreams for this summer—and next year. . ." Her voice dwindled. "And for the years after that."

"No need to give up the dreams." Ingeborg watched her beloved daughter wrestling with forces against which she had no power.

"But. . .but what if. . ."

The ticking clock sounded loud in the silence. Ashes crumbled in the freshly blacked cast-iron range.

Mary lifted tear-filled eyes and looked directly at her mother. "What if he doesn't come back?"

"Then with God's strength and blessing you go on with your life, always remembering Will with fondness and pride." Ingeborg crossed to her daughter. "You would not be the only woman in the country with such a burden to bear. Or the world, for that matter. Perhaps if our boys get in and get the job done, there won't be so many women longing for husbands, lovers, and sons."

"How will I do this?" Mary whispered.

"By the grace of God and by keeping busy making life better for others. That is how women always get through the hard parts of life."

Mary looked up at her mother, wondering as always at the quiet wisdom Ingeborg lived. Her mother didn't say things like that lightly. She who so often sat beside the dying in the wee hours of the morning had been there herself when one child was stillborn and another died in infancy. Mary put her arms around her mother's waist and pillowed her cheek on the familiar shoulder. "Oh, Mor, I've missed you more than words could say."

Ingeborg patted her daughter's back. "God always provides, child, remember that."

After supper that night, Mary and Will strolled down the street in the sweet evening air. They'd talked of many things by the time they returned to her front fence, but one question she had not been able to utter. Finally she blurted it out.

"When will you be leaving?"

"Next week, on Monday."

"But this is already Thursday."

"I know."

Mary swallowed all the words that demanded speech. "Oh." Did a heart shatter and fall in pieces, or did it just seem so?

Chapter 3

Would her heart never quit bleeding? Mary stood waving long after the train left. Will had hung half out the side to see her as long as he could. The memory of the sun glinting off his hair and him waving his cap would have to last her a good long time. She had managed to send him off with a smile. She'd promised herself the night before that she would do that. No tears, only smiles.

"We are all praying for him," a familiar voice said from behind her.

"Mrs. Norgaard, how good of you to come." Mary wiped her eyes before turning around. She sniffed and forced a smile to her face.

"He's been one of my boys for more years than I care to count," Mrs. Norgaard said with a thump of her cane. "And I'll be right here waiting when he returns, too." A tear slid down the parchment cheek from under the black veil of her hat. With her back as ramrod straight as ever, Mrs. Norgaard refused to give in to the ravages of time, albeit her step had slowed and spectacles now perched on her straight nose.

"Now, then, we can stand here sniveling or we can get to doing something worthwhile. I know you were praying for him as I was, and we will continue to do that on a daily, or hourly if need be, basis. God only knows what's in store for our boy, but we will keep reminding our Father to be on the lookout." She stepped forward and, hooking her cane over her own arm, slid her other into Mary's. "Mrs. Hanson has coffee and some kind of special treat for all of us, so let us not keep her waiting."

431

And with that the Moens, Dag and Clara, the doctor and his wife, and several others found themselves back at "the mansion," enjoying a repast much as if they'd just come for a party. With everyone asking her about school and life in Fargo, Mary felt her heart lighten. If she'd done what she planned, she'd have been home flat out across her bed, crying till she dried up.

Dr. Harmon came up to her, tucking a last bite of frosted cake into his mouth. Crumbs caught on his mustache, and he brushed them away with a nonchalant finger. "So, missy, what are you planning for the summer?"

"I was planning on picnics with Will, helping my mother with the canning and garden, and going riding with Will."

Doc nodded his balding head. "That so." He continued to nod. "I 'spect that's changed somewhat." The twinkle in his eye let her know he understood how she felt. "You given thought to anything else?"

Mary looked at him, her head cocked slightly sideways. "All right, let's have it. I've seen that look on your face too many times through the years to think you are just being polite."

"He's never been 'just polite' in his entire life." Gudrun Norgaard said from her chair off to the side. "What is it, Harmon? Is there something going on I don't know about?"

"How could that be? You got your nose into more business than a hive's got bees."

"Be that as it may, what are you up to?" Mrs. Norgaard crossed her age-spotted hands over the carved head of her cane. Dag had made the cane for her the year her husband died, when she hadn't much cared if she'd lived either.

"I think the two of you are cooking something up again." Clara Weinlander, wife of Dag and mother of their three children, stopped beside her benefactress's chair. "I know that look."

Doc attempted an injured air but stopped when he saw the knowing smile lifting the corners of Gudrun's narrow lips. "All right," he said to the older woman. "You know the Oiens?"

"Of course, that new family that moved into the Erickson property. He works for the railroad, I believe. And she has some kind of health problem—ah, that's it." Gudrun nodded as she spoke. "A good idea, Harmon."

Mary looked from one to the other as if a spectator at that new sport she'd seen at school. Even the women played tennis—well, not her, but those who had a superfluous amount of time and money.

Clara came around to Mary and slipped an arm through hers. "Why do I get the feeling they are messing with someone else's life again?"

"It never did you any harm, did it?" Doc rocked back on his heels, glancing over to where Dag, owner of the local livery and blacksmith, now stood talking with the Reverend Moen. Sunlight from the bay window set both their faces in shadow, but the deep laugh could only come from Dag.

"No, that it didn't." Clara agreed. It had taken her a long time to get Dag to laugh so freely. "So, what do you have planned for Mary here?"

"I thought since she didn't have a position for the summer, she might be willing to help the Oiens care for their children. There are two of them: a boy, four, and the girl, two. And perhaps she could do some fetching for the missus. Mrs. Oien resists the idea of needing help, but I know this would be a big load off her mind."

"What is wrong with her?" Mary asked.

"I just wish I knew. She keeps getting weaker, though she has some good days. You think you could help them out?"

"I'll gladly do what I can."

"I figured as much. After all, you are your mother's daughter." Doc Harmon gave her a nod of approbation. "I'll talk with them tomorrow."

That night Mary wrote her first letter to Will, telling him about the party at the mansion and how it looked like she would be very busy that summer after all. As her letter lengthened, she thought of him on the train traveling east. Hoping he was thinking of her as she was him, she went to stand at her window.

"Look up to the Big Dipper every night," he'd said, "and think of me standing right on that handle, waving to you."

Mary closed her eyes against the tears that blurred the stars above. "Oh, God, keep him safe, please, and thank You." She looked out again, and the heavens seemed brighter, especially the star right at the end of the dipper handle.

Each morning she greeted the day with, "Thank You for the day, Lord, and thank You that You are watching over Will." After that, she was usually too busy to think.

The Erickson house sported a new coat of white paint, and the yard had not only been trimmed, but the flower beds along the walk were all dug, ready for planting the annuals now that the likelihood of a last frost was past.

I could do that for them, Mary thought as she lingered so as to arrive at the time Doc Harmon had set. *After all, two little children won't take all my time. And Mrs. Norgaard said a woman came to clean and do some of the cooking. I know Clarissa will come help me if I need it.* Clarissa was her younger sister, after Grace. With six kids in their family, there was always someone to help out, even with all the work they did around home.

The two cars arrived at nearly the same time. The man getting out of the first wore a black wool coat as if it were still winter. A homburg hat covered hair the color of oak bark and shaded dark eyes that seemed to have lost all their life. His smile barely touched his mouth, let alone his eyes. Tall and lean, he stooped some, as if the load he bore was getting far too heavy.

Dr. Harmon crossed the grass to take Mary's arm and guide her to meet her host. "Kenneth Oien, I want you to meet Mary Moen, the young woman who has agreed to help you for the summer." As the introductions were completed, Mary studied the man from under her eyelashes. Always one to bring home the stray and injured—both animals and people—Mary recognized pain when she saw it.

"Thank you for coming on such short notice. As the doctor might have told you, my wife, Elizabeth, has not wanted to have help with the children. I finally prevailed upon her to let me hire a woman to clean and do some of the cooking. I'm hoping you can make her days a bit easier. She frets so."

"I hope so, too."

"I. . .I haven't told her you were coming."

Mary shot a questioning look at the doctor, who just happened to be studying the leaves in the tree above. *I thought this was all set up. What if she hates me?*

"Perhaps you could just meet her and visit awhile, then come back tomorrow after I see how she responds?"

"Of course," Mary answered, still trying to catch the good doctor's attention.

"I'd best be going then—got a woman about to deliver out west aways." Doc tipped his hat. "Nice seeing you, Kenneth, Mary." He scooted off to his automobile before Mary could get in a word edgewise.

Mr. Oien ushered Mary into the front room of the two-story square home. "Elizabeth, I brought you company."

"Back here," the call came from a room that faced north and in most houses like this one was a bedroom. A child's giggle broke the stillness, followed by another.

When they entered the room, the little ones were playing on a bench at the foot of the bed where Elizabeth lay.

"I'm sorry, Kenneth, I was so weak, I had to come back to bed before I fell over."

"Did you eat something?"

She shook her head.

"Have the children eaten?"

"We ate, Papa." The little boy lifted his head from playing with the Sears catalog.

The little girl scooted around the bed and peeped over the far side.

"Elizabeth, Jenny, and Joey, I brought you some company. This is Mary Moen, just returned from college where she is studying to be a teacher."

Elizabeth smoothed her hair back with a white hand. "I. . .I wasn't expecting company. Please forgive me for. . .for—" She made a general gesture at her dishevelment and the toys spread about the room.

"I'm sorry, but I have to get back to my job. There is no one else there, you see, and I—" Mr. Oien dropped a kiss on his wife's forehead, waved to the children, and vanished out the door.

Mary heard the front door close behind him. So much for that source of help. She looked around for a chair to draw up to the bed. None. The little girl, Jenny, peered at her from across the bed, nose buried in the covers so all Mary could see was round brown eyes and uncombed, curly hair.

"Jenny don't like strangers," Joey announced from his place on the bench.

"I'm sorry, Miss Moen, I—" Elizabeth sighed. "I know Kenneth is trying to help, but he so often doesn't know how." She shook her head. "But then who would?"

"Sometimes talking to another woman helps." Mary came closer to the bed. "Doctor said you have a woman who comes in to clean."

"She is nice enough, a good worker, but she speaks Norwegian, and I don't. My grandmother came from Sweden and Kenneth's grandparents from Norway. He only knows the table grace and a few phrases. Dear God, I don't know what we are going to do."

Mary nodded. "Well, I know what I am going to do. I didn't come here just to visit. I came to help, and you and I will do much better if we are honest up front. Dr. Harmon and Mrs. Norgaard have a habit of fixing things in people's lives, and they decided I could help you and that way I would be too busy this summer to miss my Will, who left on the train three days ago to fight the Germans."

She felt a thrill at saying the words *my Will* out loud. In the secret places of her heart, he'd been her Will since she was ten and he stuck up for her the first time. She looked around the room again. "How about if I move a chair in here for you to sit in while I fix your hair? Then you can hold Jenny while I brush hers."

"I combed my own hair." Still Joey didn't look up. Though he just kept turning the pages of the catalog, he was obviously keeping track of the conversation.

"Are you sure you want to do this?" Elizabeth asked, the ray of hope peeping from her eyes belying the words.

"Ja, I am sure."

By noon when Kenneth came home for dinner, his wife had a smile on her face, Jenny wore a ribbon in her hair, and Joey had helped set the table. Mary took the chicken and dumplings from the stove and set the pot in the middle of the table.

"My land, why I. . .I—" He clasped his wife's hand and sat down beside her at the table.

"Thank you, Kenneth. You brought us a miracle worker."

"Mary said—" Joey slid into his place.

"Miss Moen," his father corrected him.

"Oh." A frown creased his forehead. "She said her name was Mary."

Mary set a platter of sliced bread next to the stew pot. "Okay, we can all say grace and then eat. How's that?" She took the chair closest to the food, just as her mother had always done, so she could serve.

"Mary, you are indeed an answer to prayer," Elizabeth said, extending her hand when Mary was ready to leave for home.

"You want me to come back then?"

"With all my heart."

Mary thought about the Oien family as she walked home in the late afternoon. Mr. Larson, the banker, tipped his hat as he passed her on the way home. Mrs. Johnson called hello from the door of the general store, and Miss Mabel waved from behind her display of hats in the ladies' shoppe. How good it felt to be home, where she knew everyone and everyone knew her.

That night around the supper table, Knute, the oldest of the Moen boys, announced, "I want to enlist like Will did, before there ain't no more Germans to fight."

Mary's heart sprung a new crack. Not her brother, too.

Chapter 4

"Y ou have a letter!" Daniel met her halfway home a few evenings later.

"From Will?" Mary broke into a run to meet him. A raised eyebrow from the hotel manager made her drop back to a decorous walk.

Daniel skidded to a stop, his cheeks pink from the exertion. "It is, it is! Read it aloud."

"How about if I read it first to myself and then to you?"

"Awww, Mary. I want to know how he is. Does he like being a shoulder?"

"Soldier, Danny boy, soldier." Mary grinned down at him. She slit the envelope with care and pulled out a flimsy sheet of paper. Well, Will certainly wasn't one to waste words on paper any more than he did in person. Working with Dag Weinlander had taught him many things through the years, including how to conserve energy and speech.

My dearest Mary. The word dearest sent a thrill clear to the toes of her black pointed shoes. *I cannot tell you how much I miss the sight of your sweet face. When you were away at school, I always knew that if I grew desperate enough, I could take a train to Fargo and see you, if only briefly. Now I am clear across the continent from you, and so I commend you to the care of our loving God, for He can be with you when I cannot.*

Mary dug in her bag for a handkerchief.

"Is Will sick? Something is wrong." Daniel backpedaled in front of her so he could watch her face.

"No, silly, it's just that I miss him."

"Oh." He turned and walked beside her, slipping his hand in hers in spite of being out in public.

Mary continued reading. *I never dreamed people could be so ferocious with each other. The sergeants here shout all the time and expect us to do the same. When I think we are being trained to kill our fellowmen, my soul cries out to God to stop this war before anyone else dies. But the Huns must be stopped or the world will never be a safe place in which to love and raise our children.*

Mary tucked the letter in her pocket. She would have to read it later when she could cry along with the heartfelt agony of the man she loved. Will had never been afraid to stand up for the weaker children, and he was carrying that same strength into the battle for freedom.

That night she could not see the Big Dipper; clouds covered the sky.

Within a week Mary had both Joey and Jenny waiting by the front windows for her arrival. Mrs. Oien brightened when her young friend walked into the room, and she seemed to be getting stronger. While she sometimes slipped into staring out the window, she more often read to the children and would pinch her cheeks to bring some color to them before Mr. Oien returned home for dinner.

"How would it be if I took the children home to play with my brothers and sisters this afternoon?" Mary asked after dinner one day. "We have a big swing in our backyard, and the cat in the stable has new kittens."

"Kittens." Joey looked from his father to his mother, his heart in his eyes.

"Now, no pets. Your mother has plenty to do already." Mr. Oien effectively doused the light in the child's eyes.

"You can play with them at my house; they are too little to leave their mother yet." Mary stepped into the breach. As far as she was concerned, an animal might make things more lively in this often-silent home. Her mother had never minded when the children brought home another stray—of any kind. In fact, she frequently brought them home herself.

"Perhaps you would like to come, too," she said to Elizabeth. "I know you would love visiting with my mother."

"Another time, dear, when I am feeling stronger." Elizabeth smiled at her children. "But you two go on and have a good time."

Walking down the street with a child's hand in each of hers, Mary pointed out the store, the post office, and the hotel. But when she passed the livery, all she could think was that Will wasn't the one pounding on the anvil out back, most likely fitting shoes to one of the farmer's horses.

Jenny refused to leave the kittens. She plunked her sturdy little body down by the nest the cat had made in the hay under the horse's manger and giggled when the kittens nursed. She reached out a fat little finger and stroked down the wriggling kittens' backs.

Ingeborg had come out to the stable with Mary to watch. "I can't believe one so little would have the patience to sit like that. She is just enthralled with the kittens."

Joey had looked them over and then gone to see what the boys were doing. Knute was hoeing weeds in the garden and Daniel followed behind on hands and knees, pulling out the weeds too close to the plants for the hoe to work. He showed Joey which were weeds, and the little boy had followed the older one from then on. When they found a worm, Joey cupped it in his hands and brought it to Mary.

"Did you ever see such a big worm?" he asked.

"I think tomorrow we will dig in your flower beds and perhaps find some there." Mary stroked the hair back from the boy's sweaty forehead. Pulling weeds in the June sun could be a hot task.

"Not this big. This is the biggest worm ever. Can I take it home to show Mama?"

Mary nodded. But when Joey stuck the wriggling worm in his pocket, she shook her head. "He'll die there. Come on, let's find a can for him, and you can put dirt in it." By the time Ingeborg called the children in for lemonade, Joey had several more worms in his can.

"Mor, could we take Joey fishing?" Daniel asked, wiping cookie crumbs from his mouth. All had gathered on the porch for the afternoon treat.

Ingeborg looked up. "I don't see why not. Mary, where is Jenny?"

Mary put her finger to her lips and pointed to the barn. When she and her mother tiptoed into the horse stall, they saw Jenny on the hay, sound asleep. The mother cat and kittens were doing the same.

"I checked on her a few minutes ago and decided to leave her there. Isn't she a darling?"

"You children used to love to sleep in the hay, too. How is their mother, really?"

Mary shook her head. "She scares me sometimes, Mor. It's as though she isn't even there, and other times she is so sad. I don't know what to do to help her." Mary pondered the same question that night when she added to the week's letter to Will. "I wonder about Elizabeth Oien," she wrote. "She loves her husband and children but seems to be slipping away from them. What makes one person have such a strong will to live, like Mrs. Norgaard, and another unable to overcome a bodily weakness? Doc says she has never been the same since Jenny was born. I guess it was a hard time and she nearly died. But the children had such fun at our house."

She went on to describe the afternoon. She closed the letter as always, "May God hold you in His love and care, Your Mary."

Joey caught two fish and a bad case of hero worship. Jenny pleaded every day, "Kittens, pease see kittens." Daniel spent as much time at the Oiens as he did at home. And Mr. Oien paid Mary double what they'd agreed.

"I cannot begin to tell you what a difference you have made in our lives," he said one evening when he handed her the pay envelope. "Elizabeth and I are eternally grateful."

The Fourth of July dawned with a glorious sunrise, and the rest of the day did its best to keep up. The parade started in the schoolyard and followed Main Street to the park, where a bandstand had been set up. There would be speeches and singing, races for the children, carnival booths set up to earn money for various town groups like the Lutheran church ladies, who sold fancy sandwiches and good strong coffee. Mary had worked in that booth since she was old enough to count the change.

The Grange sold hot dogs, the school board ice cream that was being hand-cranked out behind the booth by members of the board, and the Presbyterian church made the best pies anywhere. Knute won the pie-eating contest for the second year in a row, and one child got stung by a bee. The fireworks that night capped a day that made Mary dream of Will even more. Last year they'd sat together, hands nearly touching while the fireworks burst in the sky to the accompaniment of the band. Did they have fireworks in the training camp he was in?

The next day an entire train car of young men left, waving to their families and sweethearts. They were on their way to an army training camp.

Mary stood next to her father, who had given the benediction at the ceremony. "Soon we won't have any young men left," she said softly. "Who is going to run the farms and provide food for the troops if all the workers leave?"

"Those of us left at home. It is the least we can do." John Moen blew his nose. "God have mercy on those boys." He used his handkerchief to wipe the sweat from his forehead. "Unseasonable hot, isn't it?"

"Yes, Father, it is hot, but you can't fool me. That wasn't all sweat you wiped from your face."

"You are much too observant, my dear. You will make a fine teacher; the children will accuse you of having eyes in the back of your head." John took his daughter's arm on one side and his wife's on the other. "Let's go home and make ice cream. I only got a taste yesterday."

The heat continued, made worse by air so full of moisture it felt like they were breathing underwater. Heat lightning danced and stabbed, but it failed to deliver the needed rain. How hot it was became the talk of the town. When the farmers came in to shop on Saturdays, their horses looked as bone-weary as the people.

Mary tried to entertain the Oien children, but Jenny fussed and pleaded to go see the kittens. Mrs. Oien lay on the chaise lounge on the back porch, where it was coolest, but daily Mary watched the woman weaken.

If only it would rain. Dust from the streets coated everything, including the marigolds and petunias she had planted along the front walk. Early each day she carried water to the struggling plants, praying for rain like everyone else.

The cornfields to the south of town withered in the heat. Storm clouds formed on the western horizon but always passed without sending their life-giving moisture to the ground below.

One day Mary came home from the Oiens to find Daniel lying in bed, a wet cloth on his forehead. He looked up at her from fever-glazed eyes. "I don't feel so good, Mary."

The letter lying on the hall table had no better news. Will was boarding the ship to Europe in two days. She checked the postmark. He was already on the high seas.

Chapter 5

He's a mighty sick boy, Ingeborg, I won't deny that." Doc Harmon looked up after listening to Daniel's labored breathing with his stethoscope. "People seem to fall into a couple of characteristics. Everything seems to settle in the chest for some, in the stomach for others. I don't understand it, but with Daniel here, it's always the chest. Onion plaster might help; keep his fever down and thump on his chest and back like this to loosen the mucous up." He cupped his hand and tapped it palm down on the boy's back.

Daniel started to cough after only a couple of whacks, giving the doctor a look of total disbelief.

"I know, son, but you will breathe better this way. Make sure he drinks a lot of water, and keep him as cool as possible. That plaster will heat him up some." He looked Daniel in the eye. "Now you do as your mother says and make sure you eat. Lots of broth—both chicken and beef—are good for building him back up."

He looked back up at Ingeborg. "You take care of yourself, too. This summer complaint is affecting lots of people. What we need is a good rain to clear the air."

The rains held off.

Daniel was finally up and around again but more than willing to take afternoon naps. His favorite place was next to Mary. Mrs. Oien seemed better, too, at least in the early morning and after the sun went down. Mr. Oien bought a newfangled gadget called an electric fan. Everyone wanted to sit in front of it, even when it only moved hot air around. Mary set a pan of water in front of the fan, and that helped them cool more.

July passed with people carrying water to their most precious plants and the farmers facing a year of no crops. At the parsonage, that meant there was no money in the church budget to pay the pastor, and Mary's wages became the lifeline for the Moens.

The weather changed when walnut-sized hailstones pounded the earth and all upon it. What the drought hadn't shriveled, the hail leveled. Ingeborg and Mary stood at the kitchen window and watched the garden they'd so faithfully watered be turned to flat mud and pulp.

"Guess we take God at His word and trust that He will provide." Ingeborg wiped a tear from her eye and squared her shoulders. "The root crops will still be good, and we already had some beans put up. I lived without tomatoes for years, so I know we can do so again. And the corn, well, next year we'll have corn again. At least the early apples were plentiful and perhaps we can buy a barrel from Wisconsin or somewhere later in the fall."

Mary knew her mother was indulging in wishful thinking. There would be no money for apples this year. "Mor, I could stay home from school and keep working for the Oiens."

Ingeborg shook her head. "No, my dear, your school is paid for, and you must finish. If it comes to that, I could go take care of her and those little ones."

Her face lost the strained look of moments before. "See, I said the Lord provides. What a good idea. All of ours are in school all day. Why I could do all their cleaning and cooking and perhaps— no, I couldn't cause someone else to lose their job. We will make do."

Mary knew this talking to herself was her mother's way of working things out, whether anyone else listened or not. She often found herself doing the same thing. Each night when she wrote her letters to Will, she sometimes spoke the words as she wrote them, as if that made him hear them sooner. Or rather see them.

It rained for two days, much of the water running off because the earth was too hard to receive it. At night she stood in front of her window and let the cool breeze blow over her skin. Cool, wet air —what a blessing. But she had to remember where the handle to the Big Dipper lay because she couldn't see it through the clouds.

Why hadn't she heard from Will? Where was he?

She still hadn't heard from him when she packed her trunk for the return to school. She wrapped the three precious letters carefully in a linen handkerchief and tied them with a faded hair ribbon. While she'd about memorized the words, she'd reread the pages until the folds were cracking from repeated bending.

Each week she mailed another letter to him, in care of the U.S. Army. Was he getting her letters? They hadn't come back.

The night before she was to leave, she walked to "the mansion" and up to the front door. Fireflies pirouetted to the cadence of the crickets. Mosquitos whined at her ear, but she brushed them away. She barely raised her hand to knock when Dag swung open the door.

"Come in, come in. Gudrun has been waiting for you." He turned to answer over his shoulder. "Yes, it is Mary." When he ushered her in, he whispered. "I told you she'd been waiting."

"Sorry, I should have come sooner."

"She's in the library."

Mary nodded. She loved coming to this house with its rich velvets and artfully carved sofas and whatnot tables. The embossed wallpaper gleamed in the newly installed electric lights that took the place of the gas jets.

Mrs. Norgaard sat behind the walnut desk that had belonged to her husband when he owned the bank. While she still owned the Soldall Bank, she employed a manager who ran it and only reported to her quarterly, unless of course, there was an emergency.

"Come in, my dear and sit down." She took off her spectacles and rubbed the bridge of her nose. "I'm glad you could humor an old woman like me this last night you have with your family."

"They will see me off in the morning." Mary took in a deep breath and voiced something that had been on her heart and mind for the last weeks. "If paying my school expenses is a hardship for you this year, I could stay—"

"Absolutely not. You will finish your year out, and then you can teach. The children of North Dakota need teachers like you. If you think a few months of drought and then a hailstorm will wipe out commerce around here, you just don't understand the world yet.

"Companies make a great deal of money during wartime—I sometimes think that is why men start them—and our bank has invested wisely. I can afford your schooling, and you will not hear of my bank foreclosing on the farmers because they can't make their payments on time this year. Or anyone else for that matter. I hear your mother is going to take over at the Oiens?"

Mary nodded.

"That is good. But I have a feeling you've been worrying about the church paying your father's salary." She tipped her head to look over the tops of her gold wire spectacles.

"Some. My mother says they will make do, but I know it is hard to feed seven mouths, and five of the children are growing so fast we can't keep them in shoes."

"You are not to worry. If I'd known John hadn't gotten paid last month, it never would have happened, and you can bet your life it won't happen again." Mrs. Norgaard sat up straighter. "Those men can bungle things up so bad sometimes, it takes me weeks to just figure it out."

Mary knew she referred to the deacons who ran the business of the congregation. "How'd you find out?" Curious, Mary leaned forward in her chair.

"I have my ways, child."

"Doc Harmon?" Mary shook her head. "No, he's not on the board. Mr. Sommerstrum?" At the twinkle in Gudrun's eye, Mary laughed. "Mrs. Sommerstrum."

"I'll never tell, but it's a good thing some men talk things over with their wives, even if it's only to share the gossip."

Mary nodded. "I see. I've often wondered how you keep such good tabs on the goings on in Soldall when you don't go out too often. Mrs. Sommerstrum tells Mrs. Hanson, and Mrs. Hanson tells you." Mrs. Hanson had been the housekeeper at the mansion ever since Mary could remember.

Gudrun nodded. She reached in a drawer, removed an envelope, and handed it across the shiny surface of the desk. "Here. And I don't want you scrimping and going without to send part of that money home, you understand me?"

447

Mary nodded, guilt sending a flush up her neck. *How did she know what I'd been thinking of?*

"Ah, caught you, did I?" At the girl's slight nod, Gudrun continued. "Now that we have that out of the way, I have a very personal question to ask. Have you heard from Will?"

"No, not since early July, and that letter had been written while he was on the ship."

"Neither have we. That's not like our Will." She stared at the desk before her. "Did he say anything about where they were sending him?"

Again, Mary shook her head.

Gudrun nodded and rose to her feet. "Well, as the old saying goes, no news is good news. Come, let's have a last cup of coffee and some of Mrs. Hanson's angel food cake. I think she has a packet ready to send with you, too."

By the time Mary said good-bye to the family in the mansion, she could hardly hold back the tears. It wasn't like she was going clear around the world or anything, but right now Fargo seemed years away.

The next morning was even worse. Daniel clung to her until they were both in tears. John finally took the child in his arms while Ingeborg hugged her daughter one last time. Mary smiled through her tears and ruffled Daniel's hair while at the same time hugging her father. She went down the line, hugging each of her brothers and sisters. "Now, promise me, all of you, that when I ask your teacher at Christmastime how you are doing, he will have a good report for me."

They all nodded and smiled at her.

"Hey, I'm not leaving forever, you know."

"It just seems like it."

The train blew its whistle, and the conductor announced, "All aboard."

Mary stepped on the stool and up the stairs. She waved one last time and hurried inside so she could wave again out the window. Slowly the train pulled out of the station, and when she could see them no more, she sank back in her seat to wipe her eyes. Why was leaving so hard when she had so much to look forward to?

As the miles passed, she thought back to the last night she had seen Will. The small package she'd given him contained one of her treasures, the New Testament given her by her parents on her twelfth birthday. "Will you keep this with you to remind you always how much I love you and how much more God loves you?"

"I will keep it in my shirt pocket," he'd replied, never taking his gaze from hers while he put the Testament next to his heart. "But I need no reminder."

The kiss they'd shared had been only sweeter with the small book tucked between them.

At Grand Forks, two of Mary's friends from the year before boarded, and they spent the remainder of the trip catching up on their summers. When Mary told them Will had gone to war, Janice said her brother had left, too. Dorie shook her head. "I can't believe all our boys are going over there. What if they don't come home? Who will we marry?"

Mary rolled her eyes. "Leave it to you to keep the most important things right out front." The three laughed, but Mary felt a pang of fear. What if Will didn't come home?

One evening, toward the middle of October, she returned to her room to find a message saying there was a gentleman waiting in the parlor. He wanted to talk with her. Mary flew back down the stairs, her heart pounding. Perhaps it was Will!

But when she slid open the heavy door, her father and Dag Weinlander sat in the armchairs facing the fireplace. From the looks on their faces, she knew.

"He's dead, isn't he?" How could she say the words? Dead, what did that mean?

John shook his head. Dag cleared his throat. "We hope not." He extended the letter bearing an official seal at the top.

Mary read it quickly, then went back to read each word one at a time. *We regret to inform you that Private First Class Willard Dunfey is missing in action and presumed dead.* The date was three months earlier.

Chapter 6

T hen he isn't dead." Mary went to stand in front of the fire. She wanted to throw the horrible letter in and let the flames devour it.

"We can pray that he isn't," John said. He stepped closer and wrapped an arm around her shoulders.

"Father, wouldn't I know if Will no longer lived on this earth? I mean, he can't have been dead for three months and me not sense it, could he?"

"I don't know, child." John shook his head. "I just don't know. The Almighty hasn't seen fit to let me know many things."

Mary looked up at her father. The lines had deepened in his face and his hair showed white all over. "What's been happening?"

"I had two funerals last week of boys shipped home to be buried. The oldest Gustafson boy and Teddy Bjorn. What can I say to those grieving parents—that this was God's will?"

He laid his cheek on the top of her head, now nestled against his shoulder. "I cannot say that war is God's will, that He is on the side of the right. He loves the Germans, too, not just the Americans and the English and French. We are all His children, so how can we go about killing each other?" His voice had softened on the last words. "How?"

Mary felt the shudder that passed through him. Her gentle father, who loved all the children of the parish and their parents and relatives. Who never preached the fire and brimstone of other churches because he said God is love and His grace is made perfect in our human weakness. This man now had to bury the ones he loved, because of man's inhumanity to man.

But was war really human? She'd sat through many discussions and heard heart-stirring speeches about fighting for freedom, but did freedom have to come at the cost of so many lives? She had no answers, only questions.

Had Will really gone to his heavenly home, or was he on earth, suffering some unspeakable agony? If he were alive, wouldn't he have contacted her?

"You may have to accept the fact that he is gone." John drew his arms away and stepped back so he could see her face more clearly.

"But not now!"

"No, not now."

Mary straightened her shoulders, reminiscent of Mrs. Norgaard. She forced a smile to her quivering lips. "How is Daniel? And Mother with the Oiens? Did Mr. Oien give in yet and let Jenny have a kitty? She loves them so. How have you been? You're looking tired." Before he could answer, she turned to Dag, who had been sitting quietly. "How are Mrs. Norgaard and Clara?" Perhaps if she asked enough questions, the greater one would disappear.

"We are all fine," her father finally managed to insert. "In fact, with the cooler weather, Daniel has been doing well. Hasn't missed a day of school, but he would have today if he could have hidden out in my pocket to come along. He is counting the days until you come home for Christmas. Said to tell you he prays for Will every night."

That nearly undid her. She blinked several times and stared into the fire until she had herself under control. "Have you had supper?" When they shook their heads, she looked up at the carved clock on the mantel. "I'm sure Mrs. Killingsworth will let me fix you something in the kitchen. Where are you staying?"

"We aren't. We will catch the eleven o'clock back north. I just felt it important to give you this news in person, not through a letter or over the telephone."

Mary placed a hand on his arm. "Father, you are so kind. How lucky I am that I was born to you and Mor." She spun away before he could answer. "Let me check on supper for you."

An hour later she waved them on their way. "Thank you for coming along with him, Dag. You are a good friend."

He tipped his black felt hat to her. "Mrs. Norgaard just wanted me to check up on her investment; this seemed as good a time as any." The twinkle in his eye let her know he was teasing.

"Well, then, since this was a business trip, thank you for bringing my father along." She hugged her father one last time. "Pass that on to everyone, okay?"

She kept the smile in place as long as they looked back, but when she closed the door, the tears could no longer be held back. She stumbled against the lower step of the staircase and sat down. Leaning her head against the newel post, she couldn't have stopped the tears had she tried.

One by one the other young women in the boardinghouse came down the stairs and clustered around her. One offered a handkerchief; another went for a glass of water. Still another slipped into the music room and, sitting down at the piano, began playing the hymns they'd learned as children.

As the music washed over them, soon one began humming and then another.

When the storm of tears finally abated, Mary listened to the humming in harmony. Had a chorus of angels come just to give her strength? She closed her eyes and leaned against the post. They drifted from melody to melody as the pianist did, until she finally let the last notes drift away.

"Amen." As the notes died away, Janice took Mary's arm and tugged her to her feet. Together, arms around each other's waists, they climbed the stairs to the bedroom they shared.

"Thank you, all," Mary whispered. Talking loudly would have broken the spell.

When despair grabbed at her in the days to come, she remembered that peaceful music and the love of her friends. In spite of the official letter, each evening Mary added tales of the day to her own letters to Will. She continued to send them, refusing to allow herself to speculate about what was happening to them.

"I guess I'm afraid that if I quit, Will will be dead, and if I keep on, there's a chance he is alive," she explained to Janice one night. They'd been studying late because exams were coming up.

"How can you keep on going and not let it drag you down?" Janice tightened the belt of her flannel robe. "The not knowing—" She shook her head so her dark hair swung over one shoulder. She combed the tresses with her fingers and leaned back against the pillows piled at the head of her bed. "Makes me glad I don't have a sweetheart yet."

"I wouldn't trade my friendship and love for Will for all the men on campus."

"There are several who would ask if you gave them the chance."

"Janice!" Mary turned in her chair and locked her hands over the back. "I haven't treated any one of them as more than a friend."

"I know that. You act like you are already married, for heaven's sake. I'm just telling you what I see. And hear."

"Oh, pooh, you're making that up." Mary turned back to her books. "Be quiet, I have to get this memorized."

But Mary recognized that her skirts hung looser about her waist and the shadows that lurked beneath her eyes grew darker, as if she hadn't enough sleep. Each night she committed Will to her heavenly Father's keeping and waved goodnight to him on the last star of the handle.

Two days before she left for home, she received a letter from her mother. *My dear Mary,* she read. *I have some sad news for you. Mrs. Oien, my dear friend Elizabeth, died from pneumonia two days ago. Dr. Harmon said she had no strength to fight it, and I could see that. I was with her when she breathed her last, as was Mr. Oien.*

He is so broken up, I want to take him in my arms like I do Daniel, to comfort him. The funeral is tomorrow. The children are with us for the time being, as Kenneth can't seem to know what to do with them. He stayed home from work for the first day but said he was going crazy in that house without her.

The rest of us are eagerly waiting for your return. God keep you, my dear. Your loving mother.

Mary laid the paper in her lap and looked out the window into the blackness. A streetlight up by the corner cast a round circle of light on the freshly fallen snow. Clouds, pregnant with moisture, covered the twinkling stars. The night felt heavy, like the news in her lap.

"Oh, Elizabeth," Mary whispered, "how you must have fought to stay with your children. And your poor husband. Good-bye, my friend. Go with God." She sat down and wrote a letter of condolence to Mr. Oien, knowing she would get back to town nearly as soon as the letter but feeling she needed to write it anyway.

"What happened now?" Janice asked when she came in some time later.

Mary handed her the letter.

"Oh, that poor man." Janice looked up from her reading. "He'll need someone to care for his children." She tilted her head slightly sideways and looked at Mary. "You won't think you have to stay home next term and care for them?"

"No, I promised Mrs. Norgaard I would finish this year. I just grew to care for Elizabeth so much last summer, and the children, Joey and Jenny, will be lost."

"Not if your mother has anything to do with it."

"Or Doc Harmon and Mrs. Norgaard. They'll probably have him married off in a month or two." Mary's smile slipped. "Men do that you know—marry again right away. I don't know how they can."

"For some I think marrying is like changing underwear. You do what's necessary."

"Janice Ringold!" Mary, feeling her jaw hit her chest, looked at her friend. The shock of the words made them both laugh. "You are outrageous, you know that?"

"I know. My mother always said my mouth would get me in trouble. 'Men don't like outspoken young ladies.' If I heard her say that once, I heard her a thousand times."

"Didn't help much, did it?" They chuckled again.

But before Mary fell asleep that night, she added an extra prayer for the Oien family along with her others, and as always, she gave Him Will.

The house smelled like cinnamon and fresh-baked bread when Mary tiptoed in through the front door. Candles in the windows were ready to be lit on Christmas Eve, a pine tree from Minnesota filled the usual spot in the corner of the parlor, and garlands of cedar trimmed the doorway. Mary felt a pang; she'd missed the house decorating again. If only she'd had her last exam early in the week like many of the others, she could have left sooner. She could hear her mother in the kitchen, removing something from the oven.

Mary shut the door softly, hoping there would be no squeak, and when that was accomplished, she crossed the room to the kitchen. "Surprise!"

"Oh, my heavens!" Ingeborg grabbed at the sheet of cookies that was headed for the floor. When she had the cookies safely on the table, she put her hand to her heart. "What are you trying to do, you naughty child, give your mother a heart attack?" But the smile that took in her whole face and her outstretched arms made light of her scolding words. "Land sakes, Mary, I didn't think you were ever coming."

A child's whimper came from the bedroom.

"Now see what you did—woke up Jenny. Joey won't be far behind."

"They are here?" Mary hugged her mother and began unwinding the bright red scarf about her neck. She hung it and then her coat on the rack by the door and reached outside for her valise. "You think they will remember me?"

"With Daniel telling them every day that Mary is coming, what do you think?" Ingeborg cocked her head and listened. "I think she'll settle down again. Give us time for a cup of coffee and some catching up."

"I have another box at the station; it was too heavy to carry."

"Mary, you didn't spend your money on Christmas presents, did you?"

"Some, and some I made, like always. There are some books there for my classroom—when I get a classroom, that is." She sat down at the table and watched her mother take down the good china cups. They only came down for special company and the Ladies' Aid. Ingeborg set the one with tiny rosebuds around the rim in front of her daughter. It had been her favorite since when she was little and they had tea once in a great while.

Oh, I'm home, Mary thought. *I never know how much I miss it and my family until I come back. But this time there will be no Will to come sweep me off my feet.* She sighed. A bit of the sunlight went out of the day. *You knew better,* she scolded herself. *You knew he wasn't here, so behave yourself. Don't take your feelings out on Mor, who is so happy to see you.*

After Ingeborg poured the coffee, she took her daughter's chin in gentle fingers and tilted her face toward the light. "Have you been sick?"

Mary shook her head.

"Working too hard and not sleeping enough?" She tilted the girl's head down and kissed the forehead. "Grieving for Will?" Her words were soft as the ashes falling in the stove.

"Oh, Mor." Mary flung her arms around her mother's waist and buried her face in the flour-dusted apron. "I can't believe he's dead. Wouldn't I know, some part of me down in my heart? Wouldn't I know for sure?"

Ingeborg stroked the soft curls and brushed the wisps of hair back that framed Mary's face. "I've heard tell of that, of mothers with their children, sometimes of those who've been married for many years, but—" She bent down and laid her cheek on Mary's head. "My dear, I just don't know."

They stayed that way, comforting each other for a time. Finally Mary drew away.

Ingeborg brushed some flour off her daughter's cheek. "Now the coffee is gone cold. Let me heat it up." She poured the brown liquid back in the pot and set it on the front burner again. "One thing I do know. When the time comes, you say good-bye, knowing that you loved him and he loved you and love goes on forever. But Will wouldn't want you to grieve overlong; he'd want you to get on with your life."

"I'll be teaching next year. Isn't that getting on with my life?"

"Ja, it is. God, I know, has special plans for you, and when we cry, He says He is right here with us. As He is all the time."

Mary watched the peace on her mother's face and heard

the faith in her voice. Ingeborg's faith never wavered. Could she ever be strong like that?

"Mary's home!" The cry rang through the house when school let out and the children ran in through the door. Jenny and Joey came out of their rooms, rubbing their eyes, and after a moment, joined the others in the circle around Mary. Everyone talked at once until the ceiling echoed with happy laughter.

Supper that night continued in the same vein. When Mr. Oien came to pick up his children, Ingeborg invited him to stay for a bite to eat. They pulled out the table and set in another leaf so there would be room.

Once or twice his smiles at the antics of the younger Moen children nearly reached his eyes. "Thank you so much," he said as he readied to leave after the meal was finished.

"You're welcome to stay longer." John leaned back in his chair and crossed his legs at the ankles.

"I. . .I'd best be going—put these two to bed, you know." He nodded toward Joey and Jenny, who were being bundled up by the Moens. "Again, thank you." He put his hat on and picked up Jenny. "Come, Joey." He took the boy's hand, and the three went down the walk to where he had parked his automobile at the front gate.

"He should have started that contraption first." Ingeborg shut the door and peeked through the lace curtain. "Knute, why don't you go out and help him crank that thing?"

The oldest Moen son did as asked. When he returned, he rubbed his hands together. "If it weren't for cranking those things, I'd want one the worst way."

"Wanting never hurt anyone." John winked at Mary. "I was hoping since you were home, you would read to us tonight."

"Of course. What are you reading?" She took the book her father handed her. "Oh, Charles Dickens and old Scrooge. How I love it." As soon as the dishes were washed and put away, the family gathered in the parlor and Mary began to read. After the chapter was finished, she picked up the Bible that lay on the end table and opened it to the Psalms. "I keep going back to this one. 'Oh Lord, thou has searched me, and known me.'"

"Psalm 139." Daniel beamed at being the first to recognize it. They'd played this game of guessing the Scripture all the years of their lives, until now they were all well-versed in Bible knowledge.

Mary continued reading and, when she finished, closed the book. "Far, will you pray tonight?"

John nodded. "Father in heaven, Thou dost indeed know us right well. We ask You to forgive us our sins and fill us with Your Holy Spirit so that we may do the works Thou hast given us." When he came to the end, he finished with a blessing and they all said, "Amen."

"Now I know I am home for sure," Mary said with a sigh and a smile.

She felt that same way in church a few nights later when they gathered to celebrate the birth of the Christ child. Singing the old hymns and hearing the words embedded in her memory from eighteen Christmases made her want to wrap her arms around every person in the room. *Please, God, if You will, send me a sign that Will is either here on earth or up there with You. I want to do Your will, and I thank You that You sent Your Son to walk this earth. All I ask, dear Father, is a small sign.*

Christmas passed in a blur of happiness, only saddened when Mary thought of Will and what he was missing. Two days later, Dag came to see them.

"I have something that came in the mail today." He stopped, swallowed hard, and continued.

Mary felt an icy hand grip her heart.

Dag held out something metal on his hand. "They say these are Will's dog tags, taken from a body buried in Germany."

Mary couldn't breathe.

Chapter 7

"Mary, are you all right?"

She heard the voice as if from a great distance. "I. . . I'm fine. Why?" Had she been sitting in the chair when. . . ? Memory crashed back and she whimpered. "No, no, please no." *Dear God, please, that's not the sign I wanted. I know I asked for a sign but. . .*

Dag stood before her, his hand clenched at his side, a small piece of chain dangling between thumb and forefinger.

Now, why would I notice something like that? Chains don't matter at this point. But that one did. The chain that Will had worn so proudly now brought agony to his beloved.

"Mary." Her father's face swam before her eyes. He cuddled her cold hands in his warm ones and waited for her to respond.

"Yes." She left off studying the shimmering hairs on the backs of his hands and looked at him. The tears fighting to overflow his blue eyes undid her. She threw herself into his arms and wept.

Minutes later—but what seemed like hours—she accepted the handkerchief from her mother and mopped at her eyes. "I wanted him to come home. I asked God, and you said God always answers our prayers. I prayed that He would bring Will home."

"I know. I did, too."

"And me." Dag lowered himself into a chair and leaned forward. "All of us prayed for that."

"Then why?" She shouted her question, shaking her fist in the face of God. "Why did He let Will die? Others are coming home—why not Will?"

John bent his head. "I don't know. I do not understand the

459

mind of God or some of His purposes. All I know is that His heart breaks, too, and He holds us close. Close like me holding your hand and even closer. And the other thing I know with all certainty is that you will see Will again."

"I know about heaven, but I want him here." Tears dripped down her face.

"I know that, too."

Mary felt her mother's hands on her shoulders, warm and secure.

"God could have saved Will." Again she felt like lashing out.

"Ja, He could have." The hands on her shoulders rubbed gently.

"Then why didn't He?" Mary hiccuped on the last word.

"I 'spect every wife, mother, friend, feels the same. None of us want someone we love to be killed." John rubbed the back of her hands with his thumbs.

"Am I being selfish?"

"No more'n anyone else. But death comes. It is part of life, and we look forward to heaven all the time."

Mary sat silently. Then she shook her head. "It's not fair. Will is such a good man."

"Yes, he was. You can be proud he was your friend and loved you with all his heart."

It bothered her that her father said "was." She couldn't think of Will as "was." *He is!* Her rebellious mind insisted. *Will is.*

When she awoke in the middle of the night, after alternately praying and crying, she found her mother sitting by the bed, sound asleep. Mary fought back tears again. This was so like her mother, keeping watch over those she loved and those who needed her. Her presence comforted the girl, and she drifted back to sleep.

Each day felt like she waded through spring gumbo three feet deep. Every part of her felt heavy, even to her eyelids and the tops of her ears. She pushed her hair back and finally braided it and coiled the braid in a bun at the base of her head to keep the weight of it from pulling her over. All she really wanted to do was sleep, for only in sleep did the knowledge disappear. But on waking, it always returned. They said Will was dead.

"You can stay home, you know." Ingeborg helped fold the undergarments to put in Mary's traveling valise.

"Would it be any better?" Mary turned from sorting through her books and deciding which had to go back with her.

"It would for me, because then I could make sure you eat and get enough rest and—"

"And cluck over me like one of your chicks?"

"You are one of my chicks." Ingeborg smoothed a ribbon into place on a nightgown. "No matter how grown-up you get—even when you have a family of your own—you will always be my eldest chick."

"But I have to grow up, and learning to keep going is part of that, isn't it?"

"Ja, and I know our heavenly Father will watch over you and keep you safe."

I hope He does a better job with me than He did with Will. Mary was horrified at her thoughts. They just snuck up on her and dashed off before she could rope them in and discipline them to behave.

Later, her bags all packed, Mary bundled up to walk over to the mansion to say good-bye to Mrs. Norgaard. The north wind bit her cheeks and tried to burrow into her bones.

"Come in, my dear, come in." Clara swung the door wide open. "Are you about frozen clear through, out walking in this cold?"

Mary stamped the snow from her boots and smiled at the diminutive dynamo in front of her. Clara Weinlander often reminded Mary of her mother. If there was something that needed doing, those two women would take it on.

"Herself is waiting for you." Mrs. Hanson secretly used that nickname for her employer, and at times, so did half the town. "We'll bring the coffee right in."

After their greetings, Mrs. Norgaard beckoned Mary to sit beside her on the sofa in front of the south windows. "I want to say something to you before the others come in."

Mary sat and turned to face her benefactress. "Yes."

"Losing one you love is one of the hardest things in life, but there's something I learned through all that. The Bible says, 'This too shall pass,' and it will. Right now you doubt me, but in a few weeks, months, the pain will be less and there will be some days when you surprise yourself because you didn't think of missing him at all."

Gudrun covered Mary's hands with her own. "Trust me, child, I know it is true. And one day you will think of Will, and the memory will be sweet. For you see, he will be closer now than he could have been when he was alive."

Mary felt the tears burning and closed her eyes. "But . . .but I still feel he might be alive, somewhere, somehow."

"I know, the mind plays tricks like that on us. Oh, how often I thought my husband would be home in half an hour. But he was gone, and finally I came to accept that. And that's when I began to live again." She looked up to see Clara and Mrs. Hanson with the serving trays. "And much of that is thanks to these two. They bullied me into wanting to live."

"That we did." Mrs. Hanson set the tray down. "And would again."

"Just think of all the exciting things you would have missed." Clara sat in the chair and leaned forward to pour the coffee from the silver pot. "Mary, help yourself to those cookies. Mrs. Hanson baked them just for you, and there's a box for you to take with you."

In spite of herself, Mary left the mansion feeling a little less weighed down by life.

With papers to write and new classes, Mary found herself busier than ever. Her friends gathered round her and made sure she ate and went with them to the lectures on campus to hear the suffragettes trying to get the suffrage bill passed through Congress. When it was defeated, they all held a wake.

When General Pershing made his triumphant entrance into Paris, they all listened to the speeches on the radio in the parlor. Surely peace would be coming soon.

But the war continued, and school drew to a close. The entire Moen tribe came down on the train for Mary's graduation from normal school. She would now be able to teach grades one through high school in the state of North Dakota. Mary almost, but not quite, kept from looking for Will in the well-wishers.

"To think, a daughter of mine has graduated from teaching school." Ingeborg clasped her hands at her waist.

"I won't be the last." Mary removed the square black mortar board that crowned her head. "I will help pay for the next one who wants to go. Has Knute talked about what he wants to do?" Her brother next in line was due to graduate from high school at the end of May. She looked down at the brother tugging on her arm. "Yes, Daniel?"

"Far said if you were to change, we could go have ice cream."

"Oh, he did, did he? Well, let me congratulate my friends over there, and we will all walk to the soda fountain."

"I think we need a place like this in Soldall," Ingeborg said after they took their places in two adjoining booths.

"That's right, Mother, you need something else to do." Mary shook her head.

"I didn't say I should do it." She looked around at the scroll-backed metal chairs and the small round tables. "But think what—"

"Don't even think such a thing." John leaned across the table to bring his face closer to his wife's. "You have far too much to do right now."

"Well."

"Mother!" Mary couldn't tell if her mother was serious or just teasing. After the young man took their order, Ingeborg leaned back against the high-backed wooden bench and turned to her daughter. "So, how are you, really?" She studied Mary's face, searching for the truth.

"I am much better. Mrs. Norgaard was right. Only by looking back can I tell how far I've come. I'm not angry at God anymore— or anyone else. I can read His Word and let it bless me again. But I still write my letters every night to Will and collect them in a box. I guess that has become my diary." She didn't tell them of not looking for the Big Dipper anymore. She still had a hard time looking up at the night sky at all. Invariably when she did, her eyes filled with tears and she couldn't make out the stars anyway.

"I could tell a difference in your letters. Your father and I want you to know how proud we are of you."

The sodas arrived, and the conversation turned to how good they tasted and what everyone was planning for the summer.

"Mr. Oien has been writing and asking if I would care for the children again this summer."

"I know," Ingeborg responded. "I think he sees that with all of my own children home, his two little ones might be too much."

"He doesn't know you very well then, does he?" Mary sipped on her straw. Her mother's straw hat had just been knocked askew by an arm belonging to one of the boys, who had been reaching over the back of the bench. Mary gave the hand a pinch and smiled at the "yeow" that her action provoked. Her mother righted the hat with a laugh and a threat to fix the perpetrator good. The booth full of children laughed at her words, knowing their mother would get even somehow, sometime when they least expected it.

Mary felt a glow settle about her heart. How she had missed them, mostly without even knowing it.

"So what will you do?" Ingeborg finally asked.

"I will care for his house and children and keep on searching for my school. I have my application in four different places, so time will tell."

"And that is what you want?"

Mary nodded. "This is what I want. Since God made sure I got through school, He must have a place in mind for me."

But the summer passed swiftly, and still Mary hadn't heard. By the end of August, she had a hard time keeping doubts at bay. Would she get a school? If not, what would she do?

Chapter 8

The letter arrived on a Wednesday.

Mary stared at the postmark, then slit open the envelope with a shaking finger. Grafton lay in the next township, but the school they mentioned was not in town. If they hired her, she would be teaching first through fourth at a country school with two classrooms. Could she come for an interview on Friday?

Could she come for an interview? Did cows give milk? Did the moon follow the sun? An interview! She finally had an interview. And she wouldn't be clear on the other side of the state. She could see the dear faces of her family on the weekends——that is, if she could afford the train. She hurried home to tell her family.

Questions bubbled to the surface. Where would she live? Oh, not with a family that made her share a room and bed with one of their children. Sometimes that was the arrangement. In some places families still took turns boarding the teacher. She'd heard some terrible stories about situations like that. Her feet slowed. If only she could teach right here in Soldall.

"Mary, that is wonderful." Ingeborg clasped her hands in delight. "And so close by."

Mary read the letter out loud, the actual sound of the words making it more of a reality. "So, will you care for the children on Friday for me?" she asked her mother.

"Of course. You must call the people in Grafton and tell them what time your train will arrive. This is late for hiring a new teacher. I wonder what happened there? I hope it was not an illness of the teacher they already had."

Or she didn't want to go back and found a position elsewhere. Mary shook her head. Thoughts like that were better barricaded behind steel doors.

On Friday, Mary boarded the early train and returned home in time for supper, the proud owner of a teaching position. She would report for duty in two weeks in order to have her classroom ready for her pupils.

"So, why did they need a teacher at this late date?" Ingeborg asked after the children were all in bed.

"Miss Brown's mother became ill in Minnesota and she had to go be with her. A man teaches the older grades—has for a long time. I will be staying with a widow about a mile from the schoolhouse and helping her in exchange for board. I met with her, and she seems very nice. She's a bit hard of hearing and speaks German as much as English, but we should do fine."

"Anyone who has you to help them is very blessed indeed. Helping doesn't mean milking cows and such, does it?" Ingeborg wiped her hands on her apron. "You never have had to do farm labor."

"If you ask me, her sons just want someone living with their mother. She said she didn't want to go live with them." Mary's eyes danced. "I think she doesn't want anyone bossing her around." She caught her mother by the hands and whirled around the kitchen with her. "Oh, Mr. Gunderson, the head of the school board, told me three times that they didn't want any fooling around. 'Our teachers must be a model of decorum.'" She deepened her voice to mimic the gentleman. "Mother, this is the twentieth century for pity's sake. He must still be back in the Dark Ages."

"So what did you tell him?"

Mary's smile slipped. "I told him my fiancé was killed in the war and all I was interested in was teaching children the three Rs."

The next afternoon when Mr. Oien came home from work, Mary gave him her good news.

"I'm so very happy for you," he said, but his face showed shock and what was it—bewilderment?

"You knew I planned on teaching school if I could find a position?"

"I did. But since you hadn't said anything, I'd hoped you would stay." He sank down in a chair by the door.

"My mother will watch the children again." Mary stepped to the window to check on the two who were playing outside in the sandbox. They were so sweet, and she would indeed miss them.

"That is not the problem." He paused, then continued in a rush. "I had not planned to mention this yet, what with your grieving for Will and all, but you love my children and you are so good with them and you are such a lovely person, and would you consider marrying me?"

"What did you say?"

"I asked you to marry me." He smoothed his sandy hair back with his hands. A smile came to his face. "I did it. I asked you to marry me."

"But you don't love me."

"How do you know? I love having you here with Joey and Jenny when I come home. I love seeing you play with them. I love hearing you laugh and I—"

"But I don't love you," Mary said the words softly, gently.

"You could, you know. I make a good living, you wouldn't have to teach school, you'd be near to your family whom I know you love dearly, you would have a nice house, and. . ."

Mary's slow shaking of the head forced him to run down.

"Please," he quickly amended, "don't say no right now. Give it some thought. Let me visit you, take you for drives. We could have a picnic—a. . .a. . ."

Mary stared at him. The thought of marrying someone other than Will brought a knot to her throat and tears to her eyes. "I have to go. Thank you for. . .fo—" She turned and bolted out the door.

"What happened to you?" Ingeborg's eyes widened when she saw her daughter's face.

"He. . .he asked me to m—marry him." Mary put a hand to her throat.

"A bit of a surprise, that?" Ingeborg shook her head. "Well, I never." She stirred the kettle simmering on the stove. "Hmm, that idea has possibilities."

"Possibilities! Mother, I don't love Kenneth."

"Yet. Sometimes the best marriages are when two people grow into love."

"Mother! You want me to marry someone I don't love?"

"I didn't say that. But I can see it is a natural choice from his point of view. You are lovely, you are familiar, you know his home, and you love his children. Many men would say that's more than enough basis for marriage. Women have married for a lot less, you know."

Mary felt like she was talking with a total stranger who somehow wore her mother's face. "I don't think I have any more to say to you." She turned on her heel and climbed the stairs to her bedroom. Flinging herself across her bed, she buried her face in her hands. *Oh, Will, why did you have to go and die?*

Time took wings during the days until Mary left, making her breathless most of the time. So much to be finished. In spite of her feelings of misgivings, she continued to care for Joey and Jenny, bringing them back to her mother's on the afternoons when she had errands to run. She wanted her classroom just perfect for her new pupils and spent hours preparing calendars and pictures, lesson assignments, and flash cards for numbers. Mr. Gunderson had said the school didn't have a large budget for supplies—the year had been hard for the farmers, in spite of the high prices for grain due to the war.

Mrs. Norgaard insisted that Dag would drive Mary to her new home so she wouldn't have to take all her things on the train. "God will be with you, child, as you share His love for those children. Don't you forget it."

"I'm not about to." Mary gave the old woman a hug. "You take care of yourself now while I'm away."

"Humph." Gudrun straightened her back, as if it needed it. "I've been taking care of myself since before your mother and father were born. I surely won't stop now." But the twinkle in her faded blue eyes turned the tear that shimmered on her lashes brilliant. She waved one slender hand. "You drive careful now, Dag, you hear?"

Clara, too, stood in the doorway, waving them off. "We'll keep supper for you, Dag. Enjoy the day."

"I wish she could have come." Mary settled back in her seat. The wind whipped the scarf she'd tied around her hat and blew the ends straight out behind her. The thrill of driving such speeds! *One day,* she promised herself, *I will have a car of my own to drive.* The picture of the black roadster driven by Kenneth Oien flashed through her mind. What would it be like, married to him? She liked him well enough. In fact, they could probably be friends. She shrugged the thoughts away. He'd said he'd write and gladly drive up to bring her home for a weekend. She deliberately pushed the thoughts out of her mind.

"So, how goes the blacksmithing?" She turned in the seat so Dag could hear her above the roar of the automobile and the rushing wind.

"Slow. I know I will have to convert more and more to repairing tractors and automobiles and trucks. With the engines improving all the time, we will see more changes than we ever dreamed of."

"I agree." She sought for another topic, but let it lie. Talking above the noise took too great an effort.

Dag carried all her boxes into the schoolroom, and then took the suitcases into the Widow Williamson's two-story square farmhouse and up the stairs to the large bedroom facing east. When he straightened, his head brushed the slanted ceiling, so he ducked a bit.

"This is very nice."

"I think so." Mrs. Williamson had even brought up a desk and chair to set in front of the window. Carved posts stood above a white bedspread, and extra pillows nearly hid the oak headboard. Braided rag rugs by the bed and in front of the high dresser would keep Mary's feet off cold floors in the winter, and there was more than enough space for her simple wardrobe in the double-doored oak chifforobe. A picture of Jesus the Shepherd hung by the door.

"Well, I'd best be on my way." Dag extended his hand. "You call if you need anything. I saw a telephone on the wall downstairs."

"Thank you for all your help." Mary walked him down the stairs, turning at the landing and on down. When his car roared to life and he drove away, she stood on the porch waving long after the dust had settled. She was on her own now—just what she had always wanted. Or had she?

Mary fell in love with her pupils the instant they shuffled through the door. She had sixteen all together: four in the first grade, all so shy they couldn't look up at her; three in the second; five in the third; and four in fourth. The fourth graders already bossed the younger ones, but when she rapped for order, they all sat at attention.

"We will stand for the flag salute." She checked her seating chart. "Arnold, will you lead us?" She put her hand over her pounding heart. Were they as nervous as she? She nodded at the boy on the outside row.

"I pledge allegiance to the flag. . ." They stumbled through the words, some having forgotten them and others having not yet learned.

One of the first graders broke into tears when Mary asked them to repeat the Lord's Prayer. And when they sang the "Star Spangled Banner," she mostly sang solo. These children had a lot to learn.

She had planned on standing in front of them and quizzing them on their reading and numbers, but at the sight of the tears, she called all the children to the side of the room and, sitting down on a chair, told them to sit in front of her. She smiled at each one when she called their names again.

"I need to know who you are, so could you please tell me something you like to do?"

The older children looked at each other wide-eyed.

"Arnold, we'll start with you. What do you like?" And so she went around the group, and by the time she reached the youngest ones, they smiled back at her. One little towheaded girl stared at her teacher with her heart in her eyes.

"You are so pretty," she whispered. "I like you."

Mary felt her heart turn over. "And I like you." She laid the tip of her finger on the little girl's button nose. "Now, let's all learn the pledge of allegiance because we are going to start every day saluting our flag."

"My brother went to war for our flag." One of the boys said. "He never comed home."

Mary knew she was going to have heart problems for certain. "That has happened to many of our young men, so when we salute the flag, we are remembering them at the same time." Thoughts of a star in the Big Dipper handle twinkled through her mind. Remembering. Yes, the sweetness promised by Mrs. Norgaard had finally come.

"A very dear friend of mine went to Europe to fight, too, and never came home." She laid a hand on the head of a little boy who had gravitated next to her knee. "Now, repeat after me, I pledge allegiance to the flag. . ." And so the morning continued. By the time recess came around, Mary felt like running outside to play with the children.

"The first day is always the hardest." Mr. Colburn, his graying hair worn long over the tops of his ears, stood in her doorway. His kind brown eyes and smile that made his mustache wiggle invited her to smile back.

"Is that a promise?" Mary stretched her shoulders. "Mr. Colburn, everyone spoke so highly of you, I feel honored to share your building."

"Yes, well, I try, and the honor is mine. I think we will do well together. My wife insisted I bring you home for supper one night soon. She is so curious about the new teacher, I made her promise not to come see you for herself. We've lived here for ten years, and we are still not considered part of the community. She's hoping you can be friends."

"Isn't that nice? I never turn down the offer of friendship."

"I'll go ring the bell." Mr. Colburn left, and immediately the bell in the tower bonged twice. The children flew to form a line starting with the larger ones and going to the smallest and marched into the building.

Mary took a deep breath and dove back in.

The days fell into a pattern. Up before dawn to make breakfast while Mrs. Williamson did the outside chores. Then walk to school, teach all day, and walk home. Evenings, after she'd washed the supper dishes, were spent preparing for the next day. On Saturday they cleaned house, and on Sunday, Mrs. Williamson's sons took turns driving them to church.

Mary didn't have time to be lonely. She continued to write her letters to Will each night, but now she planned to send them to her mother. Ingeborg would love to hear the stories of her daughter and her small charges.

When Mr. Colburn discovered she could play the piano, he rolled the heavy instrument into her room on the condition that she teach music. The students at Valley School loved to sing. So every afternoon, if all had done their assignments, everyone gathered in Mary's classroom for singing and then Mr. Colburn read to them. His mellow voice played the parts as he read first *The Jungle Book*, by Rudyard Kipling, and then *Oliver Twist*, by Charles Dickens. Mary was as entranced as the children.

Letters came weekly from Kenneth Oien, and Mary grew to look forward to them. While she had yet to go home to visit, his letters were like a window into the life of Soldall. He wrote of the antics of Joey and Jenny and their new friend, Mews, a half-grown cat that had shown up on their doorstep one day. He described the changing of the colors with the frost and the geese flying south. He said they all missed her and looked forward to her coming home.

There's a poet hiding in that man's soul, Mary thought as she read the latest letter. *But can I ever think of him as more than a friend?*

When the phone rang one evening and Mrs. Williamson called up the stairs to say it was for her, Mary felt her heart leap into her throat. Was something wrong at home? Was Daniel sick again?

"Hello?" She knew she sounded breathless, only because she was.

"Mary, this is Kenneth."

"Kenneth? Oh, Mr. Oien. . .uh, Kenneth." She felt like an idiot. Surely they could be on a first-name basis by now, in fact should have been a long time ago.

"I wondered if I could come and get you on Friday afternoon, if you would like to come home, that is. I would take you back on Sunday, after church. I. . .ah, that is—"

Mary took pity on his stammering. "I would love that. Thank you for the invitation."

"Would you like me to come to the school?"

"No, I'll meet you here at Mrs. Williamson's." She gave him the directions and hung up the receiver. She'd heard a click on the party line. Now everyone around would know the new teacher had a beau. Whether he was or not did not matter.

"I think of you a lot," Kenneth said when he stopped the automobile in front of the parsonage that Friday night. Dark had fallen before they reached Soldall, and traveling the rough roads by lamplight had made them drive even more slowly.

What could she say? "I enjoy reading your letters. And thank you for the ride home. Will you be coming to dinner on Sunday?"

"Yes." He smiled at her in the dimness. "And we have been invited to supper on Saturday at the mansion. That is, if you would like to go."

"Why, of course." Mary fumbled for her purse. "Thank you again for the ride."

He got out and came around to open her door, leaving the motor running. "Till tomorrow then." He helped her out and carried her valise to the door. "Jenny and Joey hope you will come see them while you are in town."

"Oh." Mary wondered what had happened to her tongue. Suffering from a lack of words was a new experience for her.

Looking back, she couldn't remember having a nicer time in a long while. While she was fully aware that all her friends and family were playing matchmakers, she couldn't fault them for it.

Kenneth Oien was a very nice man.

But a few weeks later, when he asked her to consider marriage, she shook her head.

"Please don't pressure me," she whispered. "I just cannot answer that yet."

"Yet?" His eager voice came through the darkness. He'd just brought her back from another weekend at home. He touched her cheek with a gentle caress.

Mary held herself still. If that had been Will, the urge to throw herself in his arms would have made her shake. All she felt was a longing to feel more. What was the matter with her?

Chapter 9

The world went crazy on Tuesday, November 11, 1918. Victory Day. The war to end all wars was over.

School bells rang, radio announcers shouted, the people cheered. Some sobbed at the thought their sons might still make it home in one piece. Others cried for those who would never return.

Mary was one of the latter. While her head said, "Thank You, Father, for finally bringing peace," her heart cried for the young man she had seen leave for war.

While the children were out on the playground after eating their lunches, she walked out beyond the coal shed and leaned against the building wall. Letting the tears come, she sobbed until she felt wrung out. When she could finally feel the cold wind biting her cheeks and tugging at her hair, she wiped her eyes and lifted her face to the sun that played hide-and-seek in the clouds.

"Will," she whispered, "I loved you then and I love you now, but I guess it is about time I got on with my life. One more Christmas is all I will ask for, and then if God wants me to marry Kenneth Oien, I will follow His bidding." She waited, almost hoping for an answer, but all she heard was the wind and it was too light to look for that star.

Kenneth and the children joined the Moens for Thanksgiving dinner after the church service. Pastor Moen had thanked God for bringing peace to a world torn asunder by war, and the congregation heartily agreed. Mary refused to let the tears come again. She sat in the front pew but didn't dare look directly up at her father, for she knew the love in his eyes would be her undoing. Why was it always so hard to keep from crying in church?

Several of the boys, now turned men, had returned from the service already, making it easy for some families to give thanks. One even brought back a French wife, and if that didn't start the gossips buzzing. . .

Mary felt sorry for the shy young woman. If only she could speak French to help her out.

They had stuffed goose for dinner, two given them by one of the hunters in the congregation. Ingeborg had been cooking for a week, or so the amount of food on the table testified. Afterward they played charades, and when the two little ones woke up from their naps, they played hide the thimble. Jenny ignored the game and came to sit on Mary's lap, leaning her head back against Mary's chest.

Mary looked up to catch a glance between her parents. *Please, don't push me,* she wanted to cry. Cuddling Jenny was so easy. Would cuddling with her father be as simple?

"You know, Kenneth is a fine young man," John said after the company had left.

"Yes, Father, I know you like him." Mary bit off the colored thread she was using to embroider a rose on a handkerchief for Mrs. Williamson. Making Christmas presents had begun.

"He will make a fine husband," Ingeborg said without looking up from her knitting.

"All right. I know how you feel and I know how he feels. All I want to know now is how God feels."

"And what about you?" John kept his finger in his place in the book. "How do you feel?"

"Like I cannot make a decision yet."

John nodded. "You don't have to."

"I want to go through Christmas first. I will make a decision after the first of the year. Then it will have been a year since we got the final word. But I know one thing for sure, no matter what my decision, I will finish my year at Valley School."

John and Ingeborg both nodded. Daniel wandered back down the stairs, rubbing the sleep out of his eyes. "I heard you talking, and it made me hungry."

Mary laughed as she rose to cut him another piece of pumpkin pie. "You should be as big as Knute with all that you eat."

The weeks before Christmas passed in a blur of preparing a school program and party for the families around Pleasant Valley. They decorated a Christmas tree someone brought from Minnesota and hung chains made from colored paper around the room. But the music made Mary the most proud. The children sang like the angels had from on high, and during the performance even the most stoic fathers dabbed at their eyes more than once.

Mary left for home with her presents completed and bearing treasures given her by her students. Her favorite, if she were allowed to pick, was a card decorated with pressed wildflowers and lettered, "To my teechur."

A snowstorm hung on the northern horizon, so she took the train, rather than allowing Dag or Kenneth to come for her. While it would take a lot of snow to stop the train, automobiles buried themselves in drifts with the ease of children finding a mud puddle.

Her father met her at the station with his horse and buggy. He took her valise and wrapped an arm around her shoulders. "Do you have anything more?"

"Father, at Christmas?" Her laugh pealed out. She pointed to two boxes tied up tightly with twine. "Those are mine. What happened to all the fancy automobiles?"

"Too much snow." John loaded the boxes into the area behind the seat and helped her up. "I sure hope we don't have a blizzard for Christmas."

She told him about the school program on the way home, her arm tucked in his and a robe covering their knees. When her story finished, she said, "You know one good thing about horses?"

"No, what's that?"

"You can talk and hear the other person answer." She leaned closer to him. "Without shouting."

"I know. Sometimes I think if the congregation offered me an automobile, I'd turn it down." He slapped the reins, clucking the gray gelding into a trot. "General, here, and I, we've been through a lot together. An automobile won't take me home if I fall asleep after a late call or listen to me practice my sermon. If he doesn't like one, he shakes his head and snorts. Then I know I need to go back to the desk and keep writing."

Big white flakes drifted before the wind, glistening and dancing in the streetlights. Two days until Christmas. This year they could truly say peace on earth and goodwill to men.

They spent the next two days baking *julekake,* the Norwegian Christmas bread, *sandbaklse,* and *krumkake* and frying *fatigman* and rosettes. The house smelled of nutmeg and cardamom, pine and cedar. No one was allowed to open a door without knocking or peek into closets or on shelves.

Ingeborg spent the late hours of Christmas Eve afternoon beating *rommegrote,* a rich pudding, until the melted butter from the cream rose to the surface. When anyone tried to sneak tastes, she batted them away with her wooden spoon. "If you want some, you'll have to wait or make your own." She'd been saying the same thing every year that Mary could remember.

When they finally trooped off on the walk to church, Mary stayed in the midst of her family. Kenneth finally sat in a pew a few behind them, a look of puzzlement on his face.

With Daniel glued to one side and Beth, her youngest sister, on the other, Mary put her arms around them and let them hold the hymnal. She didn't need to see the words; she'd known the carols all her life. And for a change she could sit with her family since other people now played the piano and organ Mrs. Norgaard had donated two years earlier. The music swelled, and the congregation joined in. "Silent night, holy night, all is calm, all is bright."

Two people stood to read the Christmas story. "And it came to pass in those days. . ."

Mary could say the words along with the readers. "And they laid the babe in the manger for there was no room for them in the inn."

A hush fell as Reverend John stepped into the pulpit. He stood there, head bowed.

Mary heard a stir in the back but kept her eyes on her father.

When he raised his head, he gasped. He looked to Mary and then to the back of the room.

The buzz grew with people shifting and murmuring.

Mary turned and looked over her shoulder.

The man coming up the center aisle walked as if he knew the way. Well he should. He'd helped lay the carpet.

He stopped at the end of the pew. "Hello, Mary. Merry Christmas."

"Will." She rose to her feet. Her gaze melded with his. Her heart stopped beating and then started again, triple-time. She shifted so there was room for him to sit beside her. Hands clamped as if they'd never let go, they raised their faces to the man standing openmouthed in the pulpit.

"Dearly beloved," John's voice broke. He blew his nose and tucked his handkerchief up the sleeve of his robe. "I'm sorry, folks, but never have those words been more true." He wiped his eyes with the back of his hand. "We have been given a gift, as you all know. Welcome home, Will Dunfey."

Mary heard no more of the sermon. *Will is alive! Thank You, God, thank You.* Over and over the words repeated in her mind. Tears ran unchecked down her cheeks, and while her chin quivered, she couldn't quit smiling. Not that she wanted to.

When the benediction sounded, she rose to her feet along with the others. At the final amen, when the organ poured out its triumphal notes, she turned to Will and melted into his arms. Proper or no, the kiss they shared spoke of all their heartache and all their joy. Will Dunfey had come home.

"It was my destiny," he said later after he'd shaken every hand and been clapped on the back a hundred times by all the congregation. He and Mary were sitting in the parlor at the parsonage with all the Moens, the Weinlanders, and Mrs. Norgaard. "I told Mary I would come home, and Dag taught me to always keep my word."

A chuckle rippled through the room.

"Where were you?" Daniel held the place of honor at Will and Mary's feet.

"In a prisoner-of-war camp. I lost my dog tags, and for a long time I didn't know who I was. I've been trying to get home ever since the signing of the peace. Kept me in a hospital for a while, then told me I was dead." He raised his left hand, leaving his right hand still holding firmly on to Mary's. "I said I might have been, but I was alive now and my name was still Willard Dunfey."

Mary laid her head on his shoulder. "Everyone insisted you were dead, but my heart didn't believe it. I thought I was going crazy, so I asked God for a sign and a couple of days later, your dog tags arrived."

"When that happened, we were sure they had buried you over there." Mrs. Norgaard took a lace handkerchief from the edge of her sleeve and wiped her eyes again. "Must be something in the air."

"Of course," Dag managed to say with a straight face.

"They would have except for this." Will took the Testament Mary had given him from his shirt pocket and held it up. A hole showed through the upper half.

"Good God," John breathed.

"It slowed the bullet so it couldn't penetrate my ribs. I bled like a stuck pig, but flesh wounds heal. So you see, Mary, you saved my life."

"The Word of God is powerful in more ways than one." Gudrun wiped her eyes again. "Pesky cold."

Later when everyone else had gone home or gone to bed, Mary and Will put on their coats and stepped out on the porch. The storm had blown over, and the stars shone like crystals against the black sky. Will pointed to the end of the Dipper.

"You don't need to look for me up there anymore because I am right here, and here I will stay. My love for you has only grown deeper, your face kept me from ever giving up, and," he patted his chest, "I have a scar to remind me how close I came to losing you."

Mary laid her hand over his. "And I you."

When he kissed her this time, she could have sworn she heard someone laughing. Was it that man dancing on the last star in the handle of the Big Dipper? Or the angels rejoicing with them?